Jacobite Sons in
New South Wales

Jacobite Sons in New South Wales

T. J. Lovat

Copyright © 2021 Terence J. Lovat

The moral right of the author has been asserted.

Apart from any fair dealing for the purposes of research or private study, or criticism or review, as permitted under the Copyright, Designs and Patents Act 1988, this publication may only be reproduced, stored or transmitted, in any form or by any means, with the prior permission in writing of the publishers, or in the case of reprographic reproduction in accordance with the terms of licences issued by the Copyright Licensing Agency. Enquiries concerning reproduction outside those terms should be sent to the publishers.

Jacobite Sons in New South Wales is a work of historical fiction. While it draws on historical events and names some figures of history, any resemblance to their character, motivations or events surrounding them is entirely coincidental.

Matador
9 Priory Business Park,
Wistow Road, Kibworth Beauchamp,
Leicestershire, LE8 0RX
Tel: 0116 279 2299
Email: books@troubador.co.uk
Web: www.troubador.co.uk/matador
Twitter: @matadorbooks

ISBN 978 1800464 223

British Library Cataloguing in Publication Data.
A catalogue record for this book is available from the British Library.

Typeset in 11pt Adobe Caslon Pro by Troubador Publishing Ltd, Leicester, UK

Matador is an imprint of Troubador Publishing Ltd

ACKNOWLEDGEMENTS

As with all novels, there is one named author but many unnamed helpers. I acknowledge here those family members, friends, and colleagues, especially Stephen, Di, Amy, and Tracey, who played some part in shaping this book. Whether through reading the entire manuscript, simply a part of it or providing feedback on my earlier novels, I could not have done it without you. Also, Tom, for your work on the graphic features. Thank you all.

FAMILY TREE

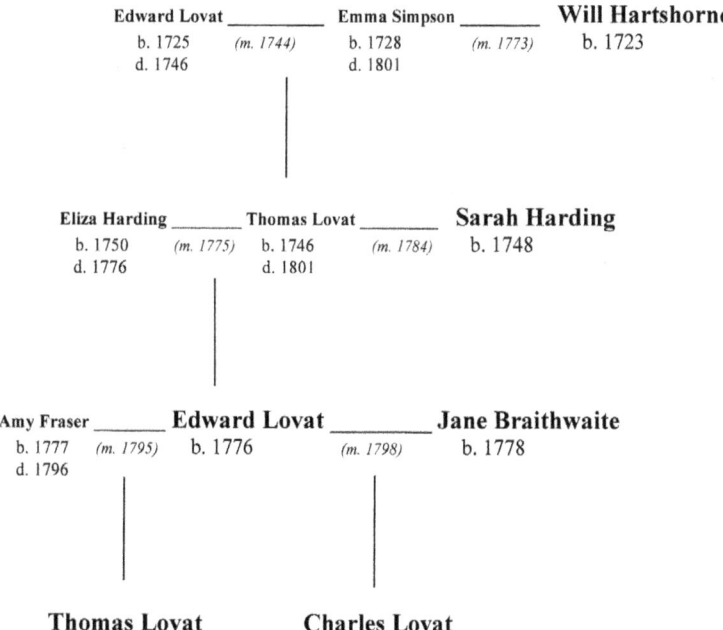

British Isles

- Inverness

SCOTLAND

Atlantic Ocean

North Sea

- Edinburgh

- Carlisle

IRELAND

- Burnley
- Preston
- Pemberton

- Dublin

- Tralee

ENGLAND

- London

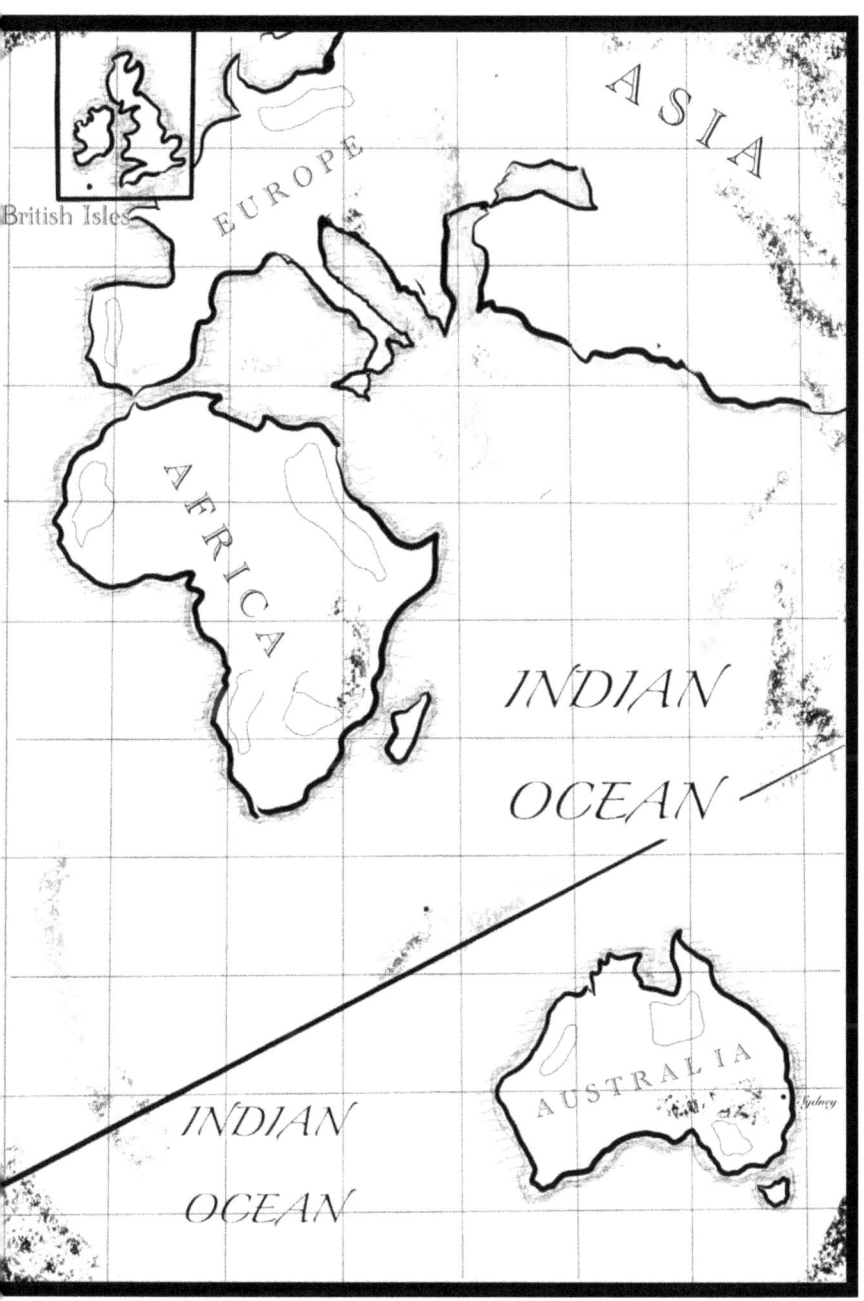

I

'He's not my son,' Jane said. 'I never even agreed to be his stepmother, much less his mother.'

'But ye ken about him when ye married me,' Edward replied. 'Surely, then, ye agreed to being *some* sort of Ma to him.'

'I don't recall ever having that conversation, Edward.'

'Well, the lad's my flesh and blood. Ye canna expect me to abandon him.'

'As I've said many times, I'm happy for you to visit him, if *our own* son's not enough for you, but the idea of him coming to live here, taking our attention away from Charles, is not something I could even consider.'

'I agree with my daughter,' Jane's mother, Elizabeth Braithwaite, said. 'Why, who knows what sort of bad behaviour's been instilled by those common Irish people? For all we know, he could be violent. He might hurt Charles. And then there's the situation of his mother.'

'Let's nay go there, Mrs Braithwaite,' Edward replied. 'Ye ken that only leads to bad blood between us.'

'Very well, I'll hold my tongue and leave it with my daughter's better sense. All I'll say is an Irish urchin sired of a rebellious heathen has no place in civilised English society. Besides, hasn't he been adopted by those Irish people? He doesn't even go by your surname. He belongs *there*; not here. *That's* all I'm saying.'

'More than enough, dear,' Charles Braithwaite said. 'I think we'd best go and let these young people sort out their own affairs.'

'Affairs indeed,' Elizabeth said, nose in the air. 'Affairs is what began this entire sorry mess. And heaven knows how many of them there were. The next thing we know there'll be some colonial child turning up and wanting to live here. If you'd married my daughter when you were supposed to, we wouldn't be having this discussion.'

'Thank you, Mummy, but I think Daddy's right,' Jane said. 'It's probably best you go. I'm sorry this pleasant evening's been spoiled by these unseemly matters.'

'Unseemly?' Edward blurted out. 'We're talking about my son. Is that so unseemly?'

'You *have* a son,' Elizabeth shot back, being dragged by her husband to the door. 'You have a son, and you should be grateful for it. And now another child on the way. Surely that's enough for you.'

This was not the first time the topic of Edward's other son, Tom, coming to live with the family in Burnley, Lancashire, had arisen. It had always been Edward's intention that Tom would eventually come and live with him and his new family.

Tom's mother, Amy, of Scottish descent, had died in childbirth in Ireland. Tom was born prematurely and needed special care. Hence, he stayed and was raised by the Prendiville family in Tralee, old family friends of the Lovats. Edward had been in no position at the time to take on the responsibilities of fatherhood, least of all a delicate child. But he was now settled with a good job on the Towneley Estate in Burnley, England, one of the finest agricultural and woodlands estates in the country. It consisted of four hundred acres of land sloping gently down to the River Calder, accommodating a mix of floral and vegetable gardens, open fields and woods that boasted more deer than anywhere else in northern England.

Edward and Jane had been married for three years, now with one child, Charles, and another on the way. They lived in a small cottage on the estate, but plans had been drawn up for a new house to be built on land Edward had purchased on Tarleton Road, a mere half mile from the estate. The plans were for a substantial residence to accommodate a growing family.

As far as Edward was concerned, it was time to bring the five-year old Tom to live with them.

The year was 1801, a momentous one for the Lovat family. Edward's father and grandmother had died on the same day in January, indeed the very day of his own twenty-fifth birthday. Just a month later, his favourite cousin and best friend, William Henry, was killed in action while on army assignment in Tunisia. This triple blow had laid Edward low with little support coming from Jane, labouring under a difficult pregnancy. Even less support was forthcoming from his mother-in-law, Elizabeth.

Charles Towneley, owner of the estate, was concerned at Edward's despondency. He was fearful he might lose his services. He arranged with the aging estate manager, Ernest Forshaw, that Edward should be appointed as his deputy with an understanding that he would succeed Forshaw as manager when the time came. Towneley hoped this might help in restoring Edward's spirits.

'But he seems very young and I wonder if he has sufficient experience,' Forshaw said.

'I take your point, Mr Forshaw,' Towneley replied. 'But then he has your excellent tutelage that, I'm certain, will see him develop the necessary skills quickly.'

'Well, this is true, sir. He is indeed fortunate in that respect.'

Towneley was aware of Edward's superior skills, despite his youth. The combination of his qualifications from Uppsala University and the Royal Agricultural Institute, together with his experience of agriculture in so many parts of the world, made him a better candidate for managing the estate's future than the largely self-trained Forshaw. Nevertheless, Forshaw had been appointed by Towneley's father, had been there for a lifetime and saw the job as a veritable birthright. Hence, Towneley was conscious of easing him out gently while assuring Edward's future.

'That's most generous of ye, sir,' Edward replied when told. 'But is Mr Forshaw comfortable with the idea?'

Edward and Forshaw enjoyed a positive relationship, but Edward had noted apprehension whenever he proposed new ideas for the estate.

'I see what you mean, young man. But we've never done things that way and I doubt Mr Towneley would approve.'

At first, Edward was inclined to back down. Tensions on the home front were sufficient to make sure he kept the work front as amicable as possible. Besides, he liked and respected Forshaw, despite his dated views about agricultural matters. For his part, Towneley had the Director of the Royal Agricultural Institute, Clive Birmingham's, ringing endorsement in his head.

'*I don't believe I have ever encountered a fitter candidate for estate management,*' were among Birmingham's words in his reference for Edward. '*He represents the future of agronomy in this country.*'

'So, what do you think, Mr Lovat?' Towneley began asking more frequently, even after Forshaw had poured cold water on the idea.

By the time Forshaw finally retired and Edward assumed the position of estate manager, he had effectively been doing the job for a while anyway. Now, he would be paid for it and might finally be able to give Jane the house and lifestyle she and her mother demanded.

As a result of the new appointment, plans for the premises on Tarleton Road were modified. There would now be six bedrooms instead of four. Elizabeth and Jane proposed that the architectural papers that went back and forth to the builders should be titled,

"Tarleton House". The two women were now fully occupied with the new residence. The Braithwaites would help with the cost while Edward would repay them through an amount extracted from his wages.

'Personally, Jane, I'd prefer we stay here in the cottage until I can afford to build without yer parents' help.'

'Well, we can't stay here, Edward. We're bursting at the seams already. You'd know that if you spent more time here.'

—ww—

'Congratulations, Mr Lovat,' the doctor said, smacking the new infant's bottom. 'You have another son.'

It was June 1801. The boy would be named William, a brother for Charles.

'Are ye *cinnteach*, darling?' Edward asked when Jane wanted intercourse just two weeks later.

'Would you be asking if I was your Scottish girl?' she replied, turning away. 'Would you have asked *her* if she was certain?'

'Jane, I'm just concerned ye might get pregnant again, that's all.'

These tensions increased as Jane's obsession with growing her family met with multiple miscarriages.

Their third child, Emma Jane, was born in 1804. This was followed by more miscarriages before the birth of young Edward in 1806. Several more miscarriages left Jane weakened, physically and mentally.

—ww—

'I think it best you have no further children,' the doctor said to Jane, Edward, and the ever-present Elizabeth.

Edward saw Jane's distress and moved to comfort her. Elizabeth beat him to it, cradling her daughter's head to her chest.

'There, there, darling, you have your four beautiful children anyway.'

'Now, we *can* operate to ensure pregnancy is rendered impossible,' the doctor said. 'But only if you wish it, of course.'

'I don't believe that will be necessary,' Elizabeth said, glaring at Edward. 'Will it?'

'I'd really like to get the young couple's view if you don't mind,' the doctor said.

'It's up to Jane,' Edward said, looking at his wife.

'It won't be necessary,' Jane replied, reaching for her kerchief.

II

During the summer of 1806, the young family moved into the partly finished Tarleton House, a classic two-storey Georgian-style red-brick residence, boasting thirty-six cross-panelled windows. There were six bedrooms upstairs with another four planned for an annex that would protrude into the back garden. The front gate, surrounded on both sides by a matching red-brick wall, led straight down a gravel pathway to the small porch and front door. The stark white door opened to a high-roofed foyer boasting a large staircase with an open balustrade on the second floor. On either side of the staircase were double doors leading to the loungeroom, parlour, study, and playroom. The dining room and kitchen were behind the staircase. They would be enlarged once the planned annex was completed.

'It's beautiful,' Jane said, standing at the gate on the day they arrived. 'Thank you, Mummy.'

Edward glanced at her. She turned to look at him.

'And you, darling. Thank you, Edward.'

'Pleasure, my dear. It's *almost* as braw as Towneley Manor. I only hope Mr Towneley dinna ken.'

Elizabeth turned to face him. Her scornful look had Edward prepared. She shook her head, sighed, and turned away.

'Perhaps it *will* be when we get those extra rooms on.'

Edward shook his head, picked up the luggage and walked towards the door.

—⚔︎—

'I'll be back in ten days,' Edward said soon after New Year's Day, 1807.

'Do you realise what ten days of managing four children all alone is like?' Jane replied.

'Ye have yer Ma. Let's face it, ye're hardly alone.'

'Well, she's not as close as she was before we moved.'

'That doesn't seem to have stopped her coming here as often. More's the pity!'

'Edward, we wouldn't be here if it weren't for Mummy and Daddy.'

'As I'm constantly reminded.'

'Oh, Edward. You're so ungrateful. But that's all beside the point. They're *your* children; not hers. *You* should be here.'

'Aye, and if wee Tom was here living with us, as *I* want, then I'd be here with ye, as *ye* want.'

Edward often wilted for the sake of peace. On this occasion, he was adamant he should be at Tom's eleventh birthday.

—⚔︎—

'Look 'o's 'ere, Thomas,' Louise shrieked from the open doorway as Edward walked down the path. 'It's yer Da.'

The shrills of excitement shook Edward out of his pensive mood. He always saw Amy's face at the window next to the front door of the Prendiville home in Tralee. It was the window of the bedroom where she had taken her last breath eleven years before. The paned window had not changed. Even the lace curtain looked the same.

'*Halo*, Louise,' Edward said, bending down to kiss her on the cheek.

'Greetin's, Teddy,' Louise replied, holding his head in a vice-like grip.

'Louise, let the poor man stand up before 'e falls over,' Mrs Prendiville called out from behind. 'And mind yer 'ead, li'l Redcoat, 'ow many times 'ave ye left a bit o' yerself on that door jamb?'

'Sorry, Teddy. It's just so good to see ye,' Louise said. 'And I'll make sure ye don't bump yer 'ead.'

'Bonnie to see ye too, darling Louise. I've missed ye. *Halo*, Mrs P.'

They walked inside. The room that served all purposes, other than sleeping, had not changed. The bare wooden dining table and six unmatching chairs in various states of repair in the middle of the room, the fireplace on one side, fuel stove on the other, with a few wicker chairs here and there between the three doors that led to bedrooms. The house always seemed smaller to Edward each time he went there.

He had hoped to see his son waiting eagerly for him. It had been several years since he had been able to travel to Ireland. His work and the difficult pregnancies and births of Emma Jane and little Edward had prevented him making the trip any earlier.

'Where are ye, Thomas?' Mrs Prendiville called. 'Come and greet yer Da. Ye've been so excited to see 'im. 'asn't 'e, Louise?'

'Yeah but 'e's still worried 'e might 'ave to go to England with 'im.'

'Oh, go away with ye, darlin',' Mrs Prendiville said. 'Our Thomas's goin' nowhere. Is 'e Edward, my boy?'

'Nay, Mrs P. I'd dare nay steal him from his Ma and Grand Ma.'

Mrs Prendiville laughed. Louise stole another opportunity to give Edward a bear hug. He had become accustomed to them since his first trip to Tralee as an infant.

'Thank ye so much, Teddy,' Louise said, shaking him from side to side. 'I just love ye so much.'

'Tell us somethin' we don't know,' Mrs Prendiville said, rollicking with laughter. 'Now, *where's that* Thomas?'

'Is he Thomas now?' Edward asked. 'What happened to wee Tom? I ken that was cute.'

'And that was the problem,' an unfamiliar voice came from the bedroom.

The three adults looked to each other and laughed.

'Oh, 'e's such a comedian,' Mrs Prendiville said. 'Just like 'is Da. Come out 'ere, funny boy, and say 'ello to yer Da before I come in there with the wooden spoon.'

'No, no, not the wooden spoon again,' Thomas feigned crying as he exited the bedroom he still shared with Louise.

'*Halo*, Tom, I mean Thomas,' Edward said, approaching his son.

'Hello, Da,' Thomas replied, hugging his father. 'I thought ye'd never come.'

'Well, I was nay going to miss yer birthday. Ye'd nay ever forgive me.'

'I'd forgive ye, Da. I've had to forgive ye before.'

Edward was struck by the maturity and poise of the son he still thought of as an infant, if not a baby. He quickly studied him, noting how much like himself he was. He was unusually tall for an eleven-year-old, thin, and fair-skinned. The light hair had darkened but he could still see some of Amy's auburn tones softening the appearance. The straight nose was his, but the blue eyes could have been taken from his mother as she lay on her death bed.

'Nay, it's nay easy with all the work I have.'

'And with yer other family. I mean yer *real* family.'

The room fell silent.

'Well, ye're my real family too, lad. And ye nay ever forget it. Is that clear?'

'Whatever ye say, Da.'

Two days later, Thomas celebrated his eleventh birthday. It happened to be Edward's thirty-first birthday as well, but he made it clear all the attention should be on his son.

Louise's sister, Mary O'Rourke, was there with her seven children. Despite being more than fulfilled as a mother, Mary had continued to be a second mother to Thomas. He had even borne the O'Rourke surname for some years, posing as a twin to Mary's third child, Bernadette, when there was a need to hide his identity.

Edward had rectified that situation on an earlier visit when the Prendivilles had feared he was going to take Thomas back to England. Edward agreed that he should stay in Tralee but insisted Thomas should be known henceforth by his proper surname, Lovat.

For a variety of reasons, Thomas felt closer to Mary than to Louise. Mary had suckled him because Bernadette was only eleven days old when he was born. So, the story went around that Mary had saved his life, something Thomas found comforting but Louise saw as threatening. Mary was also easier to be around, less smothering than Louise. Louise found this perturbing as well, granted she gave Thomas so much more attention than Mary's very divided one.

'When's li'l Tom comin' 'ome?' Louise would ask her mother on the regular occasions the boy went to stay at Mary's house.

'It was only yesterd'y 'e went there, darlin'.'

'Why'd 'e rather be there than 'ere, Ma?'

'I'm sure 'e loves the company of the other children, darlin'; that's all.'

Mrs Prendiville knew full well that Thomas felt more secure with Mary than with the ever-fussing Louise.

'D'ye think 'e loves Mary more than me, Ma?'

'Of course not, darlin'.'

Also present at Thomas's birthday was Denis, Mrs Prendiville's grandson. Though only twelve years older than Thomas, Denis had been the closest Thomas had to a father figure as he was growing up. It was an early experience of witnessing the nurturing relationship between them that had awakened Edward to his own failings as a father.

When Amy had died in childbirth, Edward had been devastated to the point he wanted nothing to do with his son. Thomas came to realise this well before he should have known about such things. The gap between father and son had never fully healed.

'Here's yer favourite boy,' Denis said to Eliza, his four-year old daughter. 'She's been like a frisky horse wanting out of the corral all morning. *When are we going, Pa? Are we going yet, Pa? Come on, Pa.*'

'Ye love yer li'l Tom, don't ye darlin'?' Mrs Prendiville said, rollicking with laughter.

'Might!' Eliza replied.

She stood rigidly on the spot, red-faced and waiting for Thomas's customary signal.

'*Halo*, Princess Eliza,' Thomas said.

'Hello, yer majesty,' Eliza replied, sidling over, and perching herself on his lap.

'She's in her favourite spot, Edward,' Denis said. 'And that's where she'll be until I wrench her away and take her home.'

Denis had married Jane Dorahy when he was seventeen. She was sixteen. They had three children, Eliza being the eldest. Jane and the other two children had gone to her parents' place for a rival event.

'How's the rest of yer family, Denis?' Edward asked.

'Very well, thank ye. They'll come over later. We were all coming over later, but Eliza wouldn't hear of it. She'd have come here alone if we'd let her.'

They laughed.

'And how's yer family?' Denis asked. 'Ye have a little one, don't ye?'

'Aye, young Edward. He's a bright wee lad.'

'Like his Da, I suppose?'

'Aye, like his Da used to be.'
'So, things are well with the others?'
'Oh, aye, just splendid.'
'Yer wife must be delighted with yer new job?'
'Aye, she's delighted,' Edward replied.

The arrival of the rest of Denis's family was the signal for the festivities proper to begin. Mrs Prendiville had asked Edward to start by saying a few words.

'Happy birthday, lad. I canna believe it's eleven years since ye were born in this very house. It was a tragic night with the death of yer dear Ma but ye've been blessed all the same to have been given the love and comfort of the wonderful Prendiville family, most especially Louise who's been the mother of all mothers to ye. I'm so happy to be here with ye, lad. Happy birthday from me and yer Ma in heaven.'

Thomas sat stony-faced. Mrs Prendiville then spoke.

'Ah, yeah, for sure. 'appy birthd'y, li'l Tom. God was so good to bring ye into our lives. Ye've been such a joy and we love ye like no-one's ever been loved.'

'Ye've been the li'l boy I never 'ad,' Louise began, blubbering before she had started. 'I was never lucky enough to 'ave my own family but ye've made up for it and I *never* want ye to go away, d'ye 'ear me?'

'Thomas, ye're a very special boy,' Denis said. 'And we know ye're gonna be a very special man. Happy birthday, man.'

'And 'appy birthday to yer Da as well,' Louise said, reaching up and kissing Edward on the cheek.

'Thank ye, Louise,' Edward replied. 'Thank ye all. Ye've all been so braw to me and my lad.'

'Go on, Eliza,' Denis said. 'I can see ye want to say something to Thomas.'

'Love ye,' she said, looking around and kissing him on the cheek from the spot she had reclaimed when the speeches began – perched atop Thomas's knee.

Edward stepped back and leant one arm on the mantlepiece. He surveyed the scene. Thomas, his own flesh-and-blood, so secure in the knowledge he was loved by every person in the room.

He noted it. He envied it.

III

'Ye'd love the Prendivilles,' Edward whispered to Jane as they settled in bed on the first night of his return to Tarleton House. 'I wish ye'd come sometime. They'd love to meet ye. They're always asking after ye.'

'And what do you tell them? That I'm a heartless wife and a careless mother, I suppose.'

'Nay, darling. As if I'd say such things.'

'I'm sorry,' Jane said, tucking herself in under his arm.

'I do love ye, ye ken?' Edward said, wrapping his arms around her.

Edward could hear and feel her sobbing. He held her tightly and began to rub her back.

'And I love you.'

Edward took her cheek by one hand and moved his lips to hers. They kissed. It lingered. More so than for a long time.

'We can't do this,' Jane said, pulling away.

'Why? Is it nay what married people do? Or is it yer time?'

'No, it's not my time. Not that a man should be thinking of such things.'

Edward sensed her mother's presence in the room – invisible but always there.

'What is it then? What on *earth* is it?'

'It's the thought of you and the Fraser girl.'

'Amy! Ye're allowed to say her name.'

'Amy, if you insist. Whenever we're together like this, I imagine you with her. And I'm certain that's what you're imagining as well, especially after having been back to that place in Ireland.'

'What on earth d'ye mean? I've nay ever imagined myself with Amy when I'm with ye.'

'Do you mean that, truly?'

'Aye, I mean it truly.'

'I'm sorry then. I've just always thought …'

'So, has that been the problem all along? Even on our wedding night when ye'd nay come near me?'

'No, I was just tired that night and I wanted to be good for you – like I'm sure she was. She was, wasn't she?'

'I seriously canna remember. It's been over ten years, ye ken?'

'I'm sorry. I'm sorry we're so unhappy.'

'Are we though? I do love ye, ye ken?'

'Truly?'

'Truly!'

Jane snuggled back in and they held tightly. Edward could feel one of her breasts pressing into his chest. He reached for the other one and cupped his hand firmly around it.

'This feels so good,' Jane said as he moved his hands down and around her lower body.

In no time, he was inside her. They were as one in a way all too rarely realised.

They slept well.

—⚘—

'My daughter told me what happened last night,' Elizabeth whispered under her breath as Edward stepped back into the house the next day.

'And ye ken that's yer business?'

'My daughter's welfare's very much my business.'

'Yer daughter's just braw, Mrs Braithwaite. Ye've nay any need to concern yerself.'

'What are you two talking about?' Jane asked as she stepped into the room.

'Nay anything, darling,' Edward replied.

Jane noted her mother turning away.

'Mummy! I told you that in confidence.'

'I'm sorry, dear. But you know what the doctor told you.'

'I think you'd best go, Mummy,' Jane said.

Elizabeth walked out, throwing a scornful glare in Edward's direction.

'Why on earth would ye be telling yer mother about our private life?'

'I'm sorry. I was just so happy I wanted to share it with someone. And Mummy's always so negative about our marriage, I wanted to give her some good news.'

'I truly doubt yer Ma ken what braw news means. I ken she wants nay anything more than our unhappiness – perhaps so it matches hers.'

'How can you say such an awful thing, Edward? Of course, she wants us to be happy. Why in heaven's name would she not?'

'Perhaps because ye'd nay have any need for her then.'

So, they went to bed that night unhappy again. Edward had thought through the day that the previous night's encounter might augur well for suggesting a trip to Tralee for the whole family. Or at least a visit by Thomas to Tarleton House.

He would have to wait for a better moment.

—⚘—

'Why can't I make my First Holy Communion too, Gran?' the four-year-old William asked.

'Because you're not old enough,' Elizabeth replied. 'And perhaps you're not good enough either. If you want to be one of God's special people, you need to be more like your brother.'

'Who? Young Edward?'

'No, cheeky boy,' Elizabeth said. 'You know I mean Charles. He'll be a priest one day, you know! And you could be one too if you were more like him.'

'Do you really think he might be a priest, Mummy?' Jane asked. 'Charles, I mean.'

'Charles? Without a doubt.'

'How would ye ken that, Mrs Braithwaite,' Edward asked. 'How on earth would ye ken that?'

'Grandmothers just know these things; that's why. And because I pray for it every day.'

'It *would* be wonderful,' Jane said. 'Imagine having our own priest in the family. Perhaps he'll be a Jesuit.'

'Well, as long as he's not like that horrid man who married you. What was his name again?'

'Father Pritchard,' Edward said. 'The best teacher I ever had.'

'Heaven knows what he taught you is all I can say,' Elizabeth replied. 'But it does explain a lot about your attitude to religion.'

'And what does that mean?'

'Well, to be frank, you don't seem to me to be very committed to your faith. You miss Mass at the drop of a hat and heaven knows how long it is since you went to confession. Jane tells me you refuse to say the rosary at night and, worst of all, you seem far too comfortable with those godless Protestants and even worse.'

'Worse? Worse than a Protestant? Oh, my Laird, is there nay anything in this world worse than a Protestant?'

'There's no need to be so rude. You know well some of the people you've liaised with over the years. That vile convict woman you met on the ship and what about those heathens you helped in Persia? What do they call them, Mozzlim or something?'

'Muslim. Aye, some of the most god-fearing people I've met. Beautiful people who don't judge others, *just like Christ*.'

'Oh, don't speak to me about Christ, boy. I know a lot more about Christ than you do.'

'Just like the self-righteous Pharisee in the eighteenth chapter of St Luke's Gospel,' Edward replied.

'What are you talking about?' Elizabeth asked.

'Just read it, Mrs Braithwaite; just read it.'

Edward did not know many gospel passages but this one was a favourite of Father Pritchard. He had often used it in sermons to make a point about religious hypocrites being the targets of Jesus' vitriol. As Edward had discovered before, pointing to a gospel passage was a proven way of confusing Elizabeth.

'All I can say is I'll clearly need to pray twice as hard if Charles is to withstand your influence,' Elizabeth said.

'By-all-means, pray to yer heart's content! And say one for me along the way.'

It had been six years since Edward lost his father, Thomas. The missing never went away. On-the-occasion-of Charles's First Holy Communion, he missed him even more. He recalled the time Thomas put on a memorable performance in this very church in Burnley. The priest, Father Cocklin, was preaching about the Crusaders in the Middle Ages who had died for their faith fighting and killing Jews, Muslims, and "other pagans". Thomas had coughed, spluttered, and blown his nose so loudly, no-one could hear the priest. As soon as the sermon was over, he stopped and when Edward glanced over with a look of concern, Thomas had winked and smiled at him. They had often laughed together about their encounter with the "Crusader priest". Father Cocklin had moved on and been replaced by Father Bannigan. Edward wished his father was here.

'Today, my children of God, you're partaking in the sacred species,' Bannigan began. 'When the Lord returned to his place at the right hand of God the Father, he left a part of himself on earth. He left us with his own precious Body and Blood to sustain us until we're with him in heaven. Through the power God gives to his priests, what looks like bread and wine are turned into the Body and Blood of Christ.

This is a gift God gives only to Catholics. Only Catholic priests have the power of transubstantiation, changing bread and wine into the sacred species. That's why you've been fasting since midnight because you'll be receiving Christ's own Body on your tongue very soon. That's why you must never chew on the host because you'd be chewing on the Lord's Body. That's why you must never desecrate the host or drop even a small crumb as you're receiving it, because then the Lord's Body would be left on the ground for people to trample on. There are Protestants who'd love nothing better than to trample on the host because they're jealous of the power that we Catholics have, and they don't.'

Edward was sitting two down from Elizabeth. She was rocking the pew with her eager head-nodding and gasps of approval. Edward was not only missing his father but Amy as well.

'It's all a hoax,' she would say. 'They want ye to believe their hocus-pocus so they have power over ye and can take yer money.'

He knew he would never find another one like her.

'Silly boy,' Father Bannigan roused.

One of the children had dropped the plate as he was receiving communion. The plate was meant to catch any particles of the "sacred species" that might drop at this time. The boy was sent scurrying back to his seat while Bannigan knelt on hands and knees retrieving miniscule particles of the Lord's body, no doubt mingled with dust and grit. He placed them on a cloth carefully positioned on the altar before resuming his role as Christ's representative.

'Anyone else who does that will be coming to see me afterwards for a punishment.'

The boy who had dropped the plate let out an audible sob.

'Where are ye, Da?' Edward thought to himself. *'Where are ye, Amy?'*

For all his scepticism, he watched with pride as he saw Charles take communion for the first time. On the way back to his seat, his son looked so caught up in the moment it was as if he was radiating godliness itself.

'Perhaps he will be a priest,' Edward thought with some horror.

―⁂―

The "communion breakfast", so-called, was as little like a breakfast as a biscuit resembles a feast. The event rivalled the wedding celebration held after Edward's and Jane's matrimony. Elizabeth had organised the breakfast, including ensuring that Father Bannigan came to this event and no rival one. The rival one was the common repast for the other children in the small hall beside the church. Charles's breakfast was held in the backyard of the Braithwaite home.

'Come now, Father,' Elizabeth said as she buttonholed Bannigan heading towards the hall. 'You're our guest of honour and we expect you to be there the entire time.'

'Yes, but I thought I'd just go in and quickly say hello to the other children.'

'Father, in that case, you'd miss saying the grace and I'm sure Mr and Mrs Towneley would be disappointed.'

'Oh, very good then,' Bannigan replied.

Proceedings began with Bannigan saying grace and repeating at least half of his theologically bereft sermon. Charles Braithwaite then spoke briefly, welcoming the guests that included the Towneleys and most of the prominent Catholics in the district. The handful who had to decline were attending their own child's insalubrious event in the church hall.

'Seriously, I would have thought they'd be here,' Elizabeth said of one family.

'I suppose they feel some small obligation to attend their own child's celebration, my dear,' her husband replied.

'Well, I suppose so!'

Finally, Elizabeth spoke, gushing about her first grandson taking his next major step into the Catholic faith and how beautiful he looked.

'Truly, I could only think what a wonderful priest he'll make.'

Edward was halfway to his feet when Jane grabbed him by the arm and dragged him back down.

'Please, not today,' she whispered through clenched teeth.

For his part, Charles seemed unaffected by the entire proceedings. He was neither revelling in them nor rebelling against them. He was his typically self-composed, almost monk-like, presence.

Even as a baby and then infant, Charles had exuded a comfortable self-assurance. Others might be fussing or fighting around him, but Charles would just do as was required of him, or as he determined for himself. It was the same today, while around him the four-year-old William and eighteen-month-old Emma Jane were causing endless fuss and the infant, young Edward, celebrated the occasion with ceaseless wailing.

Throughout it all, Charles sat serenely like a medieval prince overseeing his kingdom. The prince's mother and grandmother sat one on either side, preening their gift from heaven. Edward meantime was eventually relegated to the outer circle with his main duties around controlling his other children.

'Looks like they're frightened you'll infect him,' Will said. 'Is your mother-in-law still insisting the poor boy'll be a priest?'

'Aye. How d'ye reckon I can spoil that plan?'

Will was Edward's step grandfather. He had married his grandmother, Emma, after her first husband, the famed Jacobite warrior, Edward Lovat, had been killed at Culloden. Emma and Will met many years later while Emma's son by Edward, Thomas, had been a student at Stonyhurst College. At the time, Will was one of the Jesuit priest teachers.

Will had been an important mentor over the years, most especially around religious matters.

'What are you two plotting?' Sarah said, walking towards the two men.

Sarah was Edward's stepmother, sister to his own mother and full-time care person for the octogenarian Will. They still lived together in the old family home in Pemberton, not so far from Burnley.

'Plotting?' Will replied. 'Oh, merely how to hasten young Charles's inevitable canonisation.'

'Oh, the poor boy,' Sarah said. 'He seems so sweet.'

'Aye, he's a bonnie lad,' Edward replied. 'Keeping him out of his Gran's clutches is the issue.'

'Well, surely you can do that.'

'Nay, we're nay so close. Jane hardly lets me near him and even when she does, Elizabeth's there, standing in the way.'

'Give it time, Edward,' Sarah said. 'Boys always come back to their father. Just look at you and *your* father. When I married Thomas, you two hardly spoke to each other. By the end, you were inseparable.'

'I hope ye're right, Sarah. I truly do love the lad, just as I love his brother in Tralee. But I canna say I'm at all close to either of them.'

'Give it time; give it time.'

IV

'Well, that's the first step to the priesthood,' Will said about Charles starting at Stonyhurst College. 'Best let me have that talk with him soon.'

'Sorry to say ye'd be the last person Elizabeth would let anywhere near him,' Edward replied. 'With ye living in sin, ye ken?'

It had been a standing joke that Elizabeth disapproved of Will and Sarah living under the same roof, albeit there had never been so much as a whiff of scandal.

'Oh, she's such a good Catholic, isn't she?' Will said. 'Full of true Christian spirit.'

'That woman!' Sarah said.

The year was 1811. The twelve-year-old Charles would begin his high school studies in August.

'How's the house coming on?' Will asked.

'The extensions should be on by the time Charles starts at Stonyhurst.'

'It seems to have taken an awfully long time,' Will said.

'Aye, well building Edinburgh Castle took some time as well,' Edward replied, shaking his head.

'Why do you need something so large anyway?' Sarah asked.

'Oh, there's always some new idea. How Charles will need a second room for his study when he's home from Stonyhurst and William will need a storeroom for his tools and Emma Jane will be studying piano and, last-but-not-least, we'll need at least two more rooms for Jane's parents when they're too old to look after themselves.'

'I'm sure that idea fills you with joy,' Will said.

'I swear I'll go and live in Tralee if that ever happens,' Edward laughed. 'Or perhaps go back to New South Wales.'

'Have you paid them back yet?' Will asked.

'Nay, more's the pity. I'd almost repaid but then the extensions 've proven costly.'

'So, you've had to borrow again?'

'Aye, *from* my in-laws *for* my in-laws' future care, nay less.'

'Oh, Edward, you're too soft,' Will said.

'No, he's not,' Sarah said. 'Too kind-hearted, perhaps. The eternal peacemaker.'

'Nay a very braw one, at that,' Edward replied with a snigger.

'Anyway, how does Charles feel about going to boarding school?' Sarah asked.

'Frankly, who can tell? Charles nay gives anything away. He just takes everything in his stride.'

'Does he know he's being lined up for the priesthood?' Will asked.

'I suppose so but it dinna seem to worry him. Nay anything really does.'

'Have you spoken with him about it?' Sarah asked.

'Aye, once or twice. I've just said, *ye ken, lad, ye dinna have to be a priest if ye dinna want. Ye're free to do whatever ye want.* He just says something like, *I know, Pa*, and that's the end of it.'

'Well, just make sure I get the chance to have that talk,' Will said.

'I don't think you'll have to have the same talk with Thomas,' Sarah said.

Sarah had become the regular go-between for Edward with his other son in Tralee. She had been there only recently, which was why Edward had come down to Pemberton to see her.

'How *is* my Irish lad?' Edward asked.

'Oh, he's no Irish lad; he's probably more a Scot than you are. The older he gets, the more he looks like you and talks like his mother. I often think how much your grandmother would have loved him, just as she adored Amy. Do you remember how Emma came alive when you brought Amy to Pemberton?'

'Oh, aye, and then when we all went up to the Highlands, they both came alive even more.'

'Emma always said how much Amy reminded her of herself,' Will said.

'Well, I'm sure Thomas would remind her of herself too, and...'

'It's alright, Sarah darling, you can say it,' Will said. 'Her own Edward.'

'Well, yes, and of course her own son as well,' Sarah replied. 'Not to mention grandson.'

'Well, if he's so much like me, my Da and Grand Da, I suppose I'd best get to see the lad before he's nay too auld to ken who I am.'

'Yes, or before he's married,' Sarah said.

'What? Ye're nay being serious, I hope. Why the lad's only ...'

'Fifteen, going on sixteen,' Sarah said. 'Your grandfather was barely eighteen when he married. And I'm told Thomas is quite the ladies' man.'

'I'd best nay delay.'

'Indeed,' Sarah and Will echoed.

'It's simply not possible,' Jane said.

Edward had suggested taking Charles to Tralee before he started at Stonyhurst.

'But I'd really like the lad to meet his brother.'

'I don't really see why. He means nothing to him, and it could be quite disturbing for Charles to be confronted with his father's past.'

'What's that supposed to mean?'

'Well, it's not what happens in normal families, is it? Suddenly, a young boy finds his father has another family, and in Ireland of all places. I'm sorry, Edward. I don't wish to be mean, but you know Charles is a sensitive boy and I think he might find it quite disturbing, especially as he's about to go into training.'

'His *training*? I ken he's going to high school. That's all.'

'Of course, that's what I meant.'

'Truly, this priesthood thing's gone too far. The lad'll grow up confused unless it stops *now*. Frankly, I ken it'd do Charles a lot of good to come to Tralee and get to ken Thomas who, I'm told, is a braw lad with all the normal inclinations a young lad should have.'

'And what's that supposed to mean? You think our son's not normal? Is that it?'

'Of course, I'm nay saying that. It's just that Thomas is a few years older and it could be a bonnie thing for Charles to ken who he is.'

'Edward, I accepted long ago that none of the children I've borne you could possibly be a match for the one you had with your Scottish girl. *All* our children will have to live in his shadow forever. *I* know that and my mother knows it too. That's why I have to protect our children from that shadow.'

'Jane, that nay makes any sense at all. It's yer mother's craziness that ye're accepting without any basis in fact.'

'Oh, so my mother's crazy is what you're saying. Is that right? My children are inferior and my mother's a mad woman.'

'Well, half of that's true, nay doubt!'

—✶—

At the Good Friday service, 1813, Charles Towneley collapsed and was rushed to hospital. Edward was normally quite happy at any event that disrupted religious services, especially when Father Bannigan was conducting them. On this occasion, he was distressed. Charles had been a benevolent overseer and mentor, a worldly man who tolerated but was largely uninfluenced by Elizabeth Braithwaite. Not so his son, Percival.

'God help us if Percival ever gets hold of the estate,' Edward had confided to Sarah and Will on one occasion. 'Elizabeth has him on a string as surely as the puppeteer.'

Any hope that Charles might rise from his bed to celebrate Christ's resurrection were dashed. Elizabeth came around at dawn on Easter Sunday to announce that Charles Towneley had died overnight.

'That's very sad,' Edward said.

'Well, the Lord knows best.'

Edward imagined a hint of happy anticipation hiding not so well behind the expected look of grief.

Percival Towneley was a strange soul. He had only recently married, in his early fifties. His mother had hoped he might become a priest because he spent an inordinate amount of time in church. He had little interest in socialising, least of all with women.

But then Constance Bledderville had come into his life. She was a widow, ten or so years younger, with three boys who had all entered the seminary largely at her behest. Each of them had exited as quickly, much to her disappointment. Having abandoned her dream to be a priest's mother, she started looking around for other ways of wielding influence. Being the First Lady of the Towneley Estate was as good as it got around Burnley. In that regard, Percival was an ideal match, granted he was the only child and guaranteed inheritor of the estate. In no time, he and Constance were married.

Percival and Constance were close to the Braithwaites. Elizabeth had been drawn to Percival many years before as a kindred spirit, at least as far as devout Catholicism went. She had also been acquainted with Constance. They shared an obsession about having a priest in the family.

'Did you have anything to do with this?' Charles Braithwaite had asked his wife when the banns of marriage were announced between Percival and Constance.

'I can't imagine what you're talking about,' Elizabeth had replied.

―∞―

Charles Towneley's funeral was held on the Tuesday after Easter and Percival was in his office on the Wednesday. He had signalled to Edward that he should come and see him to talk about some changes needed on the estate.

'As you're aware, Edward, I've inherited all the responsibilities of the estate from my father.'

'Aye, sir.'

'And as I'm sure you'd expect, I have some ideas of my own. Some changes I'd like to see effected. Indeed, ones I will require you to support.'

Edward sat and watched Percival shifting uncomfortably in his chair, rolling the ends of his oversized moustache with his fingers, looking everywhere but in Edward's eyes. He noted the stiff collar on a shirt several sizes too large, the bow tie loosely appended at an odd angle. He was reminded of a character in a comedic play he'd once seen in Preston.

'How does such a substantial father have such an insubstantial son?' Edward thought to himself.

―∞―

'A strange coincidence,' Edward said to Jane after she asked him how the meeting had gone. 'Almost everything he said I've heard your mother say over the years.'

'I'm sure it's coincidence, Edward.'

Things were never the same again for Edward. He was careful not to butt heads with a man he did not respect and knew he could not trust, and whom he also knew was having his strings pulled by Elizabeth.

Percival had no real interest in the practicalities of the estate, so Edward kept to himself more and more. Whereas he would regularly have spent much of his working day in Charles Towneley's office consulting with him about future planning, he now spent almost all day with the flora and vegetable crops, occasionally wandering into the woods. He was happiest when on his knees, hands in the soil or just sitting on a log waiting for a deer to appear. It gave him time to think, to remember.

On occasion, he found himself conversing with the deer. They seemed to understand better than most around him.

V

'Teddy. We thought ye'd never come,' Louise shouted as she rushed out the door.

She ran up and gave Edward the kind of bear hug he had not had since last in Tralee.

'*Halo*, Louise. It's so bonnie to see ye.'

It was over two and a half years since Edward had been there. Between work, family tensions and settling Charles into Stonyhurst, it had been impossible to make the trip. In the end, he pushed against all the forces to be at his son's eighteenth birthday. It was late January 1814.

'So, where's yer Ma?' he asked.

'By the fire where she normally is these days.'

'And where's that lad of mine?'

'The Lord only knows,' Mrs Prendiville called out from the old chair in front of the fire that her husband used to sit in.

'*Halo*, Mrs P,' Edward said, walking across the small open room to greet her. 'It's so good to see ye. I'm sorry it's been so long.'

'Pardon if I don't stand to greet ye, li'l Redcoat. It's all I can do to stand up to go to the *jacks* these days. Now, as for yer boy, well that's anyone's guess.'

'I'm sorry, has he been a bother to ye?'

'No, no, not at all,' Louise jumped in. 'Thomas's a really good boy. The best. We just love 'avin' 'im, don't we, Ma?'

'Well, to be honest, my boy, yer Thomas's been a bit of a 'andful of late.'

'No, no, Ma, 'ow can ye say that?' Louise said.

'Maybe 'cause it's true, dear.'

'What sort of handful?' Edward asked.

'Don't get me wrong. 'E's doin' very well in 'is trade, for sure. 'e's been workin' with Stan Murphy, the builder. Stan took 'im on as an apprentice. 'e says 'e's never 'ad a more reliable worker. But it's more what 'e's been doin' outside o' work. 'e comes 'ome awfully late some nights and 'e won't tell us where 'e's been. Often, we can smell alco'ol on 'is breath but 'e insists 'e 'asn't been to the pub. We're just worried what 'e might be gettin' up to. I think 'e needs a man to talk to. Denis can normally get through to 'im but 'e's even been tight-lipped with 'im lately.'

'Ye'll get through to 'im, Teddy,' Louise said, using the excuse to give him another hug.

'Ye still love yer Teddy, don't ye darlin'?' Mrs Prendiville said.

Louise's cheeks flushed and she let Edward go.

'And I love my Louise, Mrs P,' Edward said, taking Louise in his arms and giving her the squeeze that she normally initiated.

'Oh, ye two,' Mrs Prendiville said.

'So where do ye ken I could find my lad now?' Edward asked.

'Well, if ye're quick, ye might catch 'im leavin' work. Where's 'e workin' at present, darlin'?' Mrs Prendiville asked her daughter.

'Up on Murray Road, I think, Ma. 'e's been workin' on those old buildin's that used to belong to the church. Ye know the ones I mean?'

'Aye, I ken those ones,' Edward said. 'They needed a lot of work when I was living here.'

It was almost dark by the time Edward made it to Murray Road. As he turned the corner, he caught a glimpse of a figure heading away in the opposite direction. He could not be sure, but it looked like Thomas. He walked quickly to try and overtake him.

'Thomas,' he called out when close enough to be heard.

The walker picked up his step and moved away more quickly.

'Thomas,' he called again.

Edward was fairly running to catch up. He was finally close enough to see it was his son.

'Thomas! Thomas! Thomas, wait, it's yer Da!'

Thomas turned around and hastened back to him.

'Hello, Da,' he said, taking his hand. 'Ye must be quiet.'

'I'm sorry, lad, but I nay could get yer attention. Where're ye going?'

'I can't say, Da. But don't worry; everything's alright.'

'I believe ye, lad, but Mrs P and Louise are worried about ye. They think ye might be getting into some trouble or drinking too much or something like that.'

Thomas chuckled.

'Oh, they're such wonderful people, but there's nothing to worry about. I promise ye. I must go. It's wonderful ye're here and I look forward to talking at home later.'

With that, Thomas turned and hurried away. Edward waited until he had turned the corner and then followed at a discreet distance.

It was getting darker by the minute and so it was more and more difficult to keep him in sight. Eventually, he saw Thomas come into the light being shed from a house window. A woman stepped down from a cart and gave him a warm greeting. Thomas then stepped back up onto the cart with the woman and a handful of other people and the cart was driven away.

Edward thought he recognised the woman. She seemed to be quite a bit older than Thomas.

—⚋—

'I'm sorry, lad, but I just need to ken ye're nay in any trouble,' Edward said.

Thomas had come in late and Edward was waiting for him.

'It really is alright, Da, as I said before. But tell me how everything is with ye? Sarah tells me ye're about to have two boys at Stonyhurst. I know ye went there so ye must be proud of that.'

'Aye, Charles's been there now for over two years and William's about to begin.'

'I look forward to meeting them sometime.'

'I'm so sorry ye've nay met them before now. It's just a long way and everyone seems to be so busy.'

'I know, Da. I understand. But one of these days, I might just land on yer doorstep anyway.'

'I'd truly love for that to happen, lad.'

'And Jane?' Thomas said more boldly than Edward was expecting. 'Would she love that as well?'

There was a moment of silence.

'There's no need to answer that, Da. I understand. But I might just do it anyway.'

'That'd be braw, lad. That'd be braw.'

'Well, I'd best get to bed,' Thomas said. 'I've an early start tomorrow. Will I see ye tomorrow night?'

'Aye, will ye be home early?'

'Not too late,' Thomas said, moving towards his bedroom. 'I look forward to catching up with more of yer news then.'

'Thomas. I ken that woman ye met tonight. I canna place her, but I ken I've met her before.'

Thomas stopped and looked back at his father.

'Did ye follow me then?'

'Aye, I'm sorry, lad. I dinna want to be spying on ye but I'm yer Da and I have to be certain ye're nay in trouble.'

'I'm not in any trouble, Da. I promise ye.'

Edward woke with a start sometime in the wee hours. He recalled the woman as the one he had known as Helen those many years before. Amy had taken him to a secret Jacobite meeting of a motley crew of Irish locals and Scottish immigrants hoping to start a new rebellion. He struggled to remember the details. There was something about a boy with the same name as Bonnie Prince Charlie whom the original Jacobites had wanted to put on the throne back in the "Auld '45". The boy would be a man by now.

And, of course, there was Roy Adair, the Scottish turncoat who had tried to pressure Amy into marrying him so he could inherit management rights of the estate in Listellick where her father had worked. Edward and Amy had begun their short-married life there.

He plays it both ways, he recalled Amy saying of Adair. It was his double-dealing with the English authorities that had forced them into hiding and why they had to keep Thomas's birth under wraps. Indeed, that was the very reason Thomas had been known as O'Rourke for a few years.

'*Surely he's nay involved with all that*,' Edward thought to himself.

He lay awake for the rest of the night. One minute, he was thinking through the worst possible scenarios for Thomas, the next filled with memories of his happy days with Amy in Listellick.

'Perhaps Thomas was being lured into a rebellious plan that would see him incarcerated or even killed. Perhaps he would be transported to New South Wales to suffer the same fate as Angus Fraser, Amy's brother, whom he had met on his own trip to the great southern land. Could it be that Roy Adair is still around, wanting to seal his ownership of the estate by disposing of Thomas?'

He recalled his first meeting with Amy when she spat Scottish Gaelic at him for his association with the British. How he had feared but loved her from that first instant. And then images of her in that yellow frock the first night they slept together. The way her words cut through to expose the naked truth against all pretension.

It's all a hoax, she said of the church and its beliefs. And here he was in the very house where she gave birth to Thomas as she lay dying.

It was a night of wringing emotion, torn between the happiest memories and the most dreaded future possibilities.

He heard Thomas preparing for work before anyone else was up.

'Her name's Helen, is it nay, lad?'

Thomas turned from the stove where he was boiling water for coffee.

'Yes, if ye must know. How do ye know her?'

Edward quickly filled him in with his concerns.

'Da, why don't ye meet me tonight, about six o'clock, at my work?'

'I'll be there.'

—⚜—

'I think ye know Helen Campbell, Da,' Thomas said as Helen alighted from the cart.

'Aye, we ken each other from a long time ago,' Helen said as she took Edward in her arms and hugged him. 'I was so very sorry to hear about Amy. Such a special lass, if ever the Laird made one.'

'Thank ye, Helen. I ken Amy trusted ye enormously.'

'We trusted each other. We had to, ye ken? And let me introduce ye to the rest of my family. This is my husband, James, and my bairns, John and Beatrice.'

Edward greeted each in turn as they made room for him in the cart. Thomas sat up next to him. James gave the horse the signal and the cart began to move down the road. Fifteen minutes later, they came to a small house, pulled around the back and alighted. Edward noted several carts and separately tethered horses.

'Welcome to our place,' Helen said. 'Come in and make yerself at home.'

Edward walked into the kitchen where a dozen or-so people were gathered close to the fuel stove.

'Everyone, this is Thomas's Da, Edward,' Helen said. 'Some of ye might even remember him as Amy Fraser's husband.'

'*Halo,*' they chorused with varying levels of enthusiasm. A couple of the older people nodded knowingly. Others looked confused.

'Now, ye might be wondering why we've brought his Da along because, as we ken, we keep these meetings secret,' James said. 'Well, the truth is Thomas actually asked us if we'd mind if he invited him. He said he'd be prepared to swear by his Da's truthfulness, so Helen and I said to ourselves later, *well, that's braw enough for us.*'

There was a unanimous mumbling of agreement.

'So,' Thomas said. 'Because I knew my Da was to be here for another week, I thought I'd talk to him in a few days and then see if he wanted to come along. But because he's an impatient Highlander, he followed me last night, saw me get in James' and Helen's cart and then confronted me as I walked back into the Prendivilles. He was worried I was getting myself into trouble or spending my hard-earned cash at the pub, or something worse that I'm sure he hasn't even shared with me.'

There was a murmur and some restrained laughter from the group.

'So, my dear concerned Da, can I introduce ye to the Highland History Society, Tralee Branch?'

Edward was introduced to the members, mostly adults of various ages. The youngest by far was James' and Helen's daughter, Beatrice, who looked about fifteen.

'So, what d'ye do then?' Edward asked.

'Oh, that braw Highland brogue,' James said. 'Is it nay music to the ears?'

'We learn all about the Highlands,' Thomas said. 'Helen and James were born there; they came here when they were young but they've memories and relations still there, including people who've kept up the old ways, even throughout the Clearances.'

'What d'ye mean by the auld ways?' Edward asked.

'The history mainly,' Helen said. 'As ye ken, our schools are nay allowed to teach anything about Scotland afore Culloden. Anything about the Rebellion's told from the English side. Even the auld dress's frowned upon.'

'And the auld language's still forbidden,' James said.

'So d'ye learn the auld language?' Edward asked, excitement in his voice.

'Shh!' several of them said.

'Da, that's why the secrecy,' Thomas said. 'We learn the old language and we could get into trouble for it, even here in Ireland. There was a move in some of the Irish schools to teach the old Irish, but it's been squashed by the authorities, even the puppet Irish ones, so we can't take any risks.'

'And the Prendivilles nay ken any of this?' Edward asked.

'No, I wouldn't want to put them at any risk.'

'So ye're nay planning another Jacobite Rebellion?' Edward asked.

'Nay. More's the pity,' James replied.

'But Helen, ye were involved in a Jacobite cause with Amy, were ye nay?' Edward asked. 'That was the meeting I attended.'

'Aye. But Roy the rogue spoiled all that. The double-dealing rotter was just using the meetings to get to Amy. Then, when ye came along and spoiled it by marrying her, he turned us over to the authorities so he could get hold of the estate.'

'Aye, Amy told me all about that,' Edward said. 'He did finally get hold of the management title, did he nay?'

'Aye,' James replied. 'Only to run it all into the ground. He and his rotten mob could nay run a dog race much less an agricultural estate.'

'So, what happened to it then?'

'I was going to take ye there if ye wanted, Da,' Thomas said. 'But ye'd be sad to see it now. The government took it over when Roy was killed but they haven't done anything with it.'

'Old Robert Fraser, Amy's Da, would be devastated,' Edward said. 'But, aye, I'd like to see it, lad. Ye ken it's where yer life began, though ye'd nay remember much about it.'

They laughed.

'So, the Jacobite cause's dead then?' Edward asked. 'What about that Charles Stuart, the wee lad that Amy used to talk about as the next king?'

'Let's just say it's on hold, Edward,' James replied. 'Some might say Lord Stuart's a bit of a disappointment at this point. He seems to like the idea of being a king but not of fighting for it. He's more interested in chasing money and, dare I say it, women?'

'Aye, ye ken he's the bastard of a bishop?' Helen asked.

'Nay,' Edward replied. 'Amy nay ever said that.'

'Amy probably dinna ken,' Helen said. 'Nay any of us ken for a while. Amy would've been shattered to think a bishop would have a bastard child.'

'I'm nay so sure,' Edward said. 'I ken that's exactly what she'd have expected of a bishop. But it surely would've ruled the lad out as befitting the Jacobite cause that he'd have been sired by one.'

'*Ceart gu leor*,' Helen said, clapping her hands. '*Leigidh e beagan obair a dheanamh.*'

Edward remembered enough Scottish Gaelic to know the group was being called to order. They all moved to sit around the large wooden table in the kitchen, with James at one end and Helen at the other. He noticed that Thomas and Beatrice took the opportunity to seek each other out and sat next to each other. Beatrice leant into Thomas's side as though magnetised.

—⚉—

Two nights later, the Prendivilles held a family celebration for Thomas's eighteenth birthday. On this occasion, it was the twelve-year-old Eliza who secured the special place seated next to him.

Louise meanwhile ensured her own special place sitting next to Edward, as close as one person could be to another.

'So, when are ye coming to teach for us, Thomas?' Paddy asked during a quiet moment in the conversation.

Paddy had recently been appointed parish priest at St Brendan's church, Blennerville, just outside Tralee. He had been suggesting for a while that teaching would be a better long-term career for Thomas than labouring.

'Don't pester him, Uncle Paddy,' Denis said. 'Just because ye're a book worm doesn't mean he is. Just look at the boy; He looks healthier and fitter than Mrs Murphy's sow.'

'Thomas a sow?' Eliza said, looking up into his eyes. 'I think he's more like a gelding.'

'We know ye think that Eliza,' Denis said. 'Ye've thought it for at least twelve years, if not longer.'

They all laughed as Thomas leant over and kissed Eliza's head. She responded by brushing her hand over the spot where his lips had landed. In the same move, she reached up and gave him a prolonged kiss on the cheek.

Edward reflected on how his son had grown in the years since he had seen him and how loved he was in this place. Thomas was receiving the same warmth and generous giving from the Prendivilles that had been so important to Edward in his own growing up years. The only difference was in the passing of the baton. Mr Prendiville was gone and Mrs Prendiville near crippled in front of the fire.

But to their children and grandchildren, they had passed on their magnanimous ways.

'So, seriously, Thomas,' Paddy continued. 'There's a place for ye anytime at St Brendan's school.'

—⁂—

Later in the evening, Mary and Louise were washing and drying up, Denis was tending to Mrs Prendiville and the smaller children were heading to bed. Paddy, Edward and Thomas, the latter with Eliza's sleeping head resting on his shoulder, were talking about Thomas's future.

'D'ye fancy teaching, lad?' Edward asked.

'I think so. It runs in the family, doesn't it?'

'Oh, aye. My own Ma was a teacher, and Da taught for years before he went into the army. Will, my step Grand Da, taught all his life, and even Sarah taught for a while when I was growing up in the Highlands.'

'I hadn't realised that Grand Da was a teacher. All I ever hear about is his time as a Redcoat and, of course, about his little Redcoat.'

'Ye mean Edward's Pa?' Paddy said. 'Oh, indeed, he talked a lot about his time in teaching. I think he really enjoyed it. He used to say he learned so much himself when he had to prepare his lessons, about new things happening in science and, of course, his liberal views on religion.'

'Religion? Truly?' Thomas queried. 'What were they?'

'Oh, how long's this night?' Edward replied. 'My Da spent time in Persia, d'ye ken?'

'Yes, I think I knew that but tell me about it.'

Edward spoke about the things his father had shared with him about his eye-opening experiences in the Middle East. About meeting and marrying his first love, Mahdiya, his Persian Princess, as he called her. About how informed and worldly-wise she was, how devout and yet open-minded. About how much he learned from her that never left him.

Paddy would occasionally add something here and there from things he had picked up over the years.

Then, Edward told Thomas about his own trip to Persia with his father to meet Mahdiya's parents. About the scuffle with her brothers and how his father saved him more than once. About how much he himself had learned from travelling to a different world.

'Alright darling, time to put ye to bed,' Denis said to Eliza, trying to wrest her away from Thomas's shoulder.

'No, Da,' she protested, clinging to Thomas's arm. 'I haven't seen Thomas for weeks.'

'Well, if ye go to bed now, ye can be up early enough to see him tomorrow. Come on now darling, don't make a fuss and spoil the night.'

'Oh, alright,' Eliza replied, turning to Thomas. 'Promise I'll see ye in the morning?'

'I promise,' Thomas said, giving her one last hug for the night.

There was a break as Eliza went to bed and Mary and Louise helped their mother up and into her room.

'And then ye went to New South Wales, didn't ye?' Thomas asked his father.

'Aye, indeed!'

'Tell me about it. I sometimes feel like doing something like that.'

The following night, Edward's last in Tralee, he and Thomas went to the Campbell's place for a second birthday celebration. It was a small one, just with the family of four.

'Happy birthday,' Beatrice said, opening the door and landing a big kiss on Thomas's cheek.

'Thank ye, Beattie,' Thomas said, taking her in his arms in a way that suggested it was not the first time.

They sat to a simple meal of haggis and vegetables, washed down with an ale that had Edward pining for the master brew of James Squire he had encountered in Sydney Cove.

'So, ye ken haggis then, Edward?' Helen asked.

'Oh, aye. Mainly when I was living in Eskadale. Now and again my Da used to say he was craving for it.'

'He probably had to smuggle it in,' James said. 'Ye ken it was banned in the Clearances?'

'Oh, aye. Da used to say he'd probably be thrown out of his job at the Military College if anyone ken he was eating it.'

'Bally English,' James snorted. 'Could ye believe the stupidity of banning what ye can eat? For the Laird's sake. The sooner we're rid of 'em, the better.'

'Hush now, Da,' Helen said. 'Ye ken we agreed nay to talk like that in front of the bairns.'

'We're nay bairns, Ma,' John said. 'When the rebellion happens, I wanna be there in the front line.'

'Hush, lad,' Helen said. 'Ye dinna ken what ye're saying.'

'Ma, he ken what he's saying and so do I,' Beatrice said with an assertiveness that took them all by surprise.

'Now look what ye've started, *ceile*,' Helen said.

'Ma, d'ye truly ken we dinna ken what ye and Da are doing at those meetings?' John said.

Helen and James looked to each other, then to Thomas and Edward.

'So, do I detect there's actually more to yer meetings than learning the old language?' Edward ventured.

'Yes, there is, Da,' Thomas said. 'But there's nothing for ye to worry about.'

'Well, let me worry about what I worry about. But I'd appreciate ye filling me in on what this is all about. Ye ken I've had firsthand experience of what talk of rebellion can lead to.'

There was silence as Helen, James and Thomas looked to each other to see who would begin and how much should be said.

'Oh, tell him, someone,' Beatrice said. 'We wanna be rid o' the English, that's all. And Thomas is gonna lead us when we start the fight.'

Thomas could see the fear in his father's eyes.

—☙—

'Yer Ma'd be proud of ye, lad,' Edward said. 'Ye're her kin, for sure. I ken it more than ever now.'

'Thanks, Da,' Thomas replied. 'It means a lot that ye'd say that.

I suppose I've sensed it since listening to Helen who talks of my Ma as though she was a saint. But ye obviously knew her best, so it's heartening to hear what ye think.'

'Well, she was nay a saint, lad,' Edward replied. 'She was nay a saint and she'd nay wanna be remembered as such.'

'So, what was she then?'

'Better than the best saint,' Edward said, head down, choking on the words. 'Yer Ma, my Amy, was the bonniest lass who ever stepped on this earth. Ye can be so proud ye spring from her loins, believe me. She was straight as an arrow, true as the sunlight, as honest as the Laird himself.'

Thomas was struck by a comfort he had not felt before, one that comes from knowing without doubt that one was the product of a rare love match.

'Even though she nay believed in him,' Edward continued, his voice still breaking. 'The Laird, I mean.'

'Truly?' Thomas asked. 'Did she *truly* not believe? I've heard Mrs P occasionally say something like that – in a kindly way, of course – but I've never taken it all that seriously.'

'Has Paddy nay ever told ye some of the things she said to him as she was dying?'

'No, Paddy's always spoken so well of her, so I've always imagined he must've approved of her beliefs.'

'Oh, Paddy's such a braw man, a bonnie priest. If all priests were only like him, yer Ma might've believed in their God. She said as much at the end.'

'So, what *did* she say when she knew she was dying?'

'Well, she told Paddy she nay wanted the church's mumbo-jumbo,' Edward laughed. 'Nay for her or her bairn.'

'She was quite the woman, wasn't she? I'm sure there are plenty who think such things but to say it – and to a priest – and when ye're dying. I love her so much. I just wish I'd known her, even for a little time.'

'Aye, she was one in a million, lad. One in ten million.'

'Well, if Mrs P's right, I suppose I'll get to know her eventually,' Thomas said.

'Aye, and if yer Ma's right, then ye'll nay,' Edward laughed.

At this point, the carriage that would take Edward back to Dublin came around the corner.

'It's been so good having ye here, Da. Please come again soon.'

'Aye, I wanna see plenty more of ye, lad. Ye remind me so much of yer Ma. I feel close to her when I'm with ye.'

The father and son shook hands and leant into each other in gesturing towards the hug they had never really had.

'But be careful, lad. I'm still concerned that Jacobite thing could get out of hand.'

'Aw, don't worry too much about that. I think it's all a bit of a fantasy.'

'Well, I dinna ken. Young Beatrice obviously sees ye as the knight in shining armour who'll be leading the charge.'

'She's only a child,' Thomas said.

'A child who's in love with ye, lad. Be careful there. And while we're on the topic, careful ye dinna crush that sweet wee Eliza.'

'Da,' Thomas said, laughing. 'She's even more of a child.'

'Lad,' Edward said, looking into his eyes. 'If ye were a jouster, ye'd be carrying her kerchief on yer lance. Ye ken what I say?'

'I know, Da. I hear ye.'

VI

'Darling, I have the best news,' Jane said, greeting Edward at the door of Tarleton House. 'Charles has been accepted into the pre-seminary classes. He'll be starting in August.'

Edward had spent some days of travel pondering on the contrast between his Tralee and Burnley families. Experiencing the comfort of the developing relationship with Thomas made the sense of distance with his other children all the starker.

Of all his offspring, Charles was the least known to him. Beyond the self-assured disposition that bordered on the mystical, Charles had been closeted between Jane and Elizabeth from birth. Between them, they decided everything for him, and he seemed content with that. Edward was little more than a threat to their schemes, especially the one about Charles' future priesthood.

'And how does Charles feel about that?' Edward asked.

'Delighted, of course,' Jane replied. 'And don't you go saying anything to spoil it. Mummy and Daddy are so excited.'

'I've nay doubt.'

Edward had thought of sharing with Jane his delight with how Thomas was growing up and developing. He had even thought he might press the case again for a meeting. Those thoughts were dashed by the news of Charles tilting at the priesthood. He could only imagine what Amy would have said about that.

'Well, I'm sorry your son's achievements are of no interest,' Jane said. 'No doubt that other son of yours is doing far more important things than becoming one of God's chosen ones.'

'Oh, for the Laird's sake, Jane. Provided the lad's happy, I'm happy. But how would I ken when ye dinna let me near him?'

'What do you mean I don't let you near him? It's you who've never been here for him. Anytime he looks around, you're heading over to Ireland. You know? That place where your heart truly lies?'

Edward had been back in the house for a little over a minute.

'I'd best go and see to the estate.'

Edward stayed in the gardens longer than normal that night. Noting the roses that had bloomed while he was away and feeling the dirt in his fingertips reminded him of those happier times when he and Amy worked together on the Listellick estate.

—∞—

'*And we've had some wonderful news through the week,*' Father Bannigan began his sermon the following Sunday. '*Young Charles Lovat, son of Jane and Edward, will be entering the pre-seminary later in the year. Some will say he's chosen to study for the priesthood but there's no such thing as choosing when it comes to the priesthood. Only God does the choosing. In his infinite wisdom, God has selected young Charles to follow his Son, the Blessed Redeemer, in his mission to bring all souls to heaven. Just as the Lord chose the twelve disciples, so he chooses those he loves most to be his disciples in the world today.*

Of course, it's from such a family as the Braithwaites that we'd expect God to find suitable candidates for the priesthood. We all know that they have brought up their children to be exemplary Catholics. Now, their daughter, Jane, who committed herself to Our Lady when she was only young, enjoys the privilege of having her eldest son chosen in this way. Let us pray for them and ask God to continue to bestow his blessings on this already blessed family.'

Edward noted that God's bestowal of blessings did not include him. He and his father-in-law were book-ended on the pew, with Jane, her mother and the two children sandwiched between them. Charles and William were at Stonyhurst, so not present. Thankfully, in the case of Charles, Edward mused.

He and Elizabeth were separated by several bodies. Edward was sure Elizabeth, no doubt looking like the cat that ate the cream, was glancing across to gauge his reaction. He avoided glancing back and sat stoically through the purgatorial sermon. He amused himself by imagining what Amy would be making of it and how his father would be behaving. He became aware of the smile on his face when he noticed the priest staring at him.

'Wonderful sermon, Father,' Elizabeth gushed as she pounced on the priest at the end of Mass. 'We were all so thrilled, weren't we darling?'

'Yes, thank you so much, Father,' Jane said, pressing an envelope into the priest's hand.

'Well, it's such a blessing for your family,' Bannigan replied. 'Having a priest in the family is a sure sign of God's providential favour. I'm sure you must agree, Edward.'

'I bow to yer greater wisdom about such things, Father. I ken we just need to remember the lad's only fifteen. He's nay ordained yet.'

'But he will be,' Elizabeth said. 'He *will* be.'

Edward excused himself and went to visit the grave in which his mother and father lay. He stood, facing the headstone, praying for strength.

SACRED TO THE MEMORY
ELIZA CATHERINE LOVAT
BELOVED WIFE OF THOMAS
AND MOTHER OF EDWARD

29ᵀᴴ DAY OF JANUARY 1776
AGED 26 YEARS
REQUIESCAT IN PACE

AND HER BELOVED HUSBAND
THOMAS EDWARD FRASER LOVAT
26ᵀᴴ DAY OF JANUARY 1801
AGED 54 YEARS
REQUIESCAT IN PACE

'Ye're certain this is what ye want, lad?' Edward asked.

'Yes, Pa, I believe so,' Charles replied.

Charles was home on the long summer break from Stonyhurst. Edward had secured a rare moment alone with him. His only chances were after work and when Jane or Elizabeth did not have him button-holed to fit him out mentally for what lay ahead – or merely fit him out with the distinctive suit, shirt, and tie of the pre-seminary class. Even the socks were special.

'Are ye sure ye're nay being influenced by anyone?'

'I don't believe so.'

'Well, just remember it's *yer* life and nay anyone can tell ye what to do with it.'

'I know, Pa. I appreciate what you're saying.'

Elizabeth and Jane kept a close eye on the three boys, as if they feared Edward's negative influence. They had designs on all three entering the pre-seminary in the second half of high school. Whether this was a back-up plan in case Charles changed his mind or a comprehensive three-priest plan for the family, Edward could never work out. Whichever it was, it soon fell away as it became increasingly obvious that William was a perennial prankster and forever in trouble. Meanwhile, young Edward showed worrying early signs of being fascinated with the opposite sex.

For all that, Elizabeth and Jane did not give up easily on their three-priest quest, so turning their attention away from the only child with no sacerdotal potential, Emma Jane. She was the one child who was not constantly shielded from their father. As her relationship with her mother took the inevitable turn of mother-daughter loving and hating in one, so Emma Jane's bond with Edward grew.

'Can I come with you, Papa?' she would ask wherever Edward was going on days when school was not calling – and even on some days when it was.

'Don't be ridiculous, girl,' Jane would say. 'You have to go to school.'

'No, you cannot,' she would say on other days. 'You have to help with the housework.'

'Absolutely not,' on other occasions. 'Work in the fields is not for young ladies.'

For all that, Emma Jane, now ten years of age, and Edward found ways of being together, sometimes because Edward would put his foot down. At other times, simply because Jane and her mother were otherwise occupied.

'Where on earth have you been?' Jane shouted angrily on one occasion when her daughter tramped mud into the house.

'With Papa on the estate.'

'Doing what? Look at your hair. Get those boots off, clean up the mess you've just made on the floor and get yourself into the bath before your grandmother sees you.'

'I don't care what Gran thinks. I was helping Papa.'

With that, Edward entered by the same door, having heard the shouting.

'What's going on?'

'Mama's cross because I was helping you, Papa.'

'Without my permission,' Jane said. 'Yes, I *am* cross. What on earth are you doing to our daughter, Edward? Do you want her to be a lady or a ruffian?'

Edward told Emma Jane to go inside and clean herself up for supper. He turned to his wife.

'I want her to be happy. And she's happy when she's helping me in the fields. Besides, ye were nay here when she asked me.'

'Well, you know what Mummy will say, don't you? She would never have let me ruin my hands by working in the dirt.'

'Perhaps that's a pity, Jane. Perhaps ye'd be happier if ye had.'

'And who said I'm not happy?'

—⁂—

The following year, 1815, Archibald Lovat died suddenly in the Highlands. Archibald was the last of the Old Fox's sons. The Old Fox, the last to bear the title of Lord Lovat, had been beheaded for treachery in 1747 after the failed Jacobite Rebellion. Though never bearing the lordly title, Archibald was nonetheless MacShimid, Head of the Fraser of Lovat Clan.

Archibald had been a career diplomat and politician, finishing his life as the House of Commons Member for Inverness. It was as a diplomat that he had mentored Edward's father, Thomas, seeing him through the Middle East and back safely. When he was not looking after Thomas first-hand, his proxies in the diplomatic establishment had been assigned to do so.

The memorial service and burial would be in the Wardlaw Mausoleum at Kirkhill, near Inverness. There, Archibald's brother, Simon, and his children, including William Henry, were buried. So was his father, the Old Fox; or so they supposed.

Edward knew he had to get to the funeral for both his father's sake and that of William Henry, Archibald's youngest son and Edward's favourite childhood friend by far. He still missed his cousin, William Henry. He used often to think of him and wished he was around to help steady him amidst his increasingly difficult home life.

'No, I'm sorry, Edward,' Jane said. 'I have four children and aging parents to look after. It's fine for you to go gallivanting off as you do but I have responsibilities here.'

'But Archibald is *family*. Dinna ye ken ye have some responsibilities there as well? And dinna tell me yer parents are aging. Frankly, I wish they would – or yer mother at least.'

'Oh, Edward, what a beastly thing to say. My parents have been so good to us. You've never appreciated what they've done. Even when my mother's gone out of her way to plead your case to Mr Towneley for better pay and conditions...'

'Or plead yours, more likely.'

'Oh, truly, there's no point in talking with you when you're in this mood. And your family hate me anyway. Why would I go to any of their funerals, least of all in the bleak old Scottish Highlands?'

'How would ye ken what the Highlands are like? Ye've nay ever been there.'

'And never want to.'

As it was, Edward arranged to go to Kirkhill with Sarah. He had hoped that Will might come and, even more in vain, had it in mind to convince Jane that it might be useful to Charles's later studies to go to a funeral. As it was, Will was too infirmed to make it, being in his mid-nineties. Edward saved himself the trouble of yet another fight over Charles and decided to go alone with Sarah.

The service in the mausoleum was symptomatic of the end of an era that Archibald's passing represented, his five sons having predeceased him. So, what hope for the lordly title being restored? His octogenarian wife and sisters were there, looking bereft and broken. Only Georgina, the Old Fox's eldest child and matriarch of the Lovats, stood tall, but she was well into her nineties. They would all be dead soon, none of them with living children.

That would be the end of the line for a family that had been the backbone of the old Lovat dynasty of which Edward felt so much a part. The salient message was that the Highland Clearances had done their job of destroying the family so associated with Jacobite treachery.

Far from being bowed by it, Edward felt a stiffening in his spine. He wondered how Thomas was going in Tralee with his clandestine Jacobite cause.

VII

'Thanks *for comin'*, *Teddy*,' Louise said, burying her head on his shoulder.

'*Halo* Louise. I was so sorry to hear about yer dear Ma. I only wish I could've been here for the funeral.'

'That's alright, dear one. Ma knew 'er li'l Redcoat would've been 'ere in spirit. And 'o's this beautiful girl?'

'This is Emma Jane.'

'Come 'ere, Emma Jane,' Louise said, reaching down to give one of her characteristic hugs. 'Look at yer long curly 'air. I always wanted 'air like that. And yer gorgeous brown eyes. She's so like ye, Teddy.'

'Teddy?' Emma Jane asked as she laughed. 'Is that what they call you, Papa?'

'Aye, or wee Redcoat, as Louise's Ma always called me. There's a few long stories there.'

Mrs Prendiville had died in mid-1816, some two and a half years since Edward's last visit to Tralee. He had sent his condolences and promised to visit as soon as possible. He had hoped to get there in the long summer break of that year and had spoken with Charles about the idea of accompanying him before he entered the Jesuit novitiate. Charles had made it known that he was keen on the idea.

Fearing they might lose this round, Elizabeth and Jane conspired with the novice master, Father Constable – well named, they would discover – to require Charles to undergo a pre-novitiate retreat. It happened to coincide with the time Edward was going to Ireland. The compromise Jane offered was for the now twelve-year-old Emma Jane to accompany him, something pleasing to both father and daughter.

'*Halo*, Mary,' Edward said as Mary appeared from the kitchen.

Louise and Thomas had come to stay with Mary and Michael O'Rourke and family after Mrs Prendiville's death. The old Prendiville home was in desperate need of repair, a project slowly being addressed by Thomas and the Prendivilles in their spare time.

'So, where's that bairn of mine?' Edward asked. 'On a building site somewhere, I suppose.'

'No, did ye not 'ear?' Louise replied. 'Paddy finally got 'is way so Thomas's started teachin' at St Brendan's school.'

'Nay, I dinna ken that,' Edward said, looking to Emma Jane. 'So, yer brother's a teacher, lass.'

'I don't like teachers,' Emma Jane replied.

'Oh, I think ye'll like this one,' Mary said, laughing. 'Everyone else does.'

'Aye,' Edward replied. 'Especially one young lass called Beatrice, if my memory serves me correctly.'

'Sounds like ye've a lot o' catchin' up to do, Teddy,' Louise said. 'Beatrice's Ma and Pa got themselves into lots o' trouble, so Beatrice and 'er brother 'ad to go 'n' stay with relatives in Dublin.'

'I'd nay heard any of that. I was always a little worried about it. I hope Thomas was nay in the same trouble.'

'Well, that's part o' the story be'ind him goin' to teach,' Mary said. 'But we'll let 'im tell ye all about that.'

Emma Jane was unexcited at the idea of having yet another brother, teacher or no teacher. The only ones she'd had were the pestering William and young Edward and, of course, the "saint", as William referred to Charles, a brother who had paid little attention to her amidst his steady path to the priesthood. On the other hand, Thomas had craved to meet his father's other family, the only siblings he had.

'Eliza's so keen to meet ye,' Thomas said to Emma Jane.

'Who's Eliza?'

'Eliza?' Louise laughed. 'Tell 'er 'o Eliza is, Thomas.'

'Eliza's Louise's niece,' Thomas said.

'And Thomas's future wife if she 'as anythin' to do with it,' Louise said, roaring with laughter as if the neighbours needed to hear.

'Shh, Louise,' Mary said. 'Ye're embarrassin' the boy.'

'Ah, so Eliza's usurped yer Beatie, has she?' Edward asked.

'No, not really,' Thomas replied. 'Ye did hear what happened to the Campbells though, did ye?'

Thomas recounted the story of the Jacobite group being broken up by the authorities. Helen and James Campbell had been arrested and were incarcerated in separate prisons. There was talk that one, or both, might be sent to New South Wales. Hence, their children, Beatrice and John, had been sent away to stay with relatives.

'And ye were nay caught up in any of that?' Edward asked.

'No, Da, I heeded yer warning and stayed away from those meetings. Beatie wasn't happy with me and things turned bad for us, even before she had to go away.'

'Well, ye still could've been in trouble though,' Mary said. 'The authorities were turnin' over every stone lookin' for those 'o'd been associated with the Campbells. It was Paddy 'o saved yer bacon.'

'It's true, Da,' Thomas said. 'I owe Paddy a debt, for sure. When they came looking for me, he told them he'd give them a surety that I'd never again be associated with the Campbells and that he was giving me a job as a teacher. That's really why I started teaching.'

Paddy arrived just in time to catch the end of the conversation.

'Well, I'd been trying for years to get ye to come and teach at St Brendan's, hadn't I?' Paddy said. 'And who's this young lady?'

'Emma Jane,' Thomas said. 'My long-lost sister. My only sister.'

'Why hello, Emma Jane,' Paddy said. 'I guess that makes ye my long-lost niece.'

'Hello, Uncle Paddy,' Emma Jane said, looking up at the over-sized, ruddy-faced priest.

'Father Paddy might give ye a blessing, lass,' Edward said. 'If ye ask him nicely.'

Louise recounted the story of the first time Edward had received one of Paddy's blessings. Edward was an infant and quite frightened by the unusual ritual.

'I fair ken he was going to hit me,' Edward said, laughing.

'Perhaps I'll have one later,' Emma Jane said.

'It's a promise, darling,' Paddy replied. 'Now, I gather young Thomas has told ye he's coming to teach for us.'

'Aye, we were just hearing all about it,' Edward said. 'Thank ye, Paddy, for looking after my lad. The Prendivilles looking after the Lovats is a wee bit of a habit.'

'It's my pleasure, I assure ye,' Paddy replied. 'And d'ye know I have another young teacher coming to the school next year?'

'No,' Thomas said. 'Who's that?'

'Have ye ever heard of Eliza Prendiville?'

'But she's still at school,' Thomas said.

'She won't be next year,' Paddy replied. 'The church is actually paying for her to train at a college in Dublin. She'll start in January and she'll then be teaching at St Brendan's straight after Easter.'

—⚞—

Edward and Emma Jane stayed for several days with the O'Rourke family in their over-crowded dwelling. Each evening, another member of the family would come by for supper. Emma Jane delighted all of them. One by one, they commented on how much like Edward she looked, a comment that became more and more pleasing to Emma Jane with every passing.

'Not to mention 'ow like our Tommy she is too,' Louise would add.

On the third night, Denis came by with Eliza, his eldest daughter, now fourteen years of age. Emma Jane was keen to meet her, wondering if she might indeed be the future sister-in-law that Louise was predicting. She had found it quite wearing competing with Mary's children for Thomas's attention. They all seemed to love him and would occupy him from the moment he stepped in the door at night. She figured that situation would be even worse with Eliza present.

'Eliza, meet my one and only sister, Emma Jane,' Thomas said.

As it was, Eliza all but ignored Thomas all evening. Even when Louise tried to engineer her being seated next to him, Eliza said she would prefer to sit next to *Emma Jane, my new friend*.

'So, is it true you're going to be a teacher?' Emma Jane asked. 'At the same school where Thomas teaches?'

'I believe so. But he might be gone by then.'

Emma Jane and Eliza chatted together the whole evening. Only on a couple of occasions did Emma Jane notice the slightest recognition, a glance or smile, between Eliza and Thomas. When Denis stood up and ordered his daughter to say her farewells, she went from one to the other with a customary kiss, nothing more for Thomas than for the others.

'It's been so lovely to meet ye, Emma Jane. I feel as though we've known each other all our lives.'

That night in the bed they were sharing, Emma Jane spoke with her father about feeling part of a real family for the first time.

'The Prendivilles have that effect on all of us, lass.'

VIII

'They're all so lovely, Mama,' Emma Jane said, rushing over to greet her mother.

Jane offered a cursory hug before pushing her away.

'Well, they didn't do much for your hygiene, I see,' Jane said, rubbing some dirt from her daughter's cheek and looking closely into her eyes. 'And you have such dark circles under your eyes. You look as though you need a good sleep.'

'We've just spent eight hours in a carriage, dear,' Edward said. 'Even ye might end up with a wee bit of dirt on yer face in that situation. And she slept like a bairn the whole time, did ye nay, lass?'

Jane gave no time for her daughter to answer. With her mother absent, she knew she would be outnumbered.

'Away with you now, girl. Go and clean up before dinner.'

'Is Charles here?' Edward asked.

'He is. He's been here for a week, just as he said he would be. You complain that you can never get near him but then when he comes to stay, where are you? In Ireland, of course! How can you expect to get close to him if you're not here?'

'He'll be here for another few days, will he nay?'

'I don't know. You'll have to ask him. It's between him and Father Constable now.'

'Oh, and ye and yer Ma'd nay have any sway over him. Is that what ye're telling me?'

'I've no idea what you mean. Anyway, Charles will be at dinner so you can ask him yourself.'

Edward turned to leave the room to clean himself up for dinner.

'And Mummy and Daddy will be here as well.'

Tarleton House was still unfinished. The dining room and kitchen area had been one of the targets of attention for some time. Jane and her mother kept on changing their minds about exactly what should go where and having new ideas about the additional wing being built. Architects and builders would come and go, either giving up or being sent on their way.

'Most unlike Delaney,' Charles Braithwaite said. 'Most unlike him. Are you sure you didn't say anything to offend him, dear?'

'Offend? Of course not. Besides, any man who can't take a tiny bit of criticism of their work shouldn't be in the business.'

No-one said anything.

'Did you enjoy yourself in Ireland, Emma Jane?' Charles asked his sister.

'Oh, we don't want to hear about that,' Elizabeth said.

'No, I'd really like to hear about it,' Charles said.

'It was lovely. They're so friendly,' Emma Jane replied. 'Eliza and I became really good friends.'

'And who's Eliza?' Elizabeth asked.

'She's Uncle Denis's child but I think she and Thomas'll get married.'

'Oh goodness me, child,' Elizabeth said. 'I can't keep up with you. Who is Uncle Denis and who on earth is Thomas?'

'Thomas is my brother, I believe,' Charles said. 'And if I'm not mistaken, Uncle Denis is Mrs Prendiville's grandson.'

The table went silent. Jane and her mother looked at each other and then glared at Edward.

'And how do you know about these things, Charles, my dear?' Elizabeth asked. 'As if we need to ask. Personally, I don't think it's befitting someone with a vocation to do God's work to be dealing with sordid details of this kind.'

Edward slammed down his knife and fork. He paused to catch his breath and form the words needed. Charles stepped in first.

'I see nothing sordid in the fact that Pa was married once before and had a child from that marriage. In fact, I find it sad that Pa lost his first wife and even sadder that he's not able to spend more time with his first-born son.'

There was a further period of silence. Jane and her mother looked at each other. Edward picked up his cutlery and resumed his meal. Charles continued eating without looking up.

'Thank ye, lad,' Edward said. 'I appreciate yer words.'

'Words that you've fed the boy, I dare say,' Elizabeth snapped.

'No, Gran,' Charles replied. 'Pa has never told me about these things, and I regret that. I'm delighted that Emma Jane's been able to support him when clearly the rest of his family hasn't. I'm also envious of the fact that she's had the opportunity to meet our brother. I was hoping I might have had the opportunity but, as you know, Father Constable was instructed to arrange a retreat for me, no doubt with some incentive.'

None of them had ever heard Charles speak in this way. Edward was delighted. Jane and her mother aghast.

'But who else told you about all this, darling?' Jane asked.

'That's for me to know for now, Mama. But let me repeat that I did *not* learn it from Pa.'

Charles looked across the table at Edward.

'I'm only sorry, Pa, that we've not had the kind of relationship that would have allowed you to confide in me.'

'Thank ye, lad. I agree.'

The rest of the meal was spent in silence.

—⚬—

'But how've ye ken these things, lad?' Edward asked his son as they walked in the gardens.

Edward had left Jane and Elizabeth with the architect to discuss the next stage of development for Tarleton House. He knew this was a risky strategy, but he was prepared to deal with the consequences if it allowed him some time with Charles.

'Sarah knows, Pa,' Charles replied. 'She gave me a package that Archibald had apparently wanted to give me. They were special diary notes from his son, William Henry, who I assume was a close friend of yours.'

'Aye. I'll nay ever have as braw a friend as William Henry. I miss him more every day.'

'I'm sorry for your loss, Pa. I know things haven't been easy for you. William Henry obviously thought the world of you. I can tell from the way he speaks about you.'

'I nay had any idea he kept diary notes.'

'Well, he did. Very extensive ones about you, your travels, your struggles, your loves and your commitments.'

'My heavens. But why did he want ye to have them?'

'Apparently, he'd left them with his father in case anything happened to him. He told him to make sure I got them when I was old enough to understand. I've no idea why he would have chosen me rather than Thomas. But, according to Archibald's note, he specifically asked that they be passed onto me.'

'Perhaps he ken ye'd be a priest and he could trust ye.'

'Or perhaps he sensed I was the one who would need most help in knowing who you were. I've always thought that you and Thomas understood each other better than we do. I know you haven't seen Thomas all that much but, whenever I've heard you speak about him, I've wished it was how you'd speak of me. And then I know you were very close to your father too. And I see your relationship with Emma Jane, which is so beautiful. And yet I've always felt we were strangers to each other.'

'I'm sorry, lad. I'd nay idea that's how ye felt.'

'There's nothing to be sorry for, Pa. It's just the way it is. I understand that Mama and Gran have been over-protective and that's not left much room for you. I'm sorry that I'm only seeing that now.'

'My dear lad, I'm so pleased ye've said these things now. I canna tell ye how important to me ye are. And I've felt the same frustrations that we dinna ken each other well enough. Least of all well enough for me to say how worried I am that ye might be being pushed into the priesthood by yer Ma and Gran without ye ken what it means.'

'Oh, you shouldn't be worried about that. It's the one thing I'm certain about.'

'Tell me about that then because it's something I dinna ken. How d'ye ken ye want to be a priest?'

'It's not what *I* want, Pa. It's God who wants it. It's hard to explain but I just know God wants me to be a priest.'

'So, it's nay yer Ma's or yer Gran's idea? Or Father Constable's?'

'No. I know it's what they want too but that's not why I'm doing it.'

They walked in silence for a time.

'Well, there's only one other thing I have to ask ye,' Edward said.

'What's that?'

'Ye ken my Step Da, Will?'

Charles nodded.

'He said to me once that he'd like to speak with ye before ye take this step. I ken ye've nay ever met Will – yer Ma and Gran've seen to that – him being a failed Jesuit and all.'

'Well, I *have* met him actually, Pa.'

'Really? When?'

'Sarah paid a visit to Stonyhurst to give me the package from William Henry and Will came along. She said Will would like a word with me and she left us alone in the grounds.'

'Truly? I'd nay idea.'

'It was only a few weeks ago. Besides, I think they didn't want you to know in case you said anything to Mama and then there'd be trouble. They both care so much about you, you know?'

'Aye, I ken that. So, what did Will have to say?'

'Much the same as you. He just wanted to be sure it was my decision and that if I ever needed anything, I should feel free to contact him. But that I'd better be quick or else I'd have to contact him upstairs. He's a grand old man, so wise and so caring.'

'Indeed. So, ye convinced him that it's yer decision?'

'I believe so.'

'Well, if ye're able to convince Will, then it must be right.'

'Thank you, Pa. That means a great deal to me.'

At the beginning of the 1817 academic year, Charles entered the Jesuit novitiate in Hodder Place, Stonyhurst, a separate and more isolated site than the school and seminary. Here, he was to spend two years preparing for Jesuit life, being steeped in the spirituality of the Jesuit founder, Saint Ignatius of Loyola.

Ignatius had grown up in a Europe fractured by the Protestant Reformation and in a part of Spain dominated for centuries by Islam. As a young man, he had joined the army and been badly wounded, giving him much time to contemplate what to do with his life, should he survive.

Ignatius's response to these influences was, in many ways, encased in his so-called "Spiritual Exercises", a series of meditations on the Christian gospels designed to have the practical impact of making one a more Christ-like person. He had been inspired in part by the greater focus on practical Christian living to be found in Protestantism and the piety and lofty cultural expressions of Islam. At a time when Catholicism was at a low ebb, he worked to reform it so it could match the high standards set by these competing religious traditions.

'Goodbye, Mama, Pa,' Charles said as he bade farewell before the "clothing" ceremony that would mark the beginning of his novitiate. 'Goodbye Gran, Grandfather.'

'Don't forget me,' Emma Jane shouted out as she ran to give him a hug and a kiss. 'Don't get too holy in there.'

'Emma Jane, shush,' Elizabeth said. 'You need to learn to be more respectful. Charles is no longer your brother. He's one of the Lord's disciples.'

'Ye give yer brother the biggest kiss ye want, lass,' Edward said. 'I ken the Laird's braw enough to share him with ye. *My* Laird anyway.'

Elizabeth turned away with a huff.

That was the last they would see of Charles for two years. They watched the long ceremony that saw him change out of his street clothes and into the Jesuit habit, prostrate himself before the head Jesuit, called the provincial, and commit himself verbally to the first stage of Jesuit life.

At the end of the ceremony, Charles and the fifteen other novices went through the sanctuary door and into the Novitiate House so they could not mix with their parents and other onlookers.

'I'm so sad I won't see him for two years,' Jane said.

'Unless he leaves,' Emma Jane said. 'I hope he leaves.'

'Hush girl,' Elizabeth said as she turned to Edward. 'More of your influence, I dare say.'

'I dinna say a word, Mrs Braithwaite. So long as the lad's happy, I dinna mind what he does.'

'Well, that's a change of heart, I must say. Don't tell me you're finally becoming a Catholic.'

'I ken I've always been one; just nay *yer* sort of one, thanks be to God.'

'Stop it, Edward,' Jane said. 'Not today, please.'

'Papa didn't start it, Ma,' Emma Jane said. 'Gran did.'

'Please don't speak about your grandmother like that, girl,' Jane said. 'You'll be confined to your bedroom when we get home. And don't call me Ma. Honestly, ever since you came back from Ireland!'

'Oh, don't punish the girl, Jane,' Elizabeth said. 'We all know it's not her fault.'

—⚜—

The family, minus Charles, had been invited to their grandparents' place for a celebratory lunch. When they arrived, they found thirty or so guests there, including the Towneleys. All of Elizabeth's Catholic friends had been invited to a celebration approximating that of a wedding. Father Bannigan, retired, was there, as was the new priest assigned to the Towneley Estate Chapel, Father Shaw. He was cut from the same cloth as Bannigan, hardly surprising since Elizabeth Braithwaite's approval was mandatory for any such appointment.

Elizabeth was put out by the fact that Father Constable, the Jesuit novice master, had declined the invitation. She seemed not to realise he would be busy with his new novices. She had made such a fuss, he promised to send a Jesuit in his stead. To Elizabeth's horror and Edward's delight, Father Anthony Pritchard, his old science master, turned up at the door. Elizabeth had clashed with Pritchard years before, thinking him altogether too liberal on matters to do with Protestantism, Islam, and the role of women in modern society.

'Thank you so much for the invitation, Mr and Mrs Braithwaite,' Pritchard said as he entered the door, dressed in a casual shirt. Only his black trousers gave away that he was a priest.

'Welcome, Father,' Elizabeth said. 'Please don't scandalise the guests with any of your modern ideas.'

'I'll do my best, Ma'am.'

'Father Pritchard,' Edward said, extending his hand. 'How braw to see ye. I ken ye were in Rome.'

'Yes, I was for a time,' Pritchard replied, loudly enough to ensure Elizabeth heard him. 'I think the idea was to convert me to the ways of the one true faith. But, of course, that was futile.'

They laughed.

'At least you'll have someone to talk to, Edward,' Elizabeth said, walking away to her safer guests.

'Father, let me introduce ye to my daughter, Emma Jane.'

'I'm so pleased to meet you, young lady,' Pritchard said, extending his hand.

'Are you really a priest?' Emma Jane asked. 'You're not dressed like one.'

'No, he is not, is he, darling?' Elizabeth called from across the room. 'Why, on earth, is something you can ask him.'

'And you don't talk like one either,' Emma Jane added.

'What a wonderful thing to say to a priest,' Pritchard said, smiling. 'And I believe you have some sons too, Mr Lovat.'

'Aye, I do,' Edward replied. 'William will be up to some mischief somewhere and if I ken my youngest lad, Edward, he'll be seeking out some female company.'

'Ooh,' Emma Jane said, screwing up her face. 'Who'd be interested in him?'

'And then, of course, there's your Charles,' Pritchard said. 'I gather he's been delivered into the care of our Father Constable.'

'Aye, Father,' Edward replied. 'Is care the right word?'

'Let me just say, Constable is a good name for him. But I'm sure he'll prepare his young charges well for life in the church.'

Pritchard noticed the worried look on Edward's face.

'But I'll be there to keep an eye on him for you, so don't be too concerned.'

'Thank ye, Father. He's a bonnie lad; he truly is but I'm nay sure he ken what he's taken on.'

'Well, none of us did at his age, believe me. None of us did. If we had, we probably wouldn't be here – or me at least – much to the pleasure of your mother-in-law, I dare say.'

IX

In late January 1818, Edward took his annual break and headed for Tralee to celebrate Thomas's twenty-second birthday. It had been fifteen months since he had been there to console the Prendivilles over the loss of their mother.

'Please don't go there without me,' Emma Jane asked when Edward announced he was going.

'Well, I wondered if we all might go,' Edward replied.

'On a ship? On the sea?' Jane said, her eyes widening with alarm.

'Unless ye ken another way of getting there, dear.'

'It's unthinkable. William's going on retreat with Father Shaw and young Edward's been unwell.'

'That's alright,' Emma Jane said. 'I don't want them to come anyway.'

'I didn't say you could go either, young lady.'

'But I did,' Edward replied.

'Hooray, I'll start packing,' Emma Jane said, running out of the room before her mother could spoil things.

There was a moment of silence and icy stares.

'I'll see what Mummy thinks,' Jane said.

'There's nay any need for that, Jane. It's nay any of her business.'

Dear Thomas,

It's your brother, Charles. I'm so sorry we have not had the opportunity to meet. I do hope we can sometime in the future. Pa's cousin and friend, William Henry, left me his diary notes with all the details about your mother and how much she and our father loved each other. I'm so happy to know that you were born of such love. It seems to me that these things are sadly rare. I'm so pleased to know we share our father's love and that I have an older brother across the seas.

Pa tells me there are many similarities between us and Sarah has said we even look somewhat alike. Indeed, she tells me that we both look like Thomas, her husband and our grandfather. I truly look forward to us meeting when we can.

Your brother, Charles.

Edward had passed on the letter that Charles had written just before he entered the novitiate. Thomas read it on the spot.

'That's wonderful. I must write one for ye to take back with ye.'

'The only problem is I'll nay be able to give it to him until he's out of the novitiate.'

'What does that mean?' Thomas asked.

'Charles is in the Jesuit novitiate, training to be a priest.'

'You'd never do that, would you, Thomas?' Emma Jane asked.

'No, I don't think so,' Thomas replied, smiling.

'Because you'll get married one day, won't you?' Emma Jane said.

'Well, now that ye mention it, can ye keep a secret?'

They both nodded.

'Well, I was going to let ye know anyway but my birthday will be a double celebration because Eliza and I are announcing our engagement.'

'That's wonderful, lad,' Edward said.

Emma Jane said nothing. She dropped her head.

'We're both so excited for ye, lad. Aren't we darling? Ye're going to have a new sister.'

'Yes, it's wonderful,' Emma Jane said, lifting her head. 'I love Eliza.'

'And she loves ye, Emma Jane,' Thomas replied. 'She was *so* happy when she found out ye were coming.'

—⚜—

'Were ye crying?' Edward asked that night in the bed they were sharing.

'No,' Emma Jane replied.

'Ye *are* happy for them, are ye nay?'

'Of course,' she replied, turning over and burying her head in the pillow.

—⚜—

Two days later, the wider family gathered at Mary and Michael O'Rourke's place to celebrate Thomas's birthday. The extended Prendiville family was there, except for Paddy who had a wedding to perform.

'Happy birthday, Thomas,' they called out in unison.

'Thank ye; thank ye for coming. And while I have ye all here, I've an announcement to make.'

Eliza had been standing at some distance but, at that signal, she moved around to stand next to Thomas.

'Well, I know this won't come as a surprise to most of ye. But a little while ago, I asked Uncle Denis if he'd mind if I asked Eliza if she'd consider marrying me and I'm pleased to say he said he wouldn't. He wouldn't mind, that is! Mind ye, that was the easy part.'

The family laughed.

'Then, I had to find the words to ask Eliza – which I'm pleased to say I did – and then…'

'Just tell us if she said yes, or did she have better sense?' Denis called out.

'Pa!' Eliza said, scowling.

'Well,' Thomas continued. 'I had to work out the best way to ask her and…'

'Oh, for heaven's sake,' Eliza interrupted. 'It wasn't that difficult. He asked me and I said yes.'

'I asked her, and she said yes.'

The family cheered so loud it woke one of the neighbours snoozing on his porch. The nearby chooks let out a startled clucking.

'It's easy to see who'll rule yer roost, boy,' Denis shouted amidst the din. 'Ye've chosen well.'

Edward had never seen Thomas look so nervous. He looked at Emma Jane.

'Are ye happy now, lass?'

'I always was, Papa. I *always* was.'

The next morning, a Sunday, the family met again at St Brendan's church where Paddy was the parish priest. He was celebrating the 10am Mass.

'*… and I'm particularly delighted to announce the marriage banns of Thomas Lovat and Eliza Prendiville. As ye'd note from the name, Eliza is a relative, my niece in fact. And ye'll of course know Thomas who grew up in my Ma and Pa's house and has been like a nephew if not a son of mine – I dare say the only son I'll ever have.*'

The congregation tittered.

'*Needless to say,*' Paddy continued. '*My entire family is extremely happy with the match which, we have no doubt, has been in the Almighty's plan since the beginning of time. And while I'm talking about my family, I'd like to welcome Thomas's father and sister, Edward and Emma Jane*

Lovat, who are here with us from England. Some of ye will remember Edward from the time he was living among us during his first marriage to Amy Lovat, God rest her eternal soul. Welcome Edward and Emma Jane.'

Edward nodded his acknowledgement while Emma Jane slouched further down in the pew.

After Mass, there was much handshaking and kisses from the parishioners. Paddy then farewelled the family that headed to its various locations. Eliza went home with her family and Louise went with the O'Rourkes to help prepare Sunday lunch. Paddy would be late as he was saying the 11am Mass.

'I'm just going over to yer Ma's grave,' Edward said.

'I'm coming too,' Thomas replied.

'And me,' Emma Jane said, grabbing Thomas's hand.

They stood at the grave, offering silent prayers of their own choosing.

'What was she like?' Emma Jane asked.

'The bravest woman,' Edward said, his voice choking. 'Just like ye, lass.'

'I hope I'm like her, Papa. I hope you love me like you loved her.'

Emma Jane was still holding Thomas's hand, standing between him and her father. She looped her other arm through her father's and leaned her head against his shoulder, without letting go of Thomas. Thomas responded by stepping closer to them both.

'Ye're fortunate, Da,' Thomas said. 'Ye have some wonderful memories. And just like Charles said, I'm happy to know I'm the product of the love ye had for my Ma.'

'What about us, Papa?' Emma Jane asked. 'What about us? Charles, me and the boys? What do we come from?'

Edward stood in silence. He reached his spare arm around her neck and drew her closer.

'Ye're loved lass. That's all that matters. Ye're loved as much as a *dhuine* can love his own kin.'

The following day, Edward and Emma Jane were invited to St Brendan's school to meet Thomas' and Eliza's classes. They were teaching at the same school. Eliza had trained for three months at the Nursery School in Dublin that specialised in preparing Infants teachers. She was teaching the youngest children in the school, aged between four and six years of age. Thomas was untrained but teaching the older children, up to thirteen years of age.

'Now, girls and boys, say good morning to Mr Lovat,' Eliza commanded her class.

'Good morning, Mr Lovat,' the class echoed.

'Good morning, girls and boys,' Edward replied.

'And this is Mr Lovat's daughter, Emma Jane,' Eliza said. 'Say good morning, Miss Lovat.'

'Good morning, Miss Lovat.'

'Mr Lovat is related to someone in this school,' Eliza continued. 'Who do ye think that might be? Don't call out now. Hands up those who think they know.'

'Miss, Miss, Miss,' all but one of the children's hands shot up quickly.

'Maudie,' Eliza looked to the one child whose hand was not up. 'Who do ye think Mr Lovat might be related to?'

Maudie looked embarrassed and said nothing. The other children became frenetic.

'Alright, James,' Eliza said. 'Would ye like to tell us who Mr Lovat is related to?'

'Mr Lovat,' James replied.

'That's right. Have ye heard of Mr Lovat, Maudie?'

Maudie maintained her silence. The rest of the class laughed.

'Girls and boys. There's nothing to laugh at. That's alright, Maudie. Now who would like to tell Maudie who Mr Lovat is?'

Maudie leaped to her feet and ran to Edward, stood in front of him and pointed straight at him.

'Very good, Maudie,' Eliza said. 'This *is* Mr Lovat. Ye're absolutely correct. But is there another Mr Lovat that ye know about?'

'Miss, Miss, Miss,' the class was calling, hands shooting up at full stretch.

'Janet, do ye know another Mr Lovat?'

'Yes, Miss, he teaches my sister, and she says he's going to marry ye.'

The class fell to a mix of laughing and confusion.

'Oh, does she now? Well, we'll see about that, won't we? Now, do ye think Mr Lovat here's Mr Lovat's brother?'

'No!' the class called back amidst much laughter.

'Then, who do ye think he is? Patrick?'

'His Pa.'

'Very good. And who do ye think Miss Lovat is? Joanne?'

'His sister.'

'Very good. Yes, this is our own Mr Lovat's father and his sister. Aren't we lucky to have them here to visit us?'

'Yes, Miss.'

'Is there anything ye'd like to ask them?'

The visit progressed and eventually Edward and Emma Jane went to visit Thomas's class where the process of identification was quicker. After the lunch break, Edward went back to the O'Rourke home while Emma Jane stayed to help with Eliza's class.

'I think I want to be a teacher,' she said to Edward that evening.

'Well, it runs in the family, ye ken? I'm sure ye'd make a fine teacher.'

'Do you think Ma and Gran would approve?'

They looked at each other and smiled.

—⚬—

Dear Charles,

Thank you for the letter you sent to me through our father. I appreciated it very much. I'm also so pleased to know I have a brother, three in fact, and of course a wonderful new sister. I love Emma Jane very much. She also tells me that we look alike so I do hope we get the chance to meet soon somewhere sometime.

You might know that I am to be married later in the year to a most wonderful girl, Eliza Prendiville. I would love for you to be at the wedding, but I am told that will not be possible. In fact, I believe we will be married by the time you receive this. Perhaps you will be able to baptise our children should we be blessed with them. I do wish you well in your vocation. I hope it is everything you desire.

Until we meet someday, we'll have to let our beloved sister be our go-between. She speaks so highly of you.

Yours sincerely, Thomas.

This was the letter that Edward was entrusted with. He promised to pass it onto Charles at the first opportunity.

'So, I do hope ye can both make it to the wedding in July,' Thomas said as Edward and Emma Jane stepped into the carriage to take them to Dublin.

'Oh, yes, please do come,' Eliza said. 'Ye too Emma Jane, my dear friend.'

'I really want to,' Emma Jane replied.

Edward and Thomas farewelled each other with a firm handshake and a gesturing hug while Eliza and Emma Jane held each other tightly.

'You're my best friend,' Emma Jane said. 'And I can't wait for us to be sisters.'

X

'But I need you here,' Percival Towneley replied when Edward made the request to attend Thomas's wedding. 'Weren't you just in Ireland anyway?'

The exchange came hot on the heels of an even tenser encounter the night before when Edward was ambushed by Jane and Elizabeth, urging him not to attend. In turn, this encounter had been preceded by yet another plea from Edward that Jane and the whole family, minus Charles, should accept the invitation that had arrived that day.

'You know I've never been to Ireland and hope never to,' Jane replied.

'And ye ken this is very important to me. It's part of my life, *yer husband's* life.'

'Oh, don't go on, Edward. You made your choices, but they don't have to be my choices.'

'Well, I'd like the bairns there at least.'

So, it went on from there, the oft-repeated squabble that ended with the compromise that the child with no potential for the priesthood, Emma Jane, could accompany him.

The next evening, as Edward stepped into the house, Elizabeth attacked him for his lack of responsibility. Leaving his wife on her own. Risking his job. Fraternising further with the dreaded Irish. Jane stood to one side, the victim, saying not a word.

'Thank ye for yer thoughts on the matter, Mrs Braithwaite. Now, I have some work to do if ye'll excuse me. Jane, I'll have my dinner later.'

Overnight, the thought occurred to him that Elizabeth might try and influence Percival, so he went straight to his office the next morning.

'I was there for ten days and another ten's all I need,' Edward replied to Percival's objection. 'This is my lad we're talking about, sir.'

'But what about your other children? And your wife? How do they feel about you always going over there?'

'With respect, sir, that's nay anyone's business but ours – nay even Mrs Braithwaite's.'

Percival was not a man of strength or conviction. His capacity to sustain a line of argumentation was limited.

'Well, how long did you say?' he asked.

'Ten days.'

'With no pay?'

'Aye!'

—⚬—

'So, you're going anyway,' Elizabeth said.

'Aye, if ye must ken, Mrs Braithwaite.'

'And how's your wife and family to survive with no income, not to mention paying your debts?'

'Now, how would ye ken anything about no income?' Edward shot back.

Elizabeth fell silent. Jane, standing just behind her, had the look of a frightened rabbit.

'Because she's been talking with Mr Towneley,' Emma Jane called out from the next room. 'Like she always does, Papa.'

'From the mouths of bairns,' Edward said.

'Jane, will you control your child, please?' Elizabeth said, brow furrowed.

'Darling, go to your room,' Jane called to Emma Jane.

'Darling, ye can stay right where ye are,' Edward said. 'In fact, ye might as well come in here, seeing as ye're coming with me to Tralee.'

'Is that so?' Elizabeth said. 'What about her schooling?'

'It's not decided yet, Mummy,' Jane said.

'It *is* decided,' Edward replied. 'She ken what family responsibility is about. I only wish some others in this family did.'

'Your family is *here*, Edward,' Elizabeth said.

'Thank ye for reminding me, Mrs Braithwaite. Now, we were talking about how ye ken I was taking unpaid leave.'

Elizabeth struggled for words. Jane reached out to embrace Emma Jane as she ran past the two women and bounded straight into the arms of her father.

'When are we going, Papa?'

—⁂—

'*Thomas and Eliza, hast thou come here freely and without reservation to give thyselves to each other in marriage?*' Paddy began the Catholic marriage rite.

'I have,' they replied in unison.

'*Shalt thou honour each other as man and wife for the rest of thy lives?*'

'I shall.'

'*Shalt thou accept children lovingly from God and bring them up according to the laws of Christ and his Church?*'

'I shall.'

'*The couple will now declare their vows before God and this congregation.*'

'I, Thomas, take thee, Eliza, to be my wife. I promise to be true to thee in good times and in bad, in sickness and in health. I will love, honour and cherish thee all the days of my life.'

'I, Eliza, take thee, Thomas, to be my husband. I promise to be true to thee in good times and in bad, in sickness and in health. I will love, honour and obey thee all the days of my life.'

'Before God and his Church, I now declare ye husband and wife. Ye may kiss the bride.'

They were a contrast in colour and size. The six-foot-plus Thomas, black suit and black tie that blended with his dark brown – almost black – hair, reached down to the five-foot-three Eliza in a light cream lacy dress and matching veil barely covering her flowing fair auburn hair. Their faces were radiant as their lips locked in a way that suggested it might not be the first time.

Edward and Emma Jane were in the front row on the groom's side of the old church. They watched as the young couple signed the register of marriage, seated at a small table to the left of the altar adorned with tall candles and flowers of various hue. The date in the register was May 7, 1819, Thomas's mother's birthday. He had deliberately chosen it.

Edward said a silent happy birthday to Amy. Emma Jane looked up and noted his watery eyes.

The wedding breakfast was called such because it started at 9am. The religious ceremony concluded by 8.50 and the guests proceeded straight to the hall next to the church. Though it was almost summer, it was a drizzly day in Tralee, so no-one was inclined to stand outside. Even the traditional pouring of rice over the new bride and groom was done as they entered the hall.

The whole event reminded Edward of his own simple wedding at Listellick over twenty-three years before. How happy Amy would have been to see her boy married in this way, and to a girl so much like herself in the ways that matter. Even the fact that it was in a Catholic church would have been tolerable, granted it was

Paddy performing the "mumbo-jumbo", as she used to describe all Catholic ritual. The contrast with the elaborate occasion of his second wedding, orchestrated by Elizabeth Braithwaite, did not escape him.

'You make such a beautiful bride,' Emma Jane gushed as she gave Eliza a sisterly hug. 'Welcome to our family.'

'And welcome to our family,' Eliza replied. 'Ye're already my favourite sister but don't tell the others just yet.'

'Ye look so beautiful,' Edward said, giving Eliza a hug.

'Thank ye, Da,' she replied.

'I'm so happy to have another daughter. If ye're as braw as my other one, then I'm a very lucky man.'

'I'll try my hardest,' she replied, reaching out to draw Emma Jane into their small circle.

Thomas had been formally welcomed into the Prendivilles by Eliza's parents.

'It seems strange welcoming ye into our family,' Denis said. 'Because ye've been part of it almost as long as I can remember.'

'Aye, it's as though it was meant to be,' Edward said. 'After all the trauma of yer birth, ye've ended up in the best place of all.'

'With the best Ma in the world,' Louise said, catching the end of the conversation. 'Oh, I mean apart from what yer own Ma would've been. I'm sorry, Teddy. I didn't mean to…'

'There's nay anything to be sorry for, Louise,' Edward said as he held her tightly to his side. 'Ye've been the grandest Ma a lad could have.'

'Indeed, Ma, ye have,' Thomas echoed.

'Yes, Auntie Louise,' Eliza said. 'Thanks for preparing my husband just as I'd have wanted him.'

—⚜—

The wedding breakfast was more like a midday feast. The roast lamb and apple pie were washed down with ample amounts of ale. It lasted through until late morning. This was why weddings in Ireland were invariably on a Saturday when at least some of the menfolk were not at work.

Thomas and Eliza did the bridal waltz soon before noon and then slipped away only to re-emerge in different clothes. She was in a long, summery pale green dress, tight around the neck but with sleeves that barely reached to the elbows. He was in a brown suit that looked as though it had been made for someone else. Indeed, it had. It was the same suit his father-in-law, Denis, had bought for his own wedding some seventeen years before. Eliza's dress, on the other hand, had been lovingly made for her by her mother, with help from Mary and Louise.

After going around the circle of guests in opposite directions, the new couple met where they had started and, smiling broadly, wrapped their arms around each other and walked out the door, followed by the guests. The carriage awaiting them had been lovingly prepared with a rough "married" sign strapped to its rear and a handful of multi-coloured ribbons attached wherever they could be tied. Just before stepping up into it, they said one last farewell to their parents and immediate families.

'Ye look so happy, lad,' Edward said. 'Ye're so very *fortanach*. She's so much like yer Ma it's remarkable.'

'Thanks, Da. She's a braw lassie, as ye'd say.'

'And I'm a braw lassie too,' Emma Jane said as she gave Thomas a kiss and a hug. 'And don't you forget it.'

'How could I forget ye, my one and only sister?'

'You only need one when you have me, big brother.'

'And ye only need one Ma when ye 'ave me, remember,' Louise said, brushing Emma Jane aside and seizing on Thomas as the constable might an escaped prisoner.

Thomas began to fall backwards. Louise saved him and then gave him one of her bear hugs.

'I'm goin' to miss ye so much, my li'l Tom,' she said, nuzzling her head somewhere near his armpit.

'And I'll miss ye too, Ma. Ye've been so good to me. Thank ye for everything.'

'Oh, Tommy, just come back and see me as often as ye can.'

'I promise.'

As Thomas was extricating himself from Louise's grip so he could bid final farewells to Eliza's family, Eliza came and stood with Edward and Emma Jane.

'Thank ye so much for coming all this way, both of ye,' she said as they shared kisses and hugs.

'We'd nay have missed it,' Edward replied.

'I wouldn't have missed it for the world,' Emma Jane said, her eyes welling up. 'I just love being here, and I love it that we're now part of the same family and I love that we're now sisters and I … just love you.'

'And I love ye too,' Eliza said. 'I love both of ye.'

Edward stood silently as he watched the carriage move into the distance. The happiness of his son was a two-edged sword, offering deep satisfaction and profound sadness. Emma Jane looked up at him and rested her head on his arm.

'I'm so glad I'm your daughter, Papa.'

Edward kissed her on the top of her head, burying some of his sadness in her sweet-smelling hair. He was consoled in the knowledge that without the sadness, he would not have the gem he was holding at this moment.

―⁂―

Thomas and Eliza drove to a place called Farmer's Bridge, not so far from Tralee but in the other direction from Blennerville where they taught. The chances of being bothered by their pupils were therefore minimal. They took up residence in a small cottage in the grounds of a large farmhouse owned by people Paddy knew.

The cottage consisted of just two rooms, a lounge room and bedroom, plus a very small kitchen. Everything they might need for their three-night stay was laid out for them and any extra food required would be brought down from the main house once a day. They spent the first three nights of their marriage in the largest bed either of them had ever slept in.

'This bed's a waste of space,' Thomas said in the middle of one night.

'Well, it is when ye spend all yer time on my side.'

'Would ye rather I sleep over here then?' Thomas said, beginning to move away.

'No, don't ye dare,' Eliza replied, grabbing him, and hauling him back to be even closer than before. 'I never want ye further from me than this. Never. Is that clear?'

'Never,' Thomas said as they snuggled in to enjoy what they had already enjoyed several times so far.

By day, they sat on the veranda and read, walked the farm tracks hand in hand, ate and drank generously from the store of goods provided, before heading to bed, their favourite place of all.

On the fourth morning, they headed back to Eliza's parents' place where they lived until they could afford something of their own. The following Monday, they rode together to St Brendan's where they would begin the school year, Eliza still with the "littlies" and Thomas with the "big children".

XI

'Charles is the tall, handsome one third along,' Elizabeth whispered more loudly than protocol demanded.

Elizabeth's parents, Richard and Cecilia Glover, had accepted the invitation to attend Charles's profession ceremony in June 1819. For these avowed Protestants, it was the first time they had been inside a Catholic church. There had been a significant rift in the family when Elizabeth began courting a Catholic, one that grew to a major fracture when she converted to Catholicism and then married him. The Glovers did not attend the wedding, so Charles Braithwaite's elderly father walked Elizabeth down the aisle.

The rift had slowly healed but only by studiously avoiding the subject of religion, something the Glovers did far better than Elizabeth. They had wondered at the wisdom of accepting the invitation to a display of the worst of medieval Catholicism. But they loved their daughter despite her obsessive ways and, in the end, saw it as an opportunity to further the healing process.

'You know you won't be able to go to Holy Communion,' Elizabeth said as she greeted them outside the church. 'Only Catholics are allowed.'

'I'm sure we can cope,' Richard replied.

'Thanks for letting us know, dear,' Cecilia added.

'I've asked Father Constable if you can sit with us in the same pew and he has said that would be fine,' Elizabeth prattled on. 'But you should just remain seated throughout. Don't stand or kneel like we will.'

Richard and Cecilia nodded their understanding and, with a quick glance at each other, made their way in.

They took their place in the same pew that Edward, Jane, and the children were inhabiting. Jane had met with her grandparents several times in the past few years, each time when Edward was away. Edward had therefore not met them, though Emma Jane had told him that she liked them.

Edward was on the end of the pew on the aisle side so Elizabeth and her parents had to shuffle past him and the children before passing Jane to take their places next to Charles Braithwaite at the other end of the pew. Elizabeth ushered them in without bothering to introduce Edward. Nonetheless, he stood and greeted each of them in turn.

'I'm so pleased to meet you at last, Edward,' Cecilia said, pressing his hand.

'Yes, we've heard so much about you,' Richard whispered as he grabbed his elbow and squeezed it.

'I've nay doubt,' Edward said as they shared a knowing smile.

'Hurry on now, Mother and Father,' Elizabeth ordered.

They took their places just in time for the procession to begin. Richard and Cecilia were awestruck by the majesty of the church, the stained-glass windows, statues, and flowers of all colours abounding everywhere they looked. The ornate altar was bedecked in gold, including candelabras that seemed almost to be touching the vaulted ceiling. The organ was playing a Bach prelude and fugue that would never be allowed in their church.

As the procession began passing their pew, there was the distinctive odour of burning charcoal and incense. Clouds of smoke were billowing in all directions from the thurifer who led the procession, swinging the thurible forward, backward, and then in semi-circular fashion around his body. It was everything their Protestant upbringing had told them was banished in the Reformation but here it was before their very eyes.

'You mean saintly, don't you?' Elizabeth said in reply to her mother's querying Charles's sickly appearance.

'No, dear, I said sickly. He looks to me as though he needs a good feed.'

'Obviously you can't see him properly,' Elizabeth said.

'Well, perhaps, if I was able to stand!'

Elizabeth ignored her, knowing her mother would find something to complain about in this popish environment.

The ceremony began with the routine prayers of a Catholic Mass. Richard and Cecilia did as they were told and sat rigidly while those around them stood, knelt, and occasionally joined them in sitting. They were perfectly happy to have it known that this was not their brand of Christianity.

After the reading of the gospel, which was from chapter five of St Luke's version where Jesus calls the disciples to follow him, Father Marmaduke Stone, the head of the Jesuits in England and Wales, proceeded to the pulpit to deliver the sermon.

'*Dear friends, welcome to this special occasion that sees the Jesuit congregation confirm these young men as worthy of membership. Welcome to you their families and their friends. Welcome to our fellow Catholics and, as well, those who might not be of our faith. Please feel entirely at home and free to join with us today in our celebration …*'

Cecilia dug her finger into Elizabeth's side as much as to say, *well, he's nicer than you.* Elizabeth flinched but otherwise ignored it.

'*… These young men will likely venture far in a world that is changing so rapidly. No longer can we assume to live out our lives in our own small villages, alongside those who look and sound like us, who share our own ways and beliefs. We live in an age of discovery, where worlds are colliding, where East, West, North, and South are merging* *and so the challenges before all of us are to step out of our narrow worlds where we think only our way of looking, sounding and believing is the right way and embrace this far more exciting world that confronts us.*

This is what the Lord himself did in his own ministry. In today's gospel, we read that he chose as his disciples those who were largely the marginalised, the unimportant and the cast out. He might have chosen the rich, the powerful, those considered most respectable, but he chose the least of people. In his parables, he tells us why this is so. It is among the rich, the powerful and the respectable that we find the hypocrites but among the least, we find the humble ....

And so, today, these young men are taking vows of poverty, chastity, and obedience to ensure their humility, that they will never glory in the power of priesthood, should they reach that point, but use the power that God will give them to emulate his Son in confounding the powerful and lifting up the humble...'

Cecilia was hanging off every word, nodding her agreement and emitting small vocal sounds that affirmed it. Elizabeth sat rigidly, ignoring her mother, and hoping to erase from her mind the unwelcome sentiments coming from the Jesuit head. She had been relieved not to see Edward's old teacher, Father Pritchard, among the assembled priests but was by this time feeling he might as well have been there.

What Elizabeth did not know was that Father Pritchard had also taught Father Stone who, like Edward, had come to see him as a mentor. Unlike Anthony Pritchard, Marmaduke Stone was a leader of men who had assumed the title of provincial, or head, of the English and Welsh Jesuits at an early age. It was at a time when being Catholic in England was difficult because Catholicism was not yet a recognised religion. Catholics were by and large considered treacherous and so being a Catholic priest was to be a leader of the traitors and a Jesuit priest the next worst thing to being a pope.

It was in this difficult world that Stone had proven to be a crafty leader. He had travelled widely to places like Russia, India, Japan, and Egypt and so seen and experienced a variety of cultures and religions. He was respected for his knowledge and understanding by his fellow clergy, even those of the Protestant traditions. Hence, he had managed to build up the Jesuit establishment in England and Wales at a time when it was least expected. Notwithstanding greater professional recognition than Anthony Pritchard, whenever asked about the biggest influences on him, he would always say, *Father P, without doubt.*

'I'm starting to think some of these Jesuits are really Protestants,' Elizabeth grumbled to Jane after the ceremony. 'I only hope Charles is not influenced by people like that.'

'Well, let's just be thankful he's been under Father Constable for the last two years,' Jane replied.

'Indeed, why on earth would the Jesuits not have him as their provincial instead of that heretic?'

—ᴍ—

'So, tell us about your professors, Charles, dear?' Elizabeth asked.

It was the first of four visitors' days allowed per year. The whole family, minus Jane's unwell father, had travelled up from Burnley. Edward had hoped Elizabeth might see it as a greater duty to be with her husband.

'Father Caldwell teaches Scholastic Philosophy, Father Lemming teaches Logic, Father Stone takes us for European Philosophy, whenever he can get here from London, and Father Pritchard for Philosophy of Science,' Charles replied.

'Oh my,' Elizabeth replied. 'I thought that man had retired.'

'Who?'

'The last one, the science one.'

'Father Pritchard?'

'Yes, whatever his name is.'

'I think he *was* retired but the priest who used to take the class had to go to Rome, so Father Pritchard stepped in. You know him, don't you, Pa?'

'I certainly do, lad. You could nay have a better teacher.'

'And he married you and Mama, didn't he?'

'He did indeed. And did a wonderful job too, I might say.'

Elizabeth and Jane turned and began walking towards William and young Edward who were throwing a ball to each other some distance away.

'So, what's yer favourite class?' Edward continued. 'Apart from Philosophy of Science, I mean.'

'I actually like them all. Father Stone's a wonderful teacher too. He's travelled so widely so he brings all sorts of experiences into his classes.'

'And Logic. How do you go with that?'

'I really like it. I think it's something everyone should do.'

'I agree, lad. There'd be a wee bit more sense in the world if they did.'

'What's Logic?' Emma Jane asked.

'It's all about the things we should believe,' Charles replied. 'And the things that make no sense even though people often believe them.'

'I don't understand,' Emma Jane replied.

'Aye, neither do lots of people,' Edward said. 'That's the problem.'

They laughed as they walked towards the others who were preparing the picnic lunch. Emma Jane walked between the two men, holding their hands.

—⚹—

There were twenty-two young Jesuits sitting with their families on the vast lawn. The families were spread out but many of them were close enough to see what some of the other families were eating. Most were eating sandwiches and cake or simple sweets. Elizabeth had organised a feast, complete with a roast chicken, vegetables, and ornate sweets, including sponge cake and chocolates.

'Eat up, Charles, darling,' Jane said. 'You look a little thin.'

'It's alright, Charles,' William said. 'I'll eat anything you don't.'

'Where's Stanley Wentworth?' young Edward asked, scanning the lawn.

'He left,' Charles replied. 'How do you remember him?'

'Oh, no reason.'

'He doesn't remember *him*,' William said. 'He remembers his sister. He didn't stop talking about her for weeks after your profession. What was her name, Charles? The tall blonde one.'

'Cecile.'

'Cecile Lovat,' William said. 'It has a ring to it, doesn't it, little brother?'

Young Edward picked up the ball and made to throw it at William.

'Oh, don't go on about such things, boys,' Elizabeth said. 'What do you mean he left, darling?'

'He was just gone one morning. Father Caldwell told us at the start of class. I don't know what happened, but he didn't seem happy the last time we spoke.'

'I'm sure he must be unwell,' Elizabeth said. 'There'd be no other reason to leave, especially so soon after his profession.'

'Would you Charles? Would you ever leave?' Emma Jane asked, wrapping her arm through his.

'Don't be silly, girl,' Elizabeth shot back. 'Charles will *not* be leaving.'

'But he might fall in love like his brother,' Emma Jane said.

'Don't be silly, girl,' Elizabeth said.

'Who's in love?' Jane asked.

'Thomas. He married Eliza.'

Edward smiled. Elizabeth and Jane were silent.

'Well, my brother's a very lucky man, isn't he?' Charles said.

'Not as lucky as you, dear boy,' Elizabeth said. 'And just you remember it.'

'Yes, Gran.'

'Or as you, little brother,' William said. 'Now you know Cecile's name.'

This time, young Edward did throw the ball. William ducked as it sailed by. It landed on Emma Jane's plate, propelling the slice of jam and cream sponge cake onto Charles's soutane.

'Aah,' Emma Jane screamed.

'Look what you've done, you silly boys,' Elizabeth said.

'Sorry, Charles,' young Edward said.

Jane jumped up and ran over with a cloth. Emma Jane was already scraping bits of jam, cream, and cake off the soutane. Charles was helping her.

'It's alright, little brother. It'll wash off.'

The next visitation day was near to Christmas that year. Mr Braithwaite was bedridden. Elizabeth had come down with a bad case of influenza. Jane felt obliged to stay with her parents and the boys had been banished for their behaviour at the last visitation day. Edward and Emma Jane went alone. It was snowing so the families all met their young Jesuits in the refectory.

'So, are ye happy, lad?' Edward said.

'Yes, Pa. Very much so, thank you.'

'It really *is* yer calling, then, is it nay?'

'It seems so. God's been good to me.'

'So, when you see those pretty girls,' Emma Jane said, pointing to different corners of the room. 'Like that one over there – or that one there, what do you think?'

'I think I have the prettiest girl in the room right here.'

Emma Jane gave Charles a kiss on the cheek.

'See, you even know the right things to say to a girl. It's such a waste giving yourself to God.'

Charles smirked but said nothing.

'I'm certain Emma Jane dinna mean it to come out like that, lad,' Edward said.

'I'm sorry, Charles,' Emma Jane said. 'I really am. It's just that I love you so much and I want you to be happy and…'

'It's alright, darling sis. I love you so much too, so I understand. But I *am* happy. This is the life I want.'

'So, it's not just because of Ma and Gran?'

'No, it's truly not. I know in my heart that God wants me to be here.'

'Tell us what Father Pritchard's been teaching you about then,' Edward said.

'I will, Pa. But first tell me about the brother I've never met. I hear he and Eliza are having a baby.'

Dear Thomas and Eliza,

I'm writing to say how pleased I was to hear about little Mary. Please do accept my heartiest congratulations. The experience of being parents for the first time must truly be one of life's most blessed moments. I thank God for the gift He has bestowed on you and I will continue to pray for Mary's health and wellbeing, and your own, at Mass each day.

I am enclosing a small medal of Our Lady of Olaz. As your Mary shares her name with the Mother of Our Blessed Lord, I'm sure she will look after her. I do hope and pray that I will get to meet her one day, my first-born niece.

Yours in Christ, Charles.

Mary Louise Lovat was born on the 6th day of February 1820, one day short of nine months after Thomas and Eliza's wedding. She came five days before the expected date.

'Can't we go, Papa?' Emma Jane kept nagging. 'I've never had a niece and I want to see her before she's too old to hold.'

'I'm sure we'll get there before then, lassie.'

XII

As it was, they did not get to Tralee until Thomas' and Eliza's second born, over two years later. John Edward Lovat was born on the 20th day of May 1822.

Edward and Emma Jane had plans to be there a year earlier, in the summer break of 1821, but events overtook their plans.

'Edward,' Jane said. 'Charles is going to Rome. He must be your priority at this time.'

Charles had been selected to go to Rome to complete his theological studies. It was considered a rare honour and flagged that the Jesuits had big plans for his future.

Dear Thomas and Eliza,

Please forgive me yet again that I will be unable to be with you as intended. I am only able to get one week off work and it happens to be the week that Charles will be embarking for Rome. Emma Jane is disgusted with me and is threatening to travel to Tralee on her own. I'm letting her fight that out with her mother and grandmother. Knowing Emma Jane, I suspect you will be seeing her soon.

My love, Da.

Emma Jane prevailed upon her brother, William, to accompany her to Tralee in early August of that year. They stayed two weeks with Thomas, Eliza, and baby Mary.

'So, was the bairn nay too big to hold?' Edward asked Emma Jane on their return.

'No, she's adorable, Papa. I think she looks like you. She and William are in love, aren't you, Will?'

'I wouldn't say that sis, but she's cute, I admit.'

'I suppose she's crawling by now,' Edward said.

'Walking's more like it,' Emma Jane replied. 'And talking. And you know what she says?'

'Mumma, Dadda, I suppose.'

'Yes, and *Papa*.'

'Truly?' Edward said, lowering his gaze.

'They talk about you all the time, Papa. They love you so much.'

'Who loves who?' Jane asked, walking into the room.

'Thomas and Eliza. And baby Mary calls out for Papa,' Emma Jane replied.

'Really? How quaint! Now, you two need to get to bed. And please be quiet. Your grandfather's asleep.'

Jane's parents had moved into the near-completed Tarleton House with the Lovat family. Her father's health had remained at a low ebb for years. His heart was said to be failing. This was used on occasion as another excuse to keep Edward from going to Tralee.

—⚜—

In late September 1822, Charles wrote for the first time since departing England.

Dear Mama and Pa,
I am now settled in Rome at the Jesuit College. It is in Borgo Santo Spirito, right next to the Tiber and a five-minute walk from Vatican

City. It is a rare privilege to be here in the centre of Catholicism. You could not believe the difference in religious atmosphere from Burnley where Catholics are looked down on. I am enjoying my studies immensely. One of my professors, Father Juliano Raverra, is considered an outstanding interpreter of St Thomas Aquinas. I am learning so many things I sometimes feel my brain will explode with the new ideas.

We are also encouraged to read the works of Barnabas Chiaramonti who is, of course, the current pope, Pope Pius VII. He is a very holy man, a Benedictine monk, and a renowned theologian. Father Juliano, who has taken me under his wing, went to school with him in Cesena. He has promised to introduce me sometime. Can you believe that? Me meeting the pope! Father Juliano says the church owes everything to Pope Pius VII. He took over when the church was under siege and went on to secure a Concordat with Napoleon. Things are now very settled here, thank the Lord, and we owe most of that to His Holiness.

Please continue to pray for me, as I do for you all. Please give my love to Gran, Grandfather, my dear brothers and, of course, my favourite sister.

I love you all, Charles.

PS. I do hope Grandfather is a little better. Please let him know I offer special prayers for him at Mass every day.

'He's getting so holy, isn't he?' Emma Jane said. 'I wish he was still here.'

'Don't be so ridiculous, child,' Elizabeth said. 'Who would want to be here when they can be in the holiest place in the world? Imagine our Charles meeting the pope? How wonderful. We truly are a blessed family, even if we don't *all* see that.'

Edward and Emma Jane shared a smile.

'He does seem so happy, doesn't he?' Jane said. 'My son a priest. I can't believe it.'

'Not quite a priest yet, dear,' Edward said, risking yet another scorning.

'He *will* be,' Elizabeth replied. 'I've always known it, haven't I?'

'You have, Mummy,' Jane replied. 'You have. And if he's praying for Daddy, then I'm sure he'll get well.'

As it was, Charles Braithwaite died in late October of that year. Elizabeth became an old woman overnight. She clung to Jane more than ever.

Edward and Emma Jane finally made it to Tralee in the autumn of 1823. Thomas and Eliza had moved back into the old Prendiville home with their two children and Louise. Thomas was still spending what spare time he had finishing the renovations with help from the family. Most of the work was now on the inside. There were new timbers on the floor in front of a larger fireplace. A new stove had also been installed. The rest was a work in progress.

'It's coming on well,' Edward said. 'But it still feels like the old place, which is braw.'

'Ye'd never want it any other way, would ye Da?'

'Nay, lad! Anyway, congratulations are in order, I hear.'

'Ye mean the new job?' Thomas replied.

'Aye, it's braw, lad. Tell me about it.'

'Yes, there's some interesting things happening in education here. The government's finally taking some interest in it and St John's is one of the first schools to benefit. Most education's been done by the Catholic Church up until now.'

'It's nay a Catholic school, then?'

'No, St John's is a Church of Ireland school, but the plan is that its funding will come straight from London. There's a young Whig called Edward Stanley who's pushing this idea of "national schools". He thinks church schools divide the population, and he's right. With some luck, it'll be the beginning of a whole new school system that'll create more opportunities for all young folk and overcome the sectarian strife. There's a way to go yet but trying it out at St John's is a great start.'

'And what does Paddy ken about ye going over to the Protestants, pray tell me?'

'Well, ye know Paddy. He must be one of the most tolerant Catholic priests God ever made. He said, *take it boy, they'll be able to pay ye far better than we can.* Besides, the diocese is building a new convent in Blennerville for the Augustinian Nuns. I'm not sure there'd have been a job for me anyway.'

'So, the pay'll be better?'

'Yes, apparently, and with us in the baby business, we have to think of that. Eliza had to stop work once we married, so I have to think of how to support this growing family.'

'How many more will you have?' Emma Jane said, cuddling baby John.

'A few more, we hope,' Eliza said. 'It's really lovely. I hope ye have lots of children too, Emma Jane. Ye're so good with them. Just look at ye. John won't go to anyone other than Thomas and me, but ye walk in and he's yers.'

'Yes, we always talk about how ye were with Mary last year,' Thomas said. 'Goodness, she just loved ye.'

'And William.'

'Oh yes,' Thomas laughed. '*Unca Will*, as she says. Unca Will was a favourite too.'

'I hope ye both have lots of children,' Eliza said. 'It's truly such a blessing.'

'Yes, make sure ye have lots o' l'il ones, Emma Jane,' Louise said, bringing in the tea.

The following week, Thomas took up his new post as the assistant headmaster at St John's Church of Ireland school in Tralee. Edward and Emma Jane stood at the gate, watching him being introduced to the children.

'Do you feel proud, Papa?'

'Aye, lass. Of him and of ye.'

Emma Jane wrapped her arm around his and rested her head on his shoulder.

'I'm so glad you're my Papa, Papa.'

'I'm so glad too,' Edward said, kissing her on the top of the head. 'So glad.'

'Are you sad not having your wife here?'

'She's here, lass.'

'I meant Mama.'

XIII

Charles was ordained in Rome on the 11th of July 1824. The whole family was planning to go but a bout of diphtheria broke out in northern England that year.

Emma Jane, who had been working as a volunteer nurse at a local orphanage, was the first in the family to contract it.

In quick succession, the two boys succumbed. Elizabeth was not coping well so went to stay with Percival and Constance at Towneley Manor. Jane went with her. Edward became a full-time nurse for his three children.

'Do you have any glycerine, Mr Lovat?' Dr Fowler asked.

'Aye, I'm sure we do.'

'I'll leave you with a small bottle of salicylic acid. If you mix the glycerine in water, about half and half, and add a drop of the acid, then try and get her to drink the mixture in small doses.'

Edward ran to the kitchen, pulling bottles off their shelves until he found half a bottle of glycerine. He grabbed a glass and ran back up to Emma Jane's room.

Simon Fowler was a local doctor who was attending the orphanage where Emma Jane had picked up the disease, or so they thought. The two had become close. Emma Jane had confided in Edward, but they had both kept it from Jane and her mother. The first meeting with Edward was when Fowler came to call as Emma Jane's doctor.

'Thank ye for coming so quickly,' Edward said.

'I'm just sorry to be meeting you in these circumstances, sir,' Fowler replied. 'Emma Jane has spoken so fondly of you. I've been looking forward to meeting you.'

'She's such a bonnie lass. The apple of my eye, as they say.'

Edward choked on the words. He was silent as he watched Fowler trying to get Emma Jane to drink the mixture.

'That's it. Just a little more.'

'Papa? Papa?' Emma Jane called.

'Does she ken I'm here?' Edward asked.

'I'm sure she does. Just sit here, if you wish, and I'll go and check on the boys.'

'Darling lassie. Dinna ye leave me. Remember that's our pact. Ye canna go before me.'

Emma Jane squeezed his hand. She tried to speak through her laboured breath.

'Dinna stress yerself, darling. I'll be here.'

'Love ... you ... Papa.'

'I ken, darling. And ye ken how much I love ye. Ye're the *is fearr* thing that's happened in my life.'

—⁂—

Fowler came back to the home late that night.

'I'm so sorry to say this, sir. More than I can say. But I don't think she'll make it through the night.'

Edward's head fell over Emma Jane's chest. He clung to her hand. Fowler could hear him weeping. A little later, Edward lifted his head.

'Would ye mind letting her Ma ken? She's at the Towneley Manor.'

'Of course, sir.'

Fowler went to the manor house. He was told that Jane was sleeping. He insisted she be woken. After some time, Percival came to the door.

'Please, sir, Mrs Lovat's daughter's extremely grave. She needs to come immediately.'

Percival guaranteed that he would convey the message in all its urgency. Fowler left to return to Tarleton House.

Edward, alone in every sense, watched his nineteen-year-old daughter take her last breath.

—⚘—

Dear Charles,

We write with the saddest news. Our darling Emma Jane died last night. She had been afflicted with diphtheria for the last week. We believe she picked it up from the orphanage where she was doing voluntary work. She knew the risks but, as we know, that would never have stopped our baby from doing what she thought was the right thing. We are devastated, as you can imagine, and we know you will be too. You two always had something special between you, even if much of it unspoken. We know that Emma Jane will be with you on your special day next week. We are sad that we cannot be there, as we had planned.

Emma Jane will be buried in a small ceremony tomorrow but perhaps we can have a more suitable celebration of her life when you are home. I suppose you will be able to perform the ceremony. Please do not let this tragic event overshadow the wonderful step you will be taking. You know Emma Jane would not want that and neither do we. We look forward so much to seeing you whenever that might occur.

All our love, Mama and Pa.

PS. Thank the Lord your brothers seem to be recovering from their own bouts of diphtheria.

Edward asked Fowler to post the letter when he came around to check on William and young Edward.

'I'm so sorry for you both,' Fowler said. 'Is Emma Jane's mother here?'

'Nay, she decided to stay at the manor house.'

'I'm not sure why she didn't come last night. I thought I made it clear that Emma Jane was extremely ill.'

Edward shook his head but said nothing.

'I know my loss is nothing compared with yours, sir,' Fowler said. 'But I do want you to know how very fond of Emma Jane I was. My parents have always thought I was too fastidious when it came to forming relationships. They're probably right. But I knew from the moment I met her …'

Fowler went silent, head down. He reached for his kerchief.

'Thank ye so much for telling me that, Simon. Yer loss is a real one then. I ken what a loyal friend Emma Jane could be. She was more than a daughter to me and, if God had willed it, I'm sure she'd have been more than a wife for ye, if I might say. I'm sorry for both of ye that fate's o'ertaken what ye might have had.'

'Thank you, sir. Would it be alright if I come to the burial?'

—⁂—

The epidemic had created panic among the people and burials were happening without delay. Emma Jane's funeral Mass was held on the 4th of July 1824, a bare thirty-six hours after her death. Edward and Jane were the only family members present. William and young Edward were still in bed and Elizabeth was too unwell. Percival Towneley and Simon Fowler were there, together with a handful of workers and families from the estate. Father Shaw was the celebrant. Granted it was one of seven funerals that day, he forsook giving a sermon.

'Of course, I'd have come if I'd known how ill she was,' Jane said.

'I thought Simon made it clear to Percival that she was unlikely to survive the night.'

'Simon? Who's Simon?'

'Simon Fowler. Dr Fowler.'

'No, he didn't. I swear he didn't. Anyway, why Simon? Do you know him, do you?'

'No, but Emma Jane did. They were close.'

'How close?'

'Quite close. I think they might have ended up together.'

'Truly? Did you know about that?'

'Aye, Emma Jane did mention it and Simon confirmed it after she died.'

'That'd be right. Dear Papa hears it all while her mother's left out in the cold.'

Edward was silent.

That evening, he made sure the boys were alright and took the sulky for the short ride to the cemetery. He lay on Emma Jane's grave and wept.

XIV

'I wonder if I might go home and visit my family, Father? Especially after the tragic time they've had.'

'*Capisco*, Charles,' Father Margolio said. 'But *Padre* Stone, he say it would be unwise. The *epidemico*, it is still *male*. And *mio fratello*, you *non bene*.'

Charles had kept his illness from the family. The last Roman winter had been severe, and he had rarely been without a respiratory condition. There had even been some consideration of postponing his ordination.

'I send you to *Reggio Calabria* for the *estate*, the summer. You help in the parish, but I write to *Padre Dinardo* to say you're there for *recuperare*.'

'Of course, Father.'

'*Bene*. Another year and, *per favore dio*, your England will be *bene* – and you'll be *bene*.'

The decision had been made that Charles would stay in Rome for an extra year to complete a Licentiate in Sacred Theology. He was earmarked for an academic career.

'Fortunately, Brother Lovat is the academic type,' one of the

English-speaking consultors had said as the Jesuits decided on the future paths for that year's ordination class. 'He's certainly not fit for the missions.'

—⁂—

Charles went south in August. He had not journeyed widely during his time in Italy but what he had seen was mainly to the north of Rome. He had visited Assisi on several occasions, as well as Bologna and Padua. The furthest south had been once to Naples. He came to see that the southernmost tip was a very different Italy. As the carriage wound its way along the high coastal road, he took in the most spectacular views he had ever seen. High cliff faces falling into a buffeting ocean, little villages here and there, their white stone houses cascading down the hillslopes all the way to the seashore. Reggio Calabria was one of the villages.

Apart from a couple of Masses on Sunday, one through the week and a few confession rosters, his time was essentially his own. The superior made it clear that Charles was there to rest and get well before heading back to a Roman winter.

He wandered the streets, took in the marketplaces, walked barefoot on the beach, and stopped for coffee at street-side cafes. It was the first time he could remember having time on his hands. He thought much about his family, especially Emma Jane, the sister he loved so much but hardly knew. And now never would. He remembered her asking him whether he might fall in love someday. He loved the frank and fearless way she could cut through, at times almost as though she knew those innermost thoughts that he rarely revealed to anyone. He had been looking forward to getting to know her better – and to her getting to know him. There was no-one else in his life quite like her.

He wondered how his mother and grandmother were coping with their tragic loss, as well as their disappointment at not making it to his ordination.

He thought especially about his father. He had come to appreciate him when it was almost too late. It was only because of the letter from William Henry that he had come to know about his past, his own sorrows, how much he kept bottled up inside him.

'*Is that where I got that from?*' he wondered.

He looked forward to being reunited with his father. To knowing him for the first time.

In mid-September, feeling much better, he travelled back to Rome to begin his licentiate. There was a letter waiting.

Dear Charles,

We write with many mixed emotions. We take great joy in the blessings of your ordination. We are so proud to have you as our brother. Congratulations on this wonderful occasion.

At the same time, our hearts are heavy with the loss of our darling sister, Emma Jane. We could not believe the news when it came and we thought of you and the shock it must have been, just as you were about to celebrate the greatest day of your life. We thank God that we came to know her so well through her visits here over the years. Our children loved her too. Mary still asks about Aunty Emma Jane and when is she coming again. Eliza and Emma Jane became so close and she is especially sad at losing her.

We also worry about our father and how he is coping. We know that he loves us all, but I think we knew and accepted long ago that Emma Jane filled a spot in his heart that could never be replaced. We feel so very sad for him. We understand you have been selected to do further studies in Rome so it will no doubt be even longer before we meet. However long it takes, we cannot wait for that day.

All our love, Thomas, Eliza, Mary and John.

Charles sat down that same day and wrote back.

Dear Thomas, Eliza and family,

Thank you so much for your kind letter. It is indeed such a sad event that our dear sister, Emma Jane, has gone to God. I pray for the repose of her soul every day at Mass. I fear you actually might have come to know her better than me, which saddens me, but I truly did love her and admired her spirit. I was looking forward to being back with her where we might have come to know each other better. God's ways are not ours, of course, and strangely I feel closer to Emma Jane since her death than at any time prior to that.

I share your concern for our dear father. He has borne too much, and I can only hope and pray that he can come to trust in God's good providence. I do pray for that more than anything. I too hope we can meet after I am back in the Isles.

Yours in Christ, Charles SJ.

After sealing the envelope, Charles took a breath before reaching for another ream of paper and dipping the quill into the now near-empty inkwell.

Dear Mama and Pa,

I am writing to let you know I am back in Rome and about to begin my Licence studies. I did ask if I might be able to come home first but was told it was considered unsafe because of the epidemic. I have been in Reggio Calabria, a beautiful spot on the tip of Italy's boot. I had my first opportunity to feel like a priest by celebrating Mass and hearing confessions. I also had the opportunity to relax for the first time in a while. I thought much about you all and especially my dear sister. I felt her presence at my ordination, and I continue to feel she is beside me. I thank God for his goodness and for giving her to us for as long as he did.

May God bless her and take her to Himself. All my loving best wishes to Gran and my dear brothers.

Your loving son, Charles SJ.

—⚜—

Charles wrote these letters on the first day back in Rome. On the second day, he began classes for his licentiate. The first lecture was taken by a newly appointed professor, Luigi Taparelli. Luigi was only a few years older than Charles. Charles had never been taught by a professor so young.

Taparelli was a devotee of the works of Thomas Aquinas. He referred to him as "The Angelic Doctor". Taparelli believed that the genius of Aquinas had been lost amidst the challenges of the Renaissance, the Protestant Reformation, and the birth of modern science. He regarded Aquinas as the key to understanding what had happened in these movements, rather than fighting against them as Catholicism had done too often. Through Taparelli, Aquinas came to life in Charles's mind. He came to see Catholicism in a different way. He came to see it as the tradition that should be leading the world's thinking, rather than reacting to it. Under the inspiration of the medieval Muslim scholars, Aquinas had provided Christianity with the means of accommodating itself with science. Science was no enemy of religion. They were bedfellows so long as religion did not retreat into narrow, reactionary ways of thinking, including about God.

Taparelli only lasted in the Jesuit College until the winter break. Some of the young priests were shocked by his approach. The Belgian and Spanish provincials complained about his theology, one even accusing him of heresy. When the Jesuit General in Rome refused to listen to them, they wrote directly to the pope. Charles was certain the pope would dismiss their spurious claims as well. He knew however that the wonderful man he had met in his first year in Rome, the holy and wise Pius VII, had been replaced by an unknown quantity. Anibale della Genga had become Pope Leo XII in late 1823. He was unwell and rarely seen. There were rumours about a shady past, including fathering several children, but Charles did not believe them.

What Charles did believe was that the new pope was anti-Jewish and anti-Muslim in a way that seemed to belong to the past. He was nonetheless confident that the Jesuits would not be forced to dismiss someone as brilliant and important to the future of Catholicism as Taparelli.

He was wrong.

Charles endured the rest of his licentiate, continuing to read the scholars that Taparelli had introduced to him. Not only Aquinas but the friar scientist Roger Bacon, the Muslims al Farabi and al Ghazali, the Jews Maimonides and Abulafia, the Protestants Luther and Zwingli, the cosmologists Copernicus and Newton, the philosophers Locke, Kant, Hegel, Voltaire, and Hume. Through the eyes of Aquinas, he came to see the synergy between all these exciting thoughts and the Catholicism he believed in. To him, it was a very Jesuit Catholicism, bold and advanced, not meek and recalcitrant. He was certain the sacking of Taparelli was an aberration, one the Jesuits would retract sooner rather than later. He could not believe that this was a mark of where the church was heading.

Charles looked forward to being at home and talking these things through with his father and Will.

Winter that year in Rome was especially bitter and extended. By Easter time, Charles's health was suffering again.

XV

In the summer break of 1825, Edward travelled to Tralee. William and young Edward accompanied him. In March of that year, Thomas and Eliza had their third child, Elizabeth Emma Jane.

We want you to know that we are dedicating this child to our beloved sister, they had written to Edward and Jane. *Please visit us when you can.*

'There'll be a special Mass said for Emma Jane,' Edward said. 'Surely ye'd come for that if nay for any other reason.'

'I'm not interested,' Jane replied. 'And neither is Mummy.'

Edward had extended the invitation to Elizabeth to accompany them.

'Ye're nay interested in our daughter, is that it?'

Jane ran from the room, crying. Edward cursed himself.

—∞—

'*We remember especially our beloved sister, aunt and friend, Emma Jane, who departed this life too early but having made her mark all the same. We thank God for the gift he bestowed on us in the person of*

Emma Jane and we pray for the repose of her eternal soul,' Paddy said during prayers at the end of Mass.

'Thank ye, Paddy. I ken Emma Jane'd be grateful.'

Paddy rested his hand on Edward's arm.

'Are ye alright, Edward?'

'Aye, thank ye.'

'It's not easy, is it?'

'Nay, but who ever said it's meant to be?'

'Let me know if there's anything I can do, won't ye?'

'I'm nay sure what I'd have ever done without the Prendivilles.'

'Well, we have to keep our Ma happy, ye know? Or else she'll haunt us for eternity.'

'What's that about 'auntin' us?' Louise said, interrupting.

'Our Ma will if we don't look after her li'l Redcoat.'

'As if we wouldn't,' Louise said, grabbing Edward's arm and squeezing it until it hurt.

'Thank ye for bringing William and young Edward with ye,' Denis said. 'All the children love them. Just look at them, will ye?'

William and young Edward were playing a noisy game of chasings with the children capable of running. Mary was five years of age and about to start her first year of school. John was three.

'How do ye like being a grandfather, Denis?' Edward asked. 'Several times over, that is.'

'It's wonderful. So much easier than being a parent, isn't it? I reckon ye have a lot more to look forward to, what with those two fine young fellas there. Surely they both have the young girls hanging off them by now?'

'Young Edward for sure. His problem's choosing between them. William seems to prefer male company at this stage.'

'Well, I ken which of them I'd rather be,' Denis laughed.

'Me too.'

'She loved it here,' Edward said. 'I ken ye gave Emma Jane the taste of family we nay ever had back home.'

'That's sad,' Eliza replied. 'But I'm so happy if that's the case. She was the loveliest sister. We were friends from the first moment.'

'I ken ye were, lass. She always said the same. She actually spoke about ye, both of ye and yer bairns, the day before she died.'

'Truly?'

'Aye, she said she had to get better because the idea of nay ever seeing ye again was more than she could bear.'

There was a moment of silence as they all looked down at the table.

'So, Charles is coming home?' Thomas asked.

'Aye, he's been appointed to Llanrothal.'

'Where's that?'

'In Herefordshire. The Jesuits have a seminary there, so he'll be teaching philosophy and theology.'

'Ye must be excited, Da, but I suppose ye'd have liked to have him closer.'

'I canna wait to see him but frankly I'm a wee bit relieved he'll nay be too close.'

'Because of his Ma?'

'And his Gran!'

—⋘—

Edward and the boys stayed to watch Thomas invested as the headmaster of St John's. The occasion brought Emma Jane to mind. The last time he had stood in this spot, three years ago, she had been at his side.

The next day, they rode to Dingle and embarked for London. They had been invited to stay with Mary Beth and Carl Solander at Highgate. Mary Beth and Carl had sailed with Edward on *HMS Gorgon* to Sydney Cove in 1791. Mary Beth was, at the time, married to the ship's commodore, John Parker. Carl was an agronomist whose mission was to collect flora from the various ports where the ship landed. His father had sailed with Captain James Cook when the British first claimed the great southern land as their own. It was to Carl that Edward owed his initial fascination with the natural world and its flora. Carl had steered him towards agronomy.

'Edward Lovat,' Mary Beth said, kissing him on the cheek and holding him close. 'It's been far too long.'

'Mary Beth, it's so wonderful to see ye. Please meet my lads, William and Edward. Young Edward, we call him, for obvious reasons.'

Mary Beth gave each of the boys a kiss and turned back to Edward.

'They both look so much like you. Such handsome boys.'

William and young Edward noted the look she gave their father.

'Come inside. Carl's so excited to catch up on everything.'

Edward had not seen either of them since their wedding twenty-six years before. It was not so long after his own marriage to Jane. The Solanders still lived in the same Highgate, London, mansion where Edward had stayed after John Parker had died. He came again and stayed after Amy had died. Edward and Mary Beth had explored a future together, but Edward chose to marry Jane instead. Soon afterwards, Mary Beth and Carl had wed.

The guests were treated to the kind of meal that Edward remembered so well. The best food and drink, all served by the domestic staff. Carl sat at one end of the large dining table and Mary Beth at the other. Edward sat on one of the long sides and the two boys were opposite.

The boys were fascinated with the long recounts of the voyage to New South Wales and back. They were things Edward had said little about over the years. They were fascinated with the idea of their father as a fifteen-year-old.

'We envy you your children,' Carl said as the guests took their chairs in the lounge room. 'We would have loved to have children ourselves.'

Mary Beth shot a scornful look her husband's way. She turned to Edward.

'Yes, it wasn't our good fortune, but you've made up for it, darling Edward.'

'Aye, it's been braw, but it has its sorrows too.'

'Oh, of course,' Carl said. 'I'm sorry for my insensitivity. You lost a child, didn't you?'

'Aye, my daughter, Emma Jane. She came down with diphtheria last year. The boys had it too but fortunately got over it. There were families who lost all their children. Families that were wiped out entirely.'

'It must be the worst thing,' Mary Beth said. 'To lose a child.'

'It nay gets any worse.'

'Losing a sister's almost as bad,' young Edward said.

They sat in silence, sipping the port.

'I'm so sorry for your loss,' Mary Beth said. 'For the loss you've all suffered.'

'But at least you have your boys, Edward,' Carl said.

Mary Beth looked again at her husband. He looked up and noticed her stare. He looked away. Edward noted the exchange before replying.

'Aye. It's true, Carl. I need to keep reminding myself. And, of course, there's Charles as well.'

'Oh, yes, I can't wait to meet him,' Mary Beth said. 'The day after tomorrow, did you say?'

'Aye, the ship's due at midday.'

—⁂—

The following day they relaxed around the house. Mary Beth took William and young Edward into the village in the morning while

Edward inspected the surrounding estate with Carl. They had lunch together on the lawn. Carl went back to work on the estate and the boys went inside. Mary Beth and Edward were left alone at the garden table.

'Darling Edward, are you happy?'

'Aye, enough!'

'Why did you stop writing?'

'I'm sorry. Life became so busy.'

'Too busy for a best friend?'

'I'm sorry, Mary Beth. Sometimes, there's too much to write to write.'

'What does that mean? Too much to write to write?'

'I mean there are too many things to say. Some of them best nay said anyway.'

Mary Beth looked away. She was silent for a moment before looking back at him.

'You're not happy, are you, darling?'

'Nay, well, losing Emma Jane was the cruellest thing imaginable. I'm nay sure I can ever be happy again.'

Edward pulled out his kerchief and blew his nose.

'Of course, darling. How stupid of me. How could you ever be happy after that?'

There was more silence.

'Tell me more about her,' Mary Beth said. 'So, you were close to her, were you?'

'So close. People used to say we were inseparable. Jane and her Ma used to get infuriated at how much time we spent together.'

'Why on earth? Wouldn't that make them happy?'

'Happy?' Edward scoffed. 'I dinna ken Jane or her Ma truly ken what the word even means.'

'Tell me about it.'

'Oh, what's the use? I recall ye telling me I'd have to lie in the bed I made. Well, here I am, lying in the bed I made.'

'Oh, darling. I'm so sad for you. So very sad for you.'

Edward sat silently, staring into his glass. Mary Beth studied him.

'Tell me more about Emma Jane.'

—⁂—

'Braw to see ye, lad,' Edward said.

'And you, Pa.'

Charles embraced his father and brothers.

'Ye ken yer sister would've been the first here.'

'I'm sure she's here. I feel she's been with me from the time she went to heaven.'

They embraced again before piling Charles's luggage onto the hired carriage and making for Highgate.

'You look like you could do with a good meal, brother,' William said.

'William's just jealous, Charles,' young Edward laughed. 'He'd love to be skin and bone, but he never will be.'

The two brothers jostled each other and laughed.

'Ye've lost weight, lad, have ye nay?' Edward asked.

'Yes, Pa. It was one of Rome's chillier winters. I succumbed to a few ailments.'

'Is that why they're sending ye to Hereford? Because they ken it's warmer?'

'Perhaps. But they're also starting a new philosophy of science program there.'

'And ye're to teach it?'

'Yes, apparently, with some help from Father Pritchard.'

'How exciting, lad. I canna wait to talk about it with ye.'

'And Father Pritchard?'

'Aye, and Father Pritchard.'

'Perhaps Gran would like to join us?' Charles laughed.

'I'm sure she would, lad.'

—⁂—

'Father Charles,' Mary Beth said. 'What a blessing to have you stay with us.'

'Thank you for your generosity, Mrs Solander. My Pa has often spoken of your kindness to him in the past.'

'We do have a shared history, your father and me,' Mary Beth replied, glancing and smiling at Edward. 'Please do make yourself at home.'

It was late on a balmy August afternoon when they arrived. After washing, and a change of clothes, they met together in the garden for drinks before dinner.

'So, how *is* Rome these days?' Carl asked.

'You've been there?' Charles replied.

'Indeed. My father loved Rome, so we often went there from Sweden. Not in summer or winter, mind you.'

'Oh, no,' Mary Beth said. 'I've been there in both and I agree, Rome is for mid-season.'

'I didn't mind the summers actually,' Charles said. 'After England, I found them quite a pleasant change. But the winters, oh my heavens.'

'So, ye were sick this last winter, were ye, lad?'

'Yes, Pa. In fact, for the last couple of winters.'

'Ye kept that to yerself.'

'Yes, I didn't want to be worrying everyone, especially Mama and Gran.'

'Mama and Gran worry?' William said. 'I can't imagine what you're talking about.'

'Least of all about you, Charles,' young Edward added. 'I'm sure they've forgotten you exist. I imagine we'll have to introduce you all over again. *Yes, Mama and Gran, remember you have another son and he just happens to be a priest.*'

They laughed. Mary Beth watched Edward smiling and enjoying his sons' banter.

It was getting dark and dinner was ready. They walked inside and took their places. They were in the same spots as the night before. Charles joined Edward on his side of the table. The roast chicken, vegetables and gravy were placed in the middle.

'Will you have a wine with your meal, Father Charles?' Carl asked.

'No, I don't drink. Just water, thank you.'

'More for us,' William said.

'Aren't you allowed to drink, Charlie?' young Edward asked.

'Yes, we're allowed to. I've just chosen not to. Anyway, enough about me. Tell me about how you all met. It was actually on the boat to New South Wales, wasn't it?'

'How long do you have?' Mary Beth said. 'Yes, it was. Almost thirty-five years ago now. But it seems like yesterday. None of us had ever met but we became the best of friends, didn't we?'

Carl and Edward nodded.

'It must have been unusual for a woman to be on a trip like that,' Charles said.

'Well, there had been a number of women make the trip,' Mary Beth replied. 'But they were all convicts. I only went along because my husband was the ship's commander, and I didn't want to be separated from him for nearly two years.'

'You were a sailor, were you, Carl?' Charles asked.

'Heavens no,' Carl replied. 'Mary Beth's talking about her first husband, John Parker. He died some years later at sea.'

'I'm so sorry,' Charles said.

'It's alright, Father,' Mary Beth said. 'John was a wonderful husband, and I was heartbroken when he died but I've been blessed to find another wonderful husband.'

Mary Beth reached out and rested her hand on Carl's forearm. As she pulled back, her eyes met with Edward's.

Mary Beth, Carl and Edward talked at length about the travel through Africa, the South Pacific, Sydney Cove and Norfolk Island.

The boys heard for the first time the extent of Carl's influence on Edward's career in agronomy. They noted the affection between the three of them. Charles especially saw the happy and relaxed father he had rarely known.

XVI

Two days later, they began the journey back to Burnley. Charles would stay for a few days before taking up his appointment in Herefordshire. Jane and Elizabeth had insisted he should stay with them at Towneley Manor.

'Ye dinna mind, do ye lad?'

'No, Pa. As long as that's alright with you.'

'Anything for peace, lad. Anything for peace.'

—⚭—

'Oh, my boy, how proud I am,' Jane said as she knelt in front of Charles. 'Please give me your blessing.'

'And me, darling boy,' Elizabeth said as she knelt next to her daughter.

'*Benedicat vos* …' Charles said as he made the sign of the cross over the two women, completing the ritual by laying his hand first on his mother, then his grandmother.

'Oh my, you're too skinny, darling,' Elizabeth said. 'Those Italians know nothing about cooking.'

'Well, they do actually, Gran.'

'And you're pale, darling,' Jane added. 'We're going to fatten you up and give you a bit of home care while you're here.'

'Thanks, Mama, but I'm fine. Truly.'

'Well, we'll see about that, dear,' Elizabeth said. 'Mr and Mrs Towneley have been kind enough to put on a special homecoming meal for you tomorrow night. We'll start the fattening up there and then.'

'Oh, I don't want to put you to any trouble, please,' Charles said.

'Just leave it to us, darling,' Elizabeth replied. 'We'll get your brothers over to join you.'

'And Pa?' Charles asked.

'Of course,' Elizabeth replied.

They had a light meal that night and went to bed early.

—※—

The following evening, Edward, William, and young Edward joined Elizabeth, Jane and the Towneleys at the manor house. It was a grand affair, as mealtime regularly was at Towneley Manor. The overly large table, more suited to a civic engagement, easily accommodated the eight guests. Percival sat at one end, Constance at the other, with Elizabeth and Jane sandwiching Charles on one side and Edward, William, and young Edward on the other side. Percival seemed more interested in his food than his guests, as was his wont. Constance had a habit of clearing her throat and staring at him to regain the modicum of attention that protocol required.

Jane and Elizabeth kept looking sideways at Charles, occasionally catching each other's eye, and smiling with excitement.

'So, you met the pope, darling boy.' Elizabeth said, opening the table conversation. 'What an amazing, blessed experience that must be.'

'Yes, I met Pope Pius VII. One of my professors was a personal friend, so he introduced me after one of the papal audiences.'

'But did you meet Pope Leo XII? He seems to me to be a wonderful pope. He knows what it means to be Catholic and he's not frightened to put those Protestants in their place.'

'No, I didn't ever meet him, Gran.'

'It must be wonderful being in Rome,' Jane said. 'So close to the centre of the church. You must feel as though God himself is there.'

'It's an amazing place. So much history.'

'I was really hoping you'd be stationed at Stonyhurst,' Jane said. 'Llanrothal seems so far away. How far is it, Constance?'

'Oh, I've no idea. It's in Wales, isn't it, Percival?'

'Almost,' Percival replied. 'I've never been there but I believe it's a bleak old place and I agree with Jane. It's too far away. Surely the Jesuits could have placed you somewhere closer to home.'

'Well, it's closer than Rome,' Edward said. 'And it's nay as if Charles's only job is to be the family's personal chaplain.'

Elizabeth held her knife and fork aloft as she scanned the room, first at Edward, then Jane, then Constance. The room was silent, expectant. Elizabeth looked to her plate before speaking.

'What will you be doing there, darling?'

'I'll be teaching theology at the school and in the seminary. They're also starting up a new program in philosophy of science and they want me to teach it.'

'Science?' Elizabeth said, looking around for support from Constance and Percival. 'Why on *earth* would a Catholic priest be teaching science?'

'Well, it's not science as such, Gran. It's philosophy of science which includes quite a bit of theology.'

'I think it's wonderful,' Edward said. 'The church finally getting its act together.'

'Well, you would think that, of course,' Elizabeth said.

Charles noted that some things had not changed at all.

'I only wish my Da was here to talk it through with ye, Charles,' Edward said. 'He had a huge interest in science.'

'And you were saying we'd get Father Pritchard over for a meal before you go,' William said, straight-faced.

Edward and Charles looked to their meal.

'*Please*, no,' Elizabeth said.

'Don't worry, Mummy,' Jane said. 'It *won't* be happening.'

On the second day, Charles celebrated a memorial Mass for Emma Jane. The whole Towneley Estate was there. Sarah came up from Pemberton.

'Will sends his apologies,' she said to Edward and Charles before the ceremony. 'He wanted to be here, but he's had a relapse.'

Will had celebrated his one hundred and first birthday a few months earlier. He was the first centenarian anyone in the district could remember.

'I'd love to have a talk with him if that's alright,' Charles said.

'Oh, please do,' Sarah replied. 'Edward, is there any chance you could bring Charles down to Pemberton on your way to Llanrothal? I hate to say it, but I don't think there can be much more time.'

'I'll see what can be done,' Edward said, lowering his voice. 'But let's keep it to ourselves.'

After the Mass, the whole congregation went to the grave. They stood in silence and then Charles said the prayers for the dead. The congregation moved away but Edward stayed a while. Sarah stood next to him.

SACRED TO THE MEMORY
EMMA JANE LOVAT
BORN 17 OCTOBER 1804
DIED 2 JULY 1824
BELOVED DAUGHTER OF EDWARD AND JANE

BELOVED SISTER OF REV. FATHER CHARLES
SJ, WILLIAM, AND EDWARD
REQUIESCAT IN PACE

'You must miss her terribly.'

'I canna say how much. There're nay any words for it.'

Sarah put her arm around his back and rested her head on his shoulder. He breathed heavily.

'Edward, are you coming?' Jane called.

'In a wee moment, dear.'

Two days later, Edward and Charles set out in a carriage to Llanrothal. The first stop was Pemberton.

'Father Lovat,' Will said. 'Congratulations. Lovely to see you.'

'And you, Will.'

Charles stooped over to embrace Will. Edward followed suit.

'So, what did your grandmother say when you told her you were coming to see me?'

'We dinna tell her,' Edward replied.

'Good idea,' Will laughed.

'I think she was more concerned about me going to see Father Pritchard,' Charles said.

'Did you?'

'No, I'll see him in Llanrothal anyway. He's going down there to help me set up the philosophy of science programme.'

'Well, we all know what that's going to look like then,' Will said. 'And I dare say your grandmother was delighted with it all.'

'No, she doesn't quite understand why a Catholic priest would be teaching anything about science at all, much less approve of Father Pritchard directing it.'

'Ah, yes, your grandmother is what we always called a "real" Catholic.'

'Poor Gran. She's really quite lost without Grandfather.'

'Poor thing. I should be more kind. So, how are you anyway, Charles? You seem to have lost some weight.'

'Yes, I was quite unwell during the winter. In fact, each of the winters. I'm not sure why. After all, Burnley winters are hardly tropical but there was something about the Roman ones that didn't agree with me at all.'

'I know all about that. It's those old monastic buildings made for wind and damp. So, tell me, they didn't try and get you to do a stint on the missions, did they? That was always the way in my day, regardless of health issues.'

'No, though I wouldn't have minded,' Charles replied. 'I'm fascinated with Pa's stories of his travels to New South Wales.'

'Well, who knows then?'

—⚊—

Sarah called them to dinner. She had been preparing it while the men talked. They helped Will out of his chair and to the table decked with a simple meal of cold meat, bread, and potatoes.

'Sorry for the ordinary fare,' she said. 'No doubt it's a long way short of what you were given at Highgate and Towneley Manor.'

'Aye, thank heavens,' Edward replied. 'Yer meals are always so delicious, and they leave me feeling much better the next day.'

'As Will keeps telling me,' Sarah said. 'Though he might just be being civil about it.'

'They're always perfect,' Will said, smiling. 'Better food than in all those hotels I frequent these days.'

Edward and Charles noted the fond glance they shared. Sarah and Will had lost their lifetime partners in 1801 when Emma and Thomas, Edward's grandmother and father, died on the same day. The four of them had lived together at Pemberton for many years. Since the deaths, Sarah and Will had lived together as companions, though increasingly Sarah had become Will's carer.

Charles noted how Will had aged since he had last seen him before entering the Jesuits.

'Tell me about young Father Taparelli,' Will said, his fork hand shaking.

'Oh, where to start?' Charles replied. 'I thought Anthony Pritchard had stretched my thinking as far as it could go, but Luigi took it even further.'

'In what ways?'

'In a word, philosophically, or perhaps theologically is more accurate. Father Pritchard is a wonderful free thinker, and his grasp of science is as good as the best scientists – better even. But he makes no pretensions at being a top theologian. I was never quite sure just where his theology was, to be frank. It seemed to be in some suspended animation, almost as though he didn't want to look too closely. With Luigi, it's his theology that drives his understanding of science.'

'How fascinating,' Will said. 'How do you explain that?'

'It's the Aquinas in him. Most of the Aquinas I learned from others made him out to be a dry old scholastic from the Middle Ages. Very Catholic; I mean conservative, almost reactionary Catholicism. The guardian of everything opposed to Protestant aberrations, not to mention Jewish and Islamic ones. He was the theologian's theologian but not very engaged in anything outside theology. Catholic theology, in fact.'

'That all sounds familiar to me,' Will said. 'And Luigi?'

'So different. For a start, it was as though he was Aquinas's best friend. He was so alive to him. And he could make us feel the same way; well, me at least. Some didn't see it like that but that's another story. Luigi could make me feel as though Aquinas was in the room, speaking through him. And it was this completely different Aquinas who'd seen the beauty and the wisdom in Jewish and Islamic thought, especially Islamic. Judaism and Islam weren't enemies; they were other ways in which God was speaking to us. And that's how he saw science as well. Not as a threat to Christian thought but as another way God was speaking. What we had to do was accommodate it, and that's where the Muslim scholars, Farabi especially, had become so important.'

'So, it's a whole different way of understanding Catholicism, then?' Will said.

'Aye, and God,' Edward added.

'Precisely,' Charles replied. 'Catholicism spends too much time making enemies.'

'Like yer Gran does,' Edward said.

'Oh, poor Gran,' Charles replied. 'But she's only following what she's been told by endless priests, if not some popes. Protestants are bad. They're out to destroy us. They're going to hell. And as for Jews and Muslims, well!'

'But we're actually all in this together,' Sarah said. 'Your grandfather used to say that so often, didn't he, Edward?'

'Oh, aye. And I saw it so clearly when we were in Persia together. How respectful he was of Islam.'

'How influenced he was by Mahdiya,' Sarah said.

'I know far too little about this,' Charles said. 'I think Mama and Gran kept a lot of this from me.'

'Aye, and I should've been there more for ye, lad.'

'Don't be hard on yourself, Pa. The important thing is we're where we are now.'

'Indeed. Thank ye, lad. It's wonderful to be where we are now. So, tell us more about this Father Taparelli. It sounds like my Da and he were cut from the same cloth.'

'Indeed,' Will said, his laughing causing him to drop his fork. 'And got into the same hot water, like your father did so often when he spoke to the parents at St Bartholomew's.'

Sarah stood up and walked around the table to retrieve Will's fork.

'This is another thing I know too little about,' Charles said. 'But hot water? That's where poor Luigi ended up. Or hot something at least. He's now in Kerala, as far south in India as you can go.'

'What's he doing there?' Will asked, smiling a thank you to Sarah.

'Working among the poor. Knowing Luigi, he'd be making the most of it and I'm certain he'd be doing a wonderful job. But the intellectual waste is unforgiveable if I might be so uncharitable as to say so.'

'Indeed, ye might, lad.'

'Ah, yes, the church and brutalising its prophets,' Will said. 'I think there's something in the gospels about it, isn't there, Charles?'

'And the Old Testament,' Charles replied. 'What shocked me was how easily my Jesuit superiors fell into line with the conservative voices of a few.'

'Well, when it's the Holy Office, it's a powerful conservative voice,' Will said.

'Yes, that too. When I first went to Rome, Pope Pius VII was there. As we know, he dragged the church out of the Middle Ages almost single-handed. He was holy and devout, but he was also connected intellectually to where the church needed to be going. He was a little like Taparelli, in fact. But, and God forgive me for saying it, our present pope is a very different prospect.'

'In what way?' Sarah asked.

'Well, I think he's unwell, so let me say that first. So, I might be being very uncharitable and forgive me if that's so.'

'Ye're forgiven, lad. And ye're among family and friends here so say whatever ye wish.'

'Well, he's extremely conservative. He wants to make the old enemies all over again. Not only Protestants, and Jews and Muslims, of course, but scientists, philosophers, liberal thinkers of any kind, including those he calls aberrant theologians. And, of course, Luigi was one of them. So, when the complaint went to the Holy Office, the Office sided with it and the Jesuits were ordered to send him as far away as they could. It's such a loss.'

'I take it you're not a fan of Pope Leo XII, then?' Will asked. 'I'm certain you kept that from your grandmother.'

'And from anyone other than trusted parties like yourself. The current pope has a reputation for being extremely harsh on anyone who offers even the mildest criticism. A number of the Jesuits have found themselves in places like Kerala for even asking questions that are deemed impertinent.'

'You'd better be careful, Charles, darling,' Sarah said.

'Aye, especially teaching philosophy of science tutored by Anthony Pritchard,' Edward added, laughing.

'Yes, I'm very aware of it. I really struggled after Luigi was sent away. I'm sure it's part of the reason I became so ill.'

—⁂—

The next day, Charles and Edward rode to Llanrothal. It was Anthony Pritchard himself who greeted them at the door of the seminary.

'Father Lovat and Father Lovat,' he said, extending his hand.

'Braw to see ye again, Father,' Edward said.

'You didn't bring your mother-in-law?' Pritchard asked.

'If she'd ken she'd meet ye, Father, I'm sure she'd have come.'

'Oh, I'm sure too,' Pritchard said, smirking. 'How are you, Charles? You look tired.'

'Good, Father. I'm fine. It's wonderful to see you. I'm so looking forward to working with you.'

'As you should be. I've been called out of retirement to help you get this programme in place. Much to the chagrin of some of my brothers in Christ, I'm told.'

'Thank the Laird ye nay ever change, Father Pritchard.'

'I think some of my brothers would say it's thanks to the devil.'

'Well, your Lord's my Lord, Father,' Charles said. 'I want to learn all I can from you.'

'Before I meet him face to face, you mean? Well, we'd better not waste any time.'

Edward stayed the night at the seminary before heading back to Burnley. He left after breakfast.

'Do look after my lad, Father,' he said quietly to Pritchard. 'I worry about him.'

―☙―

Three weeks later, they were together again at Will's funeral. He had gone to bed early one night, even before supper. Sarah found him in the morning. The doctor said it was a peaceful death. The news reached Edward later in the day. He set about preparing to attend the funeral.

'You're taking your own children into a Protestant church?' Elizabeth queried.

'Will was like a Grand Da to me.'

'All the same, I wouldn't allow it if they were *my* children.'

Jane turned and walked out of the room.

―☙―

'Does Gran know Charles is going to be there?' William asked as they drove to Pemberton.

'Nay, I ken that'd be far too much for yer Gran.'

'And for Ma?'

Edward remained silent.

Charles travelled up from Llanrothal. He took his place in the second-row pew of St John the Divine's Church of England in Pemberton. William and young Edward sat next to him. Edward sat next to Sarah in the front pew.

'Welcome, Father,' the Reverend Bolton-Smith said to Charles afterwards. 'I'm certain you must be the first Jesuit to ever set foot in this church, or possibly any of the King's churches in Lancashire. What did your superiors say when you told them?'

'Told them what?'

XVII

Constance Towneley died unexpectedly in the early winter of 1826. Edward and the two boys attended the funeral in the Towneley Chapel. They sat two rows back from Elizabeth and Jane who sat with Percival in the front row. Any thought that Elizabeth and Jane might return to Tarleton House were dashed. Their priority was to support Percival.

Edward planned to travel to Tralee early the following year, and to bring Charles with him. Thomas and Eliza had welcomed their fourth child, Johannah, just a month before, on the 5th of December. By this time, William and young Edward were both working on the estate, so Edward could get away for longer periods.

He was to pick Charles up in Llanrothal and they would embark the ship at Holyhead for Dingle, the closest Irish port to Tralee. They had kept the plans to themselves to save Jane and Elizabeth the consternation they knew it would cause. Finally, the two half-brothers were to meet.

'*Halo*, Father,' Edward said. 'I'm here for Father Lovat.'

'I'm sorry, Mr Lovat. Father Lovat's in hospital.'

Charles had contracted a bout of influenza that had turned to pneumonia. Edward went to see him. He was reassured Charles was recovering but would be unable to accompany him to Tralee. He was sleeping and should not be disturbed.

'Please tell him I'll be back in a few weeks' time.'

―⁂―

It was bitterly cold on the Irish Sea, but Edward chose to spend much of the trip outside near the bow. He thought of his father on their many sea voyages, choosing to spend time looking into the ocean, imagining his Persian wife and unborn child down there.

Edward pondered on his own losses, a first wife dead, a second virtually estranged and his only daughter in heaven. He worried for Charles, seeming to struggle with health and forbearance in times hostile to his intellectual disposition. The disappointment of Charles not finally meeting up with his half-brother was bearing down on him.

He stayed too long on the bow. By the time the ship arrived in Dingle, the bitterness had eked into his bones.

'Da, ye're not looking well,' Thomas said.

'*Halo*, lad. So braw to see ye. I'll be fine.'

'Where's Charles?'

'It's a long story. I'll tell ye later.'

Thomas had hired a carriage to bring his father and Charles home. He had brought the seven-year-old Mary and John, five years of age, with him.

'Say hello to yer Grand Da, *clann*.'

'Hello, Grand Da,' they echoed.

'*Halo*. My, how ye've grown. Ye do remember me, dinna ye?'

Mary nodded. John shook his head.

'Well, we're going to ken each other this time.'

Thomas wrapped Edward in a blanket and placed his children, one on each side, to keep him warm. He then drove the carriage as fast as he could to get his father home to the warmth.

—⚘—

Edward was bedridden for three days, sleeping much of the time. He was tended to by the whole family but especially by Louise. She sat through most of one night with him. The doctor had come to the house and said Edward needed the fever to be brought down. Louise did not sleep, replacing one cool cloth with the next, as required.

'*Halo*, Louise,' he said, finally waking on the third day. 'Still looking after me after all these years.'

'As if I wouldn't, Teddy. Ye must know that by now.'

'I do, darling Louise. How can I ever repay ye?'

'Ye 'ave, Teddy. Ye 'ave,' Louise said, reaching to hold his hand, her head down. 'Just don't ever die on me, will ye?'

—⚘—

'So, ye've finally decided to be sociable,' Paddy said, extending his hand.

'*Halo*, Paddy, what d'ye mean?'

'Well, when I was here two days ago, ye ignored me. Even when I offered to hear yer confession, I might add,' Paddy laughed.

'I'm sorry. I dinna ken ye were here.'

'Oh, yes. Louise came running to the presbytery to get me. *He's gonna die, Paddy*, she was saying. *Ye'd better come and give him the rites.*'

'Like Ma, like daughter, eh, Paddy?'

'Well, I couldn't let ye die and go to 'ell, could I?' Louise called from the other room.

'Sorry, Louise, I was nay meaning to make fun of ye. I love ye way too much for that.'

Louise rushed in from the other room and threw herself over

Edward's body. Edward caught his breath underneath the weight, wrapping his arms around her back.

'I couldn't live if ye died, Teddy.'

'What's wrong with Aunty Louise?' Mary asked, stepping into the room.

'She just loves yer Grand Da, Mary,' Thomas replied, standing in the doorway.

'As much as she loves ye, Da?'

'Perhaps even more, darling.'

—⚬—

'What a shame Charles couldn't make it,' Paddy said over dinner. 'I was so looking forward to meeting him. I haven't had so much to do with Jesuits, I must say. We ordinary parish priests don't mix with the likes of them.'

Paddy chuckled. The children loved watching Paddy's tummy wobble when he laughed.

'Aye, I ken he'll be disappointed too,' Edward replied. 'I ken he so wants to get here. And he's nay the typical Jesuit. Even Will said that.'

'Thank the Lord,' Paddy said.

'He seems to have had a lot of bad health, Da?' Thomas said.

'Aye, he was *go leor* sicker in Rome than he let on.'

'Is he happy, do ye think?' Eliza asked.

'I dinna ken, lass. I ken he has his difficulties.'

'What sort of difficulties,' Paddy asked.

'I ken he has different ideas from a lot of his fellow priests.'

'Well, being of yer stock – and yer father's, it's hardly surprising,' Paddy said, grinning.

'What d'ye mean, Da?' Thomas asked.

'There was a priest in Rome who influenced him but then he was sacked from his job at the college and sent to India – as a punishment, it seems.'

'Who was that?' Paddy asked.

'Father Taparelli. I forget his Christian name.'

'Can't say I've heard of him. What sort of influence?'

'Oh, about theology and science and things like that. I dinna fully understand it all but Will seemed to. I ken Charles is a wee bit free in his ideas and feels he's out of kilter with those around him, if not the church generally.'

'Well, with the current pope, he just might be,' Paddy said.

'Why's that, Paddy?' Thomas asked.

'The Holy Father's a very conservative fellow there's no doubt. Pardon me for saying what I couldn't preach on Sunday, but I think he goes a bit too far with some of his accusations.'

'But 'e's the pope, Paddy,' Louise said, her brow furrowing. "Doesn't 'e know everythin'?'

'Of course, dear, but he's only a man too,' Paddy replied. 'And they say he's not well.'

'One of the teachers at school says he has women living with him,' Thomas whispered.

'Oh, I knew ye shouldn't teach in that Protestant school, Tommy,' Louise said, brow more furrowed and eyes ablaze. 'They 'ate the pope and they'd say anythin'. Ye shouldn't take any notice of 'em.'

'I'm just saying what they say.'

'Well, I think ye should go to confession. Shouldn't 'e, Paddy?'

'I'm not sure, darling. That's between Thomas and God.'

Edward noticed Paddy taking a deep breath and looking into the whisky glass before taking a sip. He thought Paddy was drinking more than he had seen in the past.

'Well, I think 'e should. Talkin' like a Protestant. And maybe Charles should too. If 'e doesn't like what the pope's sayin'. God f'give me for sayin' that about a priest but we 'ave to be strong, we Catholics.'

'Well, I just hope ye get the opportunity to tell Charles in person, Ma,' Thomas said. 'I hope he can come here sometime – or perhaps I'll have to go to him.'

'I'd love that too, lad,' Edward replied. 'I so much want to see ye two lads together. It's been way too long.'

—⚏—

'They love ye so much, Teddy,' Louise said.

Mary and John were fighting for Edward's attention. His right knee was the focus of the competition they were waging.

'How about John sits here and ye, Mary, sit there,' Edward said, demonstrating he had a second knee.

'But I want to sit on that one.'

'Well, alright, wee one; how about ye take it in turns then? Ye sit there first and then John can sit there in a few minutes.'

The squabble was resolved. Mary sat for a few seconds in the winning spot, then went off to do something else. John had both knees to himself.

'Ye've done such braw things to the house, lad,' Edward said to Thomas.

'Yes, Da. The time I spent as a building apprentice came in handy.'

The old Prendiville home had been renovated over time. Thomas had put in new doors and windows and painted the inside. The dank mud brick look of the past was now a bright white throughout.

'I love this old house,' Edward said. 'It has so many memories.'

'How old were ye when ye first came here, Da?'

'Six,' Louise interrupted. 'The cutest li'l boy God ever made. Apart from John, of course. And ye, Tommy.'

'So, now I'm only second best?' Edward laughed. 'Or perhaps third best.'

'Close second and third, fourth and fifth,' Louise said, looking him in the eye. 'Very close.'

The love Edward had always felt in this house was passing down the generations. He thought for a moment of his life in Burnley then put it out of his mind.

Two weeks later, Edward sailed back the way he had come. He landed at Holyhead and made his way to Llanrothal.

'Father Charles has gone to Burnley, Mr Lovat,' the priest at the door said. 'His mother came and took him last week.'

Edward was told that the doctor would only release him from the hospital if he could be guaranteed rest and recuperation. Jane, Elizabeth, and Percival Towneley had ridden down in a carriage to collect him. Percival had brought his personal physician along.

Edward hurried back to Burnley.

'He's at Towneley Manor, Pa,' young Edward told him on arrival at Tarleton House. 'He was taken straight there, and no-one's allowed to see him.'

Edward made his way to the manor house and knocked on the door.

'I'll get Mr Towneley, sir,' the butler said.

Edward stood in the large foyer. He could hear voices upstairs.

'No, he doesn't wish to see his father,' Elizabeth could be heard saying.

Edward made his way up the stairs, following the voices. He opened the door.

'Charles is unwell, Edward,' Elizabeth said. 'We have strict orders from the doctor that he's not to be disturbed.'

'From yer personal physician, nay doubt. I'm nay leaving this house until I see him. Ye're free, of course, to call the constable.'

'Please, Mummy,' Jane said as she walked into the room. 'I'm sure it'll be alright. Come with me, Edward.'

They walked silently down the corridor and entered the room at the end. The door opened to one of the manor house's large guest rooms. Charles was awake, propped up in the four-poster bed at the far end of the room. A roaring fire was going in the fireplace.

'My heavens, lad. Are ye nay roasting in here?'

'He needs to be kept warm, Edward,' Jane said. 'That's what the doctor said.'

'Surely nay with hellfire,' Edward replied. 'Anyway, how are ye, lad?'

'Hello, Pa. It's good to see you. What was all the commotion about out there?'

'Oh, just yer Gran and me having one of our convivial conversations.'

'Oh, Edward,' Jane said. 'Will this never end? Now please don't tire him. He's been extremely unwell.'

'What happened? How did ye ken he was sick?'

'We received an urgent message from the Jesuits that the doctor wouldn't release him unless he could be guaranteed total rest and he didn't believe that could happen at the college. But how did *you* know he was here?'

'I called into Llanrothal on the way home. They told me there.'

'A strange way for you to come home,' Jane said, looking askance. 'Anyway, I'll leave you alone but just for ten minutes or so. I know you won't want to stay too long near the hellfire, will you?'

Jane turned and walked out the door, closing it behind her.

'I'm so sorry, Pa; I've let you down again. I was desperately trying to get well before you came to collect me and then I collapsed and ended up in hospital.'

'So, yer Ma still dinna ken our plan about Tralee?'

'No, I thought it best to keep that to ourselves.'

'Extremely wise, lad.'

'How were things there, anyway?'

'Braw, they have a bonnie new bairn, Johannah, and the other three are as braw as ever. They're just disappointed naturally that ye were nay able to make it.'

'No more than me. And please let them know that.'

'I will, lad. I will. But tell me about yerself. When will ye go back to Llanrothal?'

'Father Sinclair's suggesting I might not. He says he thinks Stonyhurst might be better for me. A warmer building and all that. Personally, I'm not so sure. I think perhaps they might just want to keep a closer eye on me.'

'Why? Have ye been a *dona* wee lad, have ye?'

'Oh, naughty I could live with. Heretic is a little more serious.'

'Truly, lad? Who would say that?'

'No less than the papal nuncio, I gather.'

'Do we even have such a thing here in England?'

'No, but there's a prelate in Rome who unofficially plays that role. And, with my luck, who would it be but Archbishop Gaspare. He's the very one who pressured the Jesuits to get Luigi out of the Roman college.'

'And he called ye a heretic?'

'According to Father Hughes, yes. Father Hughes is our official emissary with the Holy Office. Apparently, the good archbishop visited our London headquarters recently. Father Hughes came up and spoke with me about some complaints that had reached as far as Rome.'

'What sort of complaints?'

'Predictable ones, I suppose. They're things we've spoken about before. My ideas about religion and science, Catholicism and Protestantism, Christianity, and other religions. I knew a lot of it would be controversial, especially with Pope Leo XII, so I've been very careful in what I teach. I just stay with the facts as I see them but there are people who don't want to deal in facts. They prefer their well-worn myths and, of course, their hatreds. It's very wearing.'

'So, is this why ye became ill, lad?'

'I suspect it's a big part of it. Naturally, I haven't breathed a word of this to Mama or Gran, and I'm not sure I'd want Mr Towneley knowing either.'

'Very wise, lad. Very wise.'

'So, as far as they're concerned, I've had pneumonia and I need to get over it completely.'

'Yer secret's safe with me, lad. I dinna confide in yer Gran anyway. Or, least of all, Mr Towneley. Would ye prefer to come and stay with me and the lads at Tarleton?'

'At some point, I truly would, Pa. I think I'd feel more relaxed there. But for now, I'm probably better off here. After all, I can't complain about the service.'

'I'm sure of that, lad,' Edward said, laughing. 'For yer Ma and Gran, having ye here'd be like having the Laird himself in the house. Dinna ken ye'd be getting that sort of treatment at Tarleton.'

'Is that a promise?'

XVIII

In the summer of 1827, Charles was appointed to Stonyhurst College.
'Professor of Mathematics and Moral Theology?' Edward asked. 'Is that a surprise?'

'I dare say they think it's safer than philosophy of science,' Charles replied.

His main assignment was to teach mathematics to the senior school students and moral theology to the seminarians.

Jane and Elizabeth were delighted to have him close by and to have a "professor" in the family. The subtleties of philosophy of science versus other enterprises were of no interest to them.

Charles settled well into his new role and maintained reasonable health, supplemented by bouts of home cooking at Towneley Manor and long conversations with Edward at Tarleton House.

Percival and Elizabeth surprised everyone, except Jane, by announcing their intention to marry in the summer of 1830. Charles was the celebrant at a lavish wedding held on the Towneley Estate just a month after the announcement.

Edward and Charles had been planning, yet again, to travel to Tralee that summer. Thomas and Eliza's fifth child had been born in early July and they had hoped Charles might do the christening.

Elizabeth's sudden announcement of a pending marriage put paid to that.

'I swear everything that woman does is designed to ruin my life,' Edward said.

'I hope there's something called love involved as well,' Charles replied, smiling. 'Do you think Mama will come home to Tarleton once they're married?'

'I dinna ken. I fear her Ma'll nay ever let her go.'

—∞—

As winter bore down in 1830, Charles became unwell again. Another bout of pneumonia saw him hospitalised and then staying for several weeks at Towneley Manor. Before going back to Stonyhurst, he stayed for a few days at Tarleton House.

'Would ye be up to a trip to Tralee when the weather warms up?' Edward asked. 'Ye ken they'd look after ye better than anyone.'

'I'd hope I might be well enough. I've had some lovely letters from them.'

They laid out tentative plans for a visit there in the summer of 1831. A week before the ship was due to embark, Elizabeth died in her sleep.

'I told ye, lad,' Edward whispered to Charles at the wake. '*Everything* that woman did. And ye'd best hear my confession after such an uncharitable thought.'

'I'm sure God will forgive you,' Charles said under his breath. 'What will Mama do now, do you think?'

'I'm nay sure.'

Jane stayed on at Towneley Manor. She said she needed to look after Percival now that her mother was gone.

'What about looking after us?' William complained.

'It's alright, lad. Yer Ma's probably happier there.'

—∞—

In late 1831, young Edward was engaged to Margaret Baron whom he had been seeing for a short time. The wedding took place six weeks after the engagement was announced. Margaret was the daughter of a well-known Burnley family. The Barons were staunch followers of the Church of England, but Margaret agreed to convert to Catholicism before the hastily convened wedding. Charles instructed and baptised her, as well as being the celebrant at the wedding. Several months later, they had a child, Mary Jane.

'She looks quite fully grown for a premature child, little brother,' William said, grinning from ear to ear.

'Margaret's an amazing bearer of children,' young Edward replied, smirking.

Young Edward and Margaret moved into one of the worker's cottages on the estate. Edward and William were left alone in the ten-room mansion that Jane had wanted so badly.

In 1831, the Stanley Bill was passed in the English Parliament. Edward Stanley was by then the Chief Secretary for Ireland and one of his first acts was to commission the national schools of which Thomas had spoken some years before. Having trialled Stanley's vision at St John's, Thomas was sought out to take up a position as Deputy Inspector of Schools for County Limerick.

'Oh, ye 'ave to take it, Tommy,' Louise butted in.

'Thanks, Ma, but it'd mean working in Limerick. I'd be away all week.'

'But I'll be 'ere. Eliza and me, we can cope.'

'I agree, darling,' Eliza said. 'I think ye have to take it. Look at the difference in salary. It'll set the children up for life.'

'But I'll be even less help to ye.'

'Look, darling. Ye're a wonderful husband but, let's face it, ye spend so much time at that school, ye might as well be in Limerick. Besides, ye'll be home every weekend.'

In August 1832, Thomas began his job as Deputy Inspector of Schools in Limerick. He was responsible for the Limerick County, as well as the counties of Clare, Cork, Tipperary, and Kerry.

'And the weeks I'm working in Kerry, I can stay here with ye.'

'I'm so proud of ye, darling,' Eliza said.

In the same week that Thomas started his new job, Charles began his at St Mary's Hall, Stonyhurst.

'Is it nay the junior school?' Edward asked.

'Yes, it seems I'm considered a threat to the seminarians' faith, but they think I should be safe teaching mathematics to the little ones.'

'Is Rome involved in this again?'

'I fear so. They've probably had their eye on me all along. And they say Archbishop Gaspare is a close confidant of the new pope, so what chance did I have?'

Pope Leo XII had died in late 1830. Charles, among others, had been hoping for a pope who could return the church to the spiritual and intellectual tradition of Pope Pius VII. There had been some optimism when Bartolomeo Cappellari was elected as Pope Gregory XVI. He was not of the Roman mold. He was a monk of the Camaldolese Order, an ascetic group that followed a strict form of the Benedictine Rule. Unlike the previous pope, there was no whiff of scandal about his private life and he was known as a reputable theologian.

Despite these portends, it became apparent soon after his election in 1831 that the new pope was more like the conservative Leo XII than the bolder Pius VII. In fact, he reacted even more harshly than his predecessor to any intellectual ideas that were not strictly Catholic, as he interpreted them. He took aim especially at what was being taught in seminaries. While Charles had been careful in his teaching of moral theology, he did apply his own understanding of Aquinas to it. This led to him promoting notions like *sensus fidelium*.

Aquinas's understanding was that the supreme guide for Christian morality was in *sensus fidelium*, the shared conscience of all God's faithful followers. Employing Aristotle's natural law theory, Aquinas proposed that God had bestowed his own will into humanity. Each person therefore possessed the capacity to judge good from evil. As a result, the discernment of conscientious Christians, taken together, was a surer guide for moral decision-making than anything else, even the dictates of the hierarchy. Did this include the dictates of a pope even? A liberal interpretation would say "yes". A conservative one, "no".

'So, the new pope's a conservative. Is this what ye're saying?' Edward asked.

'Hardly surprising, is it? Especially if he's taking his advice from the likes of Archbishop Gaspare.'

'But I thought the Jesuits were supposed to have a mind of their own, especially here in the British Isles.'

'Well, they do but only up to a point. So much of our work happens in dioceses and they're controlled by bishops who are all controlled by Rome. So, yes, in theory, the Jesuits could ignore the pressure of Rome but then might end up losing their parishes, for instance. Catholics could even be forbidden from sending their children to Jesuit schools. Things like that. Frankly, nothing's beyond Rome, even in a very Protestant Britain.'

'Oh, the politics. Will always said if the church played the gospel as well as it plays the politics, Christianity truly might rule the world.'

'He was a wise man,' Charles said.

'So, what will ye do, lad?'

'Do my best teaching mathematics to the young ones. Fortunately, I love the subject.'

1835 was a big year for the Lovats on both sides of the Irish Sea.

Thomas was appointed as Inspector of Schools in Limerick, with even wider responsibilities. A few weeks after taking up the post, they found out that Eliza was pregnant with their sixth child.

'I'll resign, darling. I have to.'

'It's alright,' Eliza replied. 'It's a wonderful opportunity and ye love yer work.'

'And I'm 'ere, Tommy love,' Louise added.

Edward travelled to Tralee to be with the family during the birth.

'Thank ye, Da. I appreciate ye being here.'

'I've done wee enough for ye, lad. It's the least I could do.'

James was born on the 14th of August. Thomas took two days off from his job to be there. Edward stayed on for another three weeks.

'I dinna ken what they'd do without ye, dear Louise.'

'I love 'em all, Teddy. 'cause they're yers, kind o'.'

Edward held his arm around Louise as she cradled the baby.

'I just wish ye could stay,' Louise said. 'We love ye more than yer Jane ever did.'

Edward was silent.

'Sorry, Teddy. I know I shouldn't say things like that. But it's true. I love ye so much. I always 'ave. And ye need someone to love ye.'

'I ken, darling Louise. I ken.'

—⚍—

'Come quickly, Mr Lovat. William's had a fall.'

Edward had been back at the Towneley Estate for only a week. William had taken the afternoon off work to ride with his friends. One of them had bought a new horse and wanted William to try it out. The horse had bolted and thrown William off. He had broken his neck.

Charles arrived at the funeral home the following day. Edward, Jane, young Edward, his wife, Margaret, and three-year-old daughter, Mary Jane, were there.

'I swear this family's cursed,' Jane said. 'How could God do this to us, Charles? Tell me, please, before I go mad.'

'I don't know, Mama. God's ways are not our ways is all I know. We have to have faith.'

For once, religious assurances did not seem to work for Jane. For Edward, they never did. Tragedy was tragedy. There are no consoling spaces into which to climb. The deaths of Amy and Emma Jane had taught him that. He cried for William, but he could not feel it was any worse than what he had borne already.

Charles celebrated the Requiem Mass the following day in the chapel on the estate. William was buried in the same grave as Emma Jane. His name was added to the headstone.

Edward organised a small wake for the mourners at Tarleton House, the over-sized mansion he would now live in alone. Jane did not attend. She went straight home with Percival to the Towneley Manor.

—⚘—

In late November of the same year, Edward received a letter from Thomas and Eliza.

> *Dear Da,*
>
> *We write with the sad news that our darling aunt, Louise, died suddenly yesterday. She had been unwell for some days, complaining of shortness of breath. We had been trying to get her to see the doctor. She went to bed on Sunday night, promising us we could call for the doctor on Monday. When she was not up to cook my breakfast before I set off for Limerick, I went in to wake her. She was on the floor next to her bed. The doctor said she was still warm when he came so she must have collapsed as she was getting out of bed to get my breakfast. She's*

never missed seeing me off on a Monday morning. We are so sad, as we know you will be too. Please come when you can.

Our fondest love, Thomas, Eliza, and the children.

PS. If Charles could come and say a special Mass for Louise, it would mean so much.

PPS. Louise spoke about you so often but especially in the last few days. We think she had a sense she would not see you again.

Edward felt as if he had been hit in the gut with a sledgehammer. Another of those who had loved him most was gone.

1835 ended with a trip to Tralee for Christmas. Charles had agreed to come but had fallen ill again. He would stay at Towneley Manor to recuperate. Young Edward and family had been invited there for Christmas.

Edward went to Tralee alone.

XIX

'It's a long way with six bairns,' Edward said.

'We know, Da,' Thomas replied. 'But it's something we've been thinking about for a long time. Paddy mentioned it in passing a year or so ago. Neither of us said anything for a while.'

Thomas paused, looking to Eliza. They smiled as if revealing their secret for the first time. Eliza spoke first.

'And then, one night, Thomas came out with it. *I wonder if we should go to New South Wales.*'

'And I thought Eliza'd jump down my throat,' Thomas interrupted. 'But she looked at me calmly and said, *I've been thinking the same thing, but we couldn't do it to Louise.*'

'So, it's as though the Almighty knows best,' Paddy said.

Paddy filled Edward in on the correspondence he had been having with Father John McEncroe, the Catholic chaplain in New South Wales. Paddy had met McEncroe at a priests' gathering in Dublin before he went to the colony. They had maintained contact and McEncroe had informed him about the dire state of education in New South Wales. Paddy had done little more than mention it to Thomas and Eliza but that was enough to sow the seed.

'So, are ye nay happy with yer job, though, lad?' Edward asked. 'Ye seem to be doing so well at it.'

'Yes, but that's another consideration. To be frank, Da, Eliza and I hardly see each other these days. There are even *weekends* that I have to spend in Limerick. So, we thought this might be a way we could solve that problem as well. Father McEncroe has said we could both teach in the same school if we wanted to. Hasn't he, Paddy?'

'Yes, he has,' Paddy replied. 'I think he'd give ye whatever ye wanted. So, what do ye think, Edward? Ye've been there. Is it a crazy idea?'

'Nay, it's a braw idea. From what I saw, having schoolteachers of yer experience'd be a godsend to the place. My main concern's for the travel. It was *garbh* enough for me on my own but with six bairns, I ken it'd be a challenge.'

'And I'd want ye to be aware of that, ye two,' Paddy said, looking to Thomas and Eliza. 'I'd feel responsible if anything happened to any of ye.'

'We've thought of all that,' Thomas replied. 'The ships are much improved since yer day, Da. They only take three months now and the crews are more experienced. Some of the ships and crews just go back and forth all the time.'

'Well, it sounds to me as though ye've made up yer mind,' Edward said.

'Or God has,' Eliza replied.

—∞—

On the last morning he was in Tralee, Edward went to Louise's still unmarked grave to pray. He reflected on the endless love she had poured on him and the hopes and dreams she harboured that had come to nought. He pondered on his own mortality.

Later in the day, he set out for Dingle and embarked the ship for Holyhead. He had arranged to stay with Sarah at Pemberton before heading home.

―⁓―

'How do you feel about them going to New South Wales?' Sarah asked.

'It's a frightening thought. All that way with a young family. I'm nay sure they ken what they're doing but they seem determined. More than determined. It's almost as though it's their mission in life.'

'Well, missions can drive us, can't they?' Sarah replied. 'I know that from your father; and from you, I might say. It sounds as though Thomas has inherited whatever that spirit was that drove you both.'

'Aye, and I canna stop them. I'd nay *want* to stop them. I ken they believe it'll be for the best for the bairns as well. New South Wales is opening up. There's nay end of land for farming and a good livelihood for anyone who's willing to work hard.'

'Would you like to go with them?'

'It's funny ye ask. The night they told me, I tossed and turned. Part of me was anxious for them but another part excited by the thought. Then, the next morning, Thomas said, *Da, I don't suppose ye'd consider coming with us?*'

'Why don't you, then? Imagine *your* skills in that country. And you could keep an eye on them.'

'Aye, but what about my responsibilities here?'

'You mean Jane?'

'Well, aye. Nay that she really needs me but if I even mentioned the idea, I'd get another sermon about how neglectful I've been and how she's had to do everything and…'

'Frankly, darling, you'll never please her. You learned that a long time ago. Whatever poor Jane's problem is there's little you can do about it.'

'Aye. It's the *bronach* truth. But then there's Charles and young Edward and his family as well.'

'They're fairly settled, aren't they? I mean young Edward seems to be doing well on the estate and Charles has his own family in the Jesuits.'

'I'm nay so certain about him, to be honest.'

'What is it? His health?'

'Well, his health's certainly part of it. He's been ill again, ye ken?'

'I didn't know that. The same thing?'

'Aye, on the surface. He always seems to come down with influenza, if not pneumonia, about once a year. But I ken it's more than that. They dinna seem to appreciate his talents. He ken it's Rome that's pressuring the Jesuits to keep him quiet, if nay silence him altogether. Ye ken he's now teaching mathematics to the juniors.'

'Oh, my heavens, that must be so dispiriting for the poor boy.'

'I ken he's mainly disappointed with the Jesuits. I mean he lived in Rome for years, so he understands what happens there. And we all ken the current pope's a *gleidhteach* man. Very conservative. But Charles ken the Jesuits would protect him, stand up for intellectual truth, as he puts it.'

'Oh my. Will would have had lots to say about the Jesuits and intellectual truth. Indeed, the whole Catholic Church and truth.'

'Aye, and I dare say Da might have something to say about that as well.'

'Indeed. How I miss him, especially when we talk about things like this.'

They reached out and held each other's hand.

'Perhaps Charles should go with you,' Sarah said.

'Where?'

'To New South Wales. It sounds as though he needs some fresh air, and the warmer climate would do no harm.'

'Imagine if I told Jane I was taking Charles with me,' Edward laughed. 'Or if I gave her the choice about who should go. There'd be no prizes for guessing who'd win and who'd lose.'

'Oh, Edward. I'm so sad for your situation,' Sarah said, squeezing his hand again.

'Ah, it's nay so *dona*, but I've bonnie memories.'

'Only memories?'

Edward looked into her eyes and smiled.

—⚜—

'I'm now being forbidden to preach,' Charles said.

'What d'ye mean, lad? How can they do that to ye?'

'Because I've refused to take this ridiculous oath, the bishop has said he'll take away my faculties for the diocese.'

'And the Jesuits are going to stand by idly and let this happen? Is that what ye're saying?'

'Frankly, they probably feel they have no choice. Even the college chapel is technically a public oratory, so the bishop has authority over who preaches in there.'

'So, all ye'd have to do is take this oath and everything'd be *ceart gu leor*?'

'Apparently!'

'What does the oath say anyway?'

'It's a denial of just about everything I hold to be true. Science, democracy, social justice, equality, liberal philosophy, so-called aberrant theology, which is really good theology. I swear Aquinas wouldn't take it. Or if he did, I'd lose faith in *him*.'

'Would the Laird take it, d'ye ken?'

'Christ? I very much doubt it.'

'So, the church would silence its own Laird?'

'I sometimes doubt the church would even know the Lord if he came back today.'

'All the same, would it nay be better to take it? Then ye can just keep on believing and saying whatever ye choose.'

'It's not so simple, Pa. Rome has its spies all over the place. They'd soon catch up with me. And, besides, didn't you always teach us to be true to ourselves? Haven't you always told us about our grandfather and how forthright he was, even under pressure?'

'Aye, I have, lad. I dinna realise ye'd picked up so much about that. I always ken yer Ma and Gran had most of the influence.'

'For a while, perhaps, but you've probably had more influence than you realise. And *your* father too. The more I come to hear about him the more I sense his influence in how I think. I'm only sorry I never knew him. Sorry he's not here now.'

'I ken he *is*, lad. The more I hear ye talk, the more I realise he is. It's the Jacobite rebel in ye. Sorry if I've inflicted that on ye. It dinna go so well with institutional conformity of any kind, church or otherwise.'

'I know but, you see, it should. If the church truly understood its mission, it would be the rebel in any civil setting. It would be the fly in the ointment, reminding kings, emperors, tsars, and prime ministers of their responsibilities before God to serve and not be served, to witness to the good, the just, the truth, whatever the cost. It would be a church boldly leading the way, rather than dragging the chain as this dear old pope seems to want.'

'Oh, my dear lad. I feel for ye. You're right, of course, but I fear there's more in the church that ken the opposite than ken like ye.'

'That doesn't make them right, though, does it?'

'Nay, lad. It dinna. Anyway, tell me, how's yer health? Are ye ready to go back to St Mary's?'

It was nearing Easter of 1836 and Charles had been recuperating at Towneley Manor with his mother tending to him.

'I don't know, Pa. I really don't know what to do.'

'Have ye told yer Ma any of this?'

'No. Anytime I share any of my doubts, she changes the subject. I think she's terrified of the idea that I might not end up the Jesuit provincial, or perhaps a bishop. She'd probably settle for that. She still refers to me as *Professor*, did you know? Even though I'm not one anymore.'

'Aye, I ken that lad. She's always had so much invested in ye being a priest. Yer Gran ensured that. Ye ken when ye were ordained in Rome, they both ken they saw a bright light on the horizon. When I said I ken it was just the sun rising, they told me I'd nay respect for the Laird's ways.'

'Well, we all know that's true,' Charles laughed.

'Look, lad, this is just an idea, but ye ken Thomas is talking about taking the family to New South Wales?'

'Yes, he wrote and told me. I think it's wonderful.'

'Ye do?'

'Indeed. Taking education where it's needed most. That's when the church truly is doing the Lord's work, in my mind.'

'Well, then. What would ye ken if you and I go as well?'

Charles stared at him.

'Truly, Pa? Are *you* thinking of going?'

'Aye, I am. Thomas actually asked me and then Sarah suggested it as well.'

'But what about Mama? What would she think?'

'Oh, lad. I nay ken she'd really care. I'm sorry to be so frank but ye ken things are nay so *math* between yer Ma and me.'

'I know, Da. I'm sad for you both. All the same, I think she'd be devastated if you went and moved to the other side of the world.'

'Well, perhaps. I'm nay so sure. But what about ye? Would ye consider it?'

'I don't know. The Jesuits have no establishment in New South Wales or any of the colonies in the southern lands. I admit I've thought of moving to one of our missions in India or China or Japan. We also have one in South America which I thought might be good for the warmer climes.'

'Well, that was one of my thoughts about New South Wales. If the doctors are saying ye'd be better in a warmer place, I can vouch for the warmth there. I've nay ever felt so hot in my life.'

In the second week of May, Charles returned to St Mary's Hall to resume his mathematics teaching. He was forbidden to preach or even to take religious instruction for the junior students.

'So, Father Charles, have you reconsidered your situation?' Father Sinclair, the Jesuit provincial, asked him.

Sinclair had made a special trip from London to deal with Charles's refusal to take the required oath. The nuncio had communicated the pope's personal displeasure at any recalcitrant Jesuits.

'I've considered the situation carefully, Father. And I've prayed about it. But I'm afraid my position remains the same.'

'I'm very sorry to hear that, Charles. Might I explore this a little further with you?'

'Certainly, Father.'

'Charles, I'm speaking as your superior but also your brother in Christ. You know that your Jesuit brothers hold you in the highest of regard. As a person of great character but also as an outstanding academic. I've heard how well you did in your studies in Rome. There are many who see you as a great sign of hope for the future of the Jesuits and indeed of the church. Your grasp of theology and philosophy and the relationship you see between them and the new sciences constitutes a rare gift. It's something we need if the church is to maintain its relevance in a world that's changing so fast. But we have the reality of a pope who's very cautious, and understandably so, and who wants to ensure that the church remains safe and whole as the world's changing around us.

I personally don't believe we have to choose between these two things. I think we can be bold in our thinking but still respect the judgement of the Vicar of Christ on earth who, after all, is guided in his thinking in a way that we can't possibly understand. I myself have struggled with the oath that's required so I understand well why you'd find it distasteful. But I've put my own misgivings aside, knowing that if I take the oath, I can continue to do all the other things God wants of me. Charles, you could do the same. If you take the oath, I personally guarantee you'll be restored to your professorship at Stonyhurst. Indeed, I've thought of a new position I'd like to offer you as Professor of Philosophical Theology, a post entirely suitable to your strengths. What would you think of that?'

Charles was silent for a time. Sinclair studied the look on his face.

'Thank you, Father. I appreciate everything you've said, and I'm overwhelmed by your generosity in offering me such an attractive post.'

He fell silent again.

'But I cannot in good conscience take an oath to recant all I firmly believe in.'

'So, you're effectively saying you believe the pope is in error. Is that the case?'

Charles noted the change in tone.

'I say with the greatest respect that it would not be the first time. And I say that in good conscience and with the utmost loyalty to the church. The pope is not after all infallible. I'm certain even the pope himself would never suggest that.'

'Clearly, no-one is suggesting that. Nevertheless, Father. I'm sure you realise this is a grave position to take.'

'I do and I'm very sorry for it. I truly am, Father.'

Sinclair fell silent. He studied the table. Charles noted the prominent veins on his temples.

'Well, Father Charles, I need to communicate to you the clear and unqualified instructions I have received from our Father General. And this does not just apply to you but to any of our brothers who refuse to take the oath.'

Sinclair placed his head in his hands and breathed deeply. Charles watched his every move.

'Father, it pains me, but I'm obliged to give you notice that if you do not change your position within three months of this day, you will be dismissed from the Jesuit Order.'

Charles' face went pale. He stared blankly at Sinclair.

'Truly?'

'I'm so sorry, Father. I never thought my job would entail such an unpleasant duty. But I have no choice.'

'I understand, Father,' Charles said.

'Please take your time to consider this carefully. You can stay here until then, although you'll be suspended from any teaching or even the saying of public Masses. If you prefer, you can go to another Jesuit house that I can arrange for you or you can take up residence with your family. Just let me know what arrangements you wish.

Today is the 29th day of June so I will require correspondence from you by or before the 29th of September, letting me know what you've decided. If you agree to take the oath, all faculties will be restored and you might well take up your post as Professor of Philosophical Theology, as I promised. Please, Father, consider it carefully. What a wonderful position you would be in to continue the work you love and to influence other young Jesuits. All you need do is compromise a little. Surely that's not asking too much.'

—⚘—

Charles chose to stay with his father at Tarleton House. Jane came around regularly.

'Charles, darling. You can't possibly be serious. Father Constable tells me you've been offered your professorship back at Stonyhurst. All Father Sinclair's asking – no, not Father Sinclair – it's the pope who's asking – is that you obey him. He's God's own representative on earth. Do you truly think you know better than God?'

'No, Mama, I don't think I know better than God, but I do think that God leaves us free to follow our own conscience. Indeed, that God demands we follow our conscience. I know this is hard for you to understand but I cannot pretend to believe things I don't believe, even if it's the pope requiring it.'

'Oh, you *are* your father's son. In the end, he's won, hasn't he? My mother was so correct in trying to protect you from his influence. But, in the end, she lost. I'm just thankful she's in her grave rather than having to live with the agony you're imposing on me.'

'I'm so sorry, Mama.'

'Please don't call me that. I'm not your mother; you're not my son. Not if you do this.'

Charles recounted this conversation to his father on the passage across the Irish Sea. They were heading to Tralee.

'I'm so sorry, lad. She dinna mean it, ye ken?'

'Well, she seemed to mean it when she said it.'

'Aye, she's a *feargach* lass, yer Ma. I dinna ken where all the anger comes from. But I've learned nay to take it too seriously.'

'I *canna believe it's taken over thirty years to have my two lads in the one place.*'

Eliza and the children went to bed early that night, leaving the two brothers and their father to talk.

'So, tell me more about your missionary plans,' Charles said to Thomas. 'It seems a big move to make, especially when you seem to be doing so well here.'

'It is Charles. My work colleagues all think I'm mad. There's a few reasons. Some of it's to do with family. I'm not seeing my children grow up except at weekends and sometimes not even then. And I miss Eliza too much. I'm a bit lost without her, to be honest.'

Edward and Charles looked at him in silence.

'You're so *fortanach*, lad. So very lucky.'

'Indeed,' Charles added, staring into the distance before looking him in the eye. 'So, you said a *few* reasons?'

'Well, far be it from me to sound too holy, least in front of a priest, but we do believe we're being called to do something special.'

'Called?' Edward asked. 'By the Laird, ye ken?'

'Yes, Da. By God. Ye do understand, Charles, don't ye?'

'I certainly do. I said to our father recently that I think you're doing more for God and the church than I am.'

'Oh, I wouldn't say that. Ye're a priest and that's not something we could ever be close to matching. But we'd like to think we're doing as much as ye could expect from lay folk.'

'Priest or lay folk, as you put it. It makes no difference. I really don't think God distinguishes. It's the Pharisee and Publican issue, you know? It's not who you are; it's what you do.'

'Mm, I'm beginning to see why ye've been in trouble, brother.'

They laughed.

'Anyway, I interrupted,' Charles said. 'Tell us more about *your* calling.'

'It was Paddy who put the idea into our heads. He's been in contact with Father McEncroe, the chaplain in New South Wales. He's been writing and asking for help with the schools out there. Well, not really schools. There are no schools in many places; that's the problem. There are some in the bigger towns and the establishment folk have their own tutors but the others, especially the convicts and their children, often have nothing.'

'It's the real work of the church, Thomas. I envy you. And I *do* think it's far more important than anything I've done. It truly is following the Lord, whereas all I've done is toady to the institution.'

'I ken ye're selling yerself short there, lad,' Edward said. 'But I ken what ye're saying and it's important for Thomas to hear it.'

'It certainly is. Thank ye, Charles. Ye're a rare priest, I have to say.'

'I think the pope might have a better adjective for me,' Charles laughed.

'Anyway, Da tells me ye might be thinking of doing more than toadying. Is that right? Ye might be joining us?'

'I don't know, Thomas. I've a lot to think about over the next few weeks. The idea's attractive in several ways but I'm not sure I'm cut out for missionary work. I'm better at sitting in an academic chair than a saddle, if you know what I mean.'

'Well, it'd be wonderful if ye did come with us. We could even travel out together.'

'When are you going?'

'Paddy's been looking into it for us. He's coming over tomorrow after Mass so he'll no doubt have some information for us. It'll probably be next year sometime.'

'And you, Pa?' Charles asked. 'When do you think you might go?'

'I'm nay really sure. I've nay even mentioned it to yer Ma yet.'

—⚹—

The next day, a Sunday, they went to the 8am Mass. Paddy was the celebrant. Charles sat in the pew, along with the rest of the family. No-one would have known he was a priest.

'I'm very pleased to meet ye, Father,' Paddy whispered under his breath outside the church. 'I'll look forward to chatting with ye over lunch.'

Eliza walked the younger children home while Edward, Thomas and Charles went over to Amy's grave. They were accompanied by Mary and John.

'So, this is my step-mother,' Charles said.

'It's a braw thing to say, lad,' Edward replied. 'Thank ye!'

They stood silently and prayed. Charles blessed the grave with discreet movements of his right hand.

'I wish I'd known my Gran,' Mary said.

'Me too,' John added.

'Ye'd have loved her, Mary, John,' Edward said. 'And she'd have *ghradhaich* ye two.'

'*Ghradhaich*?' John asked. 'What's that mean, Grand Da?'

'Adored ye. She'd have given her life for ye.'

'She proved that didn't she, Grand Da?' Mary said. 'She gave her life for our Da.'

'Aye, she did and are ye nay glad of that?'

'Well, we wouldn't be here otherwise, would we?' John said.

'Spoken like a true Highlander,' Edward said, reaching out and embracing John and Mary, in turn.

They walked over to Louise's grave. A headstone had been erected.

LOUISE GRACE PRENDIVILLE
DIED IN THE LORD, 6TH NOVEMBER 1835
AGED 68 YEARS
MISSED BY HER SISTERS AND BROTHERS
ADORED BY HER STEPCHILDREN
REQUIESCAT IN PACE

'Adored's right,' Thomas said. 'I wish ye could've known her, Charles.'

'I'm so sorry I never did. But I know she'll welcome me home one day.'

'Aye, we have the best friend anyone could have in heaven,' Edward said, his voice choking on the words. 'She'll have the biggest bear hug for us all when we get there.'

'Especially for her Teddy, eh, Da?' Thomas said.

'Yes, especially for her Teddy,' Mary repeated, wrapping her arm through Edward's. 'Not a day went by without her talking about her Teddy.'

Edward used his spare hand to grab his kerchief.

—⁂—

'So, you have some big decisions to make, Charles?' Paddy asked when the men sat down to talk after lunch.

'Yes, Paddy. Do you have any thoughts?'

'Well, I'm an old man now, ye realise, and a simple old one at that.'

'Nay so old or simple, in my experience, Paddy,' Edward interrupted.

'Thank ye, Teddy,' Paddy laughed. 'Look, Charles, I know Rome can be a mystery to all of us at times, and frankly popes come and go, and one can never know what the next one's going to bring with him but, for mine, the pope's still the pope and we have to go along with that or else we might as well all become Protestants.'

They were silent. Charles was staring into his teacup. Paddy watched him.

'So, you think I should take this oath even though it goes against everything I believe in? As a Catholic, I might add.'

'With yer fingers crossed behind yer back, if ye must. But yes. Look on it as the politics that keeps the church going.'

'And what about the gospel? What about truth? Does any of that matter?'

'Yes, but that all just happens anyway. Ordinary folk live out the gospel, whatever popes do or don't do, whatever oaths are taken or not.'

'And truth?'

'Truth will conquer all. In time. If your view of the world's right, that's what'll come to pass. If the pope's wrong, things'll correct themselves in time. What matters for ye is where ye'll be left standing either way. If ye take the oath, ye'll be in the centre of the church's work going forward. If ye don't, then who knows where ye'll end up? But it won't be as a Professor of Theology in one of the British Isles' most prestigious seminaries.'

There was silence again. Eliza brought in a fresh pot of tea.

'To be honest, I'm not sure I *want* to be a Professor of Theology anyway. It's not really why I became a priest. And yet it's all I've done. When I was in Llanrothal, I spent a couple of weeks in a parish because the parish priest was sick. I said Mass, I heard confessions, I visited some of the homes, people came to the door because they needed help. And, you know, I felt like a priest for the first time. I was happy. People seemed to appreciate what I was doing. It had a different feel to it.'

'So, brother, perhaps ye do need to come to New South Wales,' Thomas said.

'Are ye seriously thinking of it?' Paddy asked.

'Oh, it's something Pa mentioned but there are no Jesuit missions there, so I'd probably go elsewhere if I was looking for something like that.'

"But if ye dinna take the oath, lad, ye'll nay be a Jesuit anyway,' Edward said. 'D'ye ken that?'

'That's true,' Charles replied, staring into his teacup before looking up. 'So, you'll be going next year, will you, brother?'

'Well, I thought so,' Thomas replied. 'But Paddy thinks we should go earlier. Isn't that right, Paddy?'

'Yes, my sources tell me there's assisted passage on a ship leaving in November. It also means ye'd be there in their late summer which'd be an ideal time to start schooling.'

'November, lad,' Edward said to Charles. 'When do ye have to give yer answer to the Jesuits?'

'September. Twenty-ninth at the latest.'

XXI

In mid-September, Charles met with Father Sinclair in London. He advised him of his decision. He would not take the oath.

Sinclair, in turn, advised Charles that he would be allowed a further six months of a process known as exclaustration. It was a kind of limbo state that would see him out of the Jesuits on a temporary basis. In that six months, he would need to find a bishop to take him on as a priest. If he could not find one, he could then return to the Jesuits, provided he took the oath, or cease functioning as a priest altogether.

'How could you do this to me, Charles?' Jane said.

Edward and Charles had arranged to meet with Jane at Towneley Manor. They were seated in the lavishly appointed parlour.

'It's what my conscience tells me's right, Mama.'

'Your conscience? *Your* conscience? It's the pope's conscience you should be worried about.'

'The lad'll still be a priest, dear,' Edward said.

'Yes, a *shamed* one! How do I explain that I once had a theology professor for a son who's now trying to find a bishop bold or foolish enough to let him into their diocese? A priest even Rome doesn't want to know. How do I do that, *tell me?*'

'Does it truly matter what ye have to explain to folk? Is it nay more important that our lad's happy with himself? With his God?'

'So, God can be happy with him even if the pope isn't? What sort of nonsense is that?'

'Please, Mama and Pa,' Charles said. 'I don't wish to cause trouble between you. There'll be no need to worry about me further because I'm going with Thomas to New South Wales.'

'*New South Wales?*' Jane screamed. 'What *utter* madness. To the other side of the world to work with savages? And who's this Thomas anyway? Not…?'

'Aye,' Edward said. 'His brother, the one ye've denied him all his life. Well, they finally met, and bonded in a way braw beyond all my dreams. They've both been called to the missions and I could nay be prouder of them.'

Jane was silent as she struggled for breath. They could see her hands shaking, her neck reddening.

'You really *have* won, Edward. You've taken *all* my children from me.'

Jane was looking down at her lap. She was shaking her head, clutching her kerchief. Edward and Charles glanced at each other. Edward spoke first.

'In that case, I might as well go with them.'

'What do you mean?' Jane said, looking up, her watery eyes afire.

'I'm going back to New South Wales.'

Jane returned to silence, the reddening neck and shaking hands almost out of control. Charles stood and moved to place his hand on her shoulder. She pushed him away.

Thomas and family received assisted passage on the *Lady Macnaghten* leaving the port of Cork on the 5th of November 1836.

Initial plans for Edward and Charles to join them founded for several reasons. The departure was earlier than originally expected. Edward had made a commitment to Percival to help on the estate throughout the winter period. Charles had failed to make the necessary arrangements with any bishop who was sending priests to the colony. He also had a bout of pneumonia in the early winter, making a November departure ill advised.

They drew up rough plans to begin their travels in the warmer weather of 1837.

Father Sinclair visited Charles in February 1837. He was recuperating from his winter ills at Tarleton House.

'Are you still of the same mind, Father Charles?'

'Yes, Father. I'm afraid I am.'

'And even the prospect of a professorial chair at Stonyhurst can't persuade you otherwise?'

'No. I'm afraid the attraction of such things has faded.'

'And have you had any success in finding a bishop to take you on?'

'No. I'm actually wanting to go to the New South Wales mission. I've written to the Benedictine Bishop Morris in Mauritius. He's the vicar apostolic for New South Wales. But I've heard nothing to this point.'

'I believe there's been a change in authority there, Father. I'll find out and write to you.'

Sinclair arranged for a three-month extension of Charles's exclaustration, using his illness as justification when writing to Rome.

'He seems a *dumhail dhuine*,' Edward said as they bade farewell to Sinclair.

'Yes, he's a decent man,' Charles said. 'If the church only had more like him.'

Sinclair wrote two months later with the news that New South Wales had become its own vicariate. The bishop was another Benedictine, John Bede Polding, who resided in Sydney. He had also learned that Polding's vicar-general, William Ullathorne, was in London seeking priests willing to go to New South Wales. Sinclair had spoken with Father Ullathorne and told him about Charles. He was staying at Bisham Abbey in London and would welcome a meeting.

Edward and Charles travelled to London to meet with Ullathorne in early May 1837.

'So, we're fellow cabin boys?' Ullathorne said to Edward.

'Aye, Father, though I ken mine was a long time before yers.'

'Yes, mine was therefore more comfortable, I'm sure. I used to hear tales about those old ships. How long did it take to get to Sydney in '91?'

'Over six months,' Edward replied.

'Oh, my heavens, and in a ship like the *Gorgon*? Majestic, no doubt, but made for battle rather than comfort, I dare say.'

'Well, nay in its day. We actually believed it was made for speed, rather than battle. It was only about nine hundred tons and ye ken it had a mere forty-four cannons?'

'Forty-four cannons and it wasn't made for battle?' Ullathorne laughed.

'Aye, and now I suppose they only have a few cannons?'

'Or none,' Ullathorne replied.

Charles sat and watched the two old seafarers sharing their love of ships. It was a world he knew little about. He could not have told them anything about the tonnage or firepower of the ships he'd travelled on to Rome and back.

It occurred to Charles that he always learned more about his father when he was forced to talk about himself.

'Are we neglecting you, Father Lovat?' Ullathorne asked.

'Not at all, Father, I'm enjoying listening to you both.'

'That's excellent but we're not here to talk about ourselves. I wonder if we might have a word alone.'

Edward left the two clergymen to themselves.

'Tell me about yourself,' Ullathorne asked Charles. 'Why would you want to commit to such an arduous mission as New South Wales, especially when you've enjoyed such prominence as a theologian?'

Charles spoke first about his health and the medical advice that warmer climes would suit him. He then spoke of his desire to be engaged in more pastoral work.

'And then there's the issue of the oath,' Ullathorne said. 'Tell me about that.'

Charles looked down at his hands. They were clutched together. He began to wring them. He noticed the perspiration between his fingers. He looked up and fixed his gaze on Ullathorne who had waited in silence for the answer to his question.

'It's a conscience issue, Father. I don't mean disrespect by it, least of all to the pope, but I can't promise to teach things I don't believe in. The oath pertains to those who teach, especially in seminaries, so I'd prefer to engage in pastoral ministry. Perhaps it's an escape but, even if so, it's one I'm willing to take.'

'To be frank, Father, Bishop Polding will be overwhelmed if I'm able to secure your services for the colony. It would be quite beyond his expectations. At the same time, I need to warn you that he'll not want a troublemaker among his clergy. The New South Wales church is delicately poised. The Catholic Emancipation Act has hardly registered there. The Protestant churches are dominant and quite anti-Catholic. They regard us as an Irish church fit for convicts, with uneducated clergy hardly better than the convicts themselves. Most of the clergy I'll be sending back will be Irish, dubiously trained I regret to say, so that's going to strengthen the

Protestant convictions. You, on the other hand, will make the Protestant clergy think twice about us. That's why Bishop Polding really wanted English Benedictines to fill the colony but, alas, I'm unable to secure their interest so have been dealing mainly with the Irish diocesan clergy.'

'Perhaps our Protestant brethren might not be too worried if I'm a little at odds with the Holy Father then,' Charles said, smiling.

'Perhaps,' Ullathorne replied, unsmiling. 'But at the same time, we don't want to give the wrong impression. At the end of the day, there is only one true church and unity within that church is essential.'

'Of course, Father.'

The two men talked on. Ullathorne quizzed Charles in some depth about his theological differences with the direction Rome was wanting to set. He also filled Charles in on the difficulties of colonial life, even exaggerating some of the details to gauge his reaction.

'It all sounds very exciting. My father's told me some of these things as well.'

'Mind you, Father, I'm sure things are much improved on what your father would have experienced in '91.'

'Can I ask, Father, if you think I'm doing the right thing and whether you think I might be acceptable to Bishop Polding?'

'The right thing is for you to ascertain, Father. I can't advise on that. As for the good bishop, let me think about it. I'll write to you.'

—⚘—

Edward had arranged for them to stay with Mary Beth and Carl in Highgate. They arrived to find Carl bedridden.

'He's had a terrible headache for days now,' Mary Beth said. 'The doctor thinks he's been overdoing things.'

Mary Beth went up to see him after dinner.

'He'd like to see you both,' she said as she re-entered the lounge room.

They entered the darkened bedroom.

'Edward, so wonderful to hear your voice. And so sorry I couldn't join you. I'm so unused to being an invalid.'

'There's nay any need for apologies, Carl. I'm sure ye'll be up and about soon. I have Charles with me too.'

'Charles? How wonderful. We've not met since those many years ago at the estate.'

'No, Carl. I meant my son, Charles, the priest ye met here some years ago.'

'Oh, of course, pardon me. Hello, Charles. Perhaps I might have a private word with you before you go. A Father Confessor word if you know what I mean. But first, tell me, Edward, is it true you're going back to New South Wales?'

'Aye, young Thomas and family are there already – well, we hope they are, at least – we're so looking forward to joining them.'

'Oh, the superb memories. Charles, it's where your father and I met. I'm sure you know. We were on the boat together. We became such good friends.'

'Aye, not to mention where ye met yer wife to be.'

'What was that?'

'Mary Beth. It's where ye met Mary Beth.'

'No, we met on the boat.'

Edward and Charles looked at each other.

'So, Edward. How have you been? How is Charles Towneley anyway? Is he still well?'

'Charles died some time ago, Carl. But his son, Percival, is doing well.'

'Ah yes, of course. And tell me, is it true you're going to New South Wales?'

'Aye.'

'I do hope you'll have a chance to continue your agronomical work.'

'Aye. I've been in contact with the Office of Colonial Affairs in London to see if there are any postings for agronomists in the colony.'

'Yes, wonderful. Is your son still here? I wonder if I might have a word.'

Edward left Charles with Carl and went downstairs.

'How was he?' Mary Beth asked.

'A wee bit confused, I ken.'

'Oh, dear. I've been hoping he'd get better, but it seems worse every day. I swear he didn't know who I was yesterday morning.'

'It must be breaking yer heart, Mary Beth.'

She reached out and grabbed him by the arm. Edward wrapped his arms around her and hugged her tightly.

'How did ye go, lad?' Edward said as Charles came back into the room.

'Yes, good.'

'Did he say anything I should know about?' Mary Beth asked.

'Umm, nothing I can share,' Charles replied.

'Oh, of course, how insensitive of me.'

'That's alright, Mary Beth. Just keep a close eye on him, won't you?'

They left the next morning after breakfast. Carl was still asleep. Mary Beth gave each of them a long hug and thanked them for coming.

'So, what do ye ken, lad?' Edward asked as the carriage moved away.

'I'm sure he's had a stroke of some sort. I think he's preparing himself.'

In late June, Charles received the letter from Father Ullathorne advising that he had been accepted into the Sydney diocese. He was invited to take a berth on the *Hindoo*, a small ship with a select complement. It was to depart from Liverpool on the 30th day of August 1837. He was told that his father was invited to join him.

'What do ye ken, lad?'

'I've no doubt this is where I'm meant to be. What about you?'

'I ken so but I'm worried about yer Ma.'

—⚋—

A week later, the two men met Jane at Towneley Manor.

'You're truly going, Charles? I can't believe it.'

'I'm sorry, Mama, but it's something I feel called to.'

'Surely God would *not* be so cruel. What about me? Does God not care about me?'

'Of course, he does, Mama. And I know he'll give you the strength you need, just as he'll give me the strength I need.'

'And you're happy with this, Edward?'

'It's what the lad wants, darling. And it's between him and his Laird. I ken ye'd understand that better than me.'

'And you're going too, I suppose? My husband finally walking out on me!'

Edward said nothing. Jane stood and walked towards the door. Edward and Charles followed. Jane shut the door behind them. They walked in silence to their horses tethered at the end of the pathway. They stood by their horses and looked at each other.

'I'm sorry it's so hard for Mama,' Charles said.

'No sorrier than me, lad.'

'So, what are you thinking now, Pa?' Charles asked. 'Will you be coming?'

'I dinna ken what's *ceart* or nay *ceart*, lad, but I surely want to.'

—⚋—

It was late July. Edward had indicated he would accompany Charles on the *Hindoo*. He received a letter from Mary Beth.

Dear Edward,

I write with the very sad news that my darling Carl died last week. He became very ill after you left, being unable to speak. The doctor believes he had suffered a series of strokes and it was only a matter of time.

I had meant to write to tell you how bad he was but I have been frantically trying to make his last days as comfortable as I could. I also knew you were preparing for your travel and there was really nothing you could have done. Carl would not have known you were here even if you had come.

It was lovely that you had the chance for a final conversation, and I know Charles's presence was surprisingly comforting too. I don't know what Charles said to him that night in the bedroom, but Carl seemed more at peace afterwards than he had been for weeks beforehand. Please do thank Charles for that and give him all my love, as I give you the same, my darling Edward.

Mary Beth.

'I have to go, lad. I'm sorry. Mary Beth and I've been there for each other at times like this.'

'I'll come with you,' Charles replied.

'Nay, lad. Ye have to prepare for yer travel.'

'Well, so do you, don't you?'

'I'm nay *cinnteach*, lad. I'll let ye ken.'

'Oh, you shouldn't have come, Edward, but it's so wonderful to see you.'

'I could nay have left without seeing ye.'

That evening, they sat as they had almost forty years before, huddled together on two corners of the overly large dining table. It was the first time they had been completely alone since then. Expectations of some awkwardness evaporated as they picked up where they had left off.

'Anyway, enough about me,' Mary Beth said as they sat on the chaise in front of the cold fireplace. 'When are you leaving on your trip?'

'I dinna ken, to be honest. I keep on changing my mind.'

'I feel as though I've been here before,' Mary Beth said, smiling.

'Aye. Why am I always like this when I'm with ye?'

'I don't know but I love it that you are. So why so uncertain? You've always wanted to be with your two boys and surely this is your big chance.'

'Aye, but there's still Jane to consider.'

'Well, now I *know* I've been here before,' Mary Beth said, smiling.

'As well as young Edward and his family,' Edward replied, smiling back.

'Well, it doesn't have to be forever. From what I'm told, it only takes three months to get there these days so you could have a wonderful six months there and be back by this time next year.'

Edward sat silently, staring into the fireless fireplace, sipping his port.

'*Tell* me about Jane,' Mary Beth said. 'If I'm not being too intrusive.'

'Ye're nay being intrusive at all. I just wish I could tell ye something that makes some sense. I ken we were in love. Ye remember me talking about it with ye. She seemed braw. She helped me get over my feelings for Amy. She seemed to want what I wanted at the time. Then we married and everything changed. Her Ma was everywhere. Like a third person in the marriage. She might as well have slept with us. It could nay have been worse.'

'Oh, Edward, my darling.'

'I canna complain, can I? It's the bed I chose to lie in. Your words!'

'I just feel so sad. When I think…'

'Think what?'

'You know what.'

'Aye, I do.'

'But then there'd be no Charles or young Edward or William or that beautiful Emma Jane. Sometimes we don't get the good without the bad.'

'I ken. I have to remind myself of that. Every day of my life.'

'Is there no hope for you and Jane? I mean if you stayed.'

'I'm nay *cinnteach*. It's been so long since we lived as *dhuine* and wife. I just dinna ken.'

'Perhaps you need to be sure before you go away forever, or even for a long time. Otherwise, you might always wonder.'

Edward stayed with Mary Beth for a week. They walked through the gardens by the day and ate and drank well at night. They talked as neither of them had talked for years. It was as easy as it had always been between them.

On the first night at home with Charles, Edward explained that he would not be accompanying him to New South Wales. He would perhaps come out later.

'No-one would be happier than me if you and Mama could be together again,' Charles said.

Edward nodded.

'And ye'll be alright, will ye nay? Ye'll have Thomas and Eliza there. They'll look after ye if ye need it.'

'Oh, I'll be fine. I'm sure the church will look after me.'

'With respect to ye and the church, lad, it seems to me the church looks after *itself* better than those who serve it.'

They invited Jane to accompany them to Liverpool to see Charles embark the *Hindoo*. She said she would prefer to say her goodbyes at home. They sat stiffly in the parlour of Towneley Manor, sipping tea.

'So, how long will it take you, Father?' Percival asked.

'About three months, give or take a week,' Charles replied.

'You must be used to sailing by now?'

'Yes, although it's been a while.'

Jane sat, saying nothing, nodding now and again. They finished tea and stood to say goodbye. Jane gave each of them a kiss on the cheek and a small hug. She stood at the door as they made their way to the carriage.

'Charles,' Jane shouted, running out to them.

She hugged Charles and held him tightly.

'I love you, darling boy. Be happy. Be good. Do well, as I know you will.'

'Goodbye, Mama. I love you. Thank you for everything you've done for me. I'll never forget you.'

They continued to hold each other. Edward looked on. His eyes were vacant.

Edward and Charles made their way to Liverpool where they spent the night. After dinner, they went to their shared room and sat by the fire.

'I hope I'll be able to follow, lad, but I dinna ken for sure.'

'I know, Pa. I hope you do but I understand it may be difficult.'

'Lad, in case I dinna make it, I'd like to give ye something important. I ken ye'd be the best one to have it in safekeeping.'

'What is it, Pa?'

'Before my Da died, he gave me a small box which I want to give to ye now.'

Edward reached down and picked up a tattered leather box and handed it to Charles. Charles unclipped the tie and opened it.

'Oh, my. These *are* special. Tell me about them.'

'Well that wee *creutair* there's Charlie Bear. So, Charlie meets Charlie, ye ken?'

'He's so cute. Why Charlie?'

'Charlie Talcott was a young lad who saved my life. He was the cabin boy on one of the boats when I was sailing to Persia with my Da. I dinna ken if I ever told ye the story. I was thrown overboard and managed to cling to a buoy hanging on the side of the ship. But I was slipping fast. My Da tried to get to me but he could nay reach me. So, Charlie clambered over the side, slid down the rope and helped me get back up. But then he fell into the sea. There was nay anything we could do. It was the *as miosa* day of my life. I felt so guilty and so helpless. I ken I've nay ever really gotten over it. Ye ken he was even younger than me. And here's me at my age and he had nay chance. It was *tarrangeach*. Tragic.'

Edward was silent for a time, staring into the crackling fire.

'Anyway, we went to see his guardian when we got back to England and she gave me this. She said it was Charlie's favourite toy and she ken he'd want me to have it. I asked her what its name was, and she said "bear". He just called it bear. So, I said I'd call it Charlie Bear and he's been with me ever since, including to New South Wales. I ken Charlie Bear'd like to go back there.'

Charles studied the tattered toy. He pressed his thumb into the socket that once contained an eye. He rubbed the arm that was hanging by a thread.

'What a life you've lived, Pa. I'm so sorry it's taken 'til now for you to tell me stories like that.'

'Aye, well ye ken yer Ma nay ever liked me talking about my past.'

'Why *is* that?'

'I dinna ken for sure, lad. She just seemed a wee bit threatened by the parts of my life that nay included her. It's nay her fault. It's more my fault for nay reassuring her more. Trust's the key to any relationship, lad. If ye have that ye can withstand all the storms of life. If ye nay have it, even the warm summers seem cold.'

Charles reached over and placed his hand on Edward's arm. He then reached into the box and pulled out a notebook.

'That's the diary my Da kept as a young lad. He started it when he went to Tripoli on his first trip to the Middle East and he kept it until my Ma died. It gives such braw insight into his experiences, including of Islam, his love for Mahdiya, his torn loyalties in the Americas. His devotion to my Ma.'

'It's invaluable, Pa, but are you sure you want me to have it?'

'Aye, lad. I dinna ken what'd happen to it if I kept it here. Who'd look after it after I …?'

Edward looked at Charles. Charles nodded. He reached further into the box.

'Oh my. It's a Qur'an, isn't it? The only ones I've ever seen were in the Roman library and they were huge. This is so small. And it's been damaged.'

'That's where the American's bullet hit when my Da had it in his pocket the day he was shot near Boston. The doctors told him this wee book saved his life. He said he took it from Mahdiya's hands just after she died. He ken she was the one who saved him that day.'

'That's so special, Pa. I've always thought I'd love to have a Qur'an of my own but could never imagine how I'd get one or how I'd carry one even. But this is perfect. I'll cherish it.'

'And anytime ye're holding it, spare a thought and a prayer for Charlie Talcott. My Da read from it, actually chanted from it, the day we buried him at sea.'

'Truly?'

'Aye, he ken the first chapter – *sura*, they call it – by heart.'

'In English?'

'Aye, but in Arabic as well.'

'Oh, my heavens. I do wish I'd known him. He really understood something of Islam, didn't he? I mean from the inside.'

'Aye, he used to say Islam taught him most of what he ken about God. It was all through Mahdiya, of course.'

'How wonderful. If only there were more who saw things this way, it'd be a far more tolerant world.'

'Aye, it would. I ken yer favourite saint had a high regard for the Muslims too?'

'Aquinas? Oh, yes. Indeed. That was part of his problem – at least as far as his critics were concerned.'

'D'ye ken if he ever read the Qur'an?'

'No, I can't be sure, but he certainly soaked up its spirit.'

The next day, they went to the dock to see the *Hindoo* for the first time.

'Thank you, Pa. I'm going to miss you so much. Do come soon if you can, won't you?'

'I have to, dinna I, lad? With my two lads there together. It's been my dream to be with ye both.'

Edward waited on the dock until the *Hindoo* sailed away and was no more than a speck on the horizon.

XXII

Thomas, Eliza and family had arrived in Sydney Cove earlier that year, late February 1837. They did not disembark, however, until late April. In the intervening months, they were in quarantine in Spring Cove, just inside Sydney Heads. The *Lady Macnaghten* of '36 would be remembered as "the fever ship", arguably the worst voyage in the fifty years of travel since the First Fleet of 1788. Over fifty of the four hundred passengers came down with typhus and were buried at sea. More than forty were children.

When the ship arrived in Sydney, ninety of the remaining passengers were still suffering from the fever. They remained on board while those in better health were put ashore in tents. The intense heat and rain forced the authorities to construct temporary shelters to prevent more illness. At one point, there were fears that most of the passengers might perish.

Thomas, Eliza and their six children were left scarred by the close brush with death, including of ones they had come to know and love on the voyage.

'Happy birthday, Mary,' James Hawkins said. 'Why don't you take some time off?'

'Then I wouldn't be happy, would I?' Mary replied, her eyes fixed on Hawkins. 'There's nowhere else I'd rather be.'

Hawkins smiled and touched her on the elbow. She placed her hand on his and clenched it.

'So, where should I start?' Mary said.

It was the 6th day of February, Mary's seventeenth birthday, and the ship's journey had about three weeks to run. Thomas and Eliza had put their teaching skills to good use by taking classes with the many children on board. Mary and John took it in turns to look after the younger children. At times, they would help their parents in their teaching duties.

When the fever first struck in mid-December, Mary began to help in nursing the sick children, many of whom she had come to know through teaching them. It was through this mainly that she came to work closely with Hawkins, the ship's surgeon. He was ten years older than her.

'Well, just stay with me but keep one eye on those three over there,' Hawkins said, pointing to the darkest corner of the cabin, strewn with double and triple bunks. 'Keep the water up to them and watch for any of those worrying signs. You know what I mean.'

'Yes, sir,' she said with a smile.

'It's been a while since you called me sir,' Hawkins replied.

'Well, it's a special occasion, isn't it? We said when I turn seventeen. Or have ye forgotten?'

'How could I forget?' Hawkins said. 'Do your parents know anything?'

'No, though I think Ma's guessed something.'

'Well, let me know when you want me to speak with your father.'

'It can wait. It's hardly the time with all this happening,' Mary replied, looking around the cabin.

Hawkins touched her on the shoulder, squeezing it before

turning to face the challenge of a day that would be like every day of the last six weeks. They were working in what had been the largest passenger cabin on the ship now turned into a makeshift hospital. Every bunk was filled, and the floor was half-filled with those for whom no bunk was available. By this time, over twenty men, women, and children had already been consigned to the sea. The twin challenge was to keep the rest of the sick alive until they reached Sydney Cove and to safeguard the remaining passengers.

Mary took her place next to Hawkins as he moved from bed to bed. She followed his instructions, a sip of water here, changing a sheet there, a damp cloth over the forehead somewhere else. When not focussed on a specific task, she watched him, taking note of his manner, his care, his attention to each sufferer, especially the children.

Occasionally, he would catch her watching and smile. The first time it happened, she looked away, embarrassed. Now, she would smile back. She waited for those moments.

—⚒—

'Be very careful, darling. It's obviously highly catching,' Eliza said.
'I know, Ma, but James always makes sure I'm safe.'
'James?'
'Dr Hawkins.'

—⚒—

It was at the brief celebration of the New Year five weeks earlier that Hawkins and Mary had slipped away to a quiet spot on the stern.

'I've been wondering,' Hawkins began, then paused.
'Wondering what?'
'Wondering if I might call on you when we're in Sydney.'

'Call on me? What does that mean?'

'Come and see you.'

'Why would ye do that?'

'Well, because I'd like to see you. Is that alright?'

'Oh, I suppose so, but I might be busy, ye know?'

'Doing what?'

'Oh, meeting lots of young, eligible bachelors. They tell me there's no end of them in New South Wales.'

'Really? Well, I suppose…'

'James, I'm only joking. Of course, I want ye to call on me. I'd love ye to call on me. But aren't ye going home on the *Lady*?'

'Well, perhaps, but I was thinking I could ask to stay with the sick until they're better and perhaps get a later ship home, or…'

'Or what?'

'Well, depending on what happens in Sydney, I could even stay. I gather they're desperate for doctors in the colony. I have a distant relative who's a doctor here, and…'

'What do ye mean *depending on what happens*?'

'Umm.'

'James, say what ye mean.'

'Depending on how *seeing you* goes.'

He looked out over the darkened ocean. She could not see his face. She rested her hand on his forearm.

'I think it'll go well,' she whispered.

Hawkins turned to face her.

'I was going to ask…'

'Ask what?'

'Well, it *is* New Year and…'

'Would ye like to kiss me?'

'Umm, only if it'd be alright.'

'I think it'd be alright.'

Hawkins took her by the shoulders and stiffly moved his face to her cheek. He kissed her and stepped away.

'Thank you,' he said.

'You're such an Englishman, James Hawkins,' Mary laughed. 'Come here.'

She reached her arms around his neck and pulled his face down. She kissed him firmly on one cheek, then the other.

'That's how the Irish kiss, did ye know?'

'Oh my. That was quite wonderful.'

'Anyway, we'd best go back inside before my parents wonder where I am.'

—⚘—

In the three weeks between Mary's birthday and the ship turning into Sydney Heads, another thirty passengers had died and over ninety others were suffering from the fever. Most were children. The captain was ordered to drop anchor in Spring Cove just inside the Heads. The sick would be kept on board and the others moved to a special facility on the nearby shore.

'I want to stay,' Mary said.

'Ye cannot, Mary,' Thomas replied. 'I forbid it.'

'Your father's right, Mary,' Hawkins said. 'You must go ashore where you'll be safer. The authorities are sending doctors and nurses to help.'

'But what about ye?' Mary asked, her eyes glazed.

'I'll be fine. And I'll see you ashore.'

Hawkins turned to look Thomas in the eyes.

'If that's alright with you, sir.'

'Of course. We'll be delighted to see ye whenever that might be.'

'Thank you, sir. Goodbye, Mary.'

Mary rushed to him and threw her arms around him.

'Please hurry to me,' she whispered.

They held tightly until Eliza rested her hand on Mary's shoulder.

'Come, dear. Be safe, Doctor.'

—⚘—

Three days later, one of the onshore doctors visited the family in their tent.

'How are things on the *Lady*, Doctor?' Thomas asked.

'No good, sir. They lost the ship's surgeon today.'

'Ye mean Dr Hawkins?'

'I think that was his name, yes.'

Mary dropped the cup she had been holding. Eliza went to her side. Thomas rushed over to stop her from falling.

'I'm sorry,' the doctor said. 'I suppose you got to know him?'

'Yes, we got to know him well,' Eliza replied, cradling Mary's head on her shoulder.

The next day, four bodies were brought ashore. Hawkins was one of them. Thomas and Eliza accompanied Mary to the burial that happened on a sandy spot above the beach.

'I love ye,' Mary whispered over the grave. 'There were never lots of others. Only ye.'

XXIII

It was a Saturday in late April that Thomas, Eliza, and family made their way to the accommodation set aside behind Government House overlooking the harbour. The next day, a service was held at St James Church of England, a few hundred yards away, to welcome the new arrivals. Most of the Catholics declined but Thomas and Eliza had become used to the Church of Ireland services back home, so were happy to attend.

Governor Richard Bourke was there to welcome the newcomers. He greeted Thomas, Eliza, and the family outside after the service.

'Ah, Mr and Mrs Lovat,' Bourke said. 'I saw your names in despatches. You're the teachers from Tralee, are you not?'

'Yes, Your Excellency,' Thomas replied. 'And these are our children, John, Elizabeth, Johannah, Thomas and James. Say hello to His Excellency, children.'

'Hello, sir,' they replied, out of unison.

'Hello, children. Welcome to New South Wales. But, now, if I'm not mistaken, you have *six* children. Is that correct?'

'Yes, sir,' Eliza replied. 'Mary's still in the church praying.'

'My heavens, is she going to be a nun?'

'No, sir. She was very close to Dr Hawkins, our ship's surgeon. Ye may know he perished soon after we arrived.'

'I did hear that. I'm so very sorry. Were they engaged?'

'No, but we think that was what they were thinking. Mary helped the doctor with the typhus cases, especially the children.'

'Oh, dear, so much tragedy. Look, I'd like to speak with you both, if I might. Would you be free to meet me at Government House sometime soon?'

'Certainly, sir,' Thomas replied.

Bourke turned to his adjutant.

'Lieutenant, could you organise with these good people to meet with me soon?'

Bourke tipped his hat as he began to walk away. He turned back.

'And please make sure to bring Mary with you. All of you are welcome, of course, but I'd like to meet Mary.'

―⚒―

Ten days later, Thomas, Eliza, Mary, and John were sitting in the parlour at Government House. The three youngest children were left in the care of the twelve-year-old Elizabeth.

Thomas recalled some of the stories his father had shared about dining at Government House forty years earlier. The simple building that he had described was clearly not this one. The four visitors had gasped as they walked through the gates. All thoughts of a backwoods colony evaporated. London itself could sport no finer residence. The sandstone exterior bedecked by a large columned porch, massive doors, and French windows, contrasted with everything they had been expecting. Even without the three months cramped in ship's quarters and a further two months in a tent, the contrast with what they were used to would have been sharp. Granted those five months of abstemious existence, it was as though they had stepped into a different world.

Inside was no less splendid. The foyer opened out to a vaulted ceiling overseeing a high staircase covered with a carpet runner leading from the door to the top of the stairs. Its colour matched the red coats of the British forces. The parlour was large enough to hold a ball, with finely padded high-backed chairs all around the available wall space.

'Please do come in,' the adjutant called.

They were ushered into a room almost as large again. The governor's desk was in the far corner, with several high-backed chairs facing him and others placed neatly around the office walls.

'Ah, Mr and Mrs Lovat,' Bourke said as he stood and walked around to greet them. 'And Master Lovat. What was your name again, lad?'

'John, sir.'

'John, yes, of course. And this must be Mary. Is that correct?'

'Yes, sir.'

'Please take a seat.'

Bourke walked back to his side of the desk and sat facing them.

'Mary, I didn't have the pleasure of meeting you on Easter Sunday. I believe you were a close friend of the good Dr Hawkins, a man I have heard such grand things about.'

Mary's eyes welled up. She nodded.

'Well, I thought you should know that Captain Hustwick tells me that many more would have died without Dr Hawkins' excellent work. I'm also told that he was a very modest man. A no fuss professional, we'd call him.'

Mary was weeping quietly. Eliza put her arm around her neck.

'I'm sure Mary is grateful to hear that,' Thomas said. 'Especially coming from ye, sir.'

'I'm sorry, sir,' Mary said, her voice choking. 'I'm so grateful. Dr Hawkins was a very special man. I miss his friendship.'

'Well, might I say, Mary, that he was a very lucky man to have someone like you remembering him so fondly.'

'Thank ye, sir.'

'And I'm sorry for your loss.'

'Thank ye,' Mary managed through her tears.

'Thomas, Eliza, Captain Hustwick told me what a wonderful job you did in running a virtual shipboard school on the voyage.'

'I'm sure Captain Hustwick was being overly kind, sir,' Thomas said. 'But thank ye anyway. And Mary and John helped us as well.'

'Well, the Captain Hustwick I've come to know over the years is not given to over-generosity,' Bourke said, smiling. 'But, apart from all that, I believe you were not only a headmaster but a school inspector in Ireland. Is that the case?'

'Yes, sir, I was the head of a Church of Ireland school in Tralee and then the inspector of schools for the Limerick regions.'

'Limerick, you say? A beautiful place. In fact, it's where I hope to retire.'

'So, were ye born in Ireland, sir?' Thomas asked. 'I thought I might have detected a bit of an accent.'

'How interesting. Most don't pick it, I gather. Probably beaten out of me in military college,' Bourke laughed. 'But, yes, I was indeed, born in Dublin. My wife's family though all come from Limerick, so I know it extremely well.'

'It's a fine district,' Thomas said. 'I was very happy there.'

'Indeed, it is. So, do tell me about the new arrangement for schools there. I've read about it but haven't had a chance to speak about it with any knowledgeable party.'

Thomas spoke about the recent history of government involvement in public education in Ireland. Eliza offered the occasional thought. Mary studied the Governor's uniform, remembering how Hawkins had looked so handsome in his uniform at the New Year celebration. John studied the portraits of former governors on the walls.

'Wonderful. Wonderful,' Bourke said. 'You no doubt know that we have no organised system of education here, like you would have been used to, but I am most committed to achieving that before my time is up. And I truly think the Irish system, as you've described it, is the way forward for a place like this. What fascinates me about your background is that you've seen education in a very churched context but also in the non-denominational sector.'

'That's right, sir. The Catholic schools remain but the Church of Ireland schools I worked in effectively became non-denominational when the government took them over.'

'Excellent, Excellent. That's what I really want for the colony. Currently, the Church of England and some of the other churches are running schools but they effectively exclude many of our citizens, including those who need them most. And here I mean the former convicts, largely Irish, mainly Catholic. The Catholics are beginning to form their own schools but there's nowhere near enough of them and Catholics are often not welcome in the other churches' schools so, at present, the population that needs schooling the most is missing out, especially in the far-flung regions.'

'Well, I actually thought I was coming here to help with setting up the Catholic schools. Our parish priest has been communicating with Father McEncroe.'

'Have you met with Father McEncroe yet?'

'No. I believe he's away at present. I had thought I might try to meet with Bishop Polding first.'

'So, you haven't met with any of the Catholic authorities yet?'

'No, sir.'

'Well, that might work in my favour, then, to be frank about it. I see trouble ahead if each of the churches ends up with its own segregated schools. The Church of England ones will educate the establishment. Let's call them the upper class. While the Catholic Church will educate the convict class and the poor. That's the formula for a perpetually divided society, wracked by intolerance of each other. We know all about that kind of society from what's at home, especially in England. We must do better here. We have the chance to do better.'

'I couldn't agree more with ye, sir, but what can I do to help?'

'Work for the government, rather than the church. I'd like to send you to set up and take charge of some of the new areas where establishment and the new workers are starting to mix, where religion is not as political as it's become here in Sydney. And let's start to form this new society with a fresh kind of education, one where Protestants and Catholics can mix and get to know each other as fellow citizens, where the toffs, as I call them, and the workers vital to the future of the colony learn to work together. What do you say?'

'It sounds very exciting,' Thomas said, looking across to Eliza.

'I agree,' she said. 'In fact, I was thinking how excited yer Da would be, darling.'

'I was thinking the same,' Thomas said.

'Ah yes,' Bourke said. 'I was told that your father was here in '91. Is that true?'

'Yes, sir, he came on the *Gorgon*. He actually dined here, or in the Government House of the day, with Governor Philip and Governor King. He went to Norfolk Island when Governor King went there the second time.'

'How remarkable that you'd end up here too. But tell me, why would he be excited with what we've been talking about?'

'Well, my Da's always fought against intolerance. And from what I know, his Da was the same. His Da was the son of a Jacobite hero, so I suppose the rebellious blood's always flowed through his veins. He doesn't like bigotry, especially religious bigotry.'

'I'm only sorry he didn't stay in the colony. We need more like him here.'

'Well, as far as we know, sir, he *will* be here. We think he's accompanying my brother who's coming out to work with Bishop Polding.'

'As a teacher?'

'As a priest, actually. He's a Catholic priest.'

'Oh, yes, I believe there's a boatload of Irish clergy heading this way.'

'Well, my brother's an Englishman actually. A former Jesuit professor, in fact.'

'A Jesuit professor here in the colony?' Bourke laughed. 'My heavens. Bishop Polding *will* be excited. On the other hand, some of the Protestant leaders won't know what to make of it. A Catholic clergyman better educated than them. I can't wait to see their reaction.'

'Is that what they think of Catholics, is it?'

'I'm afraid so. I have to say between us that many of our religious leaders are extremely intolerant. One might even say unchristian. And it really doesn't help in creating the kind of society we need here. We're isolated. Very much dependent on our own resources. And we must pull together. I'd have hoped religion might be a kind of glue in that situation but it's too often the opposite. That's why I want *schooling* to be the glue. I want it to help everyone out of their denominational trenches and working together. We have an opportunity to do that here and schooling's what can do it. So, do I have your support, Thomas?'

'Indeed, sir. And I know ye'll have the support of my father and brother too.'

'Even the Jesuit professor?'

'Yes, to be honest, the main reason he's coming is because of his own liberal views on these things. He's not Rome's favourite priest at present.'

'Goodness me. I wonder if Bishop Polding knows what he's taking on.'

'I hope so, sir.'

Bourke turned to the children.

'So, what do you think of Sydney town, Mary? Do you feel at home here yet?'

'It's better here than it was in Spring Cove. It was so hot.'

'Oh, my, yes, you were there in February, weren't you? I dare say you never had a summer like that in Tralee. And what about you, John? Tell me what you hope to do now you're here.'

'I'd like to be a farmer, sir.'

'Not a teacher like your parents?'

'No, they have to work too hard.'

'Teachers never breed teachers, they say, sir,' Eliza laughed.

'Well, John, there's no shortage of land in this place, as you no doubt know. We still don't know all of it, but it seems the whole country would stretch from London to Moscow in one direction and London to Cairo in the other.'

'That's exciting, sir,' John replied.

Bourke turned to face Thomas and Eliza.

'Now, have you thought of where you're going to live?'

'Not really, sir,' Thomas replied. 'We thought we'd speak with Father McEncroe about that.'

'Well, I'd like to put a proposition to you.'

Thomas and Eliza looked at each other.

'I dare say you're wondering what I'm going to say.'

'Yes, sir,' they chorused.

'Well, one of the most important areas for our survival is what we call the Hawkesbury. It's between forty and fifty miles out west, in the foothills of the mountains. My predecessor, Lachlan Macquarie, named it after Lord Hawkesbury. Are you familiar with him?'

'No,' Thomas replied, looking to check with the others.

'Well, that's not important. The Hawkesbury area has proven to be wonderful farming country, with the river providing easy access to and from Sydney. Many people have moved out there, including a great number from former convict families. And I can see the excitement in your face already, John.'

'Yes, sir.'

'Before you set up your farm out there, I'm hoping your parents might establish a school or two. There's really nothing out there at present. Some of the children travel into Parramatta to some church schools but most of the children are getting no education. I know both the Church of England and Catholic bishops would like to establish church schools out there, but I'd really like to see some non-denominational schools there instead, or as well. Now, if you were interested to help in establishing one, as I think you've agreed, I would make sure you had suitable housing for the family and, of course, all the help you would need. Planners, builders, accountants, equipment. And an appropriate wage, naturally. If you agree, we can talk out more of the details.'

There was silence. Thomas and Eliza looked at each other. An almost imperceptible nod passed between them.

'I think we're very interested, sir,' Thomas said. 'My only concern is that Father McEncroe will be expecting us to work among the Catholic population. And I think Bishop Polding will want the same.'

'Well, what about if I talk with Bishop Polding about this? He's a reasonable man and I'm sure he'll see the benefit for the Catholics out that way. He knows the church would struggle to provide the kind of education that the government can set up.'

—⚒—

By early August, the family was settled in a township called Richmond in the Hawkesbury Valley. By then, the government had built a schoolhouse there, barely suitable to a family of eight. It was made of a distinctive light brown sandstone found in the foothills of the Blue Mountains. The single storey residence had wide verandas on three sides. The front door opened to a hallway leading past two bedrooms, one on either side, and to a lounge-dining room and kitchen at the rear. All floors were timbered with no coverings. The internal walls were also timbered with a chair rail down either side of the hallway and running into the living rooms.

'So, what do ye think?' Thomas asked Eliza as they inspected the house, room by room. 'Do ye think we'll fit?'

'We'll have to, won't we? It's small but … compared to what we had at home.'

'So, do you like it?'

'It's wonderful, darling. It just needs a bit of a woman's touch.'

'Leave that to us, Pa,' Mary said, putting her arm through her mother's. 'We need something to do before the school opens anyway.'

They stepped out of the house and walked to the edge of the property. In the adjoining paddock, the first sod was being turned for a school due to take its first pupils at the beginning of 1838. Thomas would be the headmaster and teacher of the older students, with Eliza and Mary sharing the teaching of infants. There was much to do before then.

XXIV

The *Hindoo* was a 300-ton barque, barely half the size of the *Lady Macnaghten* and far smaller than the *Gorgon* on which Edward had sailed in '91. It was designed for relative comfort and speed. The *Hindoo* was one of many ships built in the 1820s and 1830s to deal with the increased movements between the British Isles and the new colonies of the great southern land. It had a full complement of only thirty-six people, fourteen of whom were children. Of the rest, there were four women, eight men, including the surgeon, and ten crewmembers. Charles was one of the four single men, the only priest and the only Catholic.

'You don't seem like a priest, if I might say, Mr Lovat,' Clarence Penthill said. 'And I don't mean to be offensive.'

Granted the nature of the ship's complement, Charles had chosen to dub himself without the priestly title. It was the captain who had let his priestly status slip and, from then on, it became a source of some curiosity on a long, relatively uneventful voyage.

'I'm not offended at all, Mr Penthill,' Charles replied. 'But what do you mean? I'm not sufficiently pious?'

'No, not at all. I just mean you seem too normal.'

'And nice,' Florence Penthill said. 'I think that's what my husband is trying to say. We've not had much to do with Catholic priests, mind you, but I've always thought of them as stern and unfriendly. Whereas you're a gentle man.'

'As well as a gentleman,' Clarence added.

'Well, thank you. I suppose I hold the view that I'm meant to be a representative of the Lord and I believe he was both a gentle man and a gentleman.'

'Indeed, well said,' Clarence replied. 'But you must agree that's not the way priests, and indeed ministers of religion generally, are always seen.'

'I suppose that's true,' Charles said. 'And that's a shame if so.'

Charles kept to himself for the most part on the long trip. He had much to think about, both on the past and the unknown future. Because there were no Catholics aboard, he had no pastoral responsibilities. He had a cabin to himself and said his own private Mass each day. Around mid-morning and mid-afternoon of most days, he would step out on the deck, walk several times around it for exercise and then either sit on a box somewhere and read his daily office, Aquinas's *Summa* or a book of his choosing. One day, he took Mahdiya's Qur'an with him. He opened it at the first *sura*, studied the fine Arabic script and ran his fingers over it as he recalled the story of his grandfather chanting it as Charlie Talcott was dispatched to the sea. He felt his grandfather's presence – and Mahdiya's – more so than ever before.

At other times, he would lean over the railing and just watch the sea. He remembered pondering on its vastness when traversing the Mediterranean to and from Rome, but nothing had prepared him for the endless watery vista of the Atlantic and Indian Oceans. There were days when its apparent anger made him fearful and days when its calm and beauty lulled him into the sense he was on another planet. Then there were those long days when he found himself immersed in his many thoughts, fears, doubts, and enchantment with the mystery surrounding his own future.

'What of Mama and Pa? Will I ever see them again? What if my health breaks down again with no-one to look after me? What if Bishop Polding demands I take the oath after all? What if I find myself overwhelmed with a situation so different from anything I've experienced? Should I have taken the oath and settled into a life I knew? Was it faith that prevented me or just pride? Arrogance even?'

Charles took most meals in his room, though once a week the captain would have a small group of the adults to his table. It was here he first conversed with the Penthills.

'Well, I *have* had quite some experience of Catholic priests,' Captain Stuart said. 'And I concur with Mr and Mrs Penthill that you seem to be cut from a different cloth.'

There was some mirth around the table at the captain's choice of words.

'Were you brought up Catholic, Captain?' Robert Smith asked.

'No, but I've encountered many Catholics in my time at sea, mainly Irish, mainly criminal, I'm sorry to say.'

'Including on voyages to the south seas, Captain?' Florence asked.

'Yes, and to other sites. I suppose my views about Catholics have been influenced by these experiences. Including about their priests, I might say. Popish is a word I'd use. But you, Mr Lovat, seem unusually non-popish if I could put it that way.'

'Well, coming from you, Captain, I'll take that as a compliment,' Charles laughed.

'Indeed, it was intended that way. Popes are not my favourite people. But tell me. Your name? It's not an English name, is it?

There are famous Scottish Lovats. Are you part of that clan, by any chance?'

'Yes, I believe so. If my father was here, as he had intended, he would have been able to tell you much more than me. His grandfather was a leader of the Jacobites at Culloden. In fact, he died at Culloden, the same day my own grandfather was born.'

'Oh, my heavens,' Florence said. 'How awfully sad.'

'Well, I agree,' Robert Smith said. 'Although I have to say I have little sympathy for the Jacobites. They were rebels, after all.'

'Yes, well, let's not start another border war,' Captain Stuart laughed. 'As you might recognise from my name, I have some Scottish ancestry myself. My own grandfather claimed a family connection with Charles Stuart, the Bonnie Prince himself. He was extremely sympathetic with the Jacobite cause. Indeed, he used to say he thought our island would have been in better hands had the Jacobites won the day. Granted there was a German on the throne at the time, one who spoke no English to boot, I always thought he had a point.'

'I think your grandfather and mine might have had a lot in common, Captain,' Charles said. 'I didn't know mine well, but my father has told me lots about him. He did many things in his life, including travelling to Persia and the Americas as an army commander but I gather he saw himself as a Highlander first and foremost.'

'Mm, stubborn people, the Scots,' Smith said. 'Especially the Highlanders. I gather. I had a friend once from Edinburgh. *Uncompromising, those Highlanders*, he used to say.'

'Ah, yes,' Captain Stuart said, raising his head to its heights. 'There's really no such thing as a Scotsman. Only Highlanders and Lowlanders, and they really don't get on so well.'

'Yes, fortunately for us,' Clarence said. 'My own father used to say if the Scots would just stop fighting each other, they'd take this country from us.'

'As indeed they almost did in the Jacobite Rebellion,' Stuart replied. 'So, tell me, Mr Lovat, why did your father not come with you?'

'A friend of his died a few weeks ago and he felt he should stay and come later.'

'Why was he going at all?' Florence asked. 'Goodness, I wouldn't be going if my husband wasn't needed there.'

'Well, my brother and his family have just moved there and with me going as well, he thought he might join us. He's been there before.'

'Truly? When was he there?' Stuart asked.

'In 1791.'

'Not on the Third Fleet, by any chance?'

'In fact, I believe it was,' Charles replied.

'Which ship, do you know?'

'Ah, yes, a strange name. Gor..?"

'The *Gorgon*?' Stuart blurted out. 'My heavens. I *do* wish he was with us. I'd love to talk with him about that. The captain of that ship was the famous Commodore Parker. He was a legendary character. I can't imagine commanding a ship of that sort all the way to New South Wales, no doubt with a band of convicts aboard. Massive, slow old boats with few comforts.'

'Yes, I gather it was a challenging trip,' Charles replied.

'Indeed. Especially on the return. Lots of sickness. Thankfully, it doesn't happen so much these days. Which ship was your brother on?'

'The *Lady Macnaghten* was the name, I believe.'

Stuart was silent, seeming to be occupied with his meal. He had heard of the *Lady Macnaghten's* fate just before leaving Liverpool. Charles had heard nothing.

'Well, I do hope he and his family are all well,' Stuart said.

—⚬—

On the second half of the trip, Charles spent even more time on deck. South of the equator in November, the days were warming up and the bright blue of the Indian Ocean was enticing. The other passengers all knew by then that he was a non-popish Catholic priest, the first variety of such a thing most of them had encountered. Many engaged him in conversation about religion, life, and their own troubles. Charles relished playing the pastor, albeit an unofficial and uncustomary one. It strengthened the sense of relief to be done with the politics of church and theological differences and to be doing what he really wanted to be – a servant of the people.

XXV

Having watched the Hindoo disappear over the horizon, Edward went home to Tarleton House, his much-oversized mansion. He had noted the thawing in Jane's manner on the day Charles left, so he harboured a slim hope that it might portend a new beginning. A few days after arriving home, he rode over to Towneley Manor.

'So, he's gone?' Jane said.

'Aye, the ship was a little late getting away is all.'

'And he seems happy?'

'Aye, as far as I can tell. He actually seemed more excited than he's been for a while. I ken the strain of everything that's happened has worn him down.'

'But what did happen, Edward? What *did* happen? He had everything and he's given it all away. I spoke to Father Constable about it. He can't believe what's happened. And Father Shaw thinks the devil's got to him.'

'Jane, ye should nay talk to these auld men. They're products of their time and they've nay an ounce of the intelligence of our lad.'

'And they both blame you for it all.'

'So, I'm the devil, am I?' Edward laughed.

'Don't joke about such things, Edward. Perhaps the devil *has* gotten into you. My mother used to wonder.'

'Yer mother? Speaking of the devil!'

'Let's not start all that, Edward.'

'Nay, let's nay.'

'So, are you going to New South Wales or not? I never know what you're doing. I thought you were going with Charles and then, suddenly, you've changed your mind.'

'I told ye Carl died so I had to make sure Mary Beth was alright.'

'Mary Beth? Oh, for heaven's sake. You'd leave me here to fend for myself but go running off to make sure Mary Beth's not fretting.'

'I'd stay here for ye if I ken ye needed me. Ye ken that.'

'Well, no, I don't know that. I've never known that.'

They stood in silence. Jane looked towards the ceiling. Edward was gazing at the floor, his right hand resting on the back of his neck. He stood straight and looked Jane in the eye.

'I'd stay now for ye if ye wanted me to,' Edward said.

Jane looked away.

'No, you go. Do what you must. Go and see Mary Beth. Then go to New South Wales if you wish. Just let me know what you're doing.'

Jane moved towards the door. Edward watched her. He opened his mouth to say something. Jane stopped and turned to look at him. He saw the grief in her eyes.

'And before you go to Mary Beth, you might want to drop in on young Edward. He's been unwell, did you know?'

'Nay. I'd nay idea.'

'Well, why doesn't that surprise me?'

'What's wrong with him?'

'Bad headaches. The doctor isn't sure what the problem is.'

'Are you alright, Jane?' Percival called from the next room.

'Yes, I'm coming. Edward is just leaving.'
'Oh, goodbye, Edward,' Percival called.
'*Mar sin leat*, Mr Towneley.'

Edward rode to the estate cottage where young Edward and his small family lived.

'Are ye alright, lad? I hear ye've been having headaches.'

'I'm feeling much better, Pa. I hope to be back at work tomorrow.'

'Well, let me ken if ye need any help on the estate.'

A few days later, Edward travelled south to stay with Mary Beth in Highgate. He stayed until January of 1838.

'I'll miss you so much,' Mary Beth said on the evening before Edward was heading home.

She reached out and rested her hand on his forearm. They were on the chaise in front of the fire. A larger than usual log had been brought in to keep it going on an especially cold night. They watched as the flames slowly caught.

'Nay more than I'll miss ye, my dear one,' Edward replied, resting his hand on hers.

'Do you have to go then?' Mary Beth said, pausing and taking a deep breath. 'Edward, I know I mustn't pressure you and I truly don't wish to. After all, it never does me any good anyway.'

She laughed. He squeezed her hand.

'But, and God forgive me for being so bold.'

Mary Beth paused again and looked into Edward's eyes.

'There *is* a life here for you whenever you want it.'

Edward lowered his head and looked back at the fire. Mary Beth continued to look at him.

'Aye, I ken,' Edward said. 'And that's what makes it so difficult. If young Edward was nay there, I'd stay. Or I'd ask ye again if ye'd come with me to New South Wales.'

'Well, and I'm sorry again to be persistent, but you know my terms for that, darling.'

'Ye drive a hard bargain, dinna ye?'

'Not really. Not at this stage of our lives, darling. There's not that much time left.'

'I just dinna ken what to do,' Edward said, finishing the port in his glass. 'So, why dinna *ye* tell me what to do?'

'Oh, Edward. I can't tell you what to do. I *shouldn't* tell you what to do. I *mustn't* tell you what to do.'

Mary Beth wrapped her arm through his and rested her head on his shoulder. Edward continued to stare at the fire. He could feel her taking deep breaths. She lifted her head and looked at him. Edward turned to meet her gaze.

'But I'm going to. I'm *going* to tell you what to do. Edward, it seems to me you're married in name only. And you're so unhappy and, from all you say, Jane is just as unhappy, *at least* as unhappy. She might be relieved to be free of it all, for all you know.'

Edward looked back at the fire.

'Do ye truly ken that? If ye were in her shoes?'

'I don't know, darling, but why don't you at least discuss it?'

Edward leant back, placed his arm around her head, and rested it on his shoulder.

'And ye'd *truly* marry me, even after my poor record as a husband?'

He could feel Mary Beth's head shaking. He could hear her laughing under her breath.

'Edward Lovat. I've loved you for forty years. And, again, I'm sorry. Oh, God, I'm sorry, but I don't feel the slightest disloyalty in saying it – I've *never* loved anyone as much.'

They were distracted by part of the log breaking off and crashing to the hearth.

'Of *course*, I'd marry you, darling Edward.'

They watched in silence as the broken off log sent embers rushing up the chimney.

'What an *amadan* I was,' Edward said. 'What a fool I've been – most of my life.'

'You haven't been a fool, darling. We're all fools when it comes to love and choosing our partner for life. I chose poor John. I was a child and all I really wanted was a father or an older brother. Not a husband who'd expect all a husband wants. I must have driven the poor man to distraction. And I *wasn't* happy. Not really. I made the most of it, but I wasn't happy; and neither was he if the truth be known.'

'I've nay ever heard ye talk like that. I suppose I guessed some of it but I'm still a wee bit shocked to hear the extent of it.'

'Well, there's no room for any more deceit between us, Edward. What we don't say now will forever be lost. And I don't want to say anything bad about John. He was a wonderful man and he tolerated and loved me even though I couldn't give him all he wanted. All I want to say, and please hear this and, if it comes to pass, let it give you the strength to do what you need to do. I *love* you. I've loved you forever. I loved you on the ship to Sydney. I knew I shouldn't. I felt wicked for the feelings I had for you. You were a mere boy, and I was a married woman.'

Mary Beth faltered. Edward pressed her head further onto his shoulder.

'But, for all that, as *God* is my witness, I fell hopelessly in love with you.'

'Truly? Why did ye nay ever say it? If nay then, then when I came to stay after Commodore Parker died. Before I even went to Tralee?'

'Oh, I don't know. I've asked myself the same question over and over – and over again. When we met in Oxford those times, I'd ask myself that night. When you wrote and told me you were married to Amy. Oh, my God, did I ask myself? And then when you told me you were marrying Jane, I persecuted myself. Why didn't I stop you and say, *Edward, I love you; I'll never be happy without you?* Why didn't I say, *Edward, I love you more than she does? Choose me instead.*'

'So, ye ken I was making a mistake? With Jane, I mean?'

'No, I'm sorry. I've no right to say that. If I'd said it then, it would have been so selfish. I'd have felt as though I was manipulating you, blackmailing you into loving me. And I never wanted that. I just wanted you to love me because you loved me.'

'As I say, what an *amadan* I've been. A sheer fool. And you've been *such* a friend. Through all of that, you were always there. Ye even came to Jane's and my wedding. How could ye've done that?'

Mary Beth raised her head from his shoulder and leant forward, staring at her clenched hands. She turned and looked him in the eye.

'It was my way of loving you, Edward. It was *all I had left*. It would have been easier in *so* many ways to have stayed away but then that would have looked like I was sulking, thinking more of myself than of you. And that wouldn't have been loving you as I wanted to. I wanted you to know that's how much I loved you that I would come and watch you marry someone else – and suffer for it.'

'But it did start something with Carl, dinna it?'

'Yes, *absolutely*. And that was such a right decision – for me, at the time. What a wonderful man he was.'

Mary Beth stared into the fire, shook her head, and took a deep breath.

'Edward, I've been very lucky; *very* lucky. I've been married twice to two wonderful men. I know that's so often not the way it is. I've friends, *many* of them, who are unhappy in their marriage, one or two married to beasts. I've *no* grounds for complaining. And I'm not.'

She continued to look at the fire. Edward could see her chest rising and falling.

'But – and *please* hear me before it's too late – that just makes my love for you so much stronger. I've *never* wanted you because I was married to a beast. I've *just* wanted you because I've loved you beyond any other kind of love I've ever had.'

Edward reached out and drew her to him. Their lips met and they held the kiss. Mary Beth pulled away and rested her head on his shoulder.

'I love you, Edward Lovat,' she sniggered. 'Or have I said that before?'

'I'm nay sure,' Edward laughed. 'Mary Beth, I do love ye, I *truly* do. I ken that as far back as the *Gorgon* as well, even though I was nay more than a bairn. Things were always so easy between us. Even when we've nay seen each other for years, it's as though we were together yesterday. I've nay felt that with anyone else – ever. And ye ken when I ken I loved ye for sure?'

'No, when?'

'At yer wedding to Carl.'

Mary Beth sat up, turned away and reached for her kerchief. She kept her head turned from him and wept.

'I can't believe that Edward.'

'I'm sorry. I should nay have told ye.'

'Oh, yes, you should. Let's never keep any more secrets between us. None, do you hear me? None!'

She came back to his shoulder. They stared into the fire.

'What might have been,' Mary Beth said. 'What might have been!'

'Or what can be,' Edward said. 'Should we nay seal it, then? I ken we've had this conversation over and over and I ken it's almost happened more than once. But, seriously, Mary Beth, should we nay seal our love? It might be our last chance.'

'Edward, my darling, so many parts of me want that too but if this is our last chance, I'd rather let it pass. To have you but not have you would be too painful. As I've said many times before, I've never wanted to be your second best, your port in a storm. When things go wrong elsewhere, here I am as your stand-in. John and Carl loved me for *me*. They chose me over all others. How could I be happy with anything else from the one I love most?'

'Of course.'

They both slept fitfully that night. The next morning, they bade farewell.

'I hope…' Edward began.

'Don't say it, darling. No promises. What will be will be!'

XXVI

The Hindoo entered Sydney Harbour, New South Wales, on the 12th day of December 1837. Unlike the ill-fated *Lady Macnaghten*, the ship was able to berth once the mandatory health check had been done. All passengers were assessed as being in good to excellent health.

'Well done, Captain Stuart,' the doctor said. 'Yet again.'

'Thank you, Doctor,' Stuart replied, turning to the others standing on the deck. 'It helps having a good ship and crew. And such delightful company if I might say.'

'Thank you, Captain,' Charles said as he turned towards the gangplank.

'It was my pleasure, Mr Lovat. Best wishes in your work. I dare say you will raise the stakes of the Catholic Church here immensely.'

'Thank you, sir. I'm not sure of that but I'll do my best.'

'I know you will, Father. But don't waste yourself on the Catholics alone. Remember there are other souls who'll need you. Ones who are not and never will be popish.'

'I'll remember that,' Charles laughed.

'Are you waiting for me, by any chance?' Charles said to the fresh-faced youngster in full clerical garb.

'*Farder* Lovat?' the young Irishman replied. 'I'm sorry, *Farder*, I was expectin' ye'd be dressed as a priest. My name's Michael O'Neill.'

'I'm afraid there was no need of a priest on board. I was the only Catholic. And how do you stand being dressed like that in this weather?'

'It's expected of us, *Farder*. We have to witness, ye know.'

'Indeed, Father.'

'Oh, sorry, *Farder*, I should've made it clear, I'm not ordained yet. I've just been entered into the diaconate.'

'Deacon O'Neill then.'

'Yes, *Farder*. Anyway, let me help ye wit' yer luggage. I've a carriage over dere. It's only a short ride to St Mary's.'

As they rode along Macquarie Street, Charles took in a scene he had never imagined. He had heard tales of the Jesuit missions implanted in Indian mountains, Chinese outposts, and South American jungles. What he saw here was pristine compared with Rome, London, and Lancashire but it was quickly taking on a look of a transplanted Europe. Massive stone structures commanded both sides of the wide thoroughfare he would come to know as Macquarie Street.

'How long have you been here, Mr O'Neill?'

'Only a few weeks, *Farder*. My friend, John Byrne, and I were studyin' at Waterford when we met Dr Ullat'orne.'

'Ah, yes. A very persuasive gentleman.'

'Well, he's a bishop actually, or I t'ink he'll be one soon,' O'Neill retorted.

'Perhaps, but bishops and gentlemen are not *always* mutually exclusive.'

Charles noted the puzzled look on the young man's face.

'Anyway, he told us not to wait for ordination. Bishop Polding'd take care o' dat once we've finished our training.'

'Where will you do that?'

'Right 'ere, *Farder*,' O'Neill replied, as they turned in the gates of the bishop's house. 'Right 'ere, wit' ye.'

'With me? What do you mean?'

'I'm sorry, *Farder*. I t'ought ye knew. It's not for me to say any more. Excuse me. Mrs 'arris will show ye to yer room. Ye have an appointment wit' Bishop Poldin' at two o'clock. Mrs 'arris will escort ye to de bishop's office.'

Charles saw the thin, greying, austere-looking woman standing where the carriage was about to finish its journey. Her stance and face spoke of agitation.

'Is this Father Lovat?' Mrs Harris asked O'Neill.

'Yes, ma'am,' Charles said as he stepped down from the carriage. 'I'm Father Lovat. I'm delighted to meet you.'

Charles held out his hand. Mrs Harris declined to take it. She was looking him up and down.

'Let me show you to your room, Father. We'll have your luggage sent straight up so you can dress appropriately for His Lordship.'

Mrs Harris walked faster than Charles could. She held the large wooden door open for him and, without another word, led him up the polished timber staircase to a room three along down a wide, equally polished timber hallway. She opened the door and ushered Charles inside.

'There's a bowl of water and a towel on the table, Father. Your luggage will be with you shortly. Once you're ready, please wait here for my return.'

Before Charles could open his mouth to respond, the door slammed shut. In no time, there was a knock.

'Come in.'

Charles heard footsteps moving away down the hallway. He opened the door to find the three valises, those containing the entirety of his worldly possessions, neatly stacked against the wall.

Charles washed and changed into his clerical dress. He sat on the one large lounge chair in the room and surveyed the four-poster bed, its timber sides polished to match the floor, a fine rug placed where one's feet would hit the floor of a morning. The wooden chair was pushed neatly under the matching desk with one ornament atop it – a silver crucifix.

'Come in,' Charles called when the knock came.

He was half-expecting there would be no response. Mrs Harris opened the door and stepped in, accompanied by a young maid holding a tray.

'Some tea and bread for you, Father. Mavis, place the tray on the table.'

'Thank you both,' Charles said.

'That will be fine, Mavis. Just leave it there. Father can pour his own tea.'

Mavis hurried back to the open door, head down. Mrs Harris was still holding the doorknob. She stood aside to let the maid move past her.

'His Lordship is expecting you at two o'clock, Father. I'll be back to escort you at ten to the hour. Is there anything else you need?'

'Ah, no, thank…'

The door shut.

—⚜—

'Welcome, Father,' Bishop Polding said, reaching out his hand and smiling. 'Welcome to the great southern land, as we describe it, especially when trying to encourage people to come here.'

'Thank you, My Lord,' Charles replied, kneeling on one knee to kiss the ring on the bishop's right hand.

John Bede Polding was an English Benedictine priest. He was only five years older than Charles, though he looked ten years or so older again. Charles was struck by his fine features and aristocratic demeanour. He looked even larger than he was in his flowing robes, a mixture of Benedictine black and episcopal purple. His hair had gone prematurely white, hanging long over his ears, and covering his collar at the back. His rimless spectacles conveyed a stern demeanour but the eyes behind them were warm, as was the smile with which he greeted Charles.

'Please take a seat, Father. How was your trip?'

'Excellent, My Lord. Better than I could have hoped for.'

'It's in the lap of the gods. Some trips are good; some abysmal. Your brother's, for instance, was possibly the worst in forty years.'

'Oh, no. I had no idea. Is he?'

'Yes, everything's fine. He and his family are in good health. But they lost almost a hundred souls on the trip, including a number after they arrived. Typhus, it was. Once it gets hold on a ship, it's very hard to control. Even the ship's surgeon was taken. I understand he and your niece were engaged. I'm told she was heartbroken.'

'Who's that? Mary?'

'I'm not sure of the name. I haven't actually met the family. I'm just going by what the Governor tells me.'

'The Governor?'

'Yes, the Governor. He was very quick to secure your brother's services. He obviously knew he'd held a senior post in the new Irish public education system. So, he's offered him a government post to set up a new school or two in some of our growing areas.'

'Not Catholic schools, you mean? I was certain Thomas thought he was coming out to work for the church.'

'Well, he was but I could hardly turn down the Governor when he prevailed upon me. After all, he was the one who'd paid the passage for the family.'

'I'm sorry to hear that. Is there anything I can do to help?'

'No, Father. Frankly, I'm quite supportive of what the Governor's trying to do. He doesn't like the denominational schools. He thinks they divide us, and he's quite right. He wants a government run school system that's for everyone. From where I sit, our Catholic people can only benefit from that.'

'I agree entirely. We've seen enough of the division at home.'

'Indeed, you're from Lancashire originally, is that correct?'

'Yes, My Lord.'

'A very divided part of the world. As is my hometown of Liverpool. Both challenging places for Catholics. I think a schooling that brought people together would be just what's needed there but one can hardly imagine it happening. Here, we have a chance to do it.'

'Absolutely. But I imagine there'll be Catholics who disagree.'

'Funny you should say,' Polding laughed. 'I'm having this very debate with some of our colleagues. Father McEncroe is spitting chips about your brother being *kidnapped*, as he puts it, to set up government schools instead of Catholic ones.'

'Yes, I've heard of Father McEncroe. He was in contact with Father Prendiville in Tralee. It was through him that Thomas first heard about the educational need in New South Wales.'

'Yes, that's right. And as far as Father McEncroe's concerned, your brother was his "find" and no-one else's. He thinks I should march over to Government House and tell the Governor he can go to hell. *Thomas Lovat is working for us, whether you like it or not – Your Excellency*.'

'Oh dear. I do hope Thomas won't be excommunicated,' Charles laughed.

'Well, if Father McEncroe had his way, he might well, and so might I,' Polding laughed. 'But enough about that. Tell me about yourself, speaking of "finds". That's precisely how Father Ullathorne described you in his despatches. What's your story, Father? You were with the Jesuits, I take it?'

'Yes, My Lord. For about twenty years. I studied at Stonyhurst and the Jesuit College in Rome, and then taught in their schools and seminaries after ordination.'

'My, my, so this is a big change for you? Tell me more.'

'Well, to be perfectly honest, My Lord. It has something to do with the oath that the Holy Father was demanding of seminary professors but there's more to it than that.'

'And to be perfectly honest with you, Father Ullathorne mentioned about the oath issue, but he assured me you weren't a heretic or turning unbeliever and I trust his judgement. All the same, I'd like to hear more about it from you. What was your problem with taking the oath?'

'It just went against everything I believe. And I know that sounds arrogant, and indeed disrespectful of the Holy Father's authority, but I was just not able in good conscience to say I don't believe in science, or liberal theology, or democracy, or social justice, or human rights and equality, and the abolition of slavery, and…'

'That's enough, Father. I get the point. And I agree, for what that's worth. And please don't quote me. Some of our colleagues would be appalled. But I agree. And I'm not a heretic or unbeliever either, though some might think I am.'

'Thank you, My Lord. It's a huge relief to hear you say such a thing. I did prevail upon Father Ullathorne to persuade me that you'd understand my position and he assured me you would. You see, My Lord, for me, it's not merely about conscience. It's actually about what I believe as a Catholic. I've read much of the Angelic Doctor's writings and taught about them too. I believe even he would have difficulty in taking an oath of this kind. I believe he'd be horrified to see the Catholic Church resisting the tide of the times, rather than leading.'

'Father, you speak about arrogance. If I might be arrogant for a moment. I think both Benedictines and Jesuits receive a theological training that's beyond the average. And it's showing in what you say. That's why I was desperate to have this new country staffed as a Benedictine mission, or perhaps a Jesuit one or one of the other intellectual Orders. Granted the other churches see Catholics as the uneducated poor, if not all of us convicts, we need a clergy here that can challenge their bigotries. As it is, Father Ullathorne couldn't manage to get the level of interest needed from any of the Orders. Hence, from next month, we'll see a stream of Irish clergy arriving, most of them with the barest of good theological training.'

'I'm sorry to hear you couldn't get more interest from one of the Orders. The Orders have been so active in India, Asia, the Americas.'

'Yes, I think we missed the boat there if you'll pardon the saying. The great missionary age in the church seems to have been replaced by a new conservatism. The church seems more concerned with saving its place in the world, or in Rome at least, than fulfilling its mission. Let's face it, the last couple of popes have been rather inward looking, I say with the greatest of respect.'

'I agree, My Lord. When I was first in Rome, Pope Pius VII was there. I actually met him. He was such an inspirational figure. So obviously a holy man but also intellectually sharp, bold even, and his sense of the church's mission was outward-looking. He did some wonderful work in the Americas, for instance. But then things changed.'

'Yes, and of course we have to believe it's all the work and wisdom of the Holy Ghost, even when it's not so obvious to us. Anyway, Father, there *is* something you can do to help in the New South Wales mission. Especially because I wasn't able to get the kind of theologically versed clergy that I wanted for the place I have something I wish to ask of you.'

Charles could sense what was coming. He regretted he had not had the chance to tell Polding how much he was looking forward to being a pastor, rather than professor.

'I need a seminary here, Father. I believe you met Mr O'Neill. He's a fine young man and I'm sure he'll make a good priest, but he has little to no theological training at this time and is unusually narrow in his views. I frankly wonder what they've been doing at Waterford that someone can get so close to ordination and know so little about the intellectual tradition of the church. And there'll be others arriving in the new year, all Irish, priests and deacons and, I'm assuming, all in need of theological fortification.'

'What is it exactly that you think I can do for them, though, especially if they're already ordained?'

'Father, you speak about Aquinas as though you know him personally. I'm not sure young O'Neill has even heard of him. We have to fix this and you're the man to do it. This is what Father Ullathorne meant when he described you as a "find".'

Charles sat in silence. He wondered if he should attempt now to state his preference for pastoral work.

'Well, what do you say, Father? I would have thought you'd be jumping at the chance to do this kind of work. I understand your last assignment with the Jesuits was teaching mathematics to the juniors. Surely what I'm offering is a step up on that.'

'Pardon my rudeness, My Lord. I'm just a little stunned. Frankly, I'd imagined my disobedience – and that's how some have described it – would disqualify me from ever holding such a post again. So, I suppose I've been imagining myself as a parish priest or chaplain or perhaps even an outback missionary.'

'Father, Rome's a long way from here. I doubt the pope even knows we exist. The nearest nuncio is on the other side of the Indian Ocean and will probably never visit here. So, I'm fairly free to make my own decisions about such things. I've heard enough about you to know you're the man I need at present. Missionary on horseback can come later if you still really want that.'

Charles looked at his own clenched hands, then looked up and straight into the eyes of the bishop.

'Then I gratefully accept your kind offer, My Lord. I can only take it as the Lord's will for me.'

'Wonderful. In that case, the room you've been assigned will be yours for the time being. You'll be officially on my staff here at St Mary's. Which means you'll get to say public Masses anyway. It won't all be teaching Aquinas.'

'Thank you, My Lord. You've been too kind.'

'Not at all, Father. I appreciate your generosity, and indeed your candour. There are times I crave for the kinds of conversations I believe I can have with you. I look forward to them.'

'Thank you again, My Lord.'

As Charles left the bishop's office, Mrs Harris handed him a letter.

'This was left for you, Father. Some weeks ago.'

Dear Charles (and Da, if you're here),

I'm told you will be reporting to Bishop Polding's office when you arrive so have left this letter for you. The bishop might have already told you that I have been appointed by the Governor to a new school out west. We are trying very hard to have it ready for pupils in the new year. Hence, there is a lot of building going on, as well as rounding up the pupils and finding extra teaching staff. I had hoped to be there to meet you when you arrived, but I was uncertain which ship you were on. Please do let us know when you have arrived and, hopefully, we can get together at some stage.

We will have much to tell you about our trip which, everyone says, was the worst in all the years of the colony. We were hit with typhus in the last month and spent day after day at makeshift funerals and despatching bodies to the sea. The number of children involved was heartbreaking to see. We were, of course, beside ourselves with worry for our own children but, thank the Lord, your prayers kept us safe.

Poor Mary had her first romantic attachment while on board. James Hawkins was our surgeon. A fine fellow. He and Mary were as much as engaged by the end but tragically he died soon after we arrived in Sydney. Mary is still getting over her heart having been broken. It would be wonderful if she could talk with you sometime. We had best away and get back to our chores. We look forward to hearing from you when you have the time.

Our love always, Thomas, Eliza, and family.

PS. We have a feeling Da is not with you. He seemed uncertain about it when we left. If he is, give him all our love and tell him he has a home here with us whenever he needs it.

Charles wrote a short note letting them know he had arrived but not their father. He also let them know about his own appointment.

> *...I'll be in contact as soon as possible and hope to meet up after Christmas.*
> *Your brother, Charles.*
> *PS. And do tell young Mary to come and see me anytime she wishes. I will pray for her and for her James.*

January 1838 came and went without the two brothers meeting. They were fifty miles apart and the only transport was by horseback or a highly unreliable carriage service. Thomas remained busy setting up his school. Charles had thought he might be able to visit when Polding invited him to accompany him to Bathurst, a hundred or so miles west of Sydney. As it happened, they took a different route and Charles had to get back to oversee the transforming of one of the buildings at St Mary's into two classrooms for the new seminary. He also had to prepare lessons according to the instructions given him by Polding.

When Polding returned, he wrote a letter to his Benedictine superior in Turvey, England.

> *Charles Lovat, a former Jesuit Professor of Moral Theology at Stonyhurst, joined us lately. He is much respected. His services are most valuable as a preacher and confessor. His good conduct in everything is admired. He has been with me as far as Bathurst to visit the hospital and to minister to the wants of the Catholics. He will be opening the new seminary next month. He is a truly great acquisition.*

On Monday, the 5th of February, both the Richmond school and St Mary's seminary opened their doors.

XXVII

'*Good morning, gentlemen,*' Charles said.
        'Good mornin', *Farder*.'

Michael O'Neill and John Byrne were joined by Michael McGrath and John Lynch who had arrived from Ireland in January. They were all deacons nearing priesthood. Charles's task was to ensure their theology was up to date and more rigorous than their bishop's estimation of it. In the two conversations he had with the bishop since his arrival, he was told of two further assignments. Several young men in the colony had expressed an interest in becoming priests and so would need training from the ground up. In addition, the bishop wished Charles to offer some advanced theological training for the already ordained. They were all Irish.

Charles anticipated difficulties with the already-ordained clergy but that was for another day.

'Gentlemen, our task is to run through some of the church's most important doctrines and the key theologians who have interpreted them for us.'

'Excuse me, *Farder*,' O'Neill shot his hand up.

'Yes, Mr O'Neill.'

'I'm sorry, *Farder*, but my understandin' was dat de doctrines of de church rested on de aut'ority of de 'oly See, and especially de 'oly *Farder*. I was taught dey needed no interpretation and dat, indeed, interpretation was what 'ad led to de Protestant 'eresies.'

'*So, this is what the bishop was talking about*,' Charles thought to himself.

'Thank you, Mr O'Neill. Does anyone else have a view on this?'

'I agree, *Farder*,' Byrne said. 'Dat was my understandin' as well.'

'Well, let's see what Saint Thomas Aquinas has to say about these things.'

In the ensuing classes, Charles focussed most attention on Aquinas. Occasionally, he would be asked about Saint Augustine, often favoured by the conservatives. He would carefully make the point that Aquinas owed much to Augustine without going too far into their differences. He glanced lightly over Aquinas's dependence on Jewish and Islamic scholarship but not sufficiently lightly.

'Excuse me, *Farder*, are we to believe dat de Angelic Doctor sought wisdom from pagans?'

'No, not from pagans, from traditions that he believed worshipped the same God as himself.'

'And do ye t'ink de same, *Farder*?'

'Well, yes, I do. With Judaism, it's obvious. The Lord himself was Jewish, after all. And Islam is the third great Abrahamic tradition. Even one of the recent popes has said as much.'

'Which pope?'

'Pope Pius VII.'

'Wit' respect, *Farder*. We've been told dat bot' Pope Leo and Pope Gregory 'ave 'ad to correct some of Pope Pius's errors. Wasn't 'e very absent-minded in the end?'

'I don't believe so. I met him not so long before he died. I was struck by his holiness and how sharp of mind he was.'

The allusion to meeting the pope steered the conversation away from something Charles found deeply troubling. He wondered what must be going on in seminaries around the world if these views were being taught.

After intense days of such teaching, he would fall into bed and asleep quickly, only to wake in the middle of the night, wondering what the next day would bring.

'And I haven't even begun with the ordained clergy,' he would think to himself.

'Please, gentlemen,' Governor Gipps said. 'I'd like to introduce you to Professor Charles Lovat, formerly from Stonyhurst College.'

Gipps had replaced Richard Bourke as Governor earlier that year. Each of the church leaders had met with the new Governor individually but this was their first meeting with him as a group. Polding had asked Charles to attend the meeting. He would normally have asked Ullathorne but, since he had not yet arrived back from England, Polding had asked Charles to stand in for him. In fact, Polding preferred that Charles attend for reasons that were quickly apparent.

Polding and Gipps had struck up a good relationship, including about the issue of non-denominational schooling. Gipps was relying on Polding's vocal support so Polding had asked if the Governor could introduce Charles in a way that optimised his status in the eyes of the Protestant leaders. Like Bourke, Gipps saw the churches as an important way of binding the population and ensuring its civility. He was especially keen for the other churches to see the Catholic Church as an ally, granted its power over the largely convict class Irish that was increasingly becoming the backbone of the working class.

'So, you were a Jesuit, Professor?' Bishop Broughton asked.

William Broughton was the Church of England Bishop of Sydney. He was accompanied by the Reverend Samuel Marsden, a pioneer clergyman, noted for his anti-Catholic sentiments.

'Yes, My Lord, I was.'

'So, why did you leave the Jesuits, if I might ask?' Marsden said.

'Oh, it's a long story, I suppose. Let's just say that Rome and I have had our disagreements.'

'I like the man already,' Marsden laughed.

The others had rarely seen Marsden smile, much less laugh. He was a serious, rather dour Christian of Wesleyan theological disposition. John Wesley was a Church of England clergyman who, a century or so beforehand, had broken away to form Methodism, an especially strict and puritanical brand of Protestantism. Marsden remained with the Church of England but promoted a very "low", least-Catholic, version of it.

'I think your man has won him over already,' Governor Gipps whispered to Polding.

Broughton overheard and smiled. Both he and the Governor had tried to rein in Marsden's excessively Protestant ways. Broughton had supported the Governor's attempts to reconcile the Catholic Church with the other denominations. The other leaders were softening to the idea, but Marsden remained resistant. Marsden held some sway over the other Protestant leaders, especially the Methodists.

'Father Lovat is, as Father Ullathorne suggested, quite a find,' Polding whispered back to the Governor.

Charles was greeted by the other leaders present. The Reverends John Lang and John McVeigh from the Presbyterians and Samuel Wilkinson and William Moore from the Methodists had been given tacit permission by Marsden to be civil to the "popish" newcomer.

They sat around the large dining table, with the Governor at one end and the Lieutenant Governor, Kenneth Snodgrass, at the other end. Roast pork was served with potato, pumpkin, and greens, washed down with red wine for those who chose to imbibe. The fact that Charles declined was another point in his favour as far as the Methodists and Marsden were concerned.

They had often expressed disfavour at the drinking habits of the Catholic clergy.

'Did you know, gentlemen, that Professor Lovat's brother has been put in charge of the new school at Richmond?' Gipps said.

'A Catholic in charge of a non-denominational school?' Marsden replied. 'Isn't that a little like putting the pope in charge of a Church of England Synod?'

'Not at all, Mr Marsden,' Gipps replied. 'Thomas Lovat has worked as an inspector in the new Irish public education system. I might also point out that he had thought he was coming to the colony to work for the Catholics but has very willingly accepted my predecessor's invitation to set up the non-denominational experiment.'

'I dare say not all your clergy were happy with that, Bishop Polding,' Broughton said.

'Indeed, Bishop Broughton. I'm not sure some of them would even hear his confession at this stage,' Polding laughed. 'Unless, of course, he repented and came back to Rome, as it were.'

'Tell me, Professor,' McVeigh asked. 'Is your brother cut from the same cloth as yourself?'

'In what way, Reverend?' Charles asked.

'Well, I've been told you have a particularly tolerant attitude when it comes to dialogue between the religious denominations.'

'Where have you heard that, Reverend?' Polding asked.

'Oh, word gets around. It's a small place, you know. I gather some of your own clergy are not entirely happy with Professor Lovat's liberalism, as it has been described to me.'

'I don't consider myself liberal,' Charles said. 'Merely a good Catholic as Catholicism should be seen. I don't consider it worthy of any Christian to be intolerant of others' beliefs. So, naturally, I don't consider it worthy of a Catholic to be that way.'

'My, my, Bishop Polding, you do have a handful here,' Broughton said. 'A good handful, in my view, but I can imagine why some of your clergy, indeed your people, would be shocked.'

'Well, they shouldn't be,' Polding said. 'Father Lovat is merely expressing what he believes to be an authentic Catholic way of being Christian, expressed by no less than Pope Pius VII quite recently.'

'But not by your current pope,' Marsden said.

'Indeed,' Polding replied.

'It's something I don't understand about you Catholics,' Marsden continued. 'How you can let your minds be ruled by an Italian who cares nothing about you.'

'I believe the pope always cares,' Charles said. 'But he's not infallible so we must interpret things that come from Rome and make them fit our circumstances. I believe the great Doctor of the Church, Thomas Aquinas, gave us a very clear formula about how that happens. How one can be obedient to the Holy Father yet follow our own consciences.'

'You mean follow the Bible, in other words?' Marsden asked.

'Yes, the Bible and the tradition.'

'Very interesting indeed,' Marsden replied. 'But tell me again, is this brother of yours cut from the same cloth?'

'Yes, I believe he is. As far as I know. I mean we don't know each other all that well. We are half-brothers. But my father assures me he's religiously tolerant. Certainly, my father is.'

'Ah, I was wanting to ask why it is that he's Irish and you're English,' Lang asked.

Charles briefly explained the history. The issue of Thomas as head of the new school was quickly overtaken by the very concept of non-denominational schooling. Polding and Broughton were in favour. Marsden was opposed. The other four sat on the fence seeming to take their cues from Marsden.

'I'm not sure the Foreign Office would approve, Governor,' Marsden said.

'Oh, I'm sure they would, Reverend,' Gipps replied, banging his glass on the table more loudly than intended. 'But let us see how things work out at Richmond under Mr Lovat's leadership.'

The lunch meeting broke up and, one by one, they started leaving. Only Charles, the two bishops and the Governor were left in the room.

'Mr Marsden's a fiery Christian,' Polding said.

'It never ceases to amaze me how he gets away with flouting your authority so blatantly, Bishop,' Gipps said to Broughton.

'Ah, the Church of England is a democracy, sir. We turn doctrinal difference into an art form. I often envy my Roman colleagues that they have a pope who can tell them what to think and believe with no opposing views entered into.'

Polding and Charles exchanged a glance, smiling.

XXVIII

Edward arrived back at Tarleton House on the 30th of January that year, 1838. He had stayed with Sarah in Pemberton on the way back from Mary Beth's. There, he had celebrated his sixty-second birthday on the 26th, the same day as the anniversary of his father's and grandmother's death thirty-seven years before. Sarah was nearing ninety and still mourning for Thomas, Edward's father. Edward wanted to be with her that day.

There was an invitation waiting for him at home. It was to a belated birthday dinner being held for him at young Edward's cottage on the night of the 1st of February. He had hoped there might be something from Jane as well. Perhaps she would be at the dinner.

In the late morning, there was a loud rapping on the door by one of the workers from the estate.

'Mr Lovat, come quickly, your son is ill.'

Edward ran to the field where young Edward had collapsed while working. He pushed his way through the workers standing around, arriving at the scene just in time to see the doctor pulling a blanket over his son's face.

'Oh, my Laird. Surely nay. Surely!'

'I'm sorry, Mr Lovat,' the doctor said. 'There was nothing anyone could have done. I believe he had a stroke.'

'Has Mrs Lovat been informed?' Edward asked.

'No, sir,' one of the workers replied. 'There's no-one home at the manor or at Mr Lovat's house. The maid at the manor said they'd all gone to Preston this morning. She didn't know when they'd be home.'

Edward lifted the blanket, ran his fingers through young Edward's hair and kissed him on the forehead. He raised his head and faced the workers. They saw the tears flowing down his cheeks.

'Please could ye take my lad to the manor? I'll go fetch the priest.'

Edward galloped to the priest's house next to the estate chapel. It was some time since he had been there. There was a notice on the door that he had not seen before. It offered instructions that all enquiries should be directed to St Mary Presbytery in Burnley.

St Mary Church in the township of Burnley had been established some years beforehand but, until recently, Father Shaw had stayed on at the estate chapel to minister separately to the flock living near the Towneley Estate. Shaw had retired and the chapel thereafter became part of the St Mary Parish. Father Patrick Wallace was the parish priest.

Edward rode to the presbytery and knocked on the door.

'Good morning, Father. I'm Edward Lovat. We've nay met.'

'Yes, Mr Lovat, I know of you,' Wallace replied. 'What can I do for you?'

'I'm afraid my youngest lad has just passed-away. Only thirty-one. I'm still in shock, I'm sorry.'

Edward paused. He reached for his kerchief.

'I'm sorry to hear that, Mr Lovat. You have my sympathy. Now, what can I do for you?'

Edward's eyes dried in an instant. He stared at the priest.

'Ah, I ken ye'd want to give him the last rites.'

'Was the boy Catholic?'

'Aye, he was christened at the Towneley chapel.'

'Yes, but was he practical?'

'Practical?'

'Did he go to Mass and confession?'

'I could nay say for sure. I've nay been here for a while.'

'And are *you* practical, Mr Lovat?'

Edward stared into the priest's eyes.

'Father, perhaps ye dinna hear me. My lad is dead. He's lying on a table at the manor house. He needs the last rites.'

'And I'm sorry for your loss, Mr Lovat. What I'm trying to ascertain is whether your son should be given the last rites as a Catholic or is he something else?'

Edward took a deep breath.

'Father, he was christened a Catholic. He's had a Catholic upbringing. He went to Stonyhurst College. His mother and grandmother are as Catholic as ye, perhaps more so.'

Wallace stiffened.

'He has a brother who's a priest,' Edward continued. 'Just how much more Catholic d'ye ken he should be?'

'Ah yes, the spoilt professor priest. Knows more than the pope, I hear. I'd like my Catholics a bit more Catholic than that, to be frank.'

'Father Wallace? That's yer name, I ken?'

'It is sir.'

'Father Wallace, I can scarcely ken my ears. There's a man lying there dead and ye're subjecting him to an examination instead of performing yer God-sworn duty to ensure he's taken to heaven. In the worst moments of the Catholic Church, I can scarcely ken any priest has ever been more derelict in his duty.'

Wallace took a deep breath and looked to the ground before raising his head and fixing his gaze on Edward.

'Mr Lovat let me fill you in on the latest advice from the Holy

Father. These things have been explained to Catholics at Mass for the last year or more. Now, I dare say there may well be a good reason why you haven't heard them. Nor perhaps your son. The Holy Father has been very clear that the sacraments of the church are to be reserved for practical Catholics, those who attend Mass and confession regularly.'

Edward stared at the priest who lowered his gaze. Edward was about to speak when Wallace looked up and continued.

'You see, Mr Lovat, people always turn to the church when it suits them. They live in sin and then come along and want to be married in the church. Parents pay no attention to their own children's immortal welfare and when they die, tragically like yours, these same parents come crawling back to the church to make everything aright. Well, that's not good enough for this pope – and, frankly, it's not good enough for me.'

Edward's gaze was fixed on the priest's face. He was struggling to breathe. Wallace looked away.

'So, to be clear, Father. And please don't turn away.'

Wallace turned back to look at Edward as he spoke.

'What ye're telling me is that ye'll nay come and give my lad the last rites. I want to hear ye clearly say that.'

The priest lowered his gaze and stood in silence. Edward stared at him until he looked up.

'Mr Lovat, I'm sorry. I'll come and say prayers over him. I'd do that for a pagan. Let me finish my lunch and I'll be over. I take it he's at Towneley Manor?'

'So, ye'll come and say prayers, as ye would to a pagan? And then?'

'Then what?'

'Would ye give him a Requiem Mass?'

'No, Mr Lovat, I would not. As I said, the Holy Father has been very clear …'

'Thank ye, Father. Dinna bother with yer prayers.'

Sarah had mentioned that the Reverend Harry Thurlow's grandson was the rector of St Peter's Church of England in Burnley. Harry Thurlow had been one of Edward's father's best friends and mentors. He was the founder of St Bartholomew's Academy for Boys where Edward's father had taught before going into the army.

'*What did she say his name was?*' Edward asked himself as he rode to St Peter's.

'*Halo*, Reverend,' he said as the door of the rectory opened. 'I'm Edward Lovat. I ken yer grandfather.'

'Edward? Are you Thomas Lovat's son?'

'Aye, I dinna ken ye ken us.'

'Oh yes, I scarcely knew my grandfather, but my own father always spoke so fondly of your father. He told me all about the lifetime of friendship between our families. Please do come in. What brings you here?'

Edward told him about young Edward's death.

'I'm so very sorry to hear that. Oh, my heavens. Your son is scarcely older than me. And his poor wife and that little girl. How old did you say the child is?'

'Just six, Reverend.'

'Oh, please call me Horace.'

'*Horace, that's it!*'

'The poor little girl. At least she'll have some memories of him. Hopefully that will comfort her. How is she taking the news? And his wife, of course? And your wife? The poor man's mother?'

'They dinna ken yet, Horace. I have to go back to Towneley Manor now and wait for them. But I have something to ask ye if I might.'

Edward told him about the reception he had received at St Mary.

'So, I'd be ever so grateful if ye'd come and say some prayers over the lad.'

'Of course, Edward. Just let me saddle up my horse and I'll follow you. I must say I find Father Wallace's attitude extraordinary.

I know my grandfather always spoke so highly of the Roman priests. I'm not sure he'd believe what we're seeing in some of them now.'

'I only wish my other son was here. He's a priest. He studied in Rome and was teaching at Stonyhurst until this new wave of conservatism hit. He'd nay doubt be able to tell us both what's going on.'

'Truly? Where is he now?'

'New South Wales. Well, I hope and pray he's there. He was due to arrive in December. Please the Laird I'll hear about it in time.'

Horace Thurlow prayed over young Edward's body while Edward knelt in silence, holding his son's hand. The butler and maid stood at the door, torn between grief and their Catholic loyalties.

'Thank ye, Horace. I appreciate it so much. I dare say ye have the jump on the popish Wallace when it comes to being the Laird in the world today.'

'Thank you, Edward. If there's anything more I can do.'

'Well, there is actually. Could I speak to ye outside?'

The two men passed the butler and maid who nodded. They stepped outside and walked to where Thurlow's horse was tethered.

'Thank ye again, Horace,' Edward said. 'I wonder if I might prevail upon ye to preside over the lad's burial as well.'

'Why, of course! Where would you like him to be buried?'

'I ken I'd be happiest if he was laid to rest in yer graveyard. The one next to yer church. Of course, I'll have to get his wife's permission, but I ken once she hears about Father Wallace, she'll agree. She's nay very Catholic herself. I ken she went to yer church as a lass anyway.'

'Why, by all means. I could have Mr Townsend from Townsend and Sons pick up the body this afternoon if you wish. His offices are just down the road from the church. They organise most of our funerals.'

Edward thought for a moment.

'If ye dinna mind, that'd be braw.'

—⚹—

The carriage arrived at Towneley Manor as night was falling. Percival and Jane stepped out. The carriage was to take Margaret and Mary Jane to their cottage where food had been prepared for Edward's birthday dinner.

'Edward? What are you doing here?' Jane said.

'I'll tell ye presently, dear. Driver, stay here, please!'

'What is it, Edward?' Jane said again.

'Margaret, would ye care to step inside?' Edward said, then turned to face the six-year-old Mary Jane. 'Come in, darling.'

'What's wrong, Edward?' Jane asked, grabbing his arm, and looking him in the eye.

'Please, just come inside.'

Edward led them into the manor house parlour and sat them down.

'Is something wrong with Pa?' Mary Jane asked.

'I'm sorry, darling. Aye, yer Pa was very sick today.'

'Where is he?' Margaret asked.

'I'm afraid he's gone to heaven,' Edward said, choking on the words.

Jane let out a cry none of them had heard before. It was so distracting that it took away any other feelings they had. It was over as quickly as it happened. Jane sat frozen to the spot. There were no tears. She stared ahead.

Mary Jane walked to her mother and buried her head on her shoulder. Margaret rested her cheek on her child's head. Percival walked out of the room without saying a word.

'What happened?' Margaret asked, her voice unsteady.

'The doctor ken he had a stroke. He asked if he'd had more headaches lately.'

'Yes, he has,' Margaret said. 'He had one this morning. I asked if he should stay home but he said Mr Towneley wouldn't be pleased. Mr Towneley has been pressuring him lately. You know how it is.'

'Oh, that's right,' Jane blurted out. 'Let's blame poor Percival for everything that goes wrong in our lives. You've taught them well, Edward.'

'Nay anyone's blaming anyone, dear.'

'Well, I'm blaming *you*. If you were a real father, you'd have been here. Perhaps if you'd been here helping him with his work…'

'That's nay fair, Jane.'

'Stop,' Mary Jane shouted, lifting her head from her mother's shoulder. 'My Pa's dead. *My Pa's dead.*'

Mary Jane burst into tears and sobbed. Margaret pulled her back to her shoulder and cuddled her.

'From the mouths of babes,' Margaret said. 'Her father's dead and you two are squabbling.'

'Better squabbling than not talking at all,' Jane said. 'Anyway, where's my boy? I need to say my goodbyes.'

'He's at Mr Townsend's place.'

Edward braced himself.

'*Townsend's*? I didn't think they did Catholic funerals.'

'They dinna.'

'Edward, *what* are you saying?'

Edward recounted the exchange with Father Wallace and the decision he had made to ask Horace Thurlow to perform the burial.

'It's your choice, Margaret. Finally, it's your choice but I could nay tolerate watching my lad be treated like a heathen. Horace granted him all the dignity ye could want for him.'

'Margaret, you *cannot* allow this,' Jane said. 'I forbid it.'

'I really don't care where he's buried,' Margaret said. 'It's the least of my concerns.'

'A Catholic buried in a Protestant graveyard?' Jane said. 'You've lost your mind, girl. Edward, this is the last straw. If this happens…! Percival. Percival. Come in here at once!'

Percival stepped back into the room.

'Percival tell them this cannot happen! Do something about it. Please talk some sense into them.'

'I heard what Edward said. I'm afraid it's consistent with what Father Wallace has been saying. I must say I don't agree with all of it myself. I try to be a faithful Catholic, but I don't like what the current Holy Father is doing with these sorts of constrictions. But, at the same time, I must say I *have* been trying to get young Edward to return to his faith, if only for appearances. There are others on the estate who've been quite unhappy that I continue to employ a lapsed Catholic. If it were not for my loyalty to Jane, I…'

'Oh, be quiet, you stupid man,' Margaret shouted, pressing Mary Jane's head further into her chest. 'That's all part of the pressure you've put on my husband. I hold *you* responsible.'

'So do I,' Mary Jane shouted at the top of her voice. '*You killed my Pa.*'

Percival staggered back on his feet.

'I, I …'

'Oh, don't be ridiculous,' Jane said in a scolding, imperious voice. 'As if Percival could have done anything about this. He's been very good keeping young Edward in a job. You should be grateful, what with our reputation in the gutter. Whatever good name we had lost with a wayward father and a renegade priest to our name.'

Edward bristled but bit his tongue before he spoke.

'I think young Mary Jane has said all that should be said at this time. Her Pa's dead. Why dinna we honour him instead of squabbling?'

'We're not squabbling,' Jane said. 'We're just being who we are. Now, Percival, let me be clear. I want you to fix this with Father Wallace. Young Edward must be buried here with his sister and brother. I *cannot* abide anything less.'

'I'm sorry,' Margaret said. 'But I *don't* want him buried here. I want him buried at St Peter's. That's where I went to church as a girl and it's where my parents still worship. I became a Catholic when we married to please you all but, frankly, I've never felt anything for your popish ways. I'm renouncing all that here and now. I want to be buried at St Peter's when the time comes, so I want my husband there.'

'But, but…,' Jane said.

'But nothing,' Margaret replied. 'My parents say Mr Thurlow's a lovely man and if he's the one who came here to say prayers while your Father Wallace thought himself too good to lower himself, then I want nothing to do with him.'

'I told young Edward not to marry a Protestant girl,' Jane said.

'Oh, you're a wicked, cold woman,' Margaret replied.

'Well, this wicked, cold woman will *not* attend.'

'Ye'll nay go to yer own lad's funeral?' Edward asked. 'Are ye serious, Jane? Are ye *serious?*'

—※—

Three days later, young Edward's funeral was held at St Peter's Church of England in Burnley. Horace Thurlow was the celebrant. Jane was in the front pew on the right-hand side. Edward and Percival were on either side of her. To Edward's left was Margaret, with Mary Jane and her other grandparents further to the left. Jane and Percival sat throughout, neither standing nor kneeling at the appointed times.

'*We gather today to commend the immortal soul of Edward Lovat to his Maker, the Almighty God, the only one who can say why he was taken from this world so soon. We grieve with his family, his wife, Margaret, his daughter, Mary Jane, and with his parents, Mr and Mrs Lovat, and parents-in-law, Mr and Mrs Baron. Mr and Mrs Baron are, of course, well known to us as parishioners here at St Peter's.*

Life is a mystery, understood fully only by God, and death is, of course, one of the most mysterious features of this mystery. In the end, we have no more control of it, its nature and timing, than we do of our birth. Only God, in his infinite wisdom, knows these things. For those of no faith, life is random and death a catastrophe. For those of us of faith, neither is the case. We know we are brought into this world with divine purpose and when that purpose is achieved, we return to the bosom from whence we came. It is not for us to question or even scrutinise when that purpose is done. God knows and we cannot but trust in his judgement.

What we do know, because it has been revealed to us in God's own words, is that life's purpose is about love. It is not about riches or power. Those are the ways of the world. It is about love. How well have we loved those around us? How well have we loved others? How well have we forgiven those who have offended us? How well have we replaced the enmities that the devil sows among us with love, the love that comes as a gift from the Almighty himself? From all I know, Edward Lovat, young Edward as he was called, was loved, and loved in turn. I'm sorry to say I didn't personally know him, but I've heard only the most gracious things said about him by his parents-in-law. They tell me their daughter has never been happier than when she first met Edward and how kind he always was to her. They also tell me of the love he always bestowed upon his daughter and of her adoration for him.

These all speak to me of someone whose main purpose in life was achieved. Why God would call him home at this time is beyond our understanding but that he now sits with God for eternity, knowing all the mysteries, is beyond doubt. It is for us, therefore, merely to give thanks for Edward's life and to celebrate his new life with God, returning from whence he and all of us have come. Let us pray for Edward, our beloved husband, father, and son, and pray that the spirit of love he has left us will continue to strengthen us in our grief and sorrow.

Praise be to the Lord. Amen.'

'Amen,' the congregation chorused.

Margaret and Mary Jane clung to each other throughout the sermon. At the mention of "his beloved daughter", Mary Jane began to sob. By the end, there were tears from all in the front row.

Even from Percival. Only Jane remained dry-eyed, immobile as a statue.

The coffin was carried out to the adjoining graveyard. Final prayers were said, and young Edward was laid to rest. Horace Thurlow shook hands with the main mourners and knelt to give Mary Jane a hug.

'Thank you,' she said.

'Thank you for your words and your kindness,' Margaret added.

'Thank ye for honouring my lad,' Edward said, shaking Horace's hand.

'Thank you, Reverend,' Percival said.

As Horace approached Jane, she turned and walked away.

XXIX

On Monday, the 5*th* day of February 1838, Thomas and Eliza opened the first non-denominational school in New South Wales, at Richmond, about fifty miles north-west of Sydney. The town was founded on the banks of the Hawkesbury River in the foothills of the Great Dividing Range. A rich agricultural area with river access to Sydney and the coast had attracted settlers from the earliest days of the colony.

The school, along with the schoolhouse, was on the edge of the town. On one side were other dwellings. On the other side was an endless vista of land, some of it being farmed with crops, cattle, or sheep while other land remained untouched. The land stretched into the distance until the surrounding hills rose to show off their perennial bluish hue. The family had become used to waking to the morning cries from kookaburras, roosters, and the mooing of cows. Kangaroos and joeys often greeted them when they stepped out of the house.

Thomas was the school headmaster and Eliza was his deputy. Thomas taught the older children and Eliza the younger ones. Fifteen-year-old John helped his father and took some learning himself. Mary, one day shy of her eighteenth birthday, helped her mother. Elizabeth, almost thirteen, and Johannah, eleven, were in their father's class while young Thomas, seven, was in his mother's class. James was not old enough for school, so he spent school days either in his mother's classroom or in the care of one of the other mothers.

There were twenty-six children in the school on the 5th of February and fifty-one by the end of the month. Some children travelled long distances each day to be there.

Opposition to the school persisted for a variety of reasons. Some parents said they did not approve of schooling done outside the church. Others did not like the idea of Catholics being included. Some of the Protestant clergy agreed with them while some of the Catholic clergy opposed their flock spending too much time alongside the Protestant children. Thomas being Catholic was consoling for some while others questioned the Governor for imposing an Irish "papist" on them. At the same time, there were those who could not see the point of schooling at all, especially if the cost was loss of the free labour their children provided for farming and other work.

The Governor's offer of free tuition and some tax relief to those who complied served to overcome most of the objections.

—⚬—

'The Governor is very happy with what you've achieved, Mr Lovat,' Rodney Kidd said.

Kidd held the post as legislator for colonial education. He was visiting Richmond later in 1838. He came with the Governor's greetings and to ascertain what extra assistance Thomas and Eliza might need.

'Thank ye, sir. So, the new Governor is just as committed to all this as Governor Bourke was?'

'Oh, indeed. Perhaps even more so.'

'Well, tell the Governor I'm most gratified,' Thomas replied. 'And could ye also tell him we're going to need more teachers to cope with the numbers?'

'Yes, especially as our family is about to grow as well,' a clearly pregnant Eliza said.

'Congratulations, Mrs Lovat, I'll certainly pass the good news onto the Governor,' Kidd replied, glancing at Eliza's stomach before looking back to Thomas. 'So, you have seventy-seven children currently. What numbers are you expecting next year?'

'It's hard to tell at this stage,' Thomas replied. 'But from what we know, it'll certainly be more than that. Ye must have had a chilly winter about five years ago because there's a huge number of four and five years' old just ready for school.'

'So, most of the extra numbers will be coming into the infants' grades, ye see, sir?' Eliza said. 'And I won't be able to teach from April or so next year. The doctor would prefer me not to teach at all.'

'I see. Of course, I'm sure you know there are not many teachers in the colony. Nowhere near enough for the kind of growth you're experiencing here. So, any suggestions you have for how we can solve this problem will be gratefully received. The Governor will spare no cost to have his dream realised. I'm sure you know that.'

'Indeed, Mr Kidd, we do,' Thomas replied. 'Well, young Mary here has learned a lot from teaching with my wife. We believe she could manage the infants' grades, with some assistance. My son, John, is also a capable teacher and can probably be given wider responsibilities. Apart from that, we know of a couple of the parents who have expressed an interest in teaching, but they'd have to give up some of their current work to do it. So, the issue of payment becomes important.'

'I'm sure the Governor will want to assist in any way.'

'And recognition, of course. And training. Could ye mention to the Governor that we're going to need some way of training future teachers and having them recognised as such?'

Kidd was taking notes. He hesitated.

'Ah, yes, Mr Lovat. Tell me what you mean exactly. How would you train a teacher? Do teachers need to be trained? I mean it's not like being a doctor, is it, where you need to understand how the body works?'

'Well, understanding how the mind works certainly helps.'

'Yes, I suppose so but what I mean is, isn't teaching just something you learn on the job, as it were, rather than something you have to be trained into?'

'It depends on what sort of teacher ye want,' Eliza interrupted. 'I mean some people would say the same about doctors, wouldn't they? That they learn most of what they need to know on the job? But if ye want the best doctors, then there's certain things they need to know and understand as well. And it's the same with teaching.'

'So, were you both trained back in Ireland?'

'I was,' Eliza said. 'I did three months training at a college in Dublin before I was given a job in a school.'

Kidd took more notes. He stopped again and looked up.

'If you'll pardon me, what did you do in this college? Wouldn't you need to be in a classroom to learn how to teach?'

'We went into classrooms in schools around Dublin, but we also sat and had lectures on all sorts of things. We had doctors from the university lecture us about physiology so a teacher has some understanding of the way the body works so we can pick when a child is sick or malnourished or even just tiring. We had one doctor who was doing new work on the mind. He talked about some of the new sciences of the mind happening in Germany. Then we had experienced teachers show us how to plan lessons, how to assess whether students are learning well or not, how to manage unruly behaviour. Some of these things can be picked up by doing the job but not all of it, especially some of the medical insights and those about the mind. D'ye see?'

Kidd was writing faster than his quill allowed. He finished writing, then dipped the quill in the ink before continuing.

'Fascinating, Mrs Lovat. And you, Thomas, were you trained?'

'Well, no, actually. But I've had my wife to guide me. I'm not sure how I would have coped without her training. And *her*, of course.'

Thomas and Eliza looked at each other and smiled. Kidd began writing again, the quill racing across the page, being dipped in the ink well each time it dried.

'Most interesting. I've written some of my own thoughts here too about the training aspect. How do you think we could do it in the colony? I mean you had the resources of a university and lots of experienced teachers?'

'It would be difficult,' Thomas said. 'But if the Governor's serious about his plan for wholesale schooling, then he needs to start thinking about training the teachers to do the job. It's like the army. There's no use wanting an effective army if you're not prepared to train the soldiers.'

'I like that, Thomas. I'm sure the Governor will understand that concept. Do you mind if I borrow that image from you?'

'Not at all,' Thomas laughed.

'So, is there anything else I should take back to the Governor?'

Thomas and Eliza looked at each other and shook their heads.

'Good, well there's something I need to put before you. And this comes directly from the Governor's desk.'

'Good heavens,' Eliza said, 'What on earth d'ye have in store for us now, Mr Kidd?'

'Well, and I need to preface it by saying the Governor did not know of your expanding family when he spoke with me about this. But would you both be interested? Ah, no, I don't think interested is the right word to convey the Governor's intentions. Would you both be *willing* to start another school?'

Thomas and Eliza looked to each other before answering.

'Ah, yes,' Thomas replied. 'I think we would. But when?'

'Next year.'

Thomas and Eliza looked to each other again.

'What time next year?' Eliza asked.

'The start of the year.'

'Ye mean in four months' time?'

'Ah, yes, four months and six days to be precise.'

'Is it even possible, Mr Kidd?' Eliza asked. 'And where's this school anyway?'

'My apologies, Ma'am. Just at Windsor, a hop, step and jump away,' Kidd laughed. 'You were probably thinking I meant right over the mountains or something, were you?'

'Well, it doesn't really matter where it is, Mr Kidd,' Thomas said. 'Even if it was right next door, it takes time to establish a school.'

'Of course, and that's why the Governor wants to give you plenty of time. I mean you had Richmond up and running from scratch in, what, five months?'

'More like six,' Eliza said.

'Well, so you'll have a few weeks less but think of how much you've learned by establishing Richmond. You now won't need to re-invent the wheel, so to speak.'

'And then there's the issue of my wife being pregnant!'

'Of course, as I said, the Governor didn't know about that.'

'Would that seriously change his mind, Mr Kidd?' Eliza asked.

'How honest would you like me to be, Mrs Lovat?' Kidd replied, smiling.

'Don't bother, Mr Kidd,' Eliza said, smiling back.

'So, what should I tell the Governor?'

'Before we answer that,' Thomas said. 'Tell us more about the plan.'

Kidd filled them in on the planning so far. A parcel of land had been set aside on the boundary of the adjoining village of Windsor. Windsor was the site of one of the Church of England's earliest churches. Its graveyard contained the remains of several of the "First Fleeters". The church had plans for a school, but they were superseded by the Governor's plan to set up a non-denominational school. Thomas was being asked to take responsibility for overseeing the building of the school over summer, as well as its staffing. He would remain headmaster of both schools for the time being.

'Do we really have any choice?' Thomas asked.

'Ah, the Governor can be a most persuasive man,' Kidd replied. 'And at least we won't have Mr Marsden railing against us this time.'

The Reverend Samuel Marsden had died on the 12th of May that year, 1838.

XXX

Charles had just finished class when the letter arrived in late May 1838.

Dear Charles,

I write with the saddest news possible that our dear son, your wee brother, Edward, died this last week. He had a stroke while working in the estate garden. Your mother and I are naturally heartbroken, just as you will be. We only wish we could be with you when you receive this news. We do hope you can find solace among your companions.

We're writing separately to Thomas and Eliza who of course met young Edward when he visited Tralee some years ago. I remember how popular he was with their bairns and how much he loved them. I'm sure they will offer you some comfort when you see them.

You will probably be surprised to hear that young Edward's funeral and burial was at St Peter's Church in Burnley. I won't burden you with all the details but, briefly, the new priest at St Mary in Burnley refused to give him the last rites or conduct the funeral Mass because he was not "practical". He claimed he was following new instructions from Rome. I must say I was shocked at this and I'm sure you would have much to say about it. One can only wonder at the future of the Catholic Church under this current pope. I take some heart in your view that these things do not reflect on the Church at its best so we can only hope for a brighter, more Christian future for it. Let's hope and pray that day comes soon.

You're probably wondering how Margaret and Mary Jane are coping. They are as good as can be expected. Margaret says Mary Jane has been calling out at night for her Pa. It's all so very sad, Charles. Three of our four bairns gone before us. It's almost more than we can bear. I do hope all is well with you. Write when you can. I hope you and Thomas are not so far from each other and can see each other often.

All our love, Pa and Mama.

PS. Please do me a favour. Sometime when you are praying for young Edward, just place your hand on Mahdiya's Qur'an. My Da believed so much in its consoling power. It will console me to think of you doing that.

PPS. I hope Charlie Bear is looking after you there.

The difficulties Charles was having with his students evaporated in an instant. He staggered and had to put his hand on the balustrade to steady himself.

'I just feel so far away,' he told Polding.

'I'm so very sorry, Charles. I wish I could let you go home for a while but of course it's out of the question.'

'Of course, My Lord. I wouldn't dream of asking.'

'I do hope the Jesuits are looking after your parents. It seems to me they owe them that much.'

'Well, the Jesuits might not even know. My Lord, there's something I need to tell you because you might hear about it in another way.'

'Certainly, Charles, anything.'

'My brother's been buried in the Church of England graveyard. His funeral service was at St Peter's in Burnley.'

'Oh, my heavens, why on earth?'

Charles relayed the message as it had been given to him.

'I must say, Charles, I'm shocked as well. I can scarcely believe a priest refusing a baptised Catholic the final sacrament under any circumstances. I'm not aware of any such instructions coming from Rome. I know we're a little out of the mainstream here, but I find it impossible to contend that a pope would ever issue such an instruction.'

'I hope it's wrong too, My Lord, but there it is.'

'How do your parents feel about it?'

'My mother will be shattered. I can barely contemplate what it would do to her. My father is a little more accepting of these things, but he says he was shocked too when the priest refused to give the last rites.'

'As indeed he should be. My heavens, I hope our Protestant brethren don't get wind of it. It's just the kind of thing they can use against the idea of integration. Our dear departed Reverend Marsden, for instance, always insisted that Catholics would never integrate into the general population because we're a closed club, as he put it.'

'Well, perhaps he was right,' Charles said. 'Especially with the current Holy Father.'

Polding raised one eyebrow but said nothing.

Dear Charles,

We were so very sad to hear of young Edward's death. We remember him so fondly. We only met him once, but he has been a constant source of fond conversation, including with our children. Mary, especially, spent almost every minute of his time with us on his lap. She burst into tears when she heard about his death. She said she felt so much for Mary Jane who is about the same age as our Mary was when young Edward visited Tralee. Poor Mary has had too many experiences of death close at hand. She still grieves over Dr Hawkins.

Charles, we are full of sympathy for your loss and we know how far away you must feel from poor Da and your Ma. Please let us know if there is anything we can do. We would love to see you. Do know you are always welcome here anytime. It seems ridiculous that we are so close but have still not seen you since you arrived. It's not so much the distance as the work that keeps us apart. We know you are very busy in yours and ours just grows by the day. All the same, we must try to see you at the first opportunity.

Our love, Thomas, Eliza, and family.

PS. Have you seen Fr McEncroe? Fr Therry tells me he is furious that I'm working for the Governor.

Postal services were slow in those days. Only once a week did the postal dray make it out to Richmond. Less so at times, depending on the weather and the state of the roads. Charles was on hospital duty when the letter arrived, so it was a fortnight later that he wrote back.

Dear Thomas, Eliza, and family,

Thank you so much for your kind letter. It has indeed been a challenging time. Hearing of young Edward's death, on top of William's and Emma Jane's, has really knocked me about. I feel so much for Pa and my mother. Things have not been easy for them, as you know. I can barely imagine how they will cope with this.

Thank you for your invitation to visit. I hope we can see each other soon. I have a week off teaching in July. Perhaps then? I know you are busy, and my work here has been more challenging than I would have thought. I've seen Fr McEncroe from time to time, but he has not mentioned your situation to me. I dare say he would not be pleased. I'm not sure he's all that pleased with me either, especially in my fraternising with our Protestant brethren. Fr McEncroe is a fierce Catholic warrior. Some have called him the Catholic Marsden. Speaking of which, I suppose you heard that poor Samuel died recently. I imagine he is stirring the pot in heaven as we speak.

Anyway, don't be worried by what some of my clergy brothers think of what you are doing. Just be assured that you have the full support of Bishop Polding and Bishop Broughton. So, you have friends in high places. You also have my fullest support, by the way. I agree with the Governor that the future of this country is in cooperation by all. Your schooling work can only be helping in this noble quest. We've all seen from our old homes, England, Ireland, Scotland, what damage denominationalism can wreak.

Thank you again for your sympathy letter, so gratefully received.

Your loving brother, Charles.

It was a cold, wet winter that year. The Hawkesbury was in flood for much of it, making roads impassable and sailing too dangerous. Plans to visit Thomas came to nothing.

—⁂—

Charles was beginning his second session in mid-July. It was to include some advanced theology classes for the new Irish clergy. Polding had insisted on them even when Charles questioned the wisdom of imposing them on an unwilling audience.

'Excuse me, *Farder*,' Father Thomas Landrigan interrupted. 'Before ye start, could ye tell us why ye refused to take *de* 'oly *Farder's oat*'?'

'I'll be very happy to explain my attitude to the oath, Father, but it might be helpful if I could continue with the lecture. Then it will be some of the church's great theologians explaining as well as me.'

'Yes but, *Farder*, ye must understand it's difficult for us to sit 'ere and listen if we can't trust yer loyalty to de church. If ye'll forgive me for bein' so frank, *Farder*. I mean I'm not sayin' ye're not loyal. God forbid, but it'd be 'elpful for us to 'ear yer explanation first so we can relax and listen to yer woise words. If ye'll forgive me, *Farder*.'

'You're forgiven, Father, be assured. Perhaps if I was just to assure you also of my loyalty to the church. Clearly, I'd not be here if I wasn't loyal. That's a simple message and I'd ask you to trust me in that. Explaining why I could not take a particular oath coming from an office in Rome that was, in my view, less than informed is a little more difficult. But I assure you I will once I've had the chance to expound on some of the church's foundational theology. Is that sufficient for now?'

There were nods of approval from five of the six clergy present.

'But if ye'll be forgivin' me again, *Farder*,' Landrigan continued. 'It was not from an office in Rome, as ye say. Our professors at St John's said it came from *de* 'oly *Farder* 'imself and so dey 'ad to take it under 'oly obedience. Now, *Farder*, I don't want to be sayin' ye're disobedient or anyt'in' like dat. I mean I know people 'ave said dat about ye but I wouldn't want to be sayin' anyt'in' o' the sort. But ye can understand why it's important for us to be assured, and…'

'Of course, Father, and let me assure you…'

Charles continued to confront opposition from some of the Irish clergy. In the first session, it was mainly from one or two of the young deacons. In the second session, it came from several of the ordained clergy. By mid-August, he felt he should make Polding aware of the difficulties he was facing.

'I'm not sure I'm the man you want for this job, My Lord.'

'Let me be the judge of that, Charles.'

'But some of the priests treat me as though I'm a heretic. Why if it's not for something I said in class, normally about the proper limits of church authority, then it's because someone saw me speaking with one of the Protestant clergy.'

'Indeed, the makings of a heretic,' Polding laughed. 'Charles, I understand it must be wearing for you, putting up with the likes of … well, I won't be uncharitable, but you can guess some of the names I was contemplating. Be assured, Charles, it's wearing for me too. I'm not used to dealing with people with such limited understanding of the church and almost no intellectual tradition behind them. That's why I wanted something different for this country.'

'I understand all that, My Lord. I truly do. But please forgive me … oh, good heavens, I'm sounding like Father Landrigan. *If ye'll forgive me for sayin' it, Farder.*'

'Yes, if you'll forgive me for what?' Polding laughed.

'I think I'm a little worn out, John. I mean, My Lord.'

'Call me John, Charles. Just not in front of the others, especially some of them.'

'John, I'm very tired. I'm not sleeping well. I'm not sure I ever got over the trip. And then it was straight into setting up the seminary and then my brother's death. I keep having all sorts of strange dreams about my mother and father. I worry deeply for them. And then I start worrying about my brother and how he's coping with his new schools, and then I start worrying about…'

'Alright, Charles, I think I get the point. You need a rest, is that it?'

'Only partly, John. I'm so sorry to bring this to you in this way, with all your other worries, but I just don't have the energy any longer for the academic side of priesthood. When I was first demoted from teaching theology at Stonyhurst, having to teach mathematics to the juniors, I was devastated. But then I realised how much less of a strain it was teaching the juniors, especially about something as indisputable as mathematics. Then I did some pastoral work in parishes and on the boat out here I was able just to be there for people. That's the kind of priest I want to be. Not having to defend myself at every turn, trying to explain Aquinas to people who don't want to understand it, who are content to live in their tiny burrows of belief. It's very tiring, John, and I fear I might become ill again, as I so often was at home. *So, if ye'll forgive me for sayin' it.*'

Polding's serious and concerned expression gave way to a burst of laughter.

'I hear you, Charles. Believe me when I say I understand the feeling more than you might think. It's just that I have no-one else at present who can do what you're doing.'

'I do understand, John.'

'Charles, let me think about it for a while. Father Ullathorne is waiting on some news at home. It might even be that he'll have secured someone suitable to replace you. I doubt it, I must say. But even if not, he might have some thoughts about how we can relieve you of some of your duties. Is that alright with you? Can you last to the end of the year?'

'Of course, John, and I apologise again for adding to your burdens.'

'Burdens is what I'm here for, Charles. I follow a Lord who bore them for all of us.'

'Indeed, John. Thank you for your care.'

—⁂—

A few days later, Polding invited Charles to come and see him.

'Charles, why don't you take a couple of weeks off and come with me to Yass?'

'Yass?'

'Yes, it's a growing village on the road to Melbourne. A hundred and fifty miles or so. There's a new church being built out there. I have to bless the foundation stone and I thought it might do you good to get away.'

'Whatever you say, John. But what should I do about my classes?'

'Oh, just give the ordained fellows a break. I'm sure they won't complain. As for the juniors, I sense you think sufficiently well of young McGrath to fill in for you.'

—⁂—

The following week, Polding, Charles, and the bishop's secretary left St Mary's early on a Wednesday morning. The bishop's carriage was out of action so Bishop Broughton had lent his for the occasion. It was larger and more comfortable, with wider, well-padded wheels that navigated the rough roads more smoothly. They stayed at the priest's house in Camden that night and in Goulburn the following night.

The three clergymen spent most of the time with their own thoughts. Charles prayed, dozed, and stared out the window, mesmerised by the countryside sliding by, remembering all the things his father had told him about this very different landscape, a sunburnt place, he said once. He had seen the odd kangaroo in Sydney but out here it was as though they owned the place. He had heard the odd kookaburra but out here the laugh of the bird was deafening.

The dry, fresh air and the rhythm of the carriage put him in a somnolent mood. He felt more relaxed than he had since his time in Reggio Calabria soon after ordination.

They arrived in Yass on Friday afternoon and settled into the makeshift presbytery, a tin hut with internal curtains for bedroom privacy. Charles spent most of his time wandering the dirt roads and paddocks, occasionally stopping to chat with a passer-by.

On Sunday, Catholics from all over the district turned up for an outdoor Mass and the blessing of the foundation stone.

Father Michael Brennan had arrived early in the morning from Goulburn.

'I'm sorry, My Lord,' Brennan said. 'Some aboriginal people have made themselves at home through the night. I'll get the local constable to move them on.'

'Is there any other way of dealing with it?' Polding replied.

'I don't really think so, My Lord. There's no point in fiddling around with these people. If ye're not strict with them, they start to think they own the place.'

'Which, in a sense, they do, of course.' Polding said.

Brennan looked at the bishop, confused.

'I wonder if I might speak with them,' Charles said.

'Would you, Charles?' Polding said. 'I'd prefer not to make a fuss if we can avoid it. Is that alright with you, Father Brennan?'

'Whatever ye say, My Lord.'

Charles grabbed a few spare clothes out of his valise and went to speak with the small aboriginal group sitting around a fire a mere few yards from where the ceremony was to take place. He sat with them for over an hour, communicating through gesture and the odd word. The two men, three women and five children took turns in sitting next to him. One of the children, a girl about three years of age, amused them all by walking up and running her hand down Charles's cheek.

'Where's Charles?' Polding asked.

'He's still out there, talking with the aborigines,' Brennan replied. 'Would ye like me to hurry him on?'

'No, leave it to him. I'm sure he'll get what he wants.'

'With respect, My Lord, I'm not sure Father Lovat understands these people. They have their own ways.'

'Well, let's see how he goes. We have time.'

'Whatever ye say, My Lord.'

Soon after, Charles walked back into the presbytery.

'How's everything out there, Father?' Brennan asked. 'Do ye need a hand?'

'No. it's all good. They've moved down the road.'

'How did you do it, Charles?' Polding asked.

'I just explained why we needed the place today … and I offered them some of my clothes.'

'Ye gave them some of yer clothes?' Brennan blurted out. 'Don't ye spoil them, Father, or ye'll never see the end of it.'

'Oh, I wouldn't say I spoilt them, Father.'

'And at least we didn't need the constable,' Polding said.

'Ye will eventually,' Brennan replied.

After the ceremony, Polding met with local officials. Brennan headed back to Goulburn. Meantime, Charles heard confessions and chatted with the locals.

On the following days, while Polding stayed in the town performing civic duties, Charles travelled out to some adjoining farms and visited the local bush hospital.

'*This is what I was ordained to do,*' he thought to himself.

The two men departed Yass on the Wednesday morning.

'You're looking better than I've seen you for a while, Charles.'

'Yes, John, I feel whole again. I'd give anything to be pastor to these people.'

Late in September, Charles came in from class to be told there was a young woman in the parlour. She had asked to see him.

'Hello, Uncle Charles,' Mary said.

'Mary, my heavens, I wouldn't have recognised you.'

'I'm not surprised. I probably look ten years older than when ye saw me. Life was so easy then.'

'Oh, my dear girl. No, it's not that you look older. Just a whole lot wiser perhaps. Your mother and father wrote and told me about your loss.'

Mary's eyes welled up. She fumbled in her cloth bag.

'Here, use mine,' Charles said, handing her his kerchief. 'Come and sit down and tell me about this young man. Only if you wish, of course.'

They sat facing each other across a small table. Mary had noticed the large-framed picture of the Sacred Heart on the wall behind her uncle. She had not seen that image of Jesus with his flamed heart since her days in the Catholic school in Tralee.

'Thank ye, Uncle Charles. I'd love to. For some reason, I can't say much at home. Ma and Da have their worries and my sisters are too young and my brothers, well, they're boys, ye know.'

'Yes, I know. So, tell me whatever you want.'

'He was just so lovely. So sweet and kind but such a good doctor too. I know doctors are meant to care for their patients but so many don't, or they care up to a point. But he cared himself to death. Literally, he died for those sick people. I've no doubt he saved some of their lives, but he shouldn't have had to die for it. It's just so unfair. And now he's left me, and I just know I'll never find anyone like him again. Sorry, Uncle …'

Mary buried her face in Charles's man-sized kerchief. Charles moved to her side of the table, crouched down, and placed her head on his shoulder.

'There, there, darling Mary. I know how you feel but you mustn't give up all hope of finding happiness again. I'm sure James wouldn't want that. If he loved you, and I'm certain he did, he'd want you to be happy.'

'But I don't want anyone else,' Mary said. 'I just want him … *I just want him.*'

'Of course, of course you do.'

'Why does it happen?'

'Death, you mean?'

'Yes, and why is it that just as we find happiness, God snatches it away?'

'It sounds cruel, doesn't it?'

'Yes, that's what I think. So, *is* God cruel, Uncle Charles? Is God *cruel*? Ye must know. Ye're a priest.'

'Well, being a priest doesn't mean I know everything about God. Far from it. There are times when I wonder why God does what he does, or lets things happen that seem so cruel.'

'Do ye really?'

'Oh, yes, really.'

'So, what do ye do when ye feel like that? Do ye feel guilty for doubting God?'

'No, I don't feel guilty. There's no point in that. There's also no point in trying to work out why things have happened. There are no easy answers for many things. Things just happen and we have to believe they're part of God's plan, even if we can't understand it at the time.'

'So, what *do* ye do then? I mean I really want to know because I get so sad and angry and unhappy and, at times, I just want to die.'

'I know, Mary. I know. What do I do? I just pray … quietly … I just let things wash over me and soak them up … and try and think of the good things. There's always good things to gladden the heart. For you, look at your family. Imagine what it must be like for so many people here who have no family. Think of all the young people who were brought here, often for no good reason. Taken from their families and brought halfway around the world. Many of them never saw them again. Think how horrific that must have been. And then think how fortunate you are to have such a wonderful family, and a nice home, and some rewarding work, from what I hear. These are the ways I cope with life's sadness.'

Mary lifted her head from Charles's shoulder. He went back to his chair on the other side of the table.

'Now, can I get you something, Mary? Do you need a meal? Are you going home tonight?'

'No, thank ye, Uncle Charles. I don't need anything. Yes, I'm getting the evening carriage back to Richmond. I'd better go. Thank ye so much. I love talking with ye.'

'Anytime, Mary. Anytime at all. Why are you in town anyway?'

'I went to visit James's grave. They moved him to the Devonshire Street Cemetery a few weeks ago. I've wanted to visit it before but the cemetery at the quarantine station was out of bounds.'

'Oh, that's good. Did it help? Seeing his grave, I mean?'

'Yes, but it also made me very sad. I'm sorry ye had to put up with me like that.'

'Not at all, Mary. Not at all. Please come whenever you want. Happy, sad, or in between. It's just lovely to see you.'

'Thank ye, Uncle Charles. Ye're so much like my Da. It's uncanny. But then ye're both so much like Grand Da.'

'I guess that explains it then. Please do give your mother and father my best wishes and tell them I hope to see them soon. Isn't it ridiculous that we've been together in this place for almost a year and we haven't seen each other?'

'I will, Uncle Charles, and please do come and visit whenever ye can.'

XXXI

'I want to be buried with young Edward and I want William and Emma Jane there too.'

'What on earth are you talking about, Edward?'

'When I come back, I want to exhume them and move them to St Peter's. I want to lie with my bairns.'

'And what about me? Or don't I have a say?'

'Jane, I'll be very happy for ye to be there too.'

—✽—

Having declined to return to work for the Towneley Estate, Edward went to Pemberton in the spring of 1838.

'Ye've always been my rock, Sarah. Ye're the only true Ma I ever had. So, what would a Ma say to me now? What should I do?'

'What are your choices, dear boy?'

'Endure the loneliest of lives or find a wee bit of happiness.'

'It doesn't really sound like much of a choice to me.'

'But there's such a thing as fidelity, isn't there?'

'Of course, but it's a two-way thing. How faithful has Jane been to *you*, would you say?'

'Oh, I ken she's done her best. And to be fair to her, I'd probably nay gotten over Amy when I married her. She always threw that at me, and I'd deny it. Of course, I'd deny it. How could I tell her the truth? But she was probably *ceart* all along. I *was* looking for an Amy. Someone who could fill the hole she left. And the truth is nay anyone could. Nay anyone.'

'Not Mary Beth?'

Edward stared at his glass. He rubbed his eyes and let out a sigh.

'Nay even Mary Beth. Nay at the time anyway.'

'She truly was the love of your life, wasn't she? Amy, I mean?'

'Oh, aye. Ye ken I still dream about her. I've nay ever stopped dreaming about her.'

'Even when you were married to Jane?'

'The first night even. Ye remember the wedding, d'ye nay?'

'Of course. Your father was worried for you!'

'Was he? How d'ye ken?'

'He said so, even at the wedding. He was watching you, watching Jane. And he said, as only he could, *they dinna love each other, ye ken?*'

'Oh, my. Why dinna he say something?'

'He probably would have if you'd asked him. But by then it was too late.'

'And what did *ye* ken?'

'I thought the same. Remember, we'd seen you with Amy when you came here, and we travelled to the Highlands. You remember that?'

'Oh, aye. How could I nay? It was the bonniest time of my life.'

'Yes, and you were so in love. Both of you. Radiant and radiantly happy. Your Gran said just those words. Even when she couldn't remember where her bedroom was. When she'd forget how to comb her hair, she still knew *how you were feeling*. Will used to say seeing you and Amy together brought her life back. And it brought his life and your father's back as well, seeing your Gran the way she was with you and Amy.'

'Oh, aye. The way she was with Amy. Amy loved her, ye ken?'

'And it was mutual.'

Edward pressed his thumb and first finger hard against his eyes.

'Nay wonder I could nay ever replace that.'

'No wonder. If she was the one, and she clearly was, there's no replacement.'

'So, I just see it out then?'

'No, I'm not saying that. There might be no replacement but there's better and worse. And it seems to me you're settling for worse right now. I mean, you *have* tried, haven't you, Edward? You really have tried to make things better with Jane?'

'Aye, I ken I have. As I say, I canna help feeling guilty because perhaps I dinna love her for herself. But then I dinna ken if it's because I *am* guilty, or I've just been made to feel that way ever since we married. Ever since we met in a way. Her Ma set out from the beginning to label me as guilty of something. I'm nay sure what. Perhaps she sensed some failing in me…'

'Or perhaps that was her way of controlling you. Some people are like that, aren't they? They like you to feel guilty, unworthy, just so they can control you.'

Sarah choked on the last word.

'Are ye alright, Sarah? Here's me talking endlessly about myself. But how are ye?'

'I'm alright, dear. I was just recalling my own experiences of being controlled. My first marriage was … oh, my heavens. But your dear father saved me from all that. Without him, I'm not sure I'd have survived. So, I do know how you're feeling. How confusing it can be when you're constantly made to feel guilty, but you don't really know why or what it's about or, least of all, be able to do anything about it.'

'Aye, so what *do* I do about it, then? I ken that's where I am at present. Ye did something about yer situation, did ye nay?'

'Well, it was done *for* me when Cecil was killed. But then that just added to the guilt. Why could I not grieve for my husband? Am I a monster? Did I somehow bring on his killing? And then I kept your dear father waiting for years while I sorted all that out. And I still don't really know what I'd have done if Cecil had lived. I might have stayed in that miserable marriage and withered away. And I'd have never had those wonderful years with your father.'

There was silence again as they stared at the cold fireplace.

'Perhaps that's what *I'm* doing. Withering away. Too afraid to make the move I ken I should.'

'Yes, but don't be too hard on yourself, dear boy. Walking out on a marriage is not something to do lightly, however bad it might be.'

'So, are ye saying I should nay do it?'

'No, it's not for me to say. All I'm saying is don't feel bad because you're torn. Any decent person would be, should be.'

More silence.

'Anyway, tell me about Mary Beth,' Sarah said. 'She's the third wheel here, isn't she?'

'Aye.'

'And she's always loved you?'

'Aye, so she says.'

'And you believe that?'

'Aye, why d'ye ask? D'ye nay ken it's true?'

'No. I don't doubt it. In fact, that was another thing your father whispered to me at the wedding. Or it might have been after the wedding. He said you spent more time with Mary Beth than Jane. At your own wedding to Jane.'

'Aye, and Jane told me that too.'

'What? That night?'

'Oh nay. We dinna talk about anything that night. She went straight to sleep.'

'You mean *straight* to sleep?'

'*Straight* to sleep,' Edward said, smiling. 'Nay, it was afterwards some time. Actually, I ken it was when we got the invitation to Mary Beth's and Carl's wedding. I came in from the estate and she was crying, and her Ma was there comforting her. And I said, *what's the matter?* And she flung the invitation on the floor. And there was all this talk from her and her Ma about me and other women. Honestly, anyone'd ken I was Lancashire's most notorious womaniser.'

'Well, you'd have some competition there,' Sarah laughed. 'But why? Why would they say that? And what was it about Mary Beth that set all that off?'

'Oh, that's when they both started talking about our wedding and how I spent all my time with Mary Beth instead of with Jane. And I'd say, *but ye were spending all yer time with yer own family. Ye dinna even talk with my family, or any of my friends.*'

'I remember that. And it was another thing your father noticed.'

'And what else did he say anyway? About me and Mary Beth?'

'Just how well you seemed to get along. How comfortable you seemed with each other. I think it was the contrast with the way you and Jane were behaving.'

'So, he saw all that?'

'Yes, he was a wise old fellow, your father. He'd seen a lot of life. He'd had his own pain. Eventually it works its way into your marrow, you know! You then see it in others, especially ones you love. And your father certainly loved you. He so wanted the best for you. He was so excited when you brought Amy over from Ireland. *My lad's happy. He's found the one*, he used to say. And, sorry, my dear, but he knew somehow that it wasn't that way with Jane.'

Edward shook his head and let out a deep breath.

'So, again, tell me. What do I do?'

'I think go to Mary Beth. Talk it all over with her. You'll know what to do.'

'I'm so sad for you, darling,' Mary Beth said as she embraced him. 'Losing one child must be unbearable. Three? I can't begin to imagine it.'

They held each other, saying nothing. Mary Beth began to loosen her grip.

'Just dinna move. Please dinna move.'

Mary Beth tightened her grip.

'It's so braw to see ye, Mary Beth. So braw,' Edward whispered into her ear.

'If I remember correctly, that means "good",' she laughed.

'Bonnie even,' he replied, standing back and looking at her, smiling.

'Come inside, darling. I've missed you so much. *So* much.'

They sat up late that night. The hearty dinner and the good wine made for ease of companionship. They talked without taking a breath. They were on the old chaise, the once bright floral pattern now faded. They were facing the fireplace, alight with the final chill of winter in the air. Mary Beth rested her head on Edward's shoulder. He fell asleep first.

It was sometime in the middle of the night when he stirred. It woke her. They were both cold. Only embers remained of the fire.

'Oh, my heavens,' Mary Beth said. 'What time is it?'

'I dinna ken but it's before first light.'

'I'm freezing. Come to bed.'

They went together to Mary Beth's bedroom, took their shoes off, and snuggled beneath the blankets. They were asleep again within minutes.

The sunlight was breaking through the edges of the shutters when they woke.

'It's so lovely having you here, my darling,' Mary Beth said, snuggling in even more tightly.

'It's braw being here. So braw.'

There was silence as they ran their arms over each other's backs.

'So braw.'

XXXII

'Charles's such a find,' Polding said. 'Just as you suggested he would be.'

'I'm so pleased to hear it,' Ullathorne replied. 'But I must say I'm surprised he's become so friendly with the Protestant clergy. I'm told he and Bishop Broughton spend an inordinate amount of time together.'

'Oh, I don't believe that's true but, yes, they've struck up a friendship of sorts and surely that can only serve our purposes well. You agree, don't you, William? I mean we are of one mind on the need for our church to find a level of respectability among the other churches, aren't we?'

'Of course, My Lord, as long as we maintain a proper distance. We might not rank highly here in the colony, but we are the Roman Catholic Church, nonetheless. That means we are the only *true* church. We wouldn't want our Protestant brethren to think it makes no difference, as though we're all just different brands of the same thing, like boot polish.'

'I don't think Charles lowers his dignity or beliefs to the level of boot polish,' Polding laughed. 'He's just a very intelligent, forward thinking theologian and that's what Broughton respects, as do I. The fact is he's about the only one of our clergy that I can send into these wider church gatherings and feel confident he'll be respected.'

'The *only* one, My Lord?'

'Apart from yourself, William, of course. That goes without saying.'

'Thank you, My Lord.'

Ullathorne had little news of the sort Polding was hoping for. There was no interest among the English religious Orders to be part of an Australian mission. The only good news was of increased interest from some of the Irish dioceses.

—⚞—

'I gather Father Ullathorne hasn't found my replacement?'

'No, Charles, I'm afraid not,' Polding said. 'I'm sorry but I'll need you to stay on for at least the first session next year. Is that alright with you?'

'Whatever you require, John. I certainly wouldn't want to leave the seminary unstaffed. I must say I do think in time there'll be some suitable staff. I'm sure you want young McGrath to get some pastoral experience, once he's ordained, but he's proven to be an excellent tutor and, frankly, seems better accepted by some of the Irish clergy than I am.'

'Thank you, Charles. I realise this is not your first choice and I *am* thinking hard about your future. The last thing I want is to lose you. I'd hate to see you heading back to England because you're not happy here.'

'Well, to be honest, John. I probably wouldn't do that anyway. I'd love to see my mother and father again but I'm aware my health seems to need the warmer climes. Or that's what the doctors tell me anyway.'

'And I'm sure they're right. You really do look so much healthier than when you arrived. And even Father Landrigan's irritations haven't taken that from you.'

They laughed.

'Thank you, John. I do feel much better, I have to say, but…'

'I know, Charles. I've seen you among the people. I know how much you relish being a pastor. And I've had so many messages that tell me how good you are too. Be it your sermons, your confessional work or just your being there for people. My problem is you're good at everything. I just need more of you and my job would be so much easier.'

'You're far too kind,' Charles said, blushing. 'It's not because I'm necessarily so good at it. It's just that increasingly I'm feeling that's what I was ordained to do.'

'That's very humble of you, Charles, and it is as I'd expect of you. Nonetheless, I'm short of people of your calibre. And that's between you and me, of course.'

'But you do have Father Ullathorne back now. That must make a huge difference.'

Polding looked to his desk.

'I must go, Charles. I have some matters to attend to. Please let me know how the first session goes.'

―⚬―

Plans for Charles and Thomas to meet sometime over the Christmas break were again forestalled. Thomas had hoped to get to Sydney but was occupied with the new school at Windsor. Charles had hoped to travel to Richmond but was busy filling in for the Sydney hospital chaplain who had fallen ill, as well as servicing new churches around Sydney. The shortage of Catholic clergy remained chronic. By mid-January 1839, he was back at St Mary's preparing for the new academic year. Polding surprised him in the classroom one day.

'My Lord?'

'How formal, Father,' Polding laughed.

'I'm sorry, John. I just haven't seen you over here before.'

'Well, I wanted to catch you in private.'

'You have me intrigued.'

'Charles, I wanted to alert you about the meeting with the Protestant leaders next week.'

'Goodness, they come around quickly. I'm assuming Father Ullathorne will accompany you.'

'Well, that's what I wanted to speak with you about. I've always taken Father Ullathorne. He *is* my vicar-general, after all. So, I'd assumed you wouldn't be coming. I'm sorry, I'd meant to mention that to you some time ago.'

'That's perfectly alright, John. I hadn't expected to go.'

'The thing is, Charles, Bishop Broughton has specifically asked that you be there.'

'Oh, well, I'm happy to if you wish.'

'I certainly do, Charles. In fact, I'd have wanted you there anyway, but I felt I shouldn't turn up with three of us. Some of our Protestant brethren might think the Romans are taking over.'

'Indeed, that's our plan, isn't it, My Lord?' Charles laughed. 'So, what do you think best?'

'Well, I'm going to mention it to Father Ullathorne, but I sense he won't like the idea.'

'Even if you say it was Bishop Broughton's idea?'

'Especially if I say it was his idea.'

'I don't understand, John.'

'Charles, between you and me, our friend, Ullathorne, is a complex man. Quite brilliant in his own way but surprisingly threatened when he feels he is not being given his due or if he feels overshadowed, which frankly he feels about you.'

'I didn't realise, John. I hope there's nothing I've done to irritate him.'

'Not at all, Charles. Not at all. It's just some idiosyncratic thing about him. God forgive me for saying it, but a lot of clergy are like that. Easily threatened. You must have seen that yourself.'

'I believe I have, John. I believe I have.'

'And they're not *all* Irish,' Polding laughed.

'Oh, yes. I can vouch for a few Romans from my own experience.'

'Anyway, I just wanted to warn you that William might be offended. And if that happens, don't take it personally, do you hear?'

'Are you certain it's wise, John? I could meet with Bishop Broughton separately if you wish. As you know, we've met on a few occasions.'

'Yes, I do know that, and I thought the same thing but, no, I'd like you there. Broughton obviously values your view of things and that's a real plus for the church.'

'By-all-means, John. Whatever you wish.'

The following week, the three clergymen, Charles, Polding and Ullathorne took the short carriage ride to Bishop Broughton's residence in Surry Hills.

'It's still very warm,' Charles said.

'Indeed,' Polding replied. 'How are you finding the weather, William? After your time back in England, I mean?'

'It's fine,' Ullathorne replied. 'I don't concern myself with matters I can't control.'

The rest of the journey was spent in silence.

'Welcome, gentlemen,' Broughton said as they entered the foyer. 'Please take off your coats and come into the cool.'

The bishop's house was a grand, three-storeyed Georgian residence of the kind one might have found in London. It stood in contrast with Polding's bare Roman-styled house at St Mary's.

Broughton ushered them into his meeting-room to the left of the large staircase. The other clergy were already in their places around the walnut oak table, so heavily polished that one could see their reflections in it, as if in glass or a still pond.

'Gentlemen, I believe we all know each other. Except for Mr Bancroft who is my new assistant bishop. He will be taking the Reverend Marsden's place at these meetings.'

The three Catholics greeted the Reverend Bancroft.

'So, the rest of us all know each other,' Broughton said. 'Is that correct?'

'Ah, I'm not sure I've met this gentleman, Bishop,' John McVeigh, the Presbyterian, said as he gestured towards Ullathorne.

'My apologies, Mr McVeigh,' Broughton said. 'This is William Ullathorne, Bishop Polding's vicar-general.'

'Oh, I say,' McVeigh replied. 'I thought Mr Lovat was the Catholic vicar-general.'

'No, I believe it's still me, sir,' Ullathorne said.

The group chuckled. Polding and Charles smiled. Ullathorne took his place at the table.

'Bishop Polding,' Broughton said. 'I've just been telling everyone that there would be three Romans at today's meeting and that the rest of us should not feel intimidated by that. It was my initiative to invite Mr Lovat even though I knew Mr Ullathorne would be accompanying you.'

'And why is that Bishop?' Reverend Wilkinson, the Methodist, asked. 'I think you were about to tell us when the three gentlemen arrived.'

'Indeed, Mr Wilkinson, I was. Well, there were a couple of reasons. I think we were generally pleased with Mr Lovat's contribution at the meeting with the Governor, and especially his openness to dialogue. It's not something we have found commonly among the Roman clergy – if I might be so frank.'

'Indeed, you might, Bishop,' Polding said.

'Thank you, Bishop Polding,' Broughton replied. 'But beyond these generalities, I believe we were especially interested in Mr Lovat's views on the Governor's plans for non-denominational schools. I believe you will remember from our earlier meeting that Mr Lovat's brother opened the first such school in Richmond this past year.'

Broughton looked around the table. The assembled clergy nodded. Ullathorne was studying his notes.

'Well, Mr Lovat tells me his brother is about to open a second one at Windsor, just down the road from St Matthew's Church of England and not far from both the Scots and Methodist churches. It seems to me to be an excellent opportunity for us to collaborate as the Governor wishes.'

'And your brother remains a Catholic, Mr Lovat?' Reverend Moore, the Methodist, asked.

'Yes, Mr Moore. As far as I know.'

'My, my! And the Governor takes no issue with this?'

'No, he doesn't, Mr Moore,' Broughton stepped in. 'I really thought we'd dealt with all this in the Governor's presence.'

'Well, to an extent perhaps,' Moore replied. 'I accept that Mr Lovat's brother possesses desirable credentials, but I really thought once he was in the job, he'd feel compromised and…'

'And what, Mr Moore?' Polding asked.

'Well…'

'Turn to one of the recognised denominations,' Reverend Lang, the Presbyterian Moderator jumped in. 'That's what Mr Moore is trying to say.'

'A recognised tradition?' Broughton said. 'You mean like the Catholic Church, Mr Lang? It's been ten years since the Catholic Emancipation Act, did you know? The Catholic Church *is* a recognised denomination.'

'In England,' Lang replied.

'And its territories, Mr Lang,' Broughton said, his eyes afire. 'Even in Scotland, I'm led to believe.'

There was silence around the table. Moore was shaking his head. Lang pulled at his beard. McVeigh reached for the jug of water. Polding's head was down. Ullathorne shuffled his papers.

Charles looked straight at Broughton who was surveying, one by one, the players around the table.

'Look, I don't think we mean any offence, Mr Lovat,' Moore said. 'But if the Governor wants this to work for the whole population, it might not be a particularly good idea starting out with a Catholic headmaster, even an English one.'

'He's not English, gentlemen,' Ullathorne said, looking up from his papers for the first time. 'He's Irish. He's Father Lovat's half-brother, I believe.'

'Oh, I'm sorry,' Moore replied. 'I'd forgotten that minor detail. But surely that merely exacerbates the issue. An Irishman and a Catholic. How can that be good for a non-denominational experiment?'

'Precisely,' Lang said. 'It might work out in the Hawkesbury but if the idea is to bring such schools in closer to Sydney, as I believe the Governor wishes to do eventually, I'm not certain of the wisdom.'

'Well, if it helps,' Charles said. 'My brother is, as am I, of Scottish heritage. Highlands in fact.'

'Lovat?' Wilkinson said. 'Surely you're not related to the old scoundrel who had his head chopped off at the Tower?'

'I believe I am, sir.'

There was another moment of silence. McVeigh looked around at Lang who was sitting next to him. McVeigh turned back to face Broughton.

'Well, I have to say, Bishop, that's good enough for me.'

McVeigh then looked across the table at Charles.

'Why, we might even make you an honorary Presbyterian, Lord Lovat,' he said, laughing.

Charles smiled and opened his mouth ready to speak.

'I'm not sure Father Lovat would altogether mind that,' Ullathorne said.

Another moment of silence. Lang spoke first.

'My, my, do we detect some rancour in the Roman ranks?'

'Not at all, Mr Lang,' Ullathorne replied. 'We Romans are one big happy family under the Holy Father's beneficence.'

'As it should be,' Broughton said. 'As it should be. Now, gentlemen, to more serious business. The Governor has asked for our common support, if it can be found, in his schooling venture. Can we speak about that, notwithstanding Mr Lovat being a Catholic? One can be certain there will be a mix of denominations among future headmasters as the system grows.'

'If indeed it does grow,' Wilkinson said.

'Do you have something more to say, Mr Wilkinson?' Broughton asked.

'Yes, I do, Bishop. And I mean no offence to Mr Lovat or his brother, but I don't think we should be distracted from this issue by Mr McVeigh's levity. I regret to say that putting the first such school in the care of a Roman Catholic will make it difficult for me to convince my synod of the wisdom of such a scheme.'

Another moment of silence.

'Perhaps I should explain a little more of the history of all this,' Charles said. 'If you could indulge me for a minute or two and I apologise that perhaps I should have said some of these things in our meeting with the Governor.'

'By-all-means, Mr Lovat,' Broughton replied. 'Please tell us what we all need to know. Are we agreed, gentlemen?'

There was nodding and grunts of approval all around.

'Well, this is the history as I understand it. I hasten to say, by the way, that I've only met my half-brother once in my life. I haven't even caught up with him in the twelve months I've been in the colony so I'm in no way his apologist. But I know much about him through my father who is also his father. Thomas gained his first teaching post in the Catholic parish of Tralee, but he was there for only a very short time when he was given a post as deputy headmaster of a Church of Ireland school in the same town. He then went on to be the headmaster of that school at a time it was being used to trial Lord Stanley's national schools plan for Ireland.

As you no doubt know, Lord Stanley was the Chief Secretary for Ireland at the time. Because of my brother's experience, he was appointed as an inspector of schools for the entire Limerick County. So, his experience is vast, unusually broad, and his focus has mainly been on the non-denominational sector. That is why the Governor handpicked him to oversee the establishment of the school at Richmond, something he has obviously done well enough to be asked to manage a second school at Windsor. He wasn't picked because he's Catholic and he is not, by any means, narrow in his Catholicism. Indeed, one or two of my clergy brothers are most distressed that Thomas is not working inside the church.'

'I can vouch for that,' Polding said. 'One of my clergy can barely mention his name without swearing under his breath.'

'And he's of Scottish descent, you say?' Lang asked again.

'Yes, Mr Lang,' Moore said. 'We know that makes him impeccable as far as you and Mr McVeigh are concerned.'

'Indeed,' Broughton said, chuckling. 'So, what can I tell the Governor, gentlemen?'

The clergymen looked to each other, some nodding, others looking at their papers or out the window. Broughton sensed an air of expectation.

'What do you think Mr Marsden would have said, Bishop?' Ullathorne said.

'Well, I think we know what he would have said,' Broughton replied. 'But he's not here, is he? And we cannot live in the past.'

'All the same,' Ullathorne said. 'For all his anti-Roman fieriness, I always had respect for Mr Marsden's wisdom about these things. He knew we Christians were *not* one big happy family and he didn't delude himself that we could be.'

There was a sustained silence, shuffling of papers and re-positioning in chairs. Polding stared at Ullathorne who refused to look his way.

'I'm frankly surprised at your tone, Mr Ullathorne,' Broughton said. 'I've not heard you speak like this before.'

Broughton looked to Polding.

'Neither have I, frankly,' Polding said. 'I'm sure Father Ullathorne is being misunderstood. We have been at pains to soften our denominational differences, knowing that the Catholic population will be the sore loser in any denominational tensions. I'm certain the Roman clergy are all at one in this view, and certainly that Father Ullathorne and I are at one in it. Is that not true, Father?'

Ullathorne stared at the desk in front of him. He raised his head and looked at his bishop.

'Of course, My Lord. Of course, we are.'

'Well then,' Broughton said. 'I think we can let the Governor know that the English and Roman churches are in favour of his plan. Is that correct?'

Polding nodded his approval.

'And you, Mr Lovat, I take it?' Broughton asked, looking across at Charles.

'By-all-means, Bishop. Not that I consider myself a decision-maker in these matters.'

Ullathorne coughed and reached for his kerchief.

'Were you wanting to say something else, Mr Ullathorne?' Moore asked.

'Not at all, Mr Moore.'

'Not that you would feel well-advised to, at least,' Moore said, glancing across at Polding.

'And what of you, gentlemen?' Broughton asked, looking at the Presbyterian and Methodist leaders.

'I believe Mr Lang and I are in substantial agreeance,' McVeigh replied. 'Is that right, Mr Lang?'

'Indeed. I think we need to review the situation as it unfolds but, broadly, I'm in agreement.'

'And Mr Lovat being Roman Catholic is not a barrier, in your view?'

Lang and McVeigh shook their heads.

'Now that we know he's a Scot by trade,' McVeigh said, smiling. 'Everything seems braw.'

'Thank you,' Broughton said, looking then to the Methodists. 'And you, gentlemen?'

'I'm not as accepting as our Presbyterian friends,' Wilkinson said. 'But I agree we should keep an open mind to these things.'

Wilkinson looked around at Moore.

'To be frank, I'm not as obliging as my colleague,' Moore said. 'I think we need to keep a very close eye on such a development. I'm conscious of Mr Ullathorne calling on Mr Marsden's spirit to caution us all. Our differences are not trivial. They're soaked in blood and we cannot pretend they can be evaporated by our children sharing a playground. I think, above all, we must maintain our own schools even if we accede to the Governor's whims at the same time.'

'Even if for diplomatic reasons,' Ullathorne said.

'Precisely,' Moore replied.

Charles felt the tension between his two Catholic colleagues as they rode back to St Mary's in silence.

'Could I see you for a moment, William?' Polding asked Ullathorne as they alighted from the carriage.

'Certainly, My Lord.'

During the short break over Easter, Polding asked to meet with Charles.

'Are you still interested in trying your hand in a parish, Charles?'

'Yes, John, to be honest, I'm aching for the opportunity.'

'So, you're really not enjoying what you're doing? Is there nothing in it for you any longer?'

'Part of me loves the work. I thrive on theological thought and investigation. There are times when I'm preparing a lecture or just doing some of my own writing when I feel as though the Angelic

Doctor himself is sitting on my shoulder, urging me on. But it's the trouble it causes that I find so dispiriting. Some of the clergy wear me down with their narrowness. I just don't understand why anyone of faith wouldn't want theological understanding to underpin it. I mean we have enough enemies in the world as it is without us fighting among ourselves. But it seems to me that all some of our clergy want is to fight, fight the Protestants, fight the native people, fight the Governor for trying to get us to work together. And if all that fails, then fight among ourselves. I'm sorry, John, but I'm tired of it.'

'It's interesting you mention the Good Doctor, Aquinas. He had his own run-ins, didn't he?'

'Oh, yes, I know. I feel as though I understand his dilemma more and more. Whatever it was that happened to him in the last years of his life. A breakdown of health or a crisis. Whatever it was that made him declare it all as straw. All his great thoughts worth nothing. I think it might have been the same wearing down by the criticism of others that I feel. Not that I'm comparing myself with him. Lord, forgive me. But I sense it might have been the same thing. The viciousness of those who wanted to condemn him even after his death. Wanting to dig him up and burn the body. And for what? For having ideas that they couldn't abide. I'm sorry, John. I'm truly sorry. Perhaps I was tired when I first came here. I'm so sorry.'

'And I'm sorry too if I've asked too much of you. I was just so excited when I heard you were coming. Not in my wildest dreams could I have imagined someone of your academic calibre coming here. Even my brother Benedictines I'd hoped to lure here. Even among them, I never hoped to get someone of your capacity. I'm sorry if my excitement blinded me to your own needs.'

'Please don't apologise, John. You've been wonderful to me and I'll be forever grateful for the opportunities you've given me. The seminary, the meetings with the other clergy, meetings with government officials. I couldn't have asked for more. I'm just so sorry to disappoint you.'

'Charles, you're not disappointing me. Even if you end up in a parish, I'll still want to call on you from time to time to work with the other clergy, help to sort out the Governor's school plans, and the like. Would that be alright with you?'

'Certainly, John. Please feel free to call on me whenever you need me. So, what, if I might ask, do you have in mind for me?'

'Well, I recall seeing you in Yass when we were there for the foundational blessing. How well you did with the people. How happy you seemed to be.'

'I must admit it was the thing I've enjoyed most since I've been here.'

'Well, things are coming along well down there. It's an area of rapid growth. The church will be ready soon and the presbytery's been fixed up. Thomas Slattery has been looking after it from Liverpool, but I think it needs its own man. How would you feel about taking up an appointment there?'

'It would be a dream come true, John. Almost too good to be true.'

'Well, you deserve it. You've truly been my greatest asset here in so many ways. So capable at what you do, such a gift when it comes to dealing with the Protestant clergy. And, if I might say, such a loyal friend to me. You've not only been my confessor, as you know, but my confidant more widely. There are not many in whom I can confide and know without a doubt that it will go no further or be used maliciously. But you truly have been that person for me, and I'll never forget you for it.'

'Thank you, John. You embarrass me but I'm so grateful to hear it. I'm honoured to have been able to support you in that way.'

'Now, I have just one final request. Would you mind staying on at St Mary's until the middle of the year? I'll make arrangements then for you to set up in the residence at Yass and that will give me time to work out what's happening at the seminary.'

'Of course, John. I'll stay so long as you need me. Dare I ask what thoughts you have about St Mary's?'

'Oh, I shouldn't say too much at this point, but you might know there's at least one person who thinks he's cut out to do your job,' Polding said, pausing and smiling. 'Perhaps even as well as you do it.'

'Or even better?' Charles said, smiling.

'I think you have it.'

'Yes, well, say no more. I'm sure some of the clergy will be delighted with the change.'

'I fear so,' Polding replied. 'Now, is there anything else I can do for you at this stage, Charles?'

'Well, John, I was going to ask if I might have a couple of days' leave to visit my brother. They're expecting their seventh child and have asked if I might be free to do the baptism.'

'Seven. The perfect number,' Polding replied. 'Whenever you need to go, Charles.'

XXXIII

On the 6th day of February 1839, Mary celebrated her nineteenth birthday. Celebrations would be scant, well overtaken by the first day of the school year in two different schools several miles apart. She was with her father for the first assembly at 8.30am at the new school in Windsor. Thomas then taught the older pupils until midday while Mary taught the younger ones.

At midday, the pupils had lunch, overseen by parents, while Thomas and Mary made their way to the other school at Richmond. About halfway along Hawkesbury Valley Road, they stopped to speak with Eliza and John going in the opposite direction.

'How are the new pupils?' Eliza asked.

'Just like the old ones,' Thomas replied. 'Some angels; some little devils in the making.'

They swapped the lists of pupils' names they had made in the morning, then proceeded to their respective schools. Eliza would replace Mary at Windsor for the afternoon, and John would replace Thomas. They would all be supported by older pupils who had graduated from Richmond the year before. The only trained teacher among them was Eliza.

'And I have a very special announcement to make,' Thomas said to the assembled pupils at Richmond before they resumed afternoon classes. 'It's Miss Lovat's birthday today. Let's all say happy birthday, Miss Lovat.'

'Happy birthday, Miss Lovat,' the ninety-three pupils chorused.

'Thank ye, girls and boys,' Mary said with a shy smile.

Thomas noted the sad eyes behind the smile. Mary had talked the night before about the seventeenth birthday she had shared with James Hawkins on the *Lady Macnaghten*.

'I just can't believe it's two years.'

'Ye still miss him, don't ye, darling?' Eliza asked.

'Just as much, Ma. Just as much.'

'Ye'd best stay home today, darling,' Thomas said to Eliza.

It was nearing Easter and Eliza was a matter of weeks away from giving birth.

'No. I said I could get through to Easter and get through to Easter I will.'

'And I don't suppose there's any point in arguing with ye?'

'What do ye think, Thomas Lovat?'

'I think I'll save my breath.'

Eliza managed to get through to Holy Thursday. On Good Friday, she woke in pain.

'John, run to Dr Baxter's, boy,' Thomas said. 'Tell him we need him here quickly.'

'No, John,' Eliza said. 'I'll let ye know when he's needed.'

'Are ye sure, darling?'

'I think after six of them, I know the signs.'

'I suppose, but it's been a few years, dear, and a number of things have happened in the meantime.'

'Only four years. It's not something a woman forgets, believe me.'

'Well, I can't argue with ye there, my darling. Much good it would do me if I tried.'

'I think ye're finally coming to know me, Thomas Lovat,' Eliza laughed.

'Ah, perhaps. Just give me a few more years.'

'Can ye believe it's only four years since James's birth?' Eliza said. 'It seems like a hundred. In a different world.'

'Do ye wish ye were back in Tralee?'

'Only for the family. I'd love to have my Ma here. And I know how she'll be fretting. But otherwise, no. This is home now and it's exciting to think we'll have our own colonial child. Fancy, he or she might never know Ireland.'

'Yes, a child of the great southern land. Who would ever have thought?'

—⁂—

Against more protesting from Thomas, Eliza made it to the makeshift church in Windsor for the 3pm service that Good Friday.

'Ye're a brave soul, Mrs Lovat,' Father Brady said after the service.

'Well, now's not the time to be getting God offside, is it, Father?'

'No time's the time to be getting God offside,' Brady replied, stern-faced.

'I don't think he saw the humour,' Thomas said as they walked away.

"I don't think humour and Father Brady have much in common,' Mary said a little louder than intended.

'Hush, child,' Eliza said. 'The poor man. I should've known better.'

'No, ye shouldn't have, dear,' Thomas said.

—⁂—

Eliza slept for most of the day, Holy Saturday.

'Don't even suggest going to Midnight Mass,' Thomas said after a light dinner.

'Why not?' Eliza replied.

'Ma,' Mary shrieked. 'No. For heaven's sake, *no*!'

Everyone was shaken out of their sleepiness.

'It's alright, darling,' Eliza said. 'I'm alright.'

'Ye have to *look after* yerself, Ma,' Mary said, choking on the words. 'I couldn't bear to lose anyone else.'

'Alright, darling,' Eliza replied. 'Ye're probably right. It's a little cold anyway.'

'Thank the Lord someone in the house has some sense,' Thomas said, moving to Mary and cradling her head on his shoulder.

'Call the doctor,' Eliza screamed.

It was a little after 11pm. John ran to the doctor's house two blocks away.

'The doctor's at church in Windsor,' one of the neighbours called out.

John ran back to the house.

'He'll be at the Church of England,' Thomas said. 'Ye know where it is?'

'Yes, Da.'

'Get there as fast as ye can, boy.'

John rode off towards Windsor. Thomas ran back into the bedroom where Mary was tending to her mother.

'Is the doctor coming?' Eliza cried out.

'He won't be long, darling,' Thomas said, glancing at Mary with a look that gave away the white lie.

'Anyway, we know what to do, don't we, Ma?' Mary said.

'What do ye mean?' Eliza said through clenched teeth. 'Are ye saying the doctor's *not* coming?'

'No, Ma. I'm just saying we probably don't need him anyway. This is yer seventh child so ye know what to do and I've done this sort of thing before.'

'Have ye truly, Mary?' Thomas asked, the look of concern deepening. 'When was *that*?'

'On the *Lady Macnaghten*. Remember? I helped James deliver a baby. I'm sure I told ye.'

'Yes, she did, Thomas. But *please* tell me the doctor's coming. Where is he, for Lord's sake?'

'He was at church, darling, but John's gone to get him.'

'Up at Windsor?' Eliza screamed. 'Up at *Windsor*? It'll take him an age to get here.'

'I'm sure he'll be here in time, darling.'

'Well, I *don't*,' Eliza said, letting out a piercing scream.

'Da,' Mary said. 'Perhaps ye'd best wake the girls.'

She had no sooner mentioned it than Elizabeth and Johannah rushed into the room, their eyes bleary and adjusting to the light. They were shaking. They had never seen their mother like this.

'What's the matter?' Elizabeth shouted.

'Why's Ma screaming?' Johannah asked.

'Girls,' Mary said, her voice steady and calm. 'Go get spare blankets, any ye can find. Pull them off yer beds if ye must. And towels, lots of them. And, Elizabeth, there's water boiling on the stove. Could ye bring me a bucket-load, please?'

The girls were still staring at their mother who was writhing, her pillow clenched to her stomach.

'Girls,' Mary said, extra authority in her voice. '*Go*, d'ye hear?'

'Do as Mary says, girls,' Thomas said. 'Elizabeth, get a pitcher of water. Johannah, as many towels and blankets as ye can find.'

—※—

By the time Dr Baxter raced in, there was little to do other than snip the umbilical cord.

'Well done, young lady,' Baxter said to Mary as he fumbled in his bag. 'You've obviously done this before.'

'Just once,' she replied, a tangible pride in her voice.

'Well, you should think about doing more of it.'

'Thank ye, Doctor,' Eliza said, struggling for breath. 'My daughter's an exceptional woman. And I'm telling ye, ye only know the half of it.'

'I look forward to knowing the other half at some time,' Baxter said, looking in Mary's direction. 'I take it you helped your mother with one of her earlier deliveries.'

'No, Doctor,' Thomas said. 'Mary served as a nurse on the ship from Ireland. The *Lady Macnaghten* actually. Ye might have heard of it.'

'Not the fever ship?' Baxter said, looking back to Mary.

'Yes, Doctor,' Mary replied. 'The fever ship.'

'Truly? Then you might have met a Dr James Hawkins?'

'Yes, Doctor,' Thomas said. 'Mary and Dr Hawkins worked closely together. Did ye know him?'

'I'd never met him, but he was a distant relative. His mother had written telling me he might be interested in settling in the colony for a time. I wrote and said he could stay with me for a while and help me in my practice. I went to the docks the day your ship was due in Sydney Cove but, of course, it was in quarantine. The next I knew, James had died. I wrote to his mother and was told she actually found out through me because the letter from the navy arrived late. She was devastated. All very sad. I believe he was a most dedicated young man.'

'He was,' Mary said. 'He was the best doctor.'

'I'm sure he was, Mary, and I'm certain you were a wonderful help to him.'

'Thank ye,' Mary said, wiping her eyes.

'Now, as to you, Mrs Lovat. You have a fine and healthy young son here. I don't suppose you've chosen a name.'

'Joseph,' Eliza and Thomas echoed.

'It was to be Joseph or Josephine,' Eliza said.

XXXIV

The two brothers finally met for the first time in New South Wales when Charles was en route to Yass in mid-August. He stayed with the family for two nights at Richmond.

'Father Brady wouldn't hear of us waiting for ye, Charles,' Thomas said.

'Well, no doubt Father Brady was only thinking of what's best for the child. It's always good to do the christening as early as possible. Just in case.'

'Of course. Mind ye, I think Father Brady might have been looking to his own interests as well. He doesn't seem too keen on the idea of any other priest meddling with his parishioners.'

'Yes, some of the clergy can be territorial,' Charles laughed.

'You know Father Brady, I suppose?' Eliza asked.

'Not so well but he did attend one or two of the classes that the bishop asked all the clergy to take.'

'Classes? For the priests?' Thomas asked. 'I'll bet they loved that.'

'Yes, well. Some of them liked them. I think.'

'And Father Brady?' Eliza asked.

'I'd rather not say,' Charles said, his eyes smiling.

'I'd love to see him sitting taking notes in class,' Thomas said. 'I get the impression he'd be happier out on the farm.'

'What were the classes about?' Mary asked.

'Theology.'

'But Father Brady hasn't been ordained all that long, has he?' Thomas asked. 'Shouldn't his theology be fairly up to date?'

'Father Brady up to date?' Mary said, laughing.

'Hush, child,' Eliza said.

'Yes, I'm sure his theology is up to date,' Thomas said, smiling. 'Even if he keeps it a secret.'

'Perhaps it is,' Charles said. 'I'm at a bit of a loss to know what's up to date and what's not these days. Regardless, Bishop Polding wants to ensure all the Catholic clergy are as theologically equipped as the Protestants. There seems to be a belief among them that we're not, especially about the Bible.'

'Is that true, though?' Eliza asked.

'About the Bible, it probably is,' Charles replied.

'So, do you teach them about the Bible, Uncle Charles?' John asked.

'Not really, John. I talk more about the great theological tradition of the church. And the great theologians. I have a particular passion for Saint Thomas Aquinas.'

'Who was he?' Mary asked.

'Probably the greatest Christian theologian of all time. He was the one who understood that religion and science are not necessarily opposed. That they're compatible and all part of God's plan.'

'So, the Protestant clergy understand this better than the Catholics?' Thomas asked. 'Is that what Bishop Polding thinks?'

'Well, no,' Charles replied. 'The Protestants hardly know anything about Aquinas. They rejected him at the time of the Reformation.'

'Why?' Thomas asked. 'If he's such a great theologian.'

'Well, the Reformers thought the Catholic Church had strayed too far from the Bible. They saw Aquinas as being partly to blame for this. Because he believed in science and philosophy, what we would call the rational arts, they saw him as part of the problem they were reacting to. The fact that the Borgia Pope, Alexander VI, was a fan of Aquinas probably didn't help.'

'Why?' John asked.

'Well, Rodrigo Borgia was the pope when people like Martin Luther and some of the other future Protestant reformers were growing up. Borgia didn't give the papacy the best of names, one might say. So, the fact he talked a lot about Aquinas didn't help his reputation among the Protestants.'

'I understand that,' Thomas said. 'But why would Father Brady not be open to Aquinas's ideas? I mean if popes like him, why wouldn't any Catholic priest?'

'Oh, I think he's just a bit challenging for anyone, Catholic or Protestant. He questioned a lot of things. He wanted everyone to think about their faith. And, you know, people don't always welcome that. They'd prefer to just go along with what they're told.'

'Even priests?' Mary asked.

'Even priests,' Charles replied. 'Even bishops,'

'What about popes?' Thomas asked.

'Yes, one or two of them too.'

'So, is this all part of why ye're heading to Yass?' Thomas asked. 'Are ye a little tired of battling it out with priests who prefer not to think too deeply?'

Charles looked deeply into the teacup before him.

'I suppose so, Thomas. It's been a difficult time for the church. So many things changing in the world. So many discoveries and new ideas that the church seems to find challenging. A little unnecessarily, in my view. That's why I rely so much on Aquinas. He lived in similar times but wasn't afraid of them. He worked through the challenges and came out the other side even stronger.

But too many in the church, and I don't just mean the

Catholics, the Protestants can be just as bad; they run away from the challenges, stick their heads in the sand. Then Christians start to look timid, scared, reacting to things happening in the world that are basically good – just different. I just don't see the Lord as timid, frightened. I think the gospels tell us about a Lord who was up to the challenges of his day, and so we should be too. Christians need to be bold and adventurous. The world's a good place. God's in charge so there's nothing to fear. That should be our message.'

Charles's gaze had been steadily on the bottom of his cup as he spoke. He looked up to see all eyes on him. The table full of adults and children staring at him, engrossed in his words as though they were coming directly from the godhead.

'Can you keep talking?' Elizabeth said.

'Yes, I love listening to you, Uncle Charles,' Johannah said.

It was the first any of them had heard from the two youngest girls.

'Well, perhaps you could come to Yass sometime and listen to me preach on a Sunday?'

'Yes, can we please?' Elizabeth asked. 'Mass is so boring here.'

'Now, darling,' Eliza said. 'Don't be disrespectful. Father Brady is...'

'Boring,' several voices echoed.

—⚜—

The following morning, the two brothers sat on the veranda, blankets around their shoulders, each sipping a cup of tea. The sun was beginning to break through to melt the frost. The fog was starting to lift. The crows were squawking, the kookaburras laughing and a variety of other birds singing. They watched a few kangaroos hopping across the field, disappearing into the mist.

'Ye know, Charles,' Thomas said. 'I was thinking last night as ye were speaking about Aquinas and the church and all that. Our

Da. He'd know what ye were saying. He's had his own difficulties with the church. And, from what he's said, it runs a little in the family. I mean our family. He's spoken about his own Da and Will, his own Da's Step Da. They all seemed to have their problems with the church. I mean the official side of it.'

'Yes, you're right,' Charles replied. 'I think it's taken me a long time to realise what an influence Pa's had on me. I was shielded from him by my mother and grandmother. So, I thought he'd not played that much of a part in my upbringing.'

'Why would they want to shield you from your own Da?'

'Oh, I think they were determined I was going to be a priest and they thought he might be a bad influence on me.'

'Charles. Can I tell ye something I've never told anyone?'

'Of course.'

'I always resented ye for the fact ye knew our Da so much better than me. He was with ye all the time, but I only saw him now and then. I had no idea he wasn't really with ye. That ye were being shielded from him. I'm sorry. That's a bit like a confession. I feel foolish saying it but at least it's off my chest.'

'Isn't that strange? The ideas we have from afar. Now it's my turn for confession.'

Charles leant over and placed his cup on the ground.

'Thomas, *I* always resented *you* because our father always seemed so much more interested in what *you* were doing than what *I* was doing. He might not have gone much to Tralee, but his heart always seemed to be there. His heart was never much in Burnley. And when my sister died, what bit of his heart had been there just left altogether.'

They sat in silence for a time.

'Thank ye for telling me that,' Thomas said. 'And I forgive ye, Father.'

'And me you,' Charles laughed. 'It seems we have more in common than merely a father.'

'Indeed, but what an influential one at that,' Thomas replied.

'And no doubt his Da before him and his Da before that. They're all in our blood, aren't they?'

'Yes, we're Jacobites, one and all, apparently,' Charles said, laughing. 'Rebels to the core.'

'I'm happy with that,' Thomas said. 'My Ma was surely one, by all accounts.'

Charles nodded and took a sip of his tea.

Charles left later in the morning. The family gathered to farewell him. He gave each of them a hug. Mary was last. She followed him around to the far side of the horse where he would mount it. For a few seconds, they were hidden from the others.

'Thank ye so much, Uncle Charles,' she whispered.

'Are you alright, Mary?'

'Yes, I think so.'

'Please come and see me anytime, won't you?'

'I'd love to.'

XXXV

It was the last week of August by the time Charles arrived in Yass as Pastor of the Argyle Mission. Polding had named him "Parish Priest of Goulburn and Yass". Goulburn was an established parish, but Father Brennan had been moved to Parramatta, leaving Goulburn vacant for a time. Charles was to live in Yass but tend, week-about, to both places. In time, the Argyle Mission expanded, the population outgrowing the priests available. Charles filled the gap gladly. The further from large cities and seminaries, the clearer the air, as far as he was concerned.

The weekend after his arrival in Yass marked exactly a year since he had been there for the blessing of the foundation stone of the church, still far from complete.

'Things are comin' on nicely, *Farder*,' the foreman, O'Byrne, said. 'Ye 'ave a study, a bedroom and a kitchen out de back. And we've enough o' de church finished for christenin's, confession and daily Mass. So long as not too many turn up, mind ye.'

'And Sunday Mass?' Charles asked.

'Dat'll 'ave to be in de court'ouse for a time, *Farder*. Sorry about dat.'

'That's perfectly alright. Religion and the law should enhance each other. Not always, mind you.'

'Whatever ye say, *Farder*. Now, d'ye want me to do somet'ing about dat mob over dere?'

'The aboriginal people, you mean?'

'Yes, *Farder*. Dey've bin told to keep deir distance from de presbytery, but dey drift back as often as we 'ustle 'em away.'

'No, that's fine, thank you.'

Charles recognised some of the group as those he had met the year before. One of them was still sporting a shirt he had given them. Another was wearing his black socks.

'Hello,' Charles said as he approached them, smiling and waving.

'*Yama*,' one of the young men said with a beaming smile. '*Giragul?*'

The man was pointing to some berries they were sharing.

'Hungry? No, thank you.'

Charles noticed an older man who looked cold and unwell.

'Is he alright?' he asked, gesturing to the old man.

'*Yingil*,' the young man said.

'Can I help in any way?' Charles said, holding the palms of his hands up.

'*Dandhangh*,' the man said, making a shivering motion.

'He's cold? Does he need more clothing?'

'*Bhadang*,' the young man nodded.

Charles went inside and came back with a black cardigan and handed it to the old man.

'*Mandaangguwu*,' the old man muttered as he took the cardigan and put it over his head. '*Mandaangguwu*,' the others echoed and laughed.

—⚭—

There was standing room only in the courthouse on the following Sunday.

'*Dear parishioners, I cannot tell you how delighted I am to be here with you. As many of you will remember, I was here with Bishop Polding just a year ago at the blessing of the foundation stone. I know we all thought the church might be finished by now but I'm sure if God can wait, then we can too. I wanted you to know that the bishop, such a good man, said to me on the way back to Sydney that he had never seen me so happy as I was when I was with you.*

And, you know, he was right. I recall so well your warmth and friendliness, how much you made me feel at home. I said to the bishop there and then that if there was ever an opportunity to work with those people, I would be delighted to accept it. And here I am. All things come in God's good time. As you know, I have a big parish, one that extends to Goulburn at present and one destined to grow even further.

For now, I will be with you during every second week, including every second Sunday. Later, I will probably be away more often, but I hope the bishop will send an assistant priest as soon as there's one to spare. Now, today's gospel tells us....'

'Thank you for the lovely sermon, Father,' was a common refrain after church.

'Please will you join us for lunch?' was another one.

'Won't you come for dinner tonight?' yet another.

The parishioners organised a roster that catered for two meals a day for as often as Charles was in the Yass environs. The Goulburn parishioners did the same for their environs. Charles was fed like never before. He put on more weight than he had ever carried.

—⚏—

Christmas that year was celebrated with a 6.30am Mass in Yass, followed by one at 4.30pm in Goulburn. When Mass finished at 5.30, the temperature was still hovering at a hundred degrees Fahrenheit.

'*Farder*, ye look exhausted,' Mrs O'Brien said. 'Please, come 'ome immediately.'

Charles stayed with the O'Brien's when in Goulburn as the presbytery was being renovated. He was no sooner in the door than he staggered, managing to reach for a chair before collapsing onto it.

He opened his eyes after an unknown time to find the entire family, two parents, five children and Granny O'Brien, staring down at him, one of the children fanning him with a newspaper. The doctor was called, and he was put to bed, a large pitcher of water by his bedside.

The summer of 1839 was recorded as the hottest since the colony was founded fifty years before. Charles had never experienced heat like it, even in the depths of a Roman summer. The fainting spell marked the beginning of a summer flu and severe dehydration.

'I really think you should stay a couple more days,' the doctor said on the Wednesday after the fainting spell. 'Will you be able to rest at home for a while?'

'No, I'm due to start my first tour of the wider parish the week after New Year.'

'Well, I advise against it, but I know what you're like, Father, so I suppose I might as well save my breath.'

'Perhaps you might,' Charles said, smiling.

―⁂―

Charles's diary for the January 1840 tour showed the first entry as "3rd – Bungendore (20 or so attend)" through to "31st – Tumut (12 attend)". There were twenty-three other towns mentioned, a journey of more than eighteen hundred miles across this hottest of summers. In time, the priest, poet and author, John Hartigan, would write of Charles in his book, *Men of '38*:

> *The ancient order of the boundary riders bandy-legged from the saddle … would without doubt hand over the Diploma of Toughness to this professor who before his initiation had ridden nothing harder or rougher than a Chair of Theology.*

Even in Bungendore, the people had noticed how tired and worn he looked.

'No, no,' he responded to their expression of concern. 'I feel wonderful. I'm where I want to be.'

He was pleased they weren't there watching the next day when his young mare, renamed "Emma Jane", stumbled on the rocky slope, throwing him headfirst down the hillside.

'Whoa, darling Emma Jane,' he muttered under his breath as he climbed back up to steady the mare. 'I'll be with you soon enough. Don't take me just yet.'

He often spoke to the mare as if to his dead sister. From the moment he had seen her in the livery on Parramatta Road, he felt closer than he had in years.

'Emma Jane's a strange name for a horse,' someone said once.

'It's after my sister who died some years ago. They have the same dark brown hair and deep brown eyes. I honestly can't tell them apart.'

He walked beside the mare until the steep slopy road levelled out. He then mounted her and trotted a way until finding a small billabong and some trees for shade. The sun was high in the sky, the temperature a hundred degrees or more. He had given up on shooing the flies away, telling himself they were God's creatures, like himself, and just as entitled to their customs as was he. Only when they strayed into his mouth would he bother to disturb them.

Charles and Emma Jane arrived in Queanbeyan, a small settlement by the Molonglo River, in the early evening. Timothy Beard, ex-convict and squatter, was the king here.

'Oh, my Lord; 'as someone died,' Beard cried as he approached Charles.

'No, sir. I'm Father Lovat from St Mary's in Yass.'

'What on earth are ye doin' 'ere, *Farder?*'

'Just the rounds of my parish.'

Beard let out a roar. He buckled over with laughter.

'What did ye do to deserve bein' sent 'ere, for 'eaven's sake?'

'Nothing. I asked for it.'

'Well, ye've got it, *Farder*, is all I can say. Anyway, I'm Timothy Beard. Pleased to meet ye.'

'Hello, Timothy. I've heard all about you.'

'Truly? All bad, I suppose.'

'Not at all. People in Yass speak highly of you.'

'Now, *Farder*, priests are not meant to lie, ye know!'

'Well, no-one ever told me that one,' Charles said as he grabbed the extended hand. 'Now, I don't suppose you need anything from me.'

'I don't t'ink so, *Farder*, but ye look as though ye need me, or at least my water supply and some food.'

'I'm not so proud as to say no,' Charles said as he limped towards Beard's dwelling. 'Thank you, Timothy.'

'Woo, *Farder*. Ye've 'urt yerself.'

'Oh, just a scratch. I was more worried about Emma Jane.'

Beard peered into the distance, squinting in face of the setting sun.

'I mean my horse.'

'Oh, for a minute I t'ought ye might 'ave a wife wit' ye. Perhaps ye'd been out 'ere so long ye didn't know ye're not s'posed to be married.'

Beard let out another raucous laugh. Charles smiled.

'My horse is enough to be looking after.'

Charles washed while Beard tended to the horse, including checking to make sure there were no injuries. They shared a meal of lamb and some potatoes and beans.

'This is fine meat, Timothy,' Charles said as he tucked in. 'Do you raise sheep?'

'Well, let's just say I 'ave some very obligin' neighbours, *Farder*.'

'Are you sure I shouldn't be hearing your confession now?' Charles said, grinning.

'It'll be alright, *Farder*. T'anks all de same. Now, where would ye like to sleep?'

'I have a rucksack. I'll be fine under the stars if you don't mind me sharing a slab of your dirt.'

'Not at all, *Farder*, but I'd rather ye sleep indoors. D'ere's quite a few browns around at dis time o' year.'

'Browns?'

'Snakes. Ye might find one of 'em tuckin' ye in if ye're not careful.'

The next morning, Charles said a short, private Mass outside under a gum tree. He came back inside. Beard handed him a large plate with several rinds of bacon and four eggs.

'Obliging neighbours?' Charles asked.

'Of course,' Beard replied, smiling. 'It's not as bad as ye t'ink, *Farder*. My neighbours and I 'ave an understandin'. We borrow from each od'er, let's say. No-one keeps a tally.'

'I'm pleased to hear it,' Charles replied.

'*Farder*, if I might say. Ye don't seem like a priest.'

'Why, on earth? Not holy enough?'

'No, not at all. It's just that ye 'aven't even asked me if I'm Cat'lic. Wit' any o' the chaplains I met while in 'er Majesty's service, it was always de first question.'

'And what would you say?'

'Oh, depending on 'o was askin' and whedder I was frightened of 'em or not, somet'in' like, *well I used to be*, or, *sorry, Farder, I'm what my Ma would 'ave called a bad Cat'lic.*'

'Do you think you're a bad man, Timothy?'

'Oh, I'm not perfect, dat's for sure, but bad? No, I don't t'ink I'm bad.'

'So, why would you describe yourself that way?'

'I'm not sure. It's just what was said when someone stopped goin' to Mass.'

'Well, if *you're* not sure, I'm certainly not going to judge you. All I know is that the last thing God would want of any of his creatures is that they'd see themselves as bad, bad anything, including Catholic.'

'As I said, *Farder*, ye don't seem like a priest.'

'Because I tell you God doesn't want you to feel bad?'

'Well, yes, to be honest. Most of de priests an' nuns I've ever met seem to want y' to t'ink ye're bad. Dat's why ye need de church. I t'ink it's what I'd call drummin' up business, ye know what I mean?'

'I find that sad, Timothy. Not that you're wrong. But it's sad if that's what the church has become. A messenger of gloom.'

They sat in silence as they tucked into the ample breakfast.

'What were ye doin' out dere dis mornin'?' Beard asked.

'Under the tree? Just saying my morning Mass.'

'Ye didn't ask me if I wanted to come?'

'I wasn't sure you would. Would you have?'

'I'm not sure,' Beard laughed. 'I'd 've 'ad to go to confession and by de time ye'd 'eard it, it'd be night-time again.'

'Would you like to go to confession?'

Beard sat in silence, holding his knife and fork aloft.

'I'd 'ave to t'ink about it, to be honest.'

'I wouldn't want you to be anything less than honest.'

They finished breakfast. Charles gathered his things and walked outside. Beard had brought Emma Jane out to the front.

'Thanks so much, Timothy. For your food and company – and for your goodness if I might say. You *are* a good man and don't ever forget it.'

'T'ank ye, *Farder*. It's bin a pleasure. Please come back anytime.'

'I certainly will. We wouldn't want to disappoint those obliging neighbours, would we?'

Beard laughed.

'So, ye're sure I'm good, are ye, *Farder*?'

'Yes, I'm sure.'

The two men shook hands. Charles mounted his mare and began cantering down the rough, pebbly road.

'Next time, *Farder*,' Beard called after him.
Charles stopped the horse and looked around.
'Under de tree,' Beard shouted.
'Under the tree.'

—⁕—

'That's far enough.'
'Hello,' Charles called out. 'I'm Father Lovat from Yass.'
The man came forward. Charles could see the single shot rifle was cocked and ready.
'What?' the man asked.
'Father Lovat. I'm the Catholic priest from Yass.'
'Whaddye want?'
'I'm just doing the rounds, finding out who's who.'
'Well, there's nothing 'ere for ye. Ye'd better be careful 'cause folks are on the lookout for scavengers, blacks especially, but not always. Ye could get yerself shot.'
'Are you sure there's nothing I can do for you? Happy to just have a yarn.'
'No, I'm not Catholic. Not anythin'. Not interested. Best ye move on.'
The man uncocked the rifle and pointed down the road.
'There's some folks about 'alf a mile down there. Place called Rob Roy. They're Irish, I think. Flaherty or O'Flaherty or some such name. I know 'e was a convict, but 'e was given a bit o' land down there.'
'Thanks. And your name?'
'None o' yer business.'
'Alright, thanks very much.'
Charles turned Emma Jane's head and gently kicked her sides. The mare began to trot towards Rob Roy. It had been another hundred plus day. Charles was running low on water. Emma Jane had drunk some dirty water by the side of the road, but Charles

thought better of it. He hoped the Flahertys or O'Flahertys were more obliging than the man with the rifle.

It was the Flannerys, in fact, James and Sally, and three children under the age of five. They had both been free from their convict past by several years but only recently been given the grant of land at Rob Roy.

'Please come in, Father,' Sally said as James helped the priest off his mare. 'My goodness, ye must be roastin'. Why on earth are ye out on a day like this?'

The Flannerys were Catholic. They had been together for over six years but had never gotten around to marrying, nor to having the children baptised. Charles obliged on both counts. The next day they had a small double ceremony, calling on a couple of neighbours to serve as witnesses and godparents. Charles stayed an extra night. Both he and Emma Jane needed the rest.

—⚏—

The heat did not let up over the next few weeks. There were several days when Charles would break off his journey by mid-morning and he and Emma Jane would rest under trees, preferably near a river or billabong.

It was around the middle of the month, an especially hot day. Charles had almost stopped at midday, but he kept going, hoping to find better shade. The rough map he was following told him there was a creek nearby. He led Emma Jane off the beaten track and down a small hill in the hope he would find it.

The first Charles knew of it was when Emma Jane reared and whinnied, ripping the reins from his hands, and throwing him to the ground. The horse galloped back up the hill. Charles fell on his back and was rolling over on his knees when he saw it. The brown was startled, snapping at the glove on Charles's right hand. He felt the fang meeting flesh. His hat had fallen off right next to where the snake was readying itself for another attack. Charles grabbed the hat and flicked it over the snake's head, taking the small moment of distraction to haul himself to his feet and run back in the direction that Emma Jane had beaten.

Having secured the mare, Charles looked to his hand. He ripped the heavy leather glove off to see a tiny tear on his small finger. He knew instinctively that without the glove, he might well be with his sister already. He mounted the mare and trotted down the road, hoping to find a homestead or hovel where someone might help.

He felt the light-headedness setting in as he rounded a corner of the road and sighted some trees ahead. He believed he could make it.

'Mister, mister,' the voice was calling.

Charles stirred, as if out of the deepest sleep, to see the aboriginal people surrounding him. There were six or so of them, two being the women attending to his hand. One of them was sucking or licking the small finger, while the other one seemed to be placing something liquid-like on it. One of those standing appeared to be engaging in a ritual of some kind, burning some small, dry branches, and waving the smoke around while singing. Charles would be asked often to describe the event but was never sure how much was fact, how much imagination. He just knew he was relieved to be alive.

He and Emma Jane stayed with the aboriginal family for three days while he recovered. He tried to get to learn their names but all they would say was *Coombah. We Coombah*. He would talk for years about the Coombah family that saved his life.

By the time the priest and his mare arrived in Tumut at the end of the month, they were both exhausted. Emma Jane would never make the trip again. She was put down early in the year, 1840. Charles felt as though he had lost his sister twice over.

—⚄—

In the autumn of 1840, having heard of his ventures through the summer and been advised of bouts of sickness and fatigue, Polding wrote to Charles, by then back in Yass.

> *Dear Father Lovat,*
>
> *As you would know, young Michael McGrath was ordained recently, his readiness in no small measure owing to your good self. I have spoken with him about an appointment to the Argyle Mission. I had thought he might serve as curate to you. If you would be happy to move more permanently to Goulburn, where the church is better established and the new presbytery almost ready, then Father McGrath could undertake the more laborious tasks associated with Yass and its far-flung responsibilities.*
>
> *Father McGrath is happy with the idea. He grew up in a rural area of Ireland and so might be more fittingly prepared for some of the rigours associated with the Yass Mission. If you are in agreeance, I could see to this arrangement in the very near future.*
>
> *Yours in Christ, +John Bede Polding OSB DD*

Charles replied immediately, asking that he be allowed to continue with a mission he was finding particularly to his liking. After some letters back and forth, Polding acquiesced, appointing McGrath to Goulburn as parish priest and separating it out from the Yass Mission.

> *...At least, this will relieve you of duties to the north. As soon as one becomes available, I will appoint another priest to assist you with duties to the east, west and especially to the vast south. +JBP.*

As it was, it would be close to ten years before the kind of help Charles needed would be available in any permanent fashion. So, that first summer coverage of his mission was only the beginning. Charles would make an annual foray of more than two thousand miles east, west, and south. It would take him over the Murray River into the adjoining colony of Victoria. Some nights he would sleep in farmhouses, others rough by the side of the road.

On occasion, he would share the campfire of an aboriginal family. Wherever he went, he would say a Mass where it was welcomed, by Catholics, those of other faiths or none. He would hear confessions, offer advice, or merely listen to people's stories of their achievements and setbacks. At times, he would perform a marriage, at other times a funeral. People would sometimes wait for special occasions if they knew a "Father Lovat visit" was imminent.

When Polding, by then an archbishop, came to open the Yass church, a much-delayed project finally completed in 1844, he enquired about Charles's fortitude.

'Are you certain this is not altogether too much for you?'

'Not at all, My Lord.'

'Charles, I feel I've asked more of you than of any of the others. And of all of them, your preparation and state of health has probably been the least fitting.'

'Perhaps, yet I'm happy in a way I've never been before.'

XXXVI

'I've arranged for Emma Jane's and William's remains to be removed to St Peter's,' Edward said on his arrival at Towneley Manor.

It was early 1839. He had spent most of the summer in London with Mary Beth and had visited with Sarah at Pemberton on the way home.

'Edward, I forbid it,' Jane replied.

'Forbid all ye wish, my dear. It's happening and that's that.'

'Percival, talk some sense into him, will you, please?'

'I'm afraid there's not much we can do, dear. It's Edward's decision.'

Jane stormed out of the room.

'Tell Jane there'll be a short ceremony at the graveyard at St Peter's next Tuesday at noon. She will be welcome, as of course will ye, Mr Towneley.'

'I'll let her know,' Percival replied. 'Though I doubt she'll be there.'

The following Tuesday, the gravediggers arrived early to exhume the remains from the Catholic graveyard on the Towneley Estate. They were placed in two new coffins and taken in the undertaker's veiled carriage the short distance to St Peter's Church of England graveyard. Reverend Horace Thurlow and Edward stood waiting. The coffins were placed atop a newly dug grave right next to young Edward's. Horace was about to begin the short service when Jane and Percival arrived. They came and stood in silence next to Edward.

'Heavenly Father, we commend again our brother, William, and our sister, Emma Jane, to the earth. We are confident they rest with thee in thine eternal paradise and that the grace thou bestowed on them in life continues in their heavenly existence. We ask thee to bless their mother, Jane, and their father, Edward, who stand here today, saddened by their deaths but gladdened in the knowledge that they live with thee in thine enduring kingdom. We now pray in the words thy Son taught us. Our Father, which art in heaven...'

Edward joined in the Church of England version of the Lord's Prayer. Jane stood mute but, at the words "as we forgive those...", she gasped and stumbled forward, grabbing onto Edward's arm. He held her arm and reached his other arm around her shoulder. She rested her head on his shoulder and wept.

'I never wanted things to be like this, Edward.'

Jane and Edward had agreed to meet that afternoon at Tarleton House. They sat facing each other in the large drawing room, a small table with a water jug and two glasses on it. Theirs were the only two chairs not covered with sheets.

'Nor did I, believe me.'

'Were you *ever* happy with me?' Jane asked.

'Of course, I was, Jane. Of *course*, I was. I chose ye, remember? I knelt on the soggy ground beneath yer window, even despite yer Ma standing there wishing me dead.'

'She never wished you dead.'

'I'm nay so sure, Jane. It's how I felt from the first meeting with her.'

'Do you blame Mummy for our unhappiness, do you?'

'Oh, what's the point in blame? *Na tha air falbh*, as they say in the Highlands. What's been is gone. And what's dead is gone forever.'

'So, are we dead, Edward? Is that what you're saying?'

'I was referring to yer Ma, Jane. There's nay use blaming the dead. It'll nay do any good at all.'

'Are we though?'

Edward looked away and stared out the window. He noticed the bird pecking on the windowsill outside.

'I ken so.'

Jane pulled the kerchief out of her knapsack. She wiped her eyes and her nose.

'So that's it?' she said, looking into his eyes.

'What do ye want me to say, love? I've asked ye time and again to come back here, to live with me in the house ye always wanted. To be with yer bairns – when we had bairns – but ye preferred to be with yer Ma, and even after she died to be with Percival. What was I to ken?'

'I know, I know. But seriously Edward, I've never felt you really wanted me. Ever! I always felt I had to settle for being your second best, maybe third best, or fourth best even. Who knows how many have loved you and that you loved more than me?'

'It's nay true, Jane. When I chose ye, I chose *ye*. There was nay any doubt in my mind. But, aye, perhaps it *was* yer Ma who poisoned ye against me. She was just always there, sticking her nose into our business, and ye always sided with her against me. It became intolerable. Ye're lucky I *dinna* take recourse to other women.'

'But you *did*. And you *have*, Edward. Tell me honestly, now, what's the nature of your relationship with Mary Beth? Are you in love with her? Are you going to leave me?'

Edward said nothing. He stared into his glass.

'We're very close. We've been close since I was a lad, as ye ken. She's been a friend and a protector.'

'That wasn't my question, Edward!'

'Let me ask *ye* a question, Jane? Do ye *want* me to stay? Does our marriage mean anything to ye?'

'Of course, it does. *Of course*, it does. But does it mean anything to *you*?'

'Aye, then come home. Do ye wanna come home?'

'Not yet.'

'Why?'

'Percival needs me. He's very lonely, you know?'

'And ye assume I dinna need ye? That I'm nay ever lonely? Even when I've lost all my bairns, dead or on the other side of the world? Maybe *I* need ye. Can ye nay see that?'

'I'm sorry, Edward. I truly am. But Percival's been so good to me. *So* kind!'

'And I've nay been kind. Is that it?'

'I'm sorry, Edward. I truly am. I can't. I don't know. Perhaps if I can speak with Mummy – or Charles. Do you think Charles might be home soon?'

Edward watched her turn and walk away. He was unable to find the words.

—⚬—

By Easter of that year, Edward was back in Highgate with Mary Beth. He had stayed at Pemberton with Sarah on the way to London.

'I don't suppose you'd accompany me to a dinner,' Mary Beth said.

'Oh, ye ken how to get to my heart, Mary Beth,' Edward replied, smiling.

'Yes, I still remember that first one. I think it was the final nail in our coffin, darling.'

'Well, I was just a wee lad. I'd nay ever mixed in those circles.'

'I recall you describing it as a complete waste of time. Not to mention your insinuations that I spent the night flirting with all the men.'

'Just to make me jealous?'

'Well, if that was it, I failed dismally, didn't I?'

'Perhaps,' Edward replied. 'Perhaps.'

Edward reached out and held her hand. They looked deeply into each other's eyes.

'Perhaps I could nay handle seeing how popular ye were with men who were so far above me. I nay ever felt so unworthy of ye as that night.'

'Oh, my darling. How badly we've understood each other at times. For two people so close, we've both made some incredibly foolish moves.'

'Perhaps it's what love does. It addles the mind.'

'Well, I'm certainly addled when it comes to you, Edward Lovat. God forgive me. I've never been able to help how I feel.'

They tightened their grip and tears welled in both sets of eyes. Mary Beth was the first to let go and sit up straight.

'Anyway, you might want to come to this one. The special guest is the Colonial Secretary. I thought he might know of things in New South Wales that would interest you.'

'Ye mean there might actually be something worth talking about? That *would* be an unusual dinner.'

'Oh, go away with you, you Highland snob.'

―⁂―

It was the Saturday night after Easter when they set out for the dinner.

'Oh my. Yer beauty nay ever fades, Mary Beth.'

Mary Beth was walking down the stairs in a black dress that reached to her ankles. The short-puffed sleeves and low neckline revealed the pale, unblemished skin on her upper chest and arms. She was pulling on long white gloves as he spoke.

'You're too kind, sir.'

'Nay at all.'

'Well, you scrub up fairly well yourself, if I might say.'

'Are ye *sure* ye'd nay rather stay in?' Edward said, winking.

'Now, what on earth would we do if we did?' Mary Beth said, smiling.

They arrived at the Kensington address of John and Esther Champion, a magnificent three-storeyed Georgian mansion. John had been a junior officer under Commodore Parker, Mary Beth's first husband. He was a member of the House of Commons. Mary Beth was on the regular guest list of the Champions. She and Carl had been regular attendees, but she had not attended since his death.

'Mary Beth, how wonderful to see you,' Esther said as they stepped inside the vaulted foyer. 'Darling, Mary Beth is here.'

'Mary Beth. How delightful,' Champion said, stepping forward from the crowd and kissing her gloved hand.

'John, Esther, I'd like you to meet my friend, Edward Lovat. Edward and I met on the *Gorgon* to New South Wales back in '91.'

'Delighted to meet you, Mr Lovat,' Champion said. 'So, you knew Commodore Parker then?'

'Indeed, I did, Mr Champion.'

'Jolly good. Jolly good. Isn't that wonderful, darling? The Commodore was such an inspiration to me. The finest captain of a ship I ever experienced.'

'Oh, don't get him started on his naval stories,' Esther said. 'You're most welcome, Mr Lovat. Any friend of Mrs Solander is a friend of ours, be assured.'

'Thank ye, Ma'am.'

'Do I detect a Scottish accent, Mr Lovat?' Esther asked.

'Highlands, actually,' Edward replied.

'And that *is* different, my dear,' Champion said to his wife. 'Never call a Highlander a mere Scot. Isn't that right, Mr Lovat?'

'Aye, it is indeed, sir.'

'Anyway, please do come and meet some of our other guests.'

Champion introduced the pair to other guests milled around between the foyer and the large function room. Mary Beth knew all of them.

'Now, just stay close to me this time,' Mary Beth whispered as they moved through the crowd. 'I still remember that first time when you snuck off to talk with the horses.'

'Aye, the only braw conversation I had that night.'

Mary Beth chuckled as she squeezed his hand.

—⚬—

Time came for them to be seated at the arranged places in the large ballroom adjacent to the foyer. Names were called in pairs.

'Mrs Solander and Mr Lovat,' the butler called.

'That's us, darling,' Mary Beth said, wrapping her arm through Edward's.

'I like the sound of it.'

'Mm,' Mary Beth replied, looking up at him. 'But it could be even better.'

They smiled as they walked through the ballroom door.

There were eight round tables, seating eight on each. For the most part, they were arranged by gender. Mary Beth was seated next to Sir Anthony Symonds, the Colonial Secretary.

'If you don't mind, Sir Anthony,' Mary Beth said. 'I might swap places with my friend, Mr Lovat. He has two sons currently in New South Wales. I thought he might like to speak with you about the situation there.'

'By-all-means, Mrs Solander. I hope we might catch up before the night's out though. Very pleased to meet you, Mr Lovat. This is my wife, Cecilia.'

'Very pleased to meet ye, Ma'am.'

Edward took his place next to Symonds. He glanced at the small bowl on the large plate in front of him. It contained a black, beady substance that was unfamiliar to him. There was a tiny fork and spoon sitting on the plate, with three glasses, one each filled with water and red and white wine. He looked up to see if Mary Beth's guidance was needed. She was busy speaking with an aging gentleman.

'So, where are your sons exactly?' Symonds asked.

'Charles is currently stationed in Sydney. He's a Catholic priest. And Thomas is headmaster at two schools near the Blue Mountains.'

'Ah, yes, I believe I've seen Thomas's name in despatches. I knew Richard Bourke, Governor of New South Wales until recently. He was very keen to establish non-churched schools in the colony. I believe your son was supporting him in that venture.'

'Yes, that's him alright. Thomas went out to work for the church but was then lured away by the Governor.'

'Oh, I dare say the church wouldn't be happy with him then. I know the current Governor, George Gipps, has had no end of trouble with some of the churches over the issue. They do like to do their own thing, I gather. Oh, I'm sorry. I don't mean any offence. You did say your other son is a priest. Roman Catholic, was it?'

'Aye. And no offence at all. Charles is highly supportive of what Thomas is doing. He doesn't approve of closed denominational thinking.'

'An unusual priest indeed,' Symonds said.

'Indeed, Charles is an exceptional man. They both are, in fact. Said with nay bias at all,'

'Of course not. So, Thomas is a Scot, I take it from your accent.'

'Nay, he was born in Tralee, in fact. And Charles was born in Preston. It's nay a wee story.'

'So, I gather. Well, I can see why Richard Bourke would have been pleased with an Irishman running his schools. He was Irish born himself, you know?'

'I dinna ken that, sir.'

'Indeed. He always referred to the way the Church of Ireland had ceded its schooling to the non-denominational system as what he wanted to achieve in New South Wales. So, tell me about your other son. Charles, was it, the priest?'

'So, it wasn't so bad, was it?' Mary Beth asked in the carriage as they headed for home.

'I'll admit I enjoyed myself,' Edward replied. 'It's all about the conversation, is it nay?'

'Well, you and Sir Anthony were certainly engrossed,' Mary Beth said, smiling. 'I felt quite abandoned.'

'Aye, that'll be the day, my dear. I saw ye flirting with that rich-looking old *dhuine*.'

Mary Beth leant into Edward's free arm, grabbing it as she laughed.

'The food was good too,' she said.

'And the wine, in case ye dinna notice.'

'Oh, yes. I noticed. So, tell me about your conversation anyway. What did you learn about New South Wales?'

'Well, Sir Anthony ken the former Governor, Bourke. He's the one who got Thomas to take on those new non-churched schools they're trying to set up there. He was nay surprised the church was less than impressed with the fact that a Catholic, Irish to boot, had sold his soul to the government.'

'Oh dear. The church can be so limited in its thinking, can't it? How *is* Thomas finding it all?'

'I ken it's been stressful but he's a strong, determined lad.'

'I wonder where he gets that from. And what about Charles? Any word from him lately?'

'Well, speaking of strong, determined lads. I ken it's even more difficult for him. An academic priest, English nay less, in a throng of non-academic Irish clergy. I ken he's finding it quite stressful. Apparently, his bishop is supportive, but he nay gets much from the rest of them. He's even talking about going to the bush, as they put it.'

'Oh dear, to go all that way and be unhappy.'

'Aye, but he's also a strong-willed lad and I'm certain he'll do well.'

'I'd so love to meet him again, and Thomas for the first time.'

'Aye, well I'm still hoping to go back there one day. And it'd nay be the same without ye there.'

'If you go, I'll go. You know that.'

'Aye, we just have a few things to sort out first, dinna we?'

'We do.'

Some weeks later, a message arrived from Percival to say that Jane was extremely unwell.

'Of course, you must go, darling,' Mary Beth said.

'I'll be back as soon as possible. And then…'

'I know, darling. Just go. Do what you must. Be back when you can.'

Again, Edward saw Sarah in Pemberton on the way home. He was shocked to see how she had aged in just a few months.

'Well, I *am* in my nineties, Edward. You must come to expect I'm not a spring chicken any longer.'

He watched her struggle out of the chair to bid him farewell.

'And neither are you, my boy. Think of that. Do what you must before it's too late. That's my advice.'

'Thank God you're here, Edward,' Percival said. 'Your wife has been quite balmy if you don't mind me saying so.'

'Why should I mind, Mr Towneley? Frankly, she's more your wife than mine these days.'

'Oh, good heavens. Surely you don't think.'

'Mr Towneley, I dinna ken and I dinna care. What's the problem ye needed me to come so far to sort out?'

'Well, some weeks ago, she began displaying strange moods. I mean stranger than normal.'

'Aye, well, I was going to say.'

'I know, I know. She's often been a little like this, but this has been worse than I've seen before. She began sleeping in extremely late. Most unlike her. Then she'd mope around the house in her nightwear. If I tried to say anything, she'd just shout at me. Incoherently. Often, I wouldn't know what she was talking about. Telling me she'd have her mother speak to me. Or Charles would come home and throw me out of the house. My own home, do you understand? After these outbursts, she'd just go quiet. Deathly quiet. Completely withdrawn. Not a word, sometimes for days.'

'Did ye call the doctor?'

'Indeed. He came several times. If she saw him coming, she'd lock herself in her room. Only once did he catch her. I had to physically restrain her while he examined her. He could find nothing wrong. He put it down to a mental disease, but he said he couldn't do anything about it. He gave me a bottle of medicine and told me to put some in her drink at night. I only did it once because the next day she was worse than ever.'

'So, what d'ye ken I can do then?'

'Well, she *is* your wife, despite what you might think. She's not my responsibility and, truly, I've had enough. I think she needs to go back to Tarleton House with you.'

Edward lowered his head. He shook it as he gathered his thoughts.

'After all these years, and ye taking advantage of her, ye want me to look after her because she's now an inconvenience. Is that it?'

'There's no need to use that tone, Edward. I believe Jane's arrangement and mine has been to our mutual benefit but I'm afraid her behaviour has rendered the situation untenable.'

'Untenable?' Edward scoffed. '*Untenable*. The hide of ye!'

'As I say, Edward, there's no need for this unpleasantness.'

'Unpleasantness?' Edward said, shaking his head again. 'Anyway, what if she'll nay come with me? What if she'll nay even talk to me? Let me in her room? What then? Will ye call the constable to remove her? Perhaps the King's Army?'

'Oh, don't be so dramatic, Edward. Of course, she'll talk to you. She talks about you all the time.'

'What? She talks about me *all the time*! What on earth d'ye mean, *dhuine*?'

'Edward, she's never stopped talking about you. Ever since she came here. She and Constance used to talk endlessly about you. How sad she was that you were so unhappy with her and how could she repair your broken relationship. Constance was good at that sort of thing. I'm not, of course, but Jane still tells me all sorts of things of that nature. I try to listen. I try to think of wise things to say. I try to think of what Constance might say but I can never remember what dear Constance would have said. She was so wise, you know?'

'Edward,' Jane screamed in apparent delight, racing towards him. 'Edward, you came back.'

'Of course, darling. I'm here. What's the matter with ye now?'

'Percival. He hates me. He's so cruel to me. He starves me and shouts at me. Please take me home, Edward. Please take me home.'

She threw her arms around him and clung more tightly than Edward could remember.

'Are ye *sure* ye want to come home? Ye've been so happy here – or so ye said.'

'No, I haven't. I've never said that. Don't you want me, Edward? Don't you want me?'

Jane began to howl. Edward stepped forward to hold her.

'Of course, darling. Of course. Let's pack up some things and we'll go home then.'

Back at Tarleton House, Edward pulled the sheets off the lounge-room chairs and sat Jane down in one of them.

'I'll just go and prepare yer room for ye,' he said.

'*Our* room?'

'Jane, we've nay shared a room for years. Even before ye went to live at Towneley Manor, we'd nay shared a room for years.'

'I don't remember that. Anyway, I want us together, Edward, like we used to be when we were happy.'

It was on the tip of Edward's tongue to say, *and when was that?*

'Alright, I'll prepare our room.'

'Thank you, darling Edward. You've always been so good to me.'

It was late so he pulled the cover sheets off the bed that Jane had used since the time she had said she wanted to sleep alone. He had no memory of how the bed even felt, whether it was hard or soft, comfortable, or not. He checked that the sheets and pillow slips were sufficiently clean.

'Come then, darling. The bed's ready for ye.'

'For *us*, Edward. For us. I want us to be together.'

'Of course, darling. Did ye want me to run ye a bath?'

'No, darling. I had a bath yesterday.'

Back in the bedroom, Jane pulled her nightwear out of one of the bags she had brought from the Towneley Manor. She prepared herself for bed.

'Aren't you coming to bed too, darling?' she said.

'Aye. I just have some things to do downstairs first.'

'Well, don't be up late, will you? I'm so looking forward to being with you tonight.'

By the time Edward came back upstairs, Jane was asleep. He slipped quietly into the bed next to her. He remembered then that he had always found this bed too soft. He could see the shape of Jane's face silhouetted against the sliver of moonlight shining through the shutters. It brought back memories. They were not all bad.

—⁂—

'Where am I?' Jane shouted, waking Edward some hours later. 'Where am I?'

Jane jumped out of the bed and ran towards the door.

'Jane, wait. Be careful, darling. Remember the stairs.'

Jane's hand was on the door handle. She stopped.

'What are you doing here, Edward? Where am I?'

'Ye're at Tarleton. Remember? Ye wanted to come back here.'

'No, I didn't. Where's Percival? What've you done with him?'

'Percival's fine. He's at his home. And ye're here because we all agreed it was best ye come home.'

Edward walked to her and took her by the arm.

'Now, come back to bed, darling. It's yer old bed, remember? It was always yer favourite.'

Edward walked her back towards the bed.

'I like this room.'

'Of course, ye do, darling. I designed it exactly as ye wanted it.'

He put her back to bed and covered her. He then walked around to his side of the bed.

'What are you doing, Edward?'

'Ye wanted me to sleep with ye, darling. D'ye nay remember?'

'Yes, I think so. That'll be nice. It's been so long.'

Edward settled into the bed, maintaining a safe distance. They lay together for several minutes in silence. Jane reached across and held his hand.

'Thank you, darling Edward. You've always been so good to me.'

XXXVII

Soon after Charles had left Thomas and Eliza's home, heading for Yass, Thomas received a message inviting him to Government House. It had been over two years since his meeting there with Governor Bourke. In that time, there had been little contact with the Governor's Office. Despite Rodney Kidd's reassurances, he continued to wonder if the new Governor, George Gipps, was as committed to non-denominational education as his predecessor.

Thomas turned up on the appointed day. He was ushered into the Governor's Office where Kidd, the colonial education legislator, was sitting opposite the Governor.

'Mr Lovat,' Kidd said. 'Delighted to renew your acquaintance.'
'Hello, Mr Kidd. How good to see ye again!'
'Mr Lovat, I don't believe you've met Governor Gipps.'
'No, I haven't. I'm delighted to meet you, Excellency.'
'Oh, too much formality,' Gipps said. 'It's Thomas, isn't it?'
'Yes, sir.'
'I've met your brother, Charles, the professor.'
'Yes, he mentioned he'd met ye, sir.'
'How is he? I understand he's chosen to have a spell in the outback.'

'He has, sir. He stayed with us a few weeks ago on his way to Goulburn and Yass.'

'My goodness, what a change for him. I dare say Bishop Polding would have been desperately unhappy to lose him from the seminary position. I know how much he was relying on him to lift the standards of clergy training. Such an impressive young man. You must be very proud of him.'

'Yes, sir. Indeed.'

'Thomas, Mr Kidd and I have been discussing the schooling situation. I know my predecessor commissioned you to set up the schools out towards the mountains. You do know why he chose that district, I presume.'

'Well, it's growing so quickly so I always assumed that was the reason.'

'Yes, that was certainly part of it, though I believe there were other reasons. I might get Mr Kidd to explain.'

'Certainly, Excellency. Thomas, Governor Bourke was having trouble convincing the churches about the benefits of non-denominational schooling. Some of the churches were especially hostile to the idea. The Presbyterians and Methodists and, at the time, a particularly fiery Church of England pastor…'

'Mr Marsden,' Thomas said.

'Ah, yes, of course. I'd forgotten you'd encountered our Mr Marsden. His bishop, Broughton, and the Catholic bishop, Polding, were always more amenable but I think a lot of their clergy were not so happy with the idea.'

'I can testify to that,' Thomas said. 'There's at least one Catholic priest who's refused even to speak with me since I accepted the Governor's position at Richmond.'

'Well, you see the problem then. Thomas, one of the main reasons your experimental school was established so far out was because the church schools are not so well established there. We could get in first, as it were. They're also a little more distant from the churches' powerbases here in Sydney.'

'I see.'

'But we're now keen to push the idea a little more under their nose, so to speak. Clearly, if the idea has merit, and we believe your highly successful operations at Richmond and Windsor show it does, then these schools must eventually be established closer to Sydney.'

'And that will involve going a little more head-to-head with the churches,' Gipps said.

'Precisely,' Kidd said. 'And that's why we wanted to call you in to speak with you about our plans.'

'And your role in them,' Gipps said. 'If you are happy with it all, of course.'

Thomas nodded.

'Thomas,' Kidd said. 'We'd like to appoint you as superintendent of schools with a brief to oversee all schools in the colony, government and church schools.'

Thomas wriggled in his chair, took a deep breath, and exhaled loudly.

'I take that as a sign of your acceptance,' Gipps laughed.

'Seriously, sir. Do ye think it possible? I mean the churches will fight ye, won't they?'

'Or fight you, Thomas,' Gipps said, replacing the laughter with a wry grin.

'I see.'

'Seriously, Thomas,' Kidd said. 'It's the only way we can see of education working as it should here, for all citizens, and as a leveller.'

'That's right, Thomas,' Gipps said. 'It's about what's best for education but also what's best for the colony and future nation if that's what it's to become. So long as the churches all educate their own lot in ghettos, we'll end up with a ghetto state, fractured, internally riven, like we've seen too much of in the world. Of all the visions your countryman, Richard Bourke, had for this place, I believe his vision of education to be the most important. You do follow me, don't you?'

'As God's my witness, sir. I saw the difference it made in Ireland and it's probably more important here.'

'Indeed, and the good news is that there *is* some important support among the churches. Bishop Polding most pronouncedly. He realises that the Catholic population can only benefit from being drawn into some form of equality with the rest. And, furthermore, that they will be the biggest losers if things go the other way. They'll forever be the convict class, the poor and dispossessed, those with fewer rights, less employment opportunities, a lowest caste virtually.'

'Not to mention seen as loyal to the pope rather than to Her Majesty,' Kidd said.

'Indeed,' Gipps replied.

Thomas nodded. He stared at the floor, gathering his thoughts. The two men watched him in silence. Thomas looked up and faced the Governor.

'And ye mention the Church of England bishop as well? Is he supportive?'

'I believe so. I'm told he had his hands tied somewhat when Marsden, I mean the Reverend Marsden, was around. I never knew this gent, but I gather he was a fierce segregationist. Church of England with a vehement Protestant streak. There are others like him who see it as their mission to form a Church of England here like no other. A particularly … what do they call it, Kidd?'

'Wesleyan.'

'Yes, Wesleyan kind of Church of England. After some chap called Wesley. What was his Christian name, Kidd?'

'John.'

'Yes, John Wesley. Does that mean anything to you, Thomas?'

'Not really, sir. My brother'd no doubt understand it.'

'Yes, well, it might be an idea to speak with him at some stage. They're a strange bunch. What I'd call wowsers. They don't drink or smoke or do anything smacking of a bit of fun. Quite humourless. And they truly believe this is what the Lord wanted. Well, I'm not an especially religious man but I don't see the Lord being that sort of character at all.'

'But Bishop Broughton is not like that, ye say?' Thomas said.

'No, I don't think so. Or if he is, he's being pushed to the sensible middle ground by the wowsers. I think frankly he has the same difficulties with some of his clergy that Bishop Polding has with the Irish. In both cases, these clergy are fiercely religious – in the worst sense, in my humble opinion. Sorry, if I'm speaking out of turn here, Thomas. I know you hail from Ireland.'

'Not at all, sir. I'm in agreement. And I know my brother would be too.'

'Oh, indeed,' Gipps said. 'He's one of the most normal clergymen I've met. So knowledgeable and sensible. Such a dignified, gentle man. And I sense it runs in the family. So, what do you say to my proposal then?'

'How can I refuse after that?' Thomas replied.

—⋘—

The rest of 1839 was especially busy for Thomas and Eliza. Thomas had to add the building and set-up of a new school and headmaster's house at Castle Hill to his ongoing responsibilities at Richmond and Windsor. His office at Castle Hill would serve as the interim superintendent's office as well. He would play the dual role as headmaster of the new school and superintendent until a new headmaster was appointed.

Eliza had to step up to take on more of the headteacher duties and Mary and John shared assistant head responsibilities. Elizabeth, Johannah and even young Thomas had to assume babysitting duties along with their studies.

Late that year, Thomas attended a meeting in Castle Hill with officials and prospective parents of the Hills district to speak about the Governor's plan for schools. It was held in the mayoral offices.

'I don't suppose ye'd be related to an Edward Lovat, sir,' the elderly, well-padded gentleman said to Thomas.

'My father's Edward. From Burnley. Do ye know him from back home?'

'No, I know him from here,' the man replied. 'I mean if it's him. Would he have been in New South Wales in '91, by any chance?'

'Yes, he was actually part of the Third Fleet, as they call it.'

'Well, well. That's amazing. I thought as I watched ye speak ye must be related. Ye look so much like him, though he was only very young at the time.'

'So, ye were part of the Third Fleet as well? On the *Gorgon* like Da?'

'Well, one could say that. But not on the *Gorgon*. The *Gorgon* was a naval vessel. I was on a convict ship.'

'As a...?'

'Convict!'

'Oh, I see. I'm sorry.'

'There's nought to be sorry for, sir. Half the colony were convicts at some stage.'

'What's yer name, sir, and how did ye meet my Da?'

'Forgive me. Bellamy's my name. William Bellamy. Yer father saved my life.'

At that point, an elderly woman and a striking middle-aged woman, infant on her hip, came up and stood next to Bellamy.

'It *is* him,' Bellamy said to the older woman. 'I mean it's his son, at least.'

'Well, we owe ye much then, sir,' the older woman said. 'Yer father saved my husband's life. He's so often talked about it.'

'Forgive me again, Mr Lovat. I'm so overwhelmed I'm forgetting my manners. This is my wife, Ann, my daughter, Sarah Clarke, and my granddaughter, Mary.'

'I'm so pleased to meet ye,' Thomas said, smiling at the infant, Mary, and rubbing her cheek with his finger. 'But please do tell me the story. How did my Da save yer life?'

'Yes, Pa. I'd like to hear this too,' Sarah said.

'Let's just say there was a time when it seemed to me that life was fairly pointless. It was after we arrived in port. Many of the crew and its passengers, all convicts, had died of the fever. I had it and was told I was probably going to die, along with a handful of others. Mr Lovat's father was put in charge of the small boat that was taking us from the ship to the quarantine base. And…'

Bellamy paused, looking at his daughter and granddaughter.

'And he decided to take matters into his own hands,' Ann said. 'As, of course, he would.'

'And it was Edward Lovat who risked his own life to bring me to my senses.'

'Pa. You've never told me that,' Sarah said. 'Oh, my God, you…?'

'Yes, I did, love. And that would've been that but for Edward Lovat diving in to save me.'

'Oh, Pa,' Sarah said, reaching out and holding his hand.

'I owe him my life,' Bellamy said. 'And he even came back several days later to check on me.'

'Well, as my mother says, we do owe yer Pa everything then,' Sarah said, looking up at Thomas. 'It seems I wouldn't be here speaking with ye otherwise.'

'Did he never tell ye that story?' Bellamy asked Thomas.

'I don't believe so, but I didn't see a great deal of my Da as I was growing up. Mind ye, he's not one to blow his own trumpet.'

'Indeed,' Bellamy said. 'That's exactly as I remember him. A good man who simply got on and did what he thought right. I recall the doctor saying to me afterwards that I was fortunate he was in charge that night. That not many of the officers would have risked their life for a convict, and one who was dying anyway.'

'Yes, he's a very special man,' Thomas said. 'I've only come to realise the extent of it lately. And thank ye so much for sharing the story. I'll tell him I've run into ye.'

'Oh, please do,' Bellamy said. 'And do pass on my very best wishes. He is well, I take it?'

'Yes, he is. Indeed, my brother and I are hopeful he might come out here soon.'

'Ye have a brother here as well?' Sarah asked.

'I do. He's a priest, in fact. He's just moved down to Yass as the parish priest.'

'Yass? I have some business interests down that way,' Bellamy said.

'What business are ye in, Mr Bellamy?'

'Agriculture, livestock and construction. I spent my misbegotten convict days learning wonderful new skills. Being sent here was without a doubt the best thing that ever happened to me. I'd have been as poor as a church mouse back home. I'll look up yer brother when I'm next down that way. What's his name?'

'Charles.'

'And please do tell yer father he'll be welcome at our place anytime should he make it back here.'

'I certainly will. He'll be most interested. So, why are ye here tonight anyway?'

'Two of my older children will be going to yer new school,' Sarah said. 'But I thought my Pa'd be interested in yer new venture. He's always going on about how divided our population is, so I knew this whole idea of schools for everyone'd appeal to him.'

'Well said, love,' Bellamy said. 'I think it's a grand plan and if I can help in any way, with advice or if ye need a donation, just let me know.'

'That's most kind,' Thomas replied.

'My husband is very careful with his money,' Ann said. 'So ye can take it as a compliment that he's opening his purse strings for ye.'

'Yes, I'm amazed to hear him being so generous so quickly,' Sarah said, resting her arm on her father's forearm.

'Well, as ye say, dear,' Bellamy said, placing his hand on top of his daughter's. 'I'm naturally inclined to the idea behind the school but knowing Edward Lovat's son's in charge of it makes me even more trusting it'll be a good thing.'

―⚬―

Early in the New Year of 1840, Thomas, Eliza, and the younger children moved into the almost completed schoolhouse in Castle Hill, ready for the start of the school year. Thomas was also beginning his tenure as superintendent of schools. The house was built in the same style as the one at Richmond, single storey, Sydney sandstone, with a wide veranda on three sides. But it was larger, with four bedrooms instead of two. Rodney Kidd had taken note of the cramped conditions when he visited the family in Richmond.

'Do ye like it, darling?' Thomas asked.

'It's lovely but…'

'I know. It needs the woman's touch.'

Mary and John stayed on in the Richmond house while finishing touches were made to the Castle Hill one. They assisted the two new headteachers at Richmond and Windsor get ready for the new year. When the Castle Hill house was completed, they moved in with the rest of the family.

'Are ye feeling at home now, Ma?' Mary asked.

'Yes, but I was hoping to get the curtains finished before school starts.'

'But we have blinds,' Thomas said. 'Do we really need curtains as well?'

Eliza and Mary glanced at each other and smiled.

―⚬―

'But ye're so good at teaching,' Eliza said to John.

'I know, Ma, but it's not what I really want to do.'

The family was enjoying Easter Dinner that year when John raised his doubts about his future.

'What do ye want to do then?' Thomas asked.

'I'd really like to turn my hand to farming.'

'I know ye've talked about that before,' Eliza said. 'But ye know nothing about it.'

'I know but I could learn. So many of the parents are on farms. Some of them have said they'd help out.'

'It costs a lot to set up a farm, ye know, John,' Thomas said. 'More than ye'll ever earn as a teacher.'

'I know, Da, and that's why I have to turn my hand to something else.'

'So, what do ye have in mind then?'

'Well, perhaps getting a job on a farm and learning the ropes or maybe working in a shop that services the farming district. I'll just be keeping my eyes out for any opportunity.'

'Alright then, boy,' Thomas said. 'We really don't want to force you to stay doing something you don't like but please stay on until the end of the year to give us time to arrange for someone to take your place.'

'Of course, Da.'

It was at a school meeting later that year that John was introduced to William and Ann Bellamy. He knew their daughter, Sarah, because he was teaching two of her children.

'My grandchildren adore ye, Mr Lovat,' Ann said.

'I concur,' Bellamy said, laughing. 'There's no use us contradicting Mr Lovat. Ye could tell them anything and they'd believe it.'

'Yes, my son's a fine teacher,' Thomas said. 'Unfortunately, he doesn't see it as something he wants to do forever.'

'Oh no,' Sarah said. 'Just as long as ye stay until my children move on. And Mary'll be starting in a couple of years too.'

Sarah and John exchanged a look and smiled.

'Don't say that, Sarah,' Bellamy said. 'Everyone has to find their own slot in life. What is it ye'd like to do, boy?'

'Farming has an appeal. I'm also interested in getting into a business of some sort. There's so many opportunities, it seems.'

'Indeed,' Bellamy said. 'It's the land of opportunities. Why don't ye come to dinner at our place and we can talk through some of those opportunities? Why don't ye *all* come? It'd be a delight to host the children and grandchildren of the man I owe it all to.'

Some weeks later, Thomas, Eliza and John visited the Bellamy homestead in Pennant Hills in Sydney's northern suburbs.

'That's the kind of farmhouse I dream of,' John said as the homestead came into view.

'Indeed,' Thomas replied. 'As Mr Bellamy himself said, it's unlikely he'd have ever lived in something like that back home.'

They were escorted up the few steps to a wide veranda that wrapped around four sides of the two-storey residence. They looked over their shoulders to see the sweeping plains of Pennant Hills stretching as far as the eye could see. They saw sheep to the right, cattle to the left, too many to count in the time they had. They stepped into a long hallway with a dark-timbered floor and papered walls of mixed hue. Hanging from the picture rails on both sides were imposing portraits of the family members. At the end of the hallway was a large room stretching the entire width of the home, lounges on one side and a long dining table on the other. The room had two fireplaces.

John was taking notes for future reference.

Sarah and her husband, Henry, joined her parents at the table. The seven diners shared a lively discussion taking in their varied experiences. Their trips from the British Isles on fever ships, the Lovats' experience on the *Lady Macnaghten* almost matched by the horrors of Bellamy's on the *Active*. Ann's trip on the *Marquis Cornwallis* was probably the best of them. They found out then that Ann came as a convict as well. In her case, the theft was of three loaves of bread for her starving siblings. It paled to insignificance compared with Bellamy's theft of six pairs of the best shoes.

'I might as well have stolen the bread as a bonus,' Bellamy laughed. 'It would've made no difference.'

'I agree,' Henry Clarke said. 'I was sent here for throwing stones at an officer. I might as well have given him a good whack, or even killed him.'

Henry's convict ship was the *Admiral Gambier*. It came via South America and its fame was for making the fastest passage from Rio de Janeiro to Sydney to that time.

There was talk of the various governors the Bellamys had experienced, the highs and lows of British authority.

'Macquarie was the best,' Bellamy said. 'Thank God for him. He cleaned out the rotten New South Wales Corps. I swear there was never a convict as crooked as most of them.'

'He was a Scot, was he not?' Thomas asked.

'Macquarie? Indeed, he was,' Bellamy replied. 'Even the Scots can turn out a good one from time to time.'

They laughed. The conversation turned to some of the Lovat Highland heritage. Bellamy remembered Edward's broad brogue.

'So, ye all have something of the rebel in ye then, don't ye?' Bellamy asked.

'Yes,' Thomas replied. 'I have it on both sides. My Ma was a Highlander as well.'

'It's a wonder ye didn't end up here in chains as well then,' Bellamy said, rollicking with laughter fuelled by an afternoon's worth of ale.

They spoke about the school situation, the battle between the government and the churches over who should control them. Bellamy took any opportunity to make mention of Edward.

'I do hope he makes it here. I'd so love to treat him to a dinner and thank him personally for his courage and his decency. Ye've no idea how decency stood out at the time.'

Bellamy paused to take another gulp of the ale.

'He made me feel I was worth something again.'

—⚏—

Sitting by the fire on the lounges, Bellamy finally asked the question that John had been waiting for throughout the meal.

'So, tell me again, young man, what are yer interests?'

John recounted what he had told him before.

'Well, I might have an opportunity for ye, if ye're of a mind to.'

Bellamy told of some of his friends and acquaintances who had been granted land in a thriving district called Greendale. There was as much wheat farming as could be managed and timber logging as well. The town centre was also growing and there were many opportunities for anyone who wanted to set up a store that might service the district's needs. Bellamy said he could introduce John to any number of people he knew out there.

'What d'ye reckon, Ma, Da?' John asked on the way home. 'Would ye be unhappy with me if I stopped teaching?'

'It's up to ye, son,' Eliza replied. 'Ye have to be happy in yer work.'

'Thanks, Ma? What about ye, Da?'

'Yer Ma's said it all. Just be sure, that's all. Ye mightn't like teaching but ye're so good at it, all the same. Ye don't want to give it away and then regret it.'

'I know but I could always go back to it.'

'So, what are ye thinking, anyway?' Eliza asked. 'I mean if ye did go to this Greendale place, what would ye want to do? Farming, logging or set up a store?'

'I don't know. It all sounds exciting. Perhaps starting with a store. As Mr Bellamy said, it's a good way to get to know the locals and work out what else I might do.'

'And get to build a house like the Bellamy's, eh, son?' Thomas said.

'Oh, yes. Perhaps by the time I'm a hundred.'

'Ye'd better make it before then if ye want us to live in it,' Eliza laughed.

John taught for another year with his mother and father. He saved whatever money he could, picking up extra work at nights and weekends. Most weekends, he was working in a general store in Penrith, owned by one of Bellamy's friends, Paul Birch. By the beginning of 1842, Birch had set up Greendale's first general store, with John as manager.

John lived in the back of the store. He worked seven long days a week, only occasionally going home for special occasions.

In time, he bought a plot of land a few miles down the road at a place called Wallacia. Like the Bellamy's land, it was ideal for dairy cattle and sheep, the kind of farming he eventually decided he wanted to do.

The land was also ideally placed for a farmhouse resembling the Bellamy one, even if not so grand.

XXXVIII

'Why doesn't Charles come to see me?' Jane asked.
'He's in New South Wales, darling,' Edward replied. 'Remember!'

'Wales is not so far. Why can't he come and see his mother? Doesn't he like me anymore?'

'It's nay Wales, dear. It's New South Wales. It's twelve thousand miles away, over the sea. It'd take months for him to come home and visit ye?'

'I don't understand. How can it take so long? I don't think he wants to come and visit me. I think he hates me. Do you hate me, Edward?'

'Nay, of course I dinna hate ye, darling.'

'I haven't been a good wife though, have I? And I'm not a good mother. If I was a good mother, God wouldn't have taken all my children from me. Why does God do things like that?'

Jane had these forlorn episodes most days. There was nothing Edward could do to console her. She never went out, even to Mass on Sundays. She did not receive visitors. Even Percival was turned away. Only Margaret and Mary Jane, by now eight years of age, were allowed visits. They gave Edward the only break in full-time care that had now become his role. In time, Margaret and Mary Jane moved into Tarleton House to help with the care of Jane.

—⚬⚬⚬—

'Are ye sure ye'll be alright here without me?' Edward asked Margaret.

'Of course, Da. You need the break. I'm not sure how you've coped alone all this time.'

'Thank ye, darling. Ye're a godsend,' Edward said, turning then to Mary Jane. 'And will ye be alright without me for a while, my dear wee lassie?'

'No, Papa. I don't want you to go.'

Mary Jane was Edward's delight and only consolation. She reminded him of the way he and Emma Jane had been, as much friends as father and daughter.

'Well, what if I promise to bring ye home something really braw?'

'As long as it's a pony,' Mary Jane replied.

'A pony? Only one?'

'No, seven!'

Edward laughed as he reached down and lifted Mary Jane into his arms.

'Ye're a funny lassie, are ye nay, my darling?'

'I'm not a lassie. That's a dog's name.'

'Oh, I ken ye were a wee doggie.'

'I'm not a doggie,' Mary Jane said.

She wrapped her arms around Edward's neck. He stood there a while as they hugged tightly.

'Oh, you two,' Margaret said. 'You should be on the stage.'

'She's my pride and joy, this one,' Edward said.

Margaret smiled as she gazed at her daughter, securely locked in Edward's arms.

'She *will* miss you. You do know, don't you?'

—⚘—

Edward travelled south to Pemberton. Sarah was still a healthy ninety plus year-old. She had a full-time nurse living in the house for her support.

'Darling Edward,' Sarah said. 'I've so been wondering how you've been coping. You don't say too much in your letters but I'm sure it must be a terrible strain, Jane being as she is.'

'Aye, I dinna ken the problem. The doctors just say it's a mental issue but they dinna ken what to do about it. *Keep her as calm as possible* is all they say.'

'And, so, you do?'

'Aye, for the most part. She only gets riled if I question her or, worse still, contradict her. There was this one time she was insisting young Edward come and see her immediately. She had something urgent to tell him. I tried to tell her calmly that he could nay come because he was dead. She just kept on insisting. It was as though she nay had any concept of being dead. In the end, I lost my temper a wee bit and said something like, *if I could raise him from the dead, dinna ye ken I'd do it?* I ken I said it louder than I should've but then she started shouting and throwing things at me.'

'Throwing things? Like what?'

'Anything she could lay her hands on. A ball of wool was the first thing because she had it on her lap. That nay got anywhere near me. Then it was a book and finally a vase. I had to duck out of the way of that one.'

'Oh, my heavens. Do you feel safe with her?'

'I ken so. It's only if I get agitated that she does things like that. The poor thing. It's just so sad, Sarah, seeing someone deteriorate like that. Her mind's fairly much gone.'

'Are there any good times?'

'Aye, occasionally, she seems quite *abheisteach*, normal almost.

She even speaks calmly about the bairns, the deceased ones and Charles. She seems to ken they're nay there anymore. Except for Charles. She finds it really hard to understand that he's alive but he canna visit. That he's too far away.'

'Oh dear, I'm so sad for you. So, what are you going to do?'

'What can I do?'

'Yes, I suppose. And what about Mary Beth? Does she know all this? Does she understand?'

'Ye ken Mary Beth. She always understands. I've nay ever ken a woman like her. Except for ye, of course, Sarah. She just understands, has the patience of a saint. She just waits. I dinna ken why.'

'I think you know why, Edward. She loves you. She *truly* loves you. If anyone has ever proven that…'

'Aye, I can scarcely believe it. How strong can love be? Surely there's a limit.'

'Perhaps, Edward. Or perhaps not. *Love conquers all*, they say. I think I believe that. I think I *know* it.

They sat in silence. Edward could see the glazed look in Sarah's eyes as she stared out the window. She looked around and smiled at him.

'You see, I think I knew that kind of love for your father. It was a little like a disease. It hurt so much. At times, made me positively ill, just like a sickness. Except it's one you don't really want a cure for. You wouldn't know what to do without it. I think that's the way Mary Beth loves you. And if that's so, then she'll wait. Wait until the sun freezes over.'

I dinna ken for sure but that's a wee bit like I felt for Amy. It was all so short I ken it was nay tested like yer love for Da or Mary Beth's for me. But that feeling ye'd do anything for someone. Ye'd stand single-handed in front of an army to protect them. That's what I remember. That's how I felt for Amy.'

'But never for Jane? I'm sorry, I don't mean to pry too much.'

'Sarah, ye could nay ever pry. Ye ken me better than anyone and I appreciate it more than I can say that I can talk about these things. Clear my muddled head. Nay, I dinna ken I ever felt like that about Jane. And ye see, that's probably where all the trouble started. She always ken my mind'd be on Amy when I was with her. She was nay always right but sometimes she was *spot air*. She was right. Oh, my Laird, the poor *cailin*.'

'Don't punish yourself too much, dear boy. It takes two to make a marriage work. And it sounds to me as though Jane was as much to blame as you. And then there was her mother.'

'Aye, and so we just go around and around, dinna we? Around and around but nay ever go forward, get out of the rut.'

'That's true. There's no use going over it too much. We are where we are. And we all have to try and make the best of it. So, what are you going to tell Mary Beth, then?'

—⚉—

A few days later, Edward was in Highgate with Mary Beth. She rushed down the stairs from the veranda and they held each other. They did not move or speak for several minutes.

'I'm sorry…'

'No. I don't want to hear it, Edward. You're here. That's all that matters. You're here.'

They walked into the house, arm in arm. They left the luggage in the foyer and went straight to the chaise in the sitting room. It was now frayed in several places.

'It's looking a wee bit the worse for wear,' Edward said, rubbing his fingers over a frayed piece of material on one of the arms.

'I'll never get rid of it,' Mary Beth replied. 'While ever two bits of the frame hold together. It knows too much.'

'Aye, it ken more than me,' Edward laughed.

'Yes, it's a wise old chair. Carl wanted to dispose of it a few times. I could never tell him quite why I couldn't let that happen. Now, I don't need to explain. I just know they'll carry me out of the house before this ever goes. Way too many memories.'

'Mainly good ones, I hope' Edward said.

'They're all good, my darling. They're *all* good.'

They sat together, as they had on so many occasions, Mary Beth's head cradled on Edward's shoulder. His right arm was around her back, his left one holding her cheek.

'So, let me explain,' Edward said.

'Only if you want to, darling. Only if you want to. Remember, I ask no more than that you're here … whenever you can be here. And even if you can't be here; that's alright too. Just always know I love you. That's all I ask.'

'What on earth have I ever done to deserve ye?' Edward asked. 'What?'

'Nothing, darling. That's not what love's about. There's no deserving. Love is love. It's free. And mine is yours.'

Edward sat in silence, pressing her closer to him.

'And if it's free, as I say, then I can't be asking anything of you. I never have; or at least I've tried never to. And I ask nothing of you now. I know what you're facing. And I can only love you for your loyalty and devotion and your nobleness. You're the man I fell in love with all those years ago. Even when I had no right to. When every civil standard said I shouldn't. I loved you then for who you are. And you're still that man. That's why you're doing what you're doing, and I understand that.'

'I dinna ken what to say.'

'You don't have to say anything. Unless it helps. Of course, I'll listen. I love listening to you. But don't feel you have to explain anything to me because you don't.'

'I just feel I've such a wee bit to offer ye. Oh, Laird. There's so much I wanted to give ye. When I left here last time, I ken what I was going to do. I ken Jane was settled with Percival. That's where she wanted to be. So, she'd be happy for me to be here, or in New South Wales. She'd nay care. It'd just be formalising what's been obvious for a long time. But then…'

'I know, darling. I know. I know. I know. Don't punish yourself.'

'That's what Sarah said … just a few days ago. Dinna punish yerself. Is that how I seem? A self-punisher?'

'Frankly, yes. You just try so hard to do the right thing, Edward. Others can slip and slide with the right thing. Most people are like that. But with you, the right thing is an unbending rod.'

'Oh, Laird. Then let me bend a wee bit.'

'But you can't, darling. You can't. And I wouldn't want you to try.'

'But what about ye? What about our plans? New South Wales and all that?'

'Oh, New South Wales doesn't matter. Except for you, of course. I know you'd love to see the boys again. And if you do ever go, I'd love to be there with you, if you wanted me there.'

'I'd want ye there, dinna fear. I'd want ye there.'

'Then perhaps it *will* happen. Who can know?'

'How long would ye wait, though? How long can ye possibly wait when things are so up in the air?'

'For you, Edward, I will wait until the sun freezes over.'

'Sarah said that too … about ye, I ken.'

Ten days later, Edward was back at Tarleton House. Mary Jane ran out to greet him. She jumped up into his arms.

'Where's the seven ponies, Papa?' she asked.

'I could nay find seven for ye, lassie, but I did get ye two very special ones.'

They went inside. Edward fossicked in his bag while Mary Jane watched.

'Two ponies in your bag?' she said.

'Well, two very special ones, remember.'

Edward pulled a rag donkey out of his bag.

'Here's one of them,' he said as he handed it to her.

'It's a donkey.'

'Oh, nay. I ken it was a pony. I'll have to take it back.'

'No, I want it.'

'Oh, alright then. And I've another one here.'

He pulled a small, wrapped parcel out of his bag. Mary Jane took it and unwrapped it. Her eyes widened.

'It's beautiful, Papa.'

'Oh, I'll be so happy if ye like it. Here, let me pin it on.'

Edward unclipped the pin and attached to Mary Jane's dress a sparkling brooch in the shape of a pony.

'You do spoil her, Pa,' Margaret said. 'Now, what do you say to Papa, Mary Jane?'

'Thank you, Papa.'

'That's alright, my darling lassie.'

'I'm not a doggie,' Mary Jane said, her smirk widening and her eyes beaming.

It was in the second month of 1841 that Edward received the message that Sarah had died suddenly in her sleep. She had been found by the nurse when she went to tend to her in the morning.

He arranged to have her remains brought to the Catholic chapel on the Towneley Estate so she could be buried where she had chosen, with her husband and sister. The execrable Father Wallace conducted the short service. He had not asked about Sarah's "practicality", though Edward had decided he would lie about it if he had to. Wallace and Edward studiously avoided eye contact throughout the ceremony.

While there, he arranged with the headstone maker to have Sarah's name added to the stone already in place.

> SACRED TO THE MEMORY
> ELIZA CATHERINE LOVAT
> BELOVED WIFE OF THOMAS

And mother of Edward
29ᵀᴴ day of January 1776
Aged 26 years
Requiescat in Pace

And her beloved husband
Thomas Edward Fraser Lovat
26ᵀᴴ day of January 1801
Aged 54 years
Requiescat in Pace

And his second wife and sister of the
above-mentioned Eliza
Sarah Margaret Lovat
11ᵀᴴ day of February 1841
Aged 93 years
Requiescat in Pace

This task reminded him that he had to arrange for a permanent stone to be placed on the grave of his three children, all resting in St Peter's Church of England graveyard.

—⁂—

Edward travelled from the funeral to Pemberton. He had owned the house there since his father had bequeathed it to him. Now that Sarah was gone, he would have to decide what to do with it.

'So, did she suffer at all?' Edward asked the lady who had nursed Sarah.

'No, sir. I don't believe she'd have known anything. She seemed perfectly alright that night. She bade me goodnight in her normal gracious way and said she'd see me in the morning. *Man proposes; God disposes*, as they say.'

'Indeed, he does. Indeed, he does.'

'She did say that if this ever happened unexpectedly, she had written you a letter and to make sure you received it.'

Dear Edward,

If you are reading this, it means I've gone to join your father. Please don't think of mourning for me in that circumstance. If I'm with your father, there is nothing to mourn for. I will be happy again, in a way that has forsaken me ever since his passing those many years ago. For forty years, I've lived without the love of my life. That's enough for anyone.

Edward, I've said this to your face many times, but I now want to say it in a way that you can keep in a drawer. You are such a special man. So courageous, loyal, and forthright. You do not bend and that is your strength and what makes you so worthy of love. It is also your lifelong challenge. You do not bend, whatever the temptation, and that is so noble but so difficult. Your current situation would be beyond what most men could endure but you have endured it. Just be careful to look after yourself, dear. Sometimes, a little bending is necessary. Take it from one who knows, especially if it is bending towards the kind of love that we all need to survive in this cruel world. Take time for yourself, even amidst your loyalty and care of others. I know I don't need to spell things out any further than this. You will know what I mean.

All my love, dearest boy. You were your father's most precious gift and you have been mine as well.

Farewell, Sarah.

The tears were rolling down Edward's cheeks as he read the letter.

He stayed several days at Pemberton. He contemplated whether he should bring Jane here, to get her away from a place so associated with their grief.

Edward had planned to keep heading south to visit Mary Beth when he received a message that Jane had taken a turn for the worse. He rushed back to Tarleton House.

'I don't think it's safe for us here anymore, Pa,' Margaret said. 'Mary Jane's quite frightened of her.'

'I understand, dear. I'd nay ever forgive myself if something happened to her. Or to ye.'

'Or to you, Pa.'

'Oh, I'll be alright. But where will ye go?'

'I'm not sure. My parents have moved to London but most of my friends, and Mary Jane's, are still in the district.'

'Perhaps I have a solution.'

Over the next few weeks, Margaret and Mary Jane re-located to Pemberton. Edward joined them whenever he could. He hoped to get down to Mary Beth at some point but, with Margaret and Mary Jane out of the house, he was managing Jane on his own.

'Sir, please don't be upset when I say you shouldn't be surprised if she doesn't make old bones.'

The doctor was giving Edward an update on Jane's condition.

'What do ye mean? Are ye telling me she's dying?'

'We just don't know but I've seen this kind of thing before. You see, the body and the mind are more connected than we've often supposed. So, when the mind is as affected as this, it often points to problems with the body as well, even if we can't detect exactly what they might be. I'm not saying she's going to die tonight. I'm just saying you need to be prepared.'

Edward had arranged for a nurse to stay with Jane for the day. He needed to ride into Burnley to meet with the manager of St Peter's graveyard about the new headstone for the family grave. Afterwards, he had lunch with Horace Thurlow, still the minister in charge of the church there.

'How is Mrs Lovat?'

'Just the same, Horace. Well, nay, she's worse if the truth be ken.'

'I'm sorry to hear that. What do the doctors say?'

'They really dinna ken the nature of her mental state, except they say she seems to be deteriorating at a faster rate than expected.'

'Is it a fatal condition, do they know?'

'Not as such, apparently. But one of the doctors was telling me recently that the worse it gets, the more I should be ready for it. Death, that is.'

'Oh, I'm so sorry. That must be such a strain. All the same if I might say, it could be a relief, I suppose.'

Edward said nothing.

'I'm sorry, Edward, that was out of turn.'

'Nay, Horace. Nay at all. I ken what ye're saying but I canna help feeling guilty when I say it … or even ken it. Why's that, then? Ye should understand guilt and all that.'

'I'm not sure I understand it better than the next man, to be truthful. I think it's all about the complexities of love. Love's never straightforward, is it? It's certainly not just about the romance, the feelings. All the things the young tend to think. Saint Paul has some interesting words about it. It's patient and kind. No boasting. Doesn't look to the self. Keeps no record of wrongs.'

'Mm. And here was I expecting a lifetime of romance,' Edward laughed. 'Why dinna they tell us these things when we're young?'

'I suppose because it'd spoil all the fun,' Horace replied, smiling. 'Imagine being young and realistic. No dreams.'

'No delusions,' Edward said.

'Indeed, anyway, did you settle things with Mr Hort, the headstone maker?'

'Yes, I did,' Edward replied. 'He'll have the new one ready by the end of the month.'

On the way home from St Peter's, Edward felt that pain in his left arm that had been coming and going for some months now. He had intended to consult a doctor about it but once it subsided, he would forget about it. He was confident it would be the same today.

He was trying to find the deep breath that often made the pain go away. He slowed the horse and alighted, moving to the side of the road to sit on a rock. He would rest there until he felt better.

He knew this could not be the end. There were too many things to look forward to. He slid off the rock and lay his head on the cool grass. It helped to soothe the pain. He felt very tired, as though he would drift off to sleep. He saw Mary Beth and himself on the clipper heading to New South Wales, Charles and Thomas waving from the dock in Sydney. Mary Beth was holding his hand, smiling. He turned his head.

Amy!

—⚊—

A passer-by found Edward lying where he had lain himself down. There were no signs of bodily injury, so the doctor put it down to a heart attack. The only doubt about the cause came from Edward's expression offering no hint of the pain that would normally accompany such an attack. It was as though he was just dozing, a tiny but unmistakeable smile on his face.

XXXIX

The letter was almost five months old by the time Charles received it in late July. He read it just after reading a letter from Edward himself, assuring him of his continued good health. He had recognised Margaret's writing on the other envelope but assumed it was no more than her regular newsy letter.

Dear Charles,

It is my saddest duty to inform you that your father died three days ago. He was found by a passer-by on the road from Burnley. He had apparently suffered a massive heart attack. It is tragic news. It has impacted on little Mary Jane especially hard. She adored her Papa so much. It has saddened me immensely too. I dare say no more than it will you.

I have tried to tell your mother, but she does not seem able to take it in. She is extremely unwell and seems to be getting worse by the day. You might have known that Mary Jane and I have been living in Pemberton for the past few weeks. Life at Tarleton became more difficult by the day and Mary Jane was not coping well with some of your mother's behaviour. I am sorry to be so frank at a time like *this, but I feel it is important for you to know what your father has been dealing with these past couple of years. He has been so strong with no real rewards coming his way. I do not know how he has survived but he has been a figure of constant and enormous strength and forbearance. As the Reverend Thurlow said at his funeral, he has been an inspiration to us all.*

I gather you will know from my reference to the Reverend that your father was buried with his three children at St Peter's in Burnley. I think you know that was his preferred burial site and I do hope you are content with that idea. I'm so sorry again to be the bearer of this unbearable news.

Your loving sister-in-law and niece, Margaret, and Mary Jane.

PS. I trust you will let your brother know. I'm not sure he will find out in any other way, although I mean to write to Father Prendiville in Ireland to inform him.

PPS. Please be assured that Mary Jane and I will stay with your mother so long as we are needed. Ironically, she seems to want to remain at Tarleton House.

'Oh, Lord no,' Charles said, slumping in his chair.

'Are ye alright, Father?' young Father McGrath asked.

'My Pa. He's died.'

'Oh, Father, I'm so sorry. Is there anything I can do?'

Charles took a moment to catch his breath. He took his kerchief from his pocket and rubbed his eyes.

'Can I get ye a cup of tea, Father?' McGrath asked.

'Thank you, Father. That would be kind.'

McGrath called to the housekeeper.

'Mrs Hennessy, could ye get Father a cup of tea and a biscuit? He's just had some sad news from home. His father's died.'

'Oh, *Farder*,' Mrs Hennessy said as she fussed around. 'Can I get ye anyt'in'?'

'Just a cuppa, Mrs Hennessy,' McGrath said.

'Yes, of course, *Farder*. I'm sorry, *Farder*. And I'll get ye a piece o' cake too. I t'ink dere's some cake left. If not, I'll run next door to Mrs Grieves. She's always got some cake in de tin. Will dat be alright, *Farder*?'

'Thank you, Mrs Hennessy,' Charles said.

'Just the cup of tea, Mrs Hennessy,' McGrath said again.

'Yes, of course. Of course.'

Mrs Hennessy rushed out in a flap.

'Father, I'm sorry to ask this of you as I know I've been away for a few weeks.'

'Anything, Father. Anything at all,' McGrath said.

'Father, I need to get to my brother. I'm not sure he knows yet. Which is awful because my father died in March.'

'Of course, Father, but I worry about ye in this weather. The Murrumbidgee's close to bursting its banks, they say, and it's going to affect all the river systems.'

'All the more reason for me to get there quickly. Would you mind taking the Masses on Sunday? I know that's asking a lot.'

'Not at all, Father. But should I try and find someone to go with ye?'

'No, thank you, Father. I really do travel faster on my own.'

'Well, ye've certainly had much practice.'

It was the 1st day of August when Charles rode up to the schoolhouse in Castle Hill. Thomas saw him through the window of his office. He ran out to meet him.

'Charles, what on earth are ye doing here? In this weather of all things.'

'I'm sorry to come unannounced, Thomas, but I need to speak with you.'

Thomas helped his sodden brother into the house.

'Come and I'll get ye a change of clothes and a cup of tea.'

'Thanks, Thomas, but before you do, I just need to let you know some sad news.'

Thomas stopped and looked into his brother's eyes.

'It's Da.'

'Yes, I'm so sorry. He died in March. I only found out this week and came straight here.'

Thomas stood as if nailed to the floor. He lowered his head. He raised his hand to his chest.

'Are you alright?' Charles asked.

'Yes. It's just such a shock. We only just received a letter from him. He sounded so well. Except for the worry of yer poor Ma, of course.'

'Yes, I had one too, possibly written about the same time. It was in the same pile as Margaret's telling me of his fate. She said he was found by the side of the road from Burnley to home.'

'So, was it the horse? Surely not! He was such a good rider.'

'I don't have all the details, but Margaret said they thought he'd had a heart attack. I agree it'd be hard to imagine him being thrown from a horse. Me, on the other hand. I mean I've fallen as often as ridden these past months.'

The two men took some relief in a moment of restrained laughter.

'We've missed ye so much, Charles. How long can ye stay?'

'I really need to be back in Yass next Sunday. Dear Father McGrath has been filling in for me now for a month or more. I'd like to say a Mass for our Pa, with you all present if possible. It seems the least we can do from this distance.'

'By all means. I'll contact Father Kennedy in Parramatta to arrange it. Would the day after tomorrow be too late?'

'That'd be good.'

'That will give me tomorrow to make some arrangements at the school and there's someone I want ye to meet. Someone who needs to know about Da.'

On the 3rd of August, another miserably wet winter's day, Charles celebrated a memorial Mass in St Patrick's church, Parramatta. Father Kennedy was there to greet the mourners. Thomas, Eliza, and family were in attendance, as were several of the school children and teachers. Charles was putting on his robes in a small room to one side when he noticed someone out of the corner of his eye.

'John? What on earth?'

'Hello, Charles,' Polding said. 'My sincerest condolences.'

'Thank you, My Lord, but how did you know?'

'Father McGrath got a message to me. He was worried about you, as would I have been if I'd known you were travelling in this weather.'

'But how did you know I'd be here?'

'Oh, I have my spies, Charles. Any bishop worth his salt does.'

'You honour me, John. Thank you for being here.'

'Anything, Charles. Anything.'

'Now, should you be celebrating? Isn't it customary for the bishop to officiate?'

'Charles, I'm here as a guest. This is your moment to honour your father. I'll just take a seat somewhere on the sanctuary.'

At that moment, Father Kennedy rushed into the room, flustered.

'My Lord, I had no idea. Do ye need vestments?'

'No, Father, I'll be fine. Just find me a seat somewhere.'

'I'm sorry we don't have a bishop's throne, My Lord.'

'I'm sure I'll survive without one, Father. It's good for the soul to be dethroned from time to time.'

Polding looked at Charles and winked. Charles smiled. Kennedy rushed outside to find a suitable seat for the bishop.

'Thank you for being here. We're remembering today and praying for the repose of the soul of my father, also the father of my brother here, Thomas, father-in-law to Eliza and grandfather to Mary, John, Elizabeth, Johannah, Thomas, James, and Joseph.

Our father was born in Lancashire but was a Highlander in

spirit. His own father was born on the last day of the Scottish Uprising known as the Jacobite Rebellion. He was born just down the road from Culloden, near Inverness, where the Scottish Army made its last stand. Thomas's father, and mine, inherited much of that fighting spirit. English-born but Scottish in his heart. And not just Scottish. He would chide anyone who referred to his Scottish heritage. "Nay, I'm a Highlander", he would say.'

The congregation chuckled.

'Our father lived a full life. He travelled to Persia as a young man, accompanying his own father who had himself travelled there when young. His own father, our grandfather, had married a Persian woman. They were only married a short time when she was killed but her influence lived on in him, and in our father. We grew up hearing the name "Mahdiya" often mentioned. She was apparently extremely wise and cultured. Through the story of Mahdiya, we grew up to understand that God's ways are not our ways. God works where he will in different ways through many different peoples. Our father used to say that if we want to understand God, we must learn to respect all the peoples of the earth, their different cultures, their different religions and beliefs.'

Father Kennedy was sitting in the front row watching his bishop's reaction. Others in the congregation wondered how a Catholic bishop would react to ideas about tolerance of non-Catholic beliefs. Polding sat motionless, except for the occasional nod that suggested he approved. Kennedy relaxed.

'Our father later joined the Royal Navy and was on one of the first fleets to sail to New South Wales. He spoke often of the many people he met on his travels, some who became lifetime friends. He was as comfortable with the aboriginal people or the convicts as he was with his fellow officers. Perhaps he was more comfortable with them, in fact. That was his Highland spirit, you understand.

Our father was challenged with many vicissitudes throughout his life, including the death of his first wife, my brother's mother, and the most-untimely deaths of three of his children, our sister and two brothers. More recently, he has been coping with the severe illness of *his current wife, my mother. As my sister-in-law said in the letter that she wrote informing me of his death, he was ever loyal, steadfast, and forthright. He knew the right and he followed it, regardless of the cost. He was everyman's friend but no-one's fool. His soul was sold to no-one. His heart he gave freely to those he loved.*

We honour him today. We will miss you, Pa/Da/Papa/Grand Da, but we are ever grateful for the time God gave you to be with us. In the name ....'

Mary was weeping freely. John sat upright, a ribbon of steel in his back. He felt a pride in a grandfather he remembered kindly but had known too little about. The words he heard that day would come to shape the rest of his life.

'Charles, I'd like ye to meet someone very special,' Thomas said after Mass. 'Someone to whom I owe a great deal. This is Mr William Bellamy.'

'Not anywhere near as much as I owe to yer father, Father Charles.'

'Mr Bellamy. Thomas has told me all about your kindness to him. And about my father saving your life. What a wonderful story.'

'What a wonderful man. Yer sermon captured his spirit. I didn't have the pleasure to know him but briefly, but he changed my life all the same. Indeed, he gave me my life back. I was ready to give up, but he wouldn't let me go.'

'Thank you so much for being here with us.'

'I wouldn't have missed it. Mind ye, I'll have some explaining to do to my Methodist minister next Sunday,' Bellamy laughed. 'But I wouldn't have missed it.'

'I don't think Reverend Ballymore would dare contradict ye, Pa,' Sarah Clarke said as she joined the group. 'He wouldn't want to see his weekly collection shrink as it would if ye withheld.'

'Father Charles, this is my daughter, Sarah. Thank yer lucky stars ye don't have a daughter, like this one, to keep ye in check.'

Charles looked at Sarah and smiled. He wondered for a short moment what that would be like.

XL

Margaret and Mary Jane would visit the grave every Sunday after attending the service at St Peter's. On her occasional better days, Jane would accompany them to the service, much to Percival's disgust. Margaret would tell her parents how unusually serene Jane would be on those occasions. Over the grave, after the service, she would stand and stare, her eyes vacant.

'Time to go, Gran,' Mary Jane said one day when it seemed Jane would stay forever.

Jane stood, fixed to the spot.

'Would you like to be here one day?' Margaret asked.

'Yes.'

Margaret and Mary Jane recounted the event after Jane died and some pressure was coming from Percival and Father Wallace to have her buried on the Towneley Estate.

'I'm certain she'd want to be with her mother,' Percival said. 'She was quite estranged from her husband in the end.'

'Her husband was the one who looked after her to the end, sir,' Margaret shot back.

The matter ended up before a magistrate. Percival was supported by Father Wallace and Margaret by the Reverend Horace Thurlow.

'What do *you* think should happen, young lady?' the magistrate asked Mary Jane.

'Gran should be with Papa and my Pa.'

'Indeed, as it should be. Mrs Lovat should be buried with her own family.'

Margaret arranged for a new headstone to be set in place.

>
> JESU MERCY
> OF YOUR CHARITY PRAY FOR THE SOULS OF
> +EDWARD LOVAT
> WHO DEPARTED THIS LIFE ON THE 13TH OF
> MARCH 1841
> AGED 65 YEARS
>
> +& OF JANE LOVAT, HIS WIFE
> WHO DEPARTED THIS LIFE ON THE 13TH OF
> APRIL 1845
> AGED 67 YEARS
>
> +& OF EMMA JANE LOVAT, THEIR DAUGHTER
> WHO DEPARTED THIS LIFE ON THE 2ND OF
> JULY 1824
> AGED 19 YEARS
>
> +& OF WILLIAM LOVAT, THEIR SON
> WHO DEPARTED THIS LIFE ON THE 24TH OF
> JANUARY 1835
> AGED 33 YEARS
>
> +& OF EDWARD LOVAT, THEIR SON
> WHO DEPARTED THIS LIFE ON THE 6TH OF
> JANUARY 1838
> AGED 32 YEARS

On whose souls may the Lord have mercy
Through thy Cross & Passion
O Jesu, deliver them

For almost a quarter of a century, Mary Beth came from London to visit the grave each year. It would be as close to Edward's birthday as the weather allowed. She had discovered a small estate on the road from Preston that sold exotic plants and flowers, including some from the great southern land. After a visit from Mary Beth, people would note and often comment on the unusually rich hue of the flowers on the Lovat grave.

Mary Beth would stand for hours by the grave. In her later years, her driver would set her up on a chair and wait, sometimes until dusk, until she was ready to leave. She would speak with Edward, just as they had on the chaise by the fire, sometimes quite loudly so people would stare. She would ponder on what might have been. She never married again.

―⁂―

Margaret and Mary Jane moved to Glasgow in 1848 for Mary Jane's schooling. In the same year, Horace Thurlow was appointed Dean of the Cathedral in Lancaster. So, when a new curator was writing a short history about the families in the graveyard, he was referred to Percival as the one in the district who knew the Lovats best. The curator recorded the following.

When gravestones and memories meet, we may expect a tale that may be of some interest to a few. It will be noted by those interested in local history that there is no mention here of Charles Lovat, the son, whose letters written from Rome in 1823 were printed by Thomas Sutcliffe, the old Burnley printer, and copies are still prized by local collectors.

Charles Lovat was not interred with the rest of the family. After returning from Rome where he had been educated for a priest, he went to serve as a missionary to one of the more distant English colonies and had since been dead to the world, even to his own family who did not long survive his departure for the colonies

... the record is a sad one to those who knew it, a very sad one! Jesu Mercy! How did the Catholic formula get into the Protestant church yard? What were the authorities doing to allow it to pass? We have other records – old letters – painful and pleasant and pitiful enough to read now, and memories not carven on gravestones that will pass away with the hearts on which they were written.

XLI

Charles spent another eight years as parish priest of Yass, with responsibilities stretching south even to the adjoining colony of Victoria. He finished the church, built a school and convent, and continued to travel as he had chosen. In the end, he spent more of his life in the rough saddle than the Chair of Theology where he had begun. He preferred it that way.

As he approached his fiftieth year, his health came against him. He was transferred to Liverpool, by then an almost urban parish, for a life judged more suited to his age and state of wellbeing. It was not his choice. He would have preferred to die in the saddle. He nonetheless gave sterling service until his death on the 20th day of June 1858. It is written that his funeral was attended by people of all faiths and those of none, an unusual event at a Catholic priest's passing. It is also recorded that the Ngunnawal people held a funerary ritual in the grounds of the church at Yass. A hollowed log was left as a mark of their respect for a man who attempted to bridge the cultures.

Charles was buried in the Devonshire Street cemetery on the western outskirts of Sydney City. Some years later, all the graves were removed to make way for Central Station, the city's main railway terminus. His grave was moved to the Catholic section of Rookwood Cemetery, halfway between Sydney and Liverpool. A new headstone, matching the others in the priests' portion, was struck.

In Memoriam
Ad Rev. Caroli Lovat
Dec qui ab hac luce migravit
Die 20 Junii AD 1858

Some years after his death, a bell was placed in the church tower at Yass. It became known as "Father Lovat's Bell", a tribute to the first parish priest. Father Hartigan, the priest biographer, grew up in the Yass district. He wrote in his book, *The Men of '38*, many years later.

The name of this holy priest is still remembered and revered in the hearts of the people and is ever associated by them with all that is saintly and good. They spoke of him as the gentle Father Lovat, the scholarly Father Lovat, the saintly Father Lovat. A splendid tribute to a Minister of God. Gentlemanliness, scholarship, sanctity bestowed by popular acclaim.

It was the regret of both Charles and Thomas that they saw so little of each other in the years after their father's death. During his time in Yass, Charles was away for three weeks out of every four. Even when his niece, Elizabeth, travelled to Yass for her wedding in 1847, it was conducted by Father McGrath because Charles was working his way along the Murray River, hundreds of miles to the south. When he came to Liverpool, he was infirmed for much of the time and rarely travelled.

Meanwhile, Thomas and Eliza spent most of this period living in Balmain, close to the heart of the city and near to the Office of the Superintendent of Schools. In 1849, the experimental non-denominational school system became by law the early form of New South Wales Public Education. Bourke's and Gipps' dream passed into reality.

In 1856, Thomas retired from his government post. He spent his retirement years helping to establish several Catholic schools that remained outside the government system. Father McEncroe finally had his way.

Thomas' and Eliza's eldest daughter, Mary, became a nurse and worked mainly in the Hills district. She never married. She lived to a grand age, at some point changing her name by deed poll to "Hawkins". She arranged to be buried with her beloved James whose remains had been moved to Waverley cemetery on the cliffs overlooking the Pacific Ocean.

Elizabeth married Colin McLaren and settled in the district around Yass. They had three children. Johannah married James McCooey from Greendale. She died childless at the age of twenty-six, predeceasing both her parents. Young Thomas also predeceased his parents, dying unmarried at twenty-eight years of age. James, the infant on the *Lady Macnaghten* that Dr Hawkins had judged to be "extremely delicate" and most prone to succumbing to the fever, married Maria Byrne, had ten children and would live well into the following century. Joseph John, the one Australian born child, lived almost to his eightieth year.

Thomas' and Eliza's eldest son, John, eventually took over the ownership of the general store in Greendale, making enough money to build his dream farmhouse on the land at Wallacia. Thomas helped oversee the building and contributed to the labour. He and Eliza lived there in their retirement years. The one time that Thomas and Charles met in those years was when Charles came out from Liverpool to bless the new home.

'John's been asking me what we should name the home,' Thomas said to his brother. 'We'd like somehow to honour Da.

We'd tossed up Tralee but that cuts ye out. Burnley or Tarleton would cut us out. Perhaps Beauly or Eskadale? What d'ye think?'

Charles thought for a moment.

'*Pemberton*. That was his real home. That's where he grew up. That's where he said he always felt most at home. It's also where his father and grandmother died. I think it's where he'd have chosen to die if he'd had any say in the matter.'

'Pemberton it is,' John said. 'I'll start on the sign in the morning.'

—⚜—

John married Catherine Dorahy in the Catholic church at Greendale in the early months of 1852. Later in the day, he carried his new bride across the parapet of Pemberton. Pemberton would go on to be the family home of generations of Lovats. Thomas and Eliza lived there until Thomas's death in 1865 and Eliza lived on as a widow, dying in 1882.

John and Catherine had eleven children. Annie was born in November 1852; she lived into her sixties. Lizzie was born in 1854, living almost a hundred years. Sarah, born in 1856, lived into her late seventies. Tommy, born in 1858, Willie, 1860, and Kate, 1863, also lived into their late seventies. Tessie, born in 1867, lived into her mid-eighties, while Joseph Patrick, born in 1872, died at the age of seventy in 1942. These children all outlived their parents.

On the other hand, young John, born in 1865, Dolly, 1869, and Vince, 1875, predeceased their parents. Dolly died of peritonitis at the age of thirty. She was a schoolteacher. Young John had died at the age of twenty-nine some six years earlier, in 1894. A little over two months later, Vince, the baby of the family, was thrown from his horse and broke his neck. He was just eighteen years of age.

John and Catherine became used to the sulky ride from Pemberton to the Greendale church to bury one of their children. They and their three predeceased children would eventually rest in the family grave next to the church at Greendale.

Joseph Patrick, Tommy and Willie, supported by Kate and Tessie, would run the farm at Wallacia after their parents died. Joseph Patrick married Sylvia Johnstone, bearing three children, Dorrie, Jack and Vince, who grew up on the farm. Pemberton survived the gold rush, miners' strikes, federation, world wars, the Great Depression, bushfires, and floods until it finally succumbed to a particularly fierce bushfire well over a century after John had carried Catherine over the parapet.

It was for a time the place where the son of a Jacobite's diary and Mahdiya's Qur'an were kept in safekeeping. When Charles's estate was settled, he had bequeathed them, along with Charlie Bear, to John. They were accompanied by a note.

Dear John,

I am asking that you keep these precious items in your safekeeping. They were given to me by my father just before I left home for New South Wales. The diary is one that your great grandfather, Thomas, kept on his first trip to Persia. It contains some wonderful reflections about the people he met and loved there, and about their culture and beliefs. He also wrote of his time in the Americas and his divided loyalties between the British and the Americans.

The ornate book with the bullet-hole on the cover is the Muslim holy book, called the Qur'an (pronounced Koran). It belonged to his first wife, Mahdiya. He cherished it for many reasons, including the fact that he said it saved his life when a bullet aimed at his heart was embedded in the book instead. I believe it meant more to him than that, however. From what my father told me, he felt close to both Mahdiya and God when he held that book.

The toy bear was very special to my father. It belonged to a young boy who he said saved his life when he fell from a ship in the Mediterranean. The boy's name was Charlie. My father said Charlie died saving him. Please do cherish these items and try and ensure they stay in the family's keeping.

Your loving uncle, Charles.

EPILOGUE

On the day in 1840 that William Bellamy first met Thomas at Castle Hill, he was accompanied by his daughter, Sarah. In Sarah's arms was William's granddaughter, Mary, two years of age. Mary grew up to marry Richard Whiticker. One of their daughter's, Martha, married George Dennis. Over a century later, one of Martha's and George's great granddaughters would marry T.J. Lovat, the author of this book.

It was as well that Edward saved William Bellamy from drowning that day in 1791.

For exclusive discounts on Matador titles,
sign up to our occasional newsletter at
troubador.co.uk/bookshop

Lightning Source UK Ltd.
Milton Keynes UK
UKHW022319230821
389349UK00001B/12/J